THE RETURN OF FITZROY ANGURSELL

THE RETURN OF FITZROY ANGURSELL

VICTORIA GODDARD

UNDERHILL BOOKS

CONTENTS

I

A CATALOGUE OF CRIMES

IN WHICH I RAID A TOMB

I prefer not to lie.

No, really—I do. Not for any strong moral compunctions, it must be said: I am, at heart, a poet. It is precisely that vocation that makes it so difficult. In life as in poetry, I much prefer the misleading wink, the sly sideways truth, the straight face smirking suggestively at a precisely chosen moment.

As a young man, I was given to great flights of hypotheticals, dizzying exaltations of absurdities, extravagant arrays of subjunctives.

When asked who I was, I used to tell people I could be the Prince of the White Forest, come to judge the righteousness and hospitality of those I encountered. (And indeed, I still maintain, I *could*.)

I acknowledged the inevitable comparisons of my physiognomy to the ninety-nine Emperors of Astandalas before my time, and never negated—how could I, in any good faith?—the family resemblance.

I conscientiously denied that I was a trickster god.

I never claimed other than that I was a poet, a wild mage, an anarchist, a revolutionary, and almost certainly a fool.

I discovered early, and subsequent experience has not disproven this, that the greatest truths, most plainly spoken, are the least likely to be believed. Few indeed are those who have told any truths more brazenly than I, or to greater applause for the depths of my cunning duplicities.

You may imagine, then, I hope, how disappointed I am in myself, how embarrassed—I, whom popular imagination believes incapable of either emotion!—when not two hours after setting off on my first real quest in thirty-odd years I was caught breaking into the tomb of one of my most esteemed ancestors and found myself unable to respond to the sarcastic guard with anything but the most stuttering, stammering, inadequate, *obvious* lie in the book.

To the flippant question I should have responded with an even more flippant truth. The guard would never have believed me had I answered "Yes"; he should certainly have found it inconceivable had I replied, "Hardly, as I was once an Emperor of Astandalas!"

I could have told him half a dozen incredible truths, but instead, when he peered in through the entrance tunnel, saw me there in amongst the grave goods, and asked, "Who do you think you are, Fitzroy Angursell?" I was so surprised to be immediately recognized that I replied with a barefaced lie, and denied it utterly.

We stared at each other, he and I, both, I reckon, somewhat startled.

On second glance the man was probably not actually a guard, but rather some form of custodian for the necropolis. He was a weedy, wiry, middle-aged sort of man, mid-brown of skin and curly of hair, dressed in a dirty cotton tunic and ragged rusty-red trews. He was peering rather apprehensively at me from the entrance tunnel.

I was standing in the central chamber of the tomb of Yr the Conqueror, first Emperor of Astandalas. It was a massive construction, all enormous blocks of rusty-black basalt, simple, heavy, and deeply impressive. On the outside it formed the shape of a grassy cone; the inside, which I was fairly certain I was the only person to have seen since it was closed, contained a short, narrow passage leading to a large single chamber.

This chamber was a hollow cube perhaps twenty feet in every direction, the basalt forming walls, floor, ceiling. I had lit a couple of mage-lights to illuminate the space, and had only just begun investigating it when I was interrupted.

The air was cold, noticeably so after the equatorial afternoon heat outside, and tasted both stale and electric, like the air before a lightning strike. Ancient magic had stirred at my entrance, but I technically had the right to enter, even if I'd never had any occasion to do so before. What the magic did if fully awoken was unclear, but judging by the eerie lack of dust inside the chamber it remained operative despite the four thousand or so years since Yr's death.

In the centre of the space was a basalt plinth on which rested a pure white alabaster sarcophagus. The lid was carved with a life-size relief of a man. He wore a knee-length kilt with a belt clearly intended to be seen as set with heavy jewels. His muscles were well-defined, his shoulders broad, his torso layered with heavy necklaces. His hands were folded on his stomach, clasping three items: the hilt of a sword whose blade ran down between his legs, a circular object I presumed represented the legendary Sun Disc, and a small mirror.

I contemplated the carving. My initial survey of the chamber had made it clear that the grave goods were primarily carved bronze, gold, and stone items representing the entire retinue an ancient emperor might want for the afterlife: horses, soldiers, servants, handmaidens, elephants, horses, dogs, falcons, horses, and thousands of items of more prosaic household use.

There was gold and jewelry and real weaponry a-plenty, but nothing quite identical to the three objects on the sarcophagus lid. If they were here, as legend claimed, then they had been sealed inside the sarcophagus with the earthly remains of the emperor.

I regarded the carved face thoughtfully. Even paying generous heed to the substantial developments in the sculptural arts over the millennia, not to mention the likelihood of flattery in the depiction here, it was remarkable how the family nose had, in fact, persisted.

"There's a curse, you know," the custodian said.

I had quite forgotten about him, and turned to see that he had edged a few steps further from the entrance. He was half-turned, obviously worried about the door closing, and leading with the unusual implement he held in his right hand. This was a handled rectangular blade with a gruesome-looking spike halfway down one side.

I have always been excessively curious, and for half my life have been prevented from asking questions for fear of the answers people might give. Delighting in the ability to do so, I nodded in the direction of his hand. "What sort of tool is that?"

He blinked and stopped his unsteady progress. "What?"

"The object in your hand. What is it?"

He lifted it, as if surprised he was holding something. "This? It's a zax, like. You use it working with slates. I was fixing the roof on Eritanyr's tomb yonder." He jerked his head in vague indication.

The Emperor Eritanyr, my unlamented uncle, had had built for himself a miniature temple, complete with silver-blue slates imported from far western Voonra, each individually dipped in gold. My ancestors had wealth; more occasionally, taste.

I nodded in appreciation of the zax. "It is certainly fearsome."

The custodian sniggered, shuffling his feet so he could lean up against the side of the tunnel mouth. "What are you holding?" His voice shifted to what I presumed was an attempt at my accent. "The *object* in your hand. What is it?"

I looked down at the item in question, a six-inch rod made of cunningly carved gold set with opaque black and white diamonds in concentric bands. It was gaudy, extravagant, visibly of the same aesthetic as the majority of objects inside this tomb, and quite likely the reason the colours of the Empire of Astandalas were black, white, and gold. The magic in it sparkled against my fingers.

"This," I said, tilting my hand so he could see it, "is called the Linchpin of the Empire. It was created by Harbut Zalarin."

The custodian pursed his lips. "Who was he, then?"

"The greatest wizard of pre-Astandalan Zunidh and the father of Yr the Conqueror." I waved the linchpin in the direction of the stone sarcophagus behind me.

"It's a magic wand, then?"

"You could say that. It was supposed to be the very core of the enchantments holding the Empire together."

A linchpin is the rod through the centre of a wheel that holds the axle in place. Harbut Zalarin was popularly supposed to have invented the wheel, though I personally believed his name was simply attached to it, as happens more often than you might think.

The custodian snorted. "Funny thing to hide away in your tomb, then."

I tucked it away into a pocket of my shoulder bag. "I brought it in with me; that's how I opened the door."

"And how did you come by it?"

"I was given it," I said blandly, omitting that this had been in the course of the ceremony that made me hundredth and last Emperor of Astandalas.

"You didn't steal it?" he said, a note of urgency coming into his voice, and he stepped towards me, zax uplifted warningly.

I didn't need to be fairly certain that he would win in any contest of physical strength, nor I in any of magic, to shake my head in denial. I did cast one final glance at the sarcophagus lid, but there is a difference—a fine one, perhaps, but clear—between robbing a tomb and desecrating a coffin.

And if I needed the mirror in the end, as I might or might not, I knew exactly where to find it.

"Look here," the custodian said, moving towards me, "I don't know what your plan is, but—"

But he had taken a step past the tunnel mouth, and despite his work on the surface the custodian had no right to be inside the chamber proper, and the magic retaliated instantly.

I moved a little less instantly, as a sudden wind shrieked past me and the figurines representing Yr the Conqueror's armies came alive and started to grow to fill the space. As an elephant stumbled over my feet I caught my breath and was able to gather my magic and composure together.

"Run, you fool!" I cried, and shoved the custodian with magic. It wasn't my full strength, but enough to propel him up the sloping tunnel and out the door into the bright sunlight.

He tumbled over. The zax embedded itself in the grass, and I half-tripped over its handle before catching myself on the stone I'd rolled away from the entrance. I whirled around, magic rousing, the linchpin leaping back into my hand from my bag as I channelled the ancient powers back into their accustomed roles.

The shrieking wind spiralled around us, pushing the custodian back to the ground, causing my garments to whip wildly around my legs, and finally picking up the boulder and slamming it into place with a definite thump.

The grass on the mound rippled and then went utterly flat as a shadow passed over the necropolis. I readied myself but, I confess, was glad I didn't have to do anything further. The shadow touched me, accepted my instinctive recognition of the custodian as under my protection, and returned to the tomb.

I took several deep breaths, recovering my composure, and turned to regard the custodian with a severe frown. That was the most physical excitement I'd experienced in decades.

The custodian ignored my frown and instead grinned crookedly at me from where he was still sprawled on his back. "Are you going to write a song about this?"

I was not even three hours away from the Imperial Apartments in the Palace of Stars. My efforts at disguise had not extended much beyond changing my clothing to something pertaining less to the iconography of emperors and more to that of folk heroes.

This consisted of a knee-length cotton tunic in sky-blue and white stripes, which was accompanied by a matching hat that more or less hid the fact that my head, as per ancient tradition, was shaven bald. The hat kept flopping over one ear and irritating me, but I felt obliged to keep it on while I was still so close to what amounted to home. It had, unsurprisingly, fallen off in my helter-skelter exit from the tomb. With great dignity I picked it up and put it back on.

I was also wearing a scarlet silk mantle, which I adjusted with even more dignity.

Black-skinned *and* bald-headed screamed, at the very least, a serious imposter of the high nobility, even if not necessarily *Last Emperor of Astandalas*.

The custodian did not have any particular reason to expect Artorin Damara or any other former Emperor of Astandalas to be standing there *sans* entourage and guards and ceremony, and did not imagine he had found him.

He had no reason to expect Fitzroy Angursell, either, but thirty years of myth-mongering after a spectacularly bizarre disappearance had apparently done much of my work for me. Not to mention that I was dressed very closely as described in several songs; sky-blue was *my* colour, and the scarlet silk mantle was nearly as famous as my Bag of Unusual Capacity.

"What makes you think I would?" I temporized.

"It's an adventure, like," he explained, getting up and experimentally tugging his zax, which was deeply embedded in the ground. "And that's what you write songs about, no?"

His tone suggested he did not really believe I was the returned Fitzroy Angursell, but that he was a canny man and was determined to cover all possibilities. And if the opportunity came to be put in a song by Fitzroy Angursell—well! He'd be a fool not to take it.

I nodded, not quite regally. "It's been known to happen."

"I'm Gus," he said, abandoning the zax in favour of impressing on me his role in the affair. "I tend the tombs, like, and it was very brave of me, don't you think, coming in to see who was inside the tomb, when everyone knows there are curses, like."

I regarded the very definitely closed stone of the tomb of Yr the Conqueror, and nodded absently.

"'Course," Gus went on, "I'm from *here*, you know, like the first emperor himself. Related, most like, from way back when."

This was unlikely. Even in those very early days—perhaps especially in those very early days—my ancestors did not tend to distribute their seed outside the marriage-bed: it is a dangerous thing to have children of the line outside of direct control.

As indeed they found with me. Not that I ever told anyone *that* truth.

"No doubt I am, too," I replied, smirking.

Ninety-three or possibly ninety-seven generations back, depending on how one counted the little-publicized instances of intergenerational incest in my family tree. There are, alas, reasons for why the features have bred as true as they have. Though I *can* say that there are other unexpected cousins than me in the history books.

The custodian appeared to find this hilarious, but eventually he recalled himself to his duties. "Are you planning on breaking into any more tombs?"

I looked at the Imperial Necropolis, where ninety-nine emperors and numerous members of their (and thus *my*) extended families and courts had tombs. (Not all of them were actually entombed here, of course; at least one, Aurelius Magnus, had disappeared into legend without leaving a corpse behind.)

"No," I said, recalling that here I was not Artorin Damara, and thus it behoved me to answer questions and attempt a certain normal courtesy. "Just that one, thank you."

That didn't sound quite correct. Oh well. I am much better at recognizing the nuances of other people's behaviour. We stood there for a moment, he toeing the ground absently, I holding my bag under my arm. I was, it was becoming increasingly clear, out of practice with this sort of thing, and wasn't quite prepared to say good-bye and walk off, especially as I wasn't entirely sure of my direction.

My plans on setting forth had focused on reaching the necropolis and retrieving the mirror. With that plan currently forestalled, my next task was to leave the world behind in furtherance of the three components of my quest, but there are no useful passages across the Borders anywhere near the capital.

"Have you been in there long?" the custodian asked at length. At my puzzled glance he clarified, "Since you disappeared, maybe. Everyone always wanted to know what happened."

Here was an excellent price of passage: to be the first person to have seen Fitzroy Angursell in thirty years! To hear the story from his own mouth!

(Assuming, that is, that I *was*.)

I bestowed upon the custodian a sly sideways smile.

"I have been in the Starry Court," I declared. "The Moon Lady offered me a place at her side, the Morning Star as my vessel. I have been adored as a god, but am now returned to the mortal lands on a quest of great moment."

Every word of this, I swear, was the honest truth.

The custodian was doubtful. "To break into tombs?"

"I will offer you gratis my method for having astonishing adventures," I told him, making his eyes light in curiosity. "First: you determine an object, in the sense of an end, or perhaps a *telos* as the philosophers would have it: a goal, that is. It might, perhaps, be something like the Three Mirrors of Harbut Zalarin. An ancient scroll I once had occasion to read tells how, in conjunction with a certain golden key Harbut Zalarin was given by his father the Sun and which I found long ago, the three mirrors permit one to open any heart. And *that*, my friend, is a quest worthy of any great poet."

I didn't mention that I'd long since subsequently also *lost* said key. It wasn't really any of his business, and I needed a back-up quest in case the first one proved easier than anticipated. Kip—my astonishingly patient and sometimes terrifyingly competent chief minister—has long since taught me the virtue of such advance preparations.

"And then?" the custodian said, unimpressed.

I found myself grinning at him, something I often felt but rarely expressed. It made me feel surprisingly light-hearted. Perhaps that was due to the momentary spike in heart-rate from the tomb magic.

"And then, one comes up with a *second* object, or perhaps even a third, and very seriously and with the utmost effort seeks after it."

Finding the three mirrors was hardly the true *telos* of my quest, either officially or personally.

The custodian laughed at my absurdity, though I could see how much he appreciated the story he would have to tell his friends. He then offered me the use of his bicycle, with the comment that I had once mentioned in a song that I had ridden the first that had ever been invented.

"I have hardly ridden one since," I objected, regarding the contraption dubiously.

"They say you never forget," the custodian replied complacently. He indicated a lever on the handle that seemed connected to a wire leading down to the front wheel. "These are brakes, to slow you down. They're newer. You probably don't have them in the Moon's country."

"I certainly never noticed them there."

"Just tell someone, wherever you leave it, that it belongs to Gus up at the Nec."

I suppose I ought to have been disgruntled at how cavalier the necropolis custodian was about his duties, but as I careened inexpertly away from Gus, descended the well-groomed slope in front of Yr the Conqueror's tomb, and sped across the open space which I had prevented many decades of well-meaning courtiers from filling with my own, I could not help but be grateful for my youthful exploits as a folk hero.

It would have been so embarrassing to be taken up before the authorities *this* soon.

~

While it was quite correct to say that I had ridden the first bicycle ever invented, I had done so after borrowing the contraption in question from the small town museum in which it was kept.

Borrow may not be quite the correct word.

Though if I recall correctly, I did eventually send it back courtesy of the post.

Gus's bicycle was largely made of bamboo and Iveline rubber, apart from the wires surrounding the brakes and the looped metal chain that powered it. It did not feel substantial, but neither did it shake itself to pieces as I bumped down into a dip.

I pedalled hard and got out of the dip again, only to be confronted with a fork in the path and the edge of the escarpment.

I tried to go left, as although I have many skills and odd powers, flight (alas!) is not one of them.

The bicycle appeared to have a will of its own. It inclined towards the righthand path, which went down in a relentless plunge.

The path was a narrow, well-beaten twist of a thing, dark red-brown against the lighter reddish stones. It was towards the end of the dry season, and the clumps of grass were green at their bases, golden-violet up their stems, to the waving violet banners of the seed-heads. I focused on the twists in front of me, hands gripping tightly to the handlebars.

Faster and faster. Some bird, somewhere, was making a loud twittering noise audible even over the noise of my passage. I jounced around on the bicycle as the path wound about larger boulders, my bag flapping against my side. The air was noticeably more sultry as I descended, warm and humid and redolent, the dominant scent something resinous and minty.

The path suddenly dropped out below the leading wheel, and for a moment I *was* flying, stomach weightless, until the bicycle landed again with a thump and a wobble. But I was going too fast to fall, faster and faster as the path unspooled down a boulder field at the base of the escarpment, and then canted left and around a huge boulder precariously balanced on top of a much smaller one, a phenomenon I just caught out of the edge of my eye before I was past it, and then in a spray of red gravel I was on a white road and narrowly avoiding a cart drawn by water buffalo.

The animals objected with a whuffling series of snorts. "Hoy!" cried their attendant.

"Sorry! Can't stop!" I called back, the honest truth, as the bicycle was pressing forward now, left and downhill along the white road, away from the escarpment and the necropolis and the cart, and my legs seemed to be pedalling without my conscious effort. Down, and down, the slope gentler now, speed a little moderated but still fast enough that the air seemed cool against my face, and I realized I was laughing madly, whooping with delight, the air echoing with it.

By all the gods, how I'd *missed* this!

The momentum from my plunge down the escarpment carried me along quite a ways down the back road I encountered at the bottom. I had never been along it before—official visits to the necropolis always followed a strict ceremonial route otherwise unused by mere mortals, and I'd never before been to the region *unofficially*—and once I caught my breath and stopped laughing, I was able to pedal along fairly decorously and enjoy my surroundings.

The land gently sloped away from the red-stone escarpment towards the fertile valley of the River Dwahaii, which runs through Solaara on its way from the Grey Mountains to the Eastern Ocean. Up here, where the scrubland was still littered with the odd boulder, ranging in size from the size of my fist to larger than the largest elephant, the basic activity appeared to be pasturage.

I saw mostly goats along with a few rangy dappled cows, their attendants dressed in wide green capes and round grey caps. They stared aghast at me as I passed, even after I stopped laughing. Well, I was grinning like a fool.

I went down a dip and up the other side, with a bit of strain in my thighs, and was glad the land sloped down again, this time presenting a splendid view of my capital city ahead and slightly to the right.

I paused there to take a drink of water from the bottle my assiduous chief attendant had packed for me, and to put away the scarlet mantle before it became damaged by dust or caught in the wheels of the bicycle, as had seemed dangerously possible more than once.

Solaara is called The City of Cities and reckoned one of the most beautiful conurbations in the whole of the Nine Worlds. It is a city of white marble and flower-garlanded arcades, intricately carved spires and elegant domes, shady squares and colourful markets. The sun-in-glory of the Palace of Stars, which crowns a central volcanic plug, was from this angle quite visible: the golden roofs of the central block, the five major wings extending out, the well-watered gardens green as a malachite brooch.

Everything was drenched in orange light, except for the river which was a streak of yellow fire. My shadow stretched in front of me, cutting the glare of the white clay road. I followed it away from the sunset, knowing night would fall soon but far too enamoured of the experience to think about practical matters.

This road seemed to be heading away from the city, which was fine by me. I had already traversed Solaara on my way to the necropolis, and though I could not exactly say I knew it *well*—my excursions into it being rather circumscribed—it was not the heart of this new adventure.

If any of the objects of my quest were to be found there, they would have to be found on my return. That is one of the classic stories, and though I am certainly no longer a young man off to seek my fortune, nevertheless the task of finding who you truly are and where you truly belong never ends.

And of course, recently escaped prisoners of state generally ought not to linger in the environs.

Thus I followed the road I was on, ignoring any side tracks leading back uphill or towards the city. It was a winding sort of road, not well-travelled—apart from the carter and the herders I had seen no one since leaving the Nec—but all the more pleasant for that. The city had been suffocating in its crowds. I am not well used to them, though this was only the second time in one thousand and twelve years I had been alone for longer than an hour at a time.

It was, dare I say it, invigorating, but the plains around Solaara are no wasteland, and my splendid independence lasted only until full dark, when I missed a turn and toppled straight into a fen.

Fortunately some passing arsonists found this amusing and rescued me.

2

IN WHICH I AM CALLED UPON TO ASSIST AN ARSONIST IN HIS CRAFT

*I*t was, I take pride in stating, a spectacular fall. I rather specialize in them.

Just at dusk I crossed a causeway marked by a line of leathery-leaved shrubs that appeared to be the source of the resinous, minty scent, for they filled the air almost to the point of intoxication as I approached. On the other side of the hedgerow the white-earth road transitioned to a wooden boardwalk.

The vibrations caused by the bicycle moving over the corrugations were pleasing. The boardwalk was level, and the boards were fairly smooth and well-fitting, so the shaking was minimal and the pedalling easy. On either side of the boardwalk were tall grasslands, chest-high to me on the bicycle, full at first of small birds flitting here and there and fireflies starting to glow as the dusk deepened. It reminded me rather of my first adventure, when I had escaped my exile and found myself in a painted city at the edge of a vast grassy estuary.

I cycled along, humming an old song of mine from those days, and reflected that that was another thing I had not been able to do for so long. Most of the time it is inappropriate for a head of state to be humming absently, and even when it isn't—in the bath, for instance—I was never *alone*. Not that my guards were anything but discreet; but it was always the case that I wasn't supposed to know Fitzroy Angursell's songs, the majority of which remain banned.

I relished my perceived isolation, moved from 'A Riot in the Painted City' to 'The Glorious Defeat of the Third Army of Astandalas' (ah, those were the days! I had yet to learn how to title songs properly but nevertheless managed to write ones that appealed to large swaths of the population), and ignored the really quite basic fact that I do not have magically enhanced night vision, and that these fens are known for their fatally attractive spirit lights.

I was aiming for an edifice illuminated by human agency, so I felt justified in looking for a congregation of lights. Once I had realized the boardwalk was taking me along the edge of the Fens towards the river, it occurred to me that I did know of a destination I could aim towards for supper—increasingly appealing—and probably the night as well.

The River-Horse Inn at the edge of the Fens was an establishment my long-suffering former secretary and present viceroy Kip had mentioned as a place he intended to take his family on their visit to him, and indeed had done so after a river excursion, to apparent pleasure all round. From this I deduced that it would be clean, aesthetically appealing, culinarily acceptable, reasonably priced, and almost certainly middle-class in clientele, all of which seemed a good idea for this first night out from the Palace.

There were very few cross-paths from the boardwalk, but whenever I came across one I always chose the route that took me towards the cluster of bright lights that I thought indicated the inn.

I should not, of course, have been following the lights.

The Solamen Fens lie to the east of Solaara, and have an ill repute.

The enclosing and binding of the fens was one of my first great acts as Lord of Zunidh. As Emperor of Astandalas I was preoccupied with other matters, and did not make use of what I may say is a considerable talent for wild magic. When I woke after the Fall, it was to find my empire disintegrated and the magic of the world maddened and uncontrolled. I began the work of restoration and reconstruction close to what had become home, with the Fens and their deadly spirits.

The River Dwahaii meanders past a line of volcanic plugs of varying heights and precipitousness in the wide valley formed between the Escarpment I had just descended and the southerly Vijurnka Hills, of which I knew little besides the fact that the hill tribes and the Plainsmen had a long and storied enmity that mostly played out nowadays in enthusiastic and often violent sporting matches. The Prince of Eastern Dair, into whose demesne Solaara and its surroundings fall, takes much more interest in them than the majority of his subjects.

The line of volcanic plugs finishes with a flourish of sorts, in the form of a double peak unimaginatively called the Twins. Although not very high, the Twins are of sufficient mass and conformation to force the river through the gap between them. On the city side of the Twins are the farms and market gardens that fed the city; on the ocean side are the Fens.

Despite what some of the songs might indicate, I do not have a wholly unreliable sense of direction. I cannot claim any great feats of orientation, it is true—I am not the person one looks to when navigation is in question—but I can, most of the time, hold a map in my mind and relate the visible geography of a place to the cartographical image.

I mention this not only to clear up a matter of longstanding irritation, but to indicate that I was not *lost*. I had come down from the Escarpment, very good. Solaara was behind me, also very good. The river was to one side of me, the sun had set behind me, and I was sloping ever downhill. The sea was some way in front of me, and before the coast was the River-Horse Inn. Also very good.

19

I expected to come to the foot-path that I had been informed led alongside the Twins for the convenience of those who wanted to stay close to the riverside as they journeyed, and after that, I thought, I would have to watch out for the Fens. But since I would be on the riverbank path, there would be no need to fear losing my way or missing the River-Horse, and I happened to know that the bindings on the fen spirits protected the bank from their depredations even at night.

What I had not taken into account was that my back-road approach had led me to the north of the Twins. Thus, when I passed through the hedgerow I had entered the Fens far from the river, and whatever lights I was heading towards had nothing whatsoever to do with the inn.

It had been a long time since my work on the Fens. I was still proud of my work, but I confess I had spent very little time thinking about the bindings since I finished them, except in a vague self-congratulatory manner. They were a network of magic holding the Fen spirits in and ensuring that travellers were safe throughout the marshes during the day, and that at least the margins were safe at night. All around the perimeter were spirit houses, where the local witches paid the small tributes of salt and wine and so on required to keep the Fen spirits occupied. It was still assuredly not a good idea to go very far past the periphery.

I have always thought it a very great work of magic indeed. The Fens had been places of horror and misery for as long as anyone had ever mentioned them, and now they were bound, even if not precisely *tamed*.

Not that anyone *can* tame the true Wild. A certain discipline may be accepted, as even my muse will accept a certain metre, but only complete destruction will obliterate something at once so beautiful and so perilous. The boardwalk path I was following led south and east through the very middle of the Fens, where I had long been assured absolutely no one had any desire or need to go. Only the Fen spirits dwelled there, I was told. The river folk muttered about skinwalkers and hobgoblins and things of that ilk, but I had never encountered any, and so, in my arrogance, thought none were there.

It is a hazard of the profession, arrogance. You can change the world, and so you begin to think you *should*.

And of course, if one is secretly also reckoned the greatest poet and one of the greatest renegades of the Nine Worlds, one's name known to the highest of the high and the lowest of the low alike, and one's friends are scattered to the winds—well, it is something of a miracle I have any sense of humour left, really.

I have Kip to guide me now, but in those days he was a lowly undersecretary of little standing and no reputation besides one for being a bit of a troublemaker, and barely a whisper of his exploits came to my ears. I was instead surrounded by people who were desperate for me to take care of all their problems, and willing to flatter me to the point where I began to think I could. Kip mentioned the Fens a few times, early in his time as my secretary, but I had not learned to listen, and I was much more concerned with—and to be frank, far more interested in—new and greater works.

I was pondering the difficulty of finding good advisors (and that heads of state have *at least* as hard a time with it as notorious criminals) when the front wheel of the bicycle dropped out from under me.

Unlike when I'd gone over the Escarpment, there was no path to catch it. The front wheel plunged down in a fountain of black water. Physical momentum ensured both rear wheel and rider followed, at an angle that flipped me over the handlebars to land flat on my back in three feet of murky water atop many more of muck.

By the time I found my bag and scrambled to my feet, the bicycle was nearly out of sight. I spent a good few minutes attempting to haul it out. It *was* borrowed, and I'd rather that Gus up at the Nec tell all his friends that Fitzroy Angursell had seen to the safe return of his cycle than to have taken it in good faith only to abandon it in the middle of a haunted swamp. The suction from the mud below the water made my efforts increasingly difficult, as did the mosquitos that had emerged out of nowhere when I stopped moving.

It was in all regards a distasteful activity. The mud was unpleasantly warm and squishy between my toes—my sandals were an early sacrifice to its depth—and full of disquieting bits of harder material that I hoped very much were fragments of plants. It also smelled. It was funky rather than vile, with a brackish edge, and it made me think of old stories about these fens.

It was said that Yr the Conqueror, the ancestor whose tomb I had just raided, had set off about conquering his empire specifically to get away from the Solamen Fens in the dry season, when they used to catch on fire.

It was just the edge of the dry season. The water was low, the mud turgid, and the mosquitos hungry. It was all very disagreeable.

I eventually stopped, with the handlebars propped uncomfortably against my shins, so that I could pay attention to the mosquitos and shift them magically. As I wiped my muddy and now sweaty brow with an equally muddy and sweaty hand, grateful to stretch my back straight, I discovered I had an audience.

This was promising.

There were three men on the boardwalk watching me. Short and wiry and midtoned of skin, insofar as I could tell in the gloaming, they reminded me rather of Gus up at the Nec; the Plainsmen are taller and have a redder hue to their skin, and the river-folk tend towards the Plainsman phenotype, though I don't believe they are all that closely related. These men were clearly shorter and stockier than the river-folk I had met in the past. The central one was holding a shielded lantern so the light fell on me, which I spied with great delight.

"I haven't seen one of those in years!" I cried, ignoring all else. "A proper thief's lantern, to be sure. How splendid. Is there much to rob in here?—Oh!" I gave them a brilliant smile, even as the lantern-bearer lifted his hand and cast the light on my face. "Good evening, good sirs. I must apologize for my presumption, I'm afraid it's a terrible habit. I don't suppose you could assist me in lifting this bicycle out of the mud? It doesn't belong to me and I shouldn't like Gus up at the Nec to think I'd absconded with it when he was so kind as to lend it to me."

"Gus up at the Nec, eh," the central one said, looking to the man on his right. I couldn't see their expressions because of the light in my face—the boardwalk put them a good two feet above me, though I was naturally taller than they—but I could see the way their bodies shifted with discomfort, wariness, and curiosity.

One thing sitting on a throne staring down at milling courtiers for hours on end does is give you a ripe appreciation for what body language can indicate. There are all sorts of games you start to play when your function is to sit up on a gold-plated throne in glory and be seen as powerful, magnificent, and divinely benevolent while your courtiers busily angle for favour. I tried to cut back on how often I held court, but that only ended up in a noticeable increase in regional warfare, so developing several variants of courtier solitaire it was.

And really, reading an audience is reading an audience regardless of whether one is a bard, a conman, a jobbing mage, or a head of state.

All this is to say that it didn't occur to me to be concerned about my physical safety.

"Yes," I went on blithely. "He let me out of Yr the Conqueror's tomb."

There was a pause. I tugged at the handlebars, which were subsiding again, and grinned up at the three men. My hat had disappeared in the tumble, and good riddance to the itchy thing, so I trusted the darkness, the situation, and the preponderance of mud to disguise me.

"*Out of* the tomb, eh," the lantern-holder said. His two companions shuffled back a step. He held his ground, but he lifted the lantern again so it shone on my face.

It is absolutely true that I strongly resemble every one of my ancestors.

He cleared his throat with a phlegmy-sounding cough. "And— excuse me—" he coughed again, and twisted around to spit the gob of phlegm off on the other side of the boardwalk, a courtesy I trust you will understand I very much appreciated. "And why were you, er, in there?"

I patted my bag, strap safely if somewhat damply snug against my side. "I had something to fetch."

The two companions stepped back again, then jostled forward when they realized they had nearly fallen off the opposite side of the boardwalk.

"Steady there," I said. "The mud isn't that pleasant. It's probably usefully exfoliating, but I'm not sure about the contents."

"Not a fan of leeches, eh?" the speaker said. It was a comment that I found wonderfully motivating.

In short order I was up beside them, the bicycle handlebars hooked on the edge of the boardwalk to keep it from disappearing. The three men had retreated several yards away, leaving me just enough light from the lantern to see that my arms and probably many more parts of my body were liberally spotted with shiny black parasitical molluscs.

"How do I get them off me?" I enquired with as much calm as I could muster, which wasn't very much. I abhor leeches. Slugs. Even snails. Anything of that mucilaginous ilk.

"Fire works," the lantern-holder began slowly, coming a half-step towards me as if to proffer his aid.

I danced away from him, rubbing my hands together and shuddering bodily when I touched one of the leeches with the side of my palm.

"Fire? Right. Yes. Fire."

"Yes, you want to—" he said, but I ignored whatever he went

on to say.

Without really thinking further I called up magic in the form of small flames and sent them dancing across my skin. Head right down to toes, and not forgetting any of the more private areas either. It's probably just as well that the clean-shaven fashion extended to all bodily hair but for eyebrows and eyelashes, as I would surely have singed it all close in an effort to be thorough. The mud baked instantly into a crackling dry glaze.

I let the last of the flames die away from my hands and took a deep, relieved breath. "There," I said. "Surely none of the leeches would have survived that!" I stretched, grateful to be out of the swamp and also—my thighs were protesting the entirely unaccus-tomed exertion—to be off the bicycle. Ah yes, the bicycle. I stared down at the handlebars, just visible in the light from the thief's lantern. I smiled hopefully at the men and gestured at the vehicle. "Would you be so good as to help me lift it up?"

"Er," said the lantern-holder, making a motion suggestive of turning to look plaintively back at his friends. My eyes were adjusting but it was a dark night, thick with clouds. I have to admit that despite being a skilled weather-worker (not to mention having lived half my life in the vicinity) I had no real idea about the weather hereabouts. General climatological patterns, yes. Daily forecasts, no. I've spent most of my time indoors.

I remembered the magic word, and smiled as winningly as I could. "Please?"

One of the non-lantern-holders laughed, a short, astonished crackle. "Why not?" he said, his voice full of ironic marvel. "An ancient man cycles into the middle of the Fens on a new-moon night and sets himself on fire to rid himself of leeches. Of *course* he'd have a strange request."

"I'm not that old," I protested, though it's true I am on the edge of retirement.

"You can't suggest you're *young*?" the new speaker asked, handing something to the third of their trio and stumping forward to squat beside the bicycle. "My cousin owes me one," he muttered, tugging at the handles. "Glory, this is stuck."

"I like that invocation," I said.

"Shorty doesn't like calling on the Emperor," the lantern-holder explained.

"Neither do I," I said, charmed. "Can I be of assistance, ah, Shorty? I'm afraid I'm not one for upper body strength, but I can try."

"You're not too shabby," Shorty replied after giving me a thorough inspection in the light his friend thoughtfully held up for him. "Can't say you've missed too many meals, but at the same time, you're obviously not totally idle."

This was highly gratifying, for all that sitting on thrones and so on does not make for a particularly active lifestyle. "Thank you," I said, which made Shorty utter his crackle again and return to his efforts with the handles. He obviously *did* have a more active lifestyle, for he was able to set his heels down against the boardwalk and with a single thrust heave the bicycle up beside him.

I was within the radius to be splattered with mud as he did so. When I lit a small magical light to see if any leeches had come with the mud, I discovered I had been somewhat overly enthusiastic earlier and had contrived to burn off all my clothes without noticing.

"Thank you," I said gravely to Shorty, refusing to be discombobulated. "Do you have any leeches that require removal?"

He brushed his hands together. "No, thank you! You might want to clean off the bike before you get back on it again, mind."

The lantern-holder snorted. "You might want to put some clothes on first."

I gave him a serene smile; I am very well-practiced at them. "Oh, I shan't be getting back on that any time soon, I assure you. I shall have to find somewhere to leave it so that Gus can find it again." At Shorty's incredulous look—his was the only expression I could see clearly—I grinned at them. "I *am* perhaps a bit underdressed for the next stage of my quest. The mosquitos, you know. One moment."

My bag was not *my* bag, the one made famous in song and story, but was a reasonable replacement. It held anything I put into it, which included all the luggage my chief groom of the chamber had thought requisite for my quest. I didn't fancy trying to clean any cloth the Fen mud got onto, however, so I forbore any of my more impressive outfits in favour of the white cotton tunic with which I had begun my travels that day.

In some ways this bag was superior to the first one. That first bag was well stuffed with all the eclectic paraphernalia that caught the eye of a magpie-minded young poet on his first adventures, but because I couldn't easily retrieve any specific item I had a tendency to provide whatever came first to hand in response to whatever had prompted the search. This made for some absolutely splendid stories.

Alas, with age and experience comes a certain tendency to expeditiousness. I put my hand into the new bag and drew out the white tunic without any trouble at all, and was just a touch disappointed. Though it must be said my audience, all three, seemed happier once I was again clothed.

"Right," I said, clapping my hands together and placing the replacement bag over my shoulder. "Thank you, Shorty. I'm afraid I have delayed your expedition quite considerably. Is there anything I can do to assist?"

The lantern-holder let the lantern swing idly for a few moments as Shorty (who was, naturally, the tallest of the three) bent down to whisper in his ear. I let them discuss without trying to listen, looking out past the two circles of lantern- and mage-light to the black water beyond. The grasses swayed in the light breeze, whispering (one story had it) the ancient secret that one emperor had donkey ears. I had always rather hoped it was Haultan the Terrible, in the running for my least favourite ancestor, but the histories are coy on the matter.

The ripples caused by the bicycle retrieval had stilled. Apart from the grasses and the whispering men in front of me, it was very quiet, no frogs or birds to be heard. In the distance more and more lights were gathering, all the palest of colours.

"But if he *is*," Shorty said suddenly out loud, attracting my attention.

"Shh!" said the lantern-holder, sending his circle of light swinging wildly.

I saw absolutely no reason to politely pretend not to have heard. "Yes?" I said, with a grin. "*If* I am—who?"

The lantern-holder scoffed. "That's a question, isn't it?"

"It's not one you have yet asked," I pointed out. "Let me give you one hint: you know my name."

Shorty elbowed the lantern-holder, as if to emphasize his intuition. The lantern-holder was not easily moved, however, and spoke with slow caution. "That's as may be, and I can't say I hope I'm wrong, but you must understand our position—we don't know what *your* purpose is."

"It's a wise man indeed who knows that," I replied, laughing. "My current purpose is to find a bite of supper and a place to spend the night. I had been aiming at the River-Horse Inn, where I had heard I might find both. However, as serendipity has led me to you, and I cannot believe that your good turn in assisting me does not cry out to be returned immediately: what can I do for you?"

"Well," said the lantern-holder, "seeing as you're obviously a man of talent with fire, will you help us burn down the swamp?"

I was barely three hours away from a long and resolutely respectable career as a competent, benevolent, and beloved head of state.

I am noted, I believe, for being reasonable.

I gave the lantern-holder and Shorty and their third friend a brilliant smile.

"Absolutely."

3

IN WHICH I AM TEMPTED TO LIE

*I*t turned out that they thought I was the revenant spirit of Yr the Conqueror, come to avenge himself on the Fens.

This put me in a somewhat tricky position. On the one hand, this was not true. On the other, what a delicious mistake.

I smiled and said nothing, in a most telling way.

The anarchist in me had only recently been loosed to do more than utter sarcastic comments in the privacy of my own mind. You cannot think I would have done anything else.

Shorty's two friends were Hank, the lantern-hold, and Wat, who was taciturn. They addressed me, with a sidelong, tentative air, as, "Sire," and I did not even think for several minutes that I should not be answering that honorific. It's so rarely that I am called by name (any name, to be honest) that I usually respond to everything else first.

They led me along the boardwalk away from the concentration of lights, with me pushing the bicycle and contemplating the fact that this was only the second time since my days with the Red

Company that I had stood barefoot outside. It was deeply satisfying to feel my feet thwack on the wooden boards.

"May I ask," I said after a bit, "why you wish to set the Fens alight?"

There was a pause. Hank was in the lead, with his lantern casting a low circle of illumination on the boardwalk in front of him, then Shorty walking on the other side of the bicycle from myself, with Wat coming along behind. After we had turned the corner that had caused me such trouble, the previously straightforward route marked by the boardwalk began to turn and angle and branch more extensively.

I had had no idea any of this construction was here. It was hard to see in the dark, but while the wooden boards seemed new, the piers looked old—very old indeed. I had bound the Fens, oh, seven hundred and fifty years ago, as the Ouranatha reckon it.

The Fall of Astandalas had a peculiar effect on temporal progression in the worlds that had once been a part of it. On Zunidh there had been a period when different areas had aged at different rates, so that one village might be generations on from the next. I did not personally feel a thousand and thirty-six years old, but that was what I was told the College of Priest-Wizards had counted.

"We've always burned the Fens, like," Hank said, a little lamely.

The three men were not youths, though hardly of my age (either real or apparent) either. Perhaps they were in their late thirties or early forties. This was not a question of high spirits or mischief, not by their solemnity and caution.

Nevertheless, I was quite sure that even I would have heard—Kip would surely have told me—if people burned the Fens on a regular basis.

"Every year?"

Hank swung the lantern slightly more vigorously than necessary, which I took to be *no*. After a moment he said aloud, "Not for a while, like. Too long."

The circle of light cast odd shadows across the grasses surrounding us. As we'd gone further into the Fens the grasses to each side grew taller, and now were a good three feet over my head. The scent was less brackish and pungent now; rather more just barely sweet, like new hay, and a touch peppery. It did not sound like the reed plains around the Painted City, which were always rustling and full of birds and frogs and insects. These Fens were dead silent and, now that the Fen lights were hidden by the grass, black but for the grey light of the thief's lantern.

It was all rather exciting. What an adventure this was turning out already!

Shorty tried to explain next. "Back when the Last Emperor— you know about him?"

I inclined my head gravely, fighting not to smile. "I do."

"Well, back a while he did this work of magic to make the Fens safe, like," Hank interjected in an explanatory manner.

Shorty nodded. "It was sore dangerous after the Fall—you know about the Fall?"

"I do."

I didn't smile this time, for much as I often disliked my empire I didn't wish for it to be destroyed in a great magical cataclysm, either, nor for myself to be forever written into the history books as the one reigning when that happened.

"Well, like Hank said, the Last Emperor made the Fens safe. But he didn't know—I guess no one told him, and he didn't come asking *us*, see—that the Fens need to burn, or else the Tigara gets ... antsy."

God, sometimes I hate how Kip is always right. He'd told me I should have talked to the inland villagers as well as the ones who lived along the river.

"And what, may I ask, is the Tigara? The Fen spirits?"

We turned another corner, and came up to a kind of wall made of giant grasses or reeds. These ones went high above our heads, out of sight of the thin illumination; the stems I could see were

31

knobbly and thick as my wrist except for the engorged joints larger than a clenched fist. I frowned at them. I think the joints meant that they were a form of grass rather than reed, but it has been a long time since I last studied botany in any way, shape, or form.

The three men stopped. Shorty put his hand on the bicycle handles to tug me to a halt before I quite crashed into Hank.

"We should tell you about the Tigara before we go any further," Hank said seriously. "Stories say—you might be able to tell us if they're true—that you never liked these Fens, is that right?"

I decided to err on the side of an always-true if not necessarily relevant utterance. "Legends are not always inaccurate."

"You see," said Shorty, in a low, satisfied hiss.

Hank ignored him except to hang the lantern on the bicycle handlebar so that he could hook his thumbs into the waistband of the loose trousers he wore. "I don't know if you ever heard tell of what was in here besides the *tipilipi*? The spirits, that is."

I thought of those stories from the river folk. "Hobgoblins and skinwalkers ..."

Hank coughed up another wad of phlegm and spat it into the grasses with a plop that sounded very loud in the stillness. "Not those bogeys from the river-folk. If you were listening to them, no wonder you hated the swamps. They don't like anything that their witches can't help them with. We have *one* skinwalker in a thousand years, *and* we saw to it, and they never can get over it."

"Hank," Shorty said in a warning tone, then added to me, "It's not good to talk about it. No offence to you—it's private. Not for outsiders, not even *you*, sire. Savvy?"

"Entirely," I replied gravely. "But the Tigara?"

The Tigara was clearly not in the same category as hobgoblins or other bogeys of the river-folk. Hank's voice filled with wary pride as he described, a little haltingly, the being at the heart of the Fens.

"In the beginning, the first men came out of a hole in the edge of the Escarpment, in a sacred cave, eh. But there were no women, and they were lonely and sad. They said, 'How can we live like this? We have cows to milk but no women to make cheese, we have clay for pots but no women to cook with them, we have straw for our houses but no women in our beds.'"

I knew better than to interrupt stories of the Beginning, so I merely murmured an encouraging sound.

Hank went on. "So they spoke and were sad. But Crow came down from the Big Sky and said, 'Go into the swamps and ask the Tigara for aid.' The first men listened to Crow and came down from the Escarpment to the edge of the swamps. They found there much clay for their pots, and grasses for their houses, and water for their cows, but they found no women, and they muttered. But Crow came down again and again said, 'Go into the swamps and ask the Tigara for aid.'"

Shorty took up the story next. "The first men made a boat out of the grasses, and they took with them milk from their cows and pots from their workings, and they poled their way deep into the swamps."

"They did not need to worry about the Fen spirits?" I asked, when he stopped there.

"Not then," said Hank, with another phlegmy cough.

"In the deep heart of the swamps the first men found a great circle of water, a lake, black and still," Shorty said. "And there was the Tigara. They asked the Tigara for aid, for women to make cheese and cook and share their beds and so on, for they were lonely and sad without them. And the Tigara said that the women had strayed to find a resting-place, but if the first men were brave they could be found and brought home."

Hank cleared his throat. "The first men were afraid of the Tigara, but one was brave enough, and he said he would go find the women for them all. So the Tigara told him to dive down into the centre of the water, down and down, until he could bring up a root of the *siriava* plant—"

Shorty interrupted him brusquely. "Which is a secret plant, sire,

33

we cannot tell you more of it, but that was what the Tigara wanted."

From the tone of his voice I gathered that this story was not often told to those outside the community, and they were not accustomed to guarding the secret knowledge.

"I understand," I assured him.

Shorty went on. "The bravest of the first men dove down as the Tigara said, and brought back the root from the bottom of the lake for the Tigara, and the Tigara taught them how to find the women and bring them home. So ever after we have honoured the Tigara."

"The Tigara is very old now, and very big, eh, they say," said Hank. "In the old days the Tigara ruled the *tipilipi*, what you call the Fen spirits, and they were ..."

There was a pause, before Shorty offered, "They were always dangerous, but not as dangerous, in the old days. Not to our people, anyways."

It was my understanding that the Fen spirits were more than the mischievous will-o'-the-wisps of other marshes, and not only drowned but also enslaved the souls of their victims as means to ensure their own reproduction.

I confess I was curious. "Were you unhappy with the Last Emperor's work?"

"Oh no, no," said Shorty. "We'd lost some of the old knowledge, see, over time, and the Tigara had fallen asleep, deep *deep* asleep, so we didn't know ... We only ever came to the edge, to get the clay and the grasses, and then only for special ceremonies when you really can't use the regular stuff. We didn't like what the *tipilipi* had become either."

This was a relief. I had obviously missed a few major items in my preparatory work, but at least I didn't feel obliged to re-do (or at least, attempt to re-do) the bindings on behalf of offended locals.

The charming origin story did not explain the need to set the Fens on fire, however, though my three present companions seemed to think it a sufficient explanation.

"Thank you for telling me that story," I said, recalling the manners appropriate to someone not the Last Emperor of Astandalas, or indeed not necessarily *not* the first, and then, when they seemed set to keep walking, added, "Ah—the fire?"

"Oh," said Shorty, in audible surprise at my density.

"The Tigara is very old and very big, like," said Hank, "and needs help to shed its skin. The shamans said now was the time."

"It's an honour," said Wat, the first time he had spoken, in a voice that made it suddenly very clear to me that they had not expected to survive their night's work.

While I have encountered dragons, sea serpents, monstrous lizards, and any number of large snakes—what sort of magic-wielding folk hero hasn't?—giant intelligent serpents from the dawn of time were new to me.

It was more than a little humbling to realize that despite being well-learned in the ways of odd, obscure, and frankly arcane magics—not to mention being personally responsible for the magical state of the world—I had never even heard of the Tigara before, let alone encountered it.

"Oh," I said as we came around the wall of grass and found the circular lake, the waters black and still as promised, and coiled up just under the surface a creature of gold and black and bronzy green. "Isn't it *magnificent*."

The Tigara was enormous. The coils were wide as a horse, filling the lake with layer upon layer of smooth, shining serpent, until nothing was visible but the glass-like surface and the curves of the great creature.

The tiny scales on the massive coils were jewel-bright from an internal glow, for neither the sky nor Hank's thief's lantern illuminated more than our immediate surroundings. The sky was invisible and the water was black, but a few feet under the water the serpent glowed with its own radiance.

I took a few steps away from the others, forgetting about the bicycle until it clattered down onto the boardwalk. I wished I could touch the scales, which were surely smooth as polished metal and soft as fine leather. I could not help myself from letting my magic rise to greet the power here, so very distinct from anything I knew as emperor or as lord magus.

This was not a being of the Schooled Magic of the Empire, or even of the hybrid magic I had wrought since the Fall. The Tigara was one of the Ancients of Days, and it tasted of the Wild.

I made it a quarter of the way around the lake before I came to the end of the boardwalk. I stopped there, and looked back at the three men gathered next to the bicycle, three upright shadows half-outlined by the thief's lantern. The Tigara's light did not reach upward out of the water; nor did the surface ripple.

The surface did not ripple, and I saw no movement, but nevertheless the Tigara lifted its head out of the water to regard me.

The head was a serpent's, not a dragon's: it bore no horns nor ruff nor ears, and its tongue, when it tasted the air, was forked and flickering. Its eyes were dark and lidless and intelligent. It regarded me, tongue flickering to take my scent, and I knew it had felt my magic stir, and recognized it.

I inclined my head to the serpent, as an equal greeting another. "I bid you good evening, Tigara," I said in my most court-formal voice.

The great serpent tilted its head to one side. The air and the water were both very still. My voice was quiet, seeming to fall into silence only a few feet away.

"So you wear a new body now, Crow?" the Tigara said at last, amusement threading through what was otherwise a breathy hiss. "It has been long and long since you sent your people to me."

I have never quite figured out just what it is about me that makes people think I'm a trickster god. Even without such a story as Hank and Shorty had just told me to bear in mind—and I would never knowingly blaspheme sacred stories told me in good faith—I have never felt it a good idea to pretend to a divinity not mine. Presumptuous I may be in many ways, but even I do not go that far.

But oh, how I was tempted to lie!

"I am not Crow," I said, firmly.

The Tigara regarded me with what I have to say struck me as an unbelieving attitude. "If you insist," it said politely, as if this were quite a usual sort of conversation to have with Crow. "Have you a name you wish to use to go along with your current form, then?"

Long experience has taught me to keep all sighs inward and silent. But then again—for the first time in thirty-odd (or a thousand) years I had the opportunity, even the obligation, to give my name of choice. "I do prefer Fitzroy Angursell," I declared happily, smiling brightly at the serpent.

The Tigara actually laughed, with a hissing, chortling sort of snicker, and its glow brightened. "I have been deep in the Dreaming," it said, "but even I have heard that name. No wonder I felt the waters stir when you touched them! Very well, old friend, keep your secrets safe in your nest. What do you intend here tonight?"

I felt on safer ground here. "I was asked to assist in the burning of the Fens."

The Tigara lifted its head, tongue flickering in the direction of Hank and Shorty and Wat. "Ah," it said, lowering itself again down to my level. "I had thought, in my sleep, that all the old ways had been forgotten. Sleep was laid on me and mine, sleep and a soft nest, and a net to hold in place. I stirred in my sleep once, twice, but no one came to the calling, and I sloughed off my old scales as best I could and burrowed deeper into the mud to soothe the itch, and I waited."

"I, too, waited," I said quietly.

The Tigara laughed again, more softly than before. "Crow, waiting! Fitzroy Angursell, counselling sleep and a soft nest! It is long since time for both of us to shed the old skin and burn down the dross."

The great serpent was beautiful and perilous. I was hardly going to offer to free it from the net entirely, not when I knew so few of the stories concerning the Tigara and the *tipilipi* Fen lights.

Kip, for one, would be deeply unhappy if I brought all riverside trade to a screeching halt because of a misplaced unbinding. I may be an anarchist by temperament but my odd friendship with that devoted bureaucrat has taught me *some* appreciation for the joys of orderly government.

Besides, if I did something like that everyone would know I was here. There was no one of sufficient magical skill currently in Solaara to tell that *I* set the Fens on fire, but anyone with half a brain could figure out that the only person who could easily and invisibly change the bindings on the Fens was the person who set them in the first place.

"These men are brave," I said then, "and they did me a good turn."

The Tigara gave me a too-knowing look with its inhuman dark eyes, and it laughed again. This time the hisses set up little running whispers in the grass around us.

My emperor has donkey ears, I thought, keeping my countenance serene.

"They have seen me," said the Tigara, lifting its head high and then arcing it down over the three men and the bicycle like a flash of lightning, jaws wide as its bronze tongue darted out over them, perhaps even to touch their heads. A faint cry came back across the black water towards me, and a motion as if one were swaying with the shock. But they did not fall, and they did not say anything else. With a motion fast as a whiplash the Tigara drew back to its former position next to me. The water stilled almost immediately.

"They are brave," the Tigara proclaimed. "And as in the past Crow has spoken for their people, and I have listened for the good to be done for me, so now do you speak for them, and I listen, for the good to be done for me. Light the grasses, Fitzroy Angursell. Shed the old skin, burn the dross, bring renewal to the waters. The people will witness, as their ancestors witnessed, and take back the news of the Ancient of Days to their sons and daughters. So shall it be."

I reviewed the phrases quickly and then agreed with all due solemnity. "So shall it be. I bid you a good renewal, Tigara."

The Tigara laughed again, and this time the whispers did not fade. "I bid you a good burning, Fitzroy Angursell. Do not forget your old friends for so long again."

Sound advice in so many ways!

I inclined my head in farewell, then turned and walked back towards the other men. The Tigara watched me go; when I reached the circle cast by the thief's lantern I felt a brief rush of wind and heard a nearly soundless *Fly with joy, old Crow* as the great head plunged past us into the water and disappeared into the endless coils.

One look at Hank's face in the lantern-light made it clear our voices had not carried. All they had seen was me talking to the Tigara, equal to equal.

I grinned brightly at them and rubbed my hands together. "Shall we? The night is wearing on, and I grow hungry. The Tigara says you are worthy of carrying the night's deeds home to your people, and grants me permission to be the fire-lighter. I trust you will not make any unnecessary confession of arson; you need only tell the truth as you have witnessed it, and blame me."

"But we asked you to help us, eh," Hank said.

It amazes me that people manage to get to adulthood without understanding the fundamental means of obfuscating a matter by telling the truth.

I said patiently, "You came across a man who had fallen into the Fens while cycling at night. He claimed to be heading towards the River-Horse Inn, but was nowhere near the river path. Whether or not you believed his story is immaterial ..."

"I understand," said Shorty, who was emerging as the most quick-witted of the two of them. (I had my doubts about the taciturn Wat. Of my most silent guards, one is a quite accomplished poet and, indeed, Commander in Chief of the Imperial Guard, and the other is steady as a foundation wall. You can imagine which was the one to assist me most.)

"Very good. Shall I begin?"

They nodded, or I thought they did. I was conscious of the no-doubt still observing Tigara, and the reputation that I apparently had even amongst originary deities, not to mention the one that has spent thirty-odd (or a thousand) years building amongst my people, and … well.

How could I resist the advice given me by the ancient serpent?

Burn down the dross, indeed.

I smiled at the three men, whose body language was both apprehensive and excited. Wary, fearful, exalted: had they anticipated *seeing* the Tigara? Had they thought they would come to the centre of the Fens and fire the dead grass and wood around them, and hope they did the right thing according to their ancient traditions even as they burned with the rest?

I squatted down, rather awkwardly, and laid both palms flat on the boardwalk. I sent my magic into the wood, running down the boards and the piers and the longer pieces (the stringers?) supporting the cross-pieces. The piers were indeed ancient, the boards younger, decades rather than centuries old. My magic touched the wood and laid protections along it, against fire but also against rot while I was about it.

The spirit houses along the edges of the Fens sparkled in my mind, their magic almost alien despite being my own. So many years—generations for the river-folk—of witches bringing their salt and wine and speaking the little spells that anchored the working. Each utterance, each offering, laying a knot in the magic that was not mine, tying the net ever tighter and holding the Fen spirits within their bounds.

I was glad withal it was myself lighting the fire, for I could ensure it did not destroy those bindings as it burned down the rest. I hoped Kip would appreciate the restraint when he realized it was me.

As a final gesture I drew my magic around the three men and myself to protect us from what was shortly to be a raging inferno. It was visible in the air, a flurry of gold and scarlet sparks. I wished I had put back on my scarlet silk mantle but it really *wasn't*—

Oh, the hell with prudence.

I reached into the bag and pulled it out first try, which was … useful … and slung it over my shoulder and around my arm with a flourish. It was hardly past midnight. One likes to dress the part as much as possible, you see.

One likes to do the whole thing properly, in fact.

I reached into my bag again and pulled out a harp. I spent a few moments checking the tuning of the strings, because playing out of tune is something I abhor. It's not as if I were actually going to perform magic by means of music—though I have met a few practitioners of that and related arts—more that I was going to accompany my magic-working with music. For the effect, I suppose you could say.

I started with fire at the roots of the grasses nearest me, and a flurry of low notes on the harp. Hank and Wat were staring at me with their mouths open; Shorty was looking madly confused. I laughed at them in wild delight as the fires caught and my fingers remembered what they were doing.

And then as the fire spiralled up the knobbly grass stems the words came, and I lifted up my voice in song, for I was always a poet before a musician, and my muse loves chaos.

The fire rose and my voice lifted and the darkness and the silence of the Fens broke open like a thunderbolt striking a forest into flame.

4

IN WHICH I MAKE A GRAND EXIT

At some point in the night the Tigara tossed a large fish, already well-charred, onto the boardwalk. My companions of the night and I ate it gratefully, and drank a bottle of wine I had in my bag. It was a much finer vintage than anything the three villagers had ever had before, and they drank deeply and with great enthusiasm. I was more moderate, as it doesn't do to mix fire, magic, and alcohol in large quantities.

Hank and Shorty fell asleep soon after. The fire had moved away from our immediate vicinity and was dancing around grasses further off, in a widening circle out from the lake. Wat watched me for a while longer, eyes wide in the light reflecting off clouds and water.

He spoke only once more that night. I stood up from where I had been sitting with them, stretching out the stiffness from the hour on the bicycle and the unaccustomed posture. I have contracted the unfortunate habit of restless pacing, so the walking had not been as foreign a movement, but my feet were not used to the friction of sandal straps and dust.

"Who are you, really?" Wat asked, as I turned in a slow pirou-

ette to consider the progress of the fire and summoned a light
breeze to shift the smoke away from us. It lay in drifts over the
black water, catching the faintest of golden glows from the Tigara's
deep-plunged coils.

I shook out the scarlet mantle and replaced it, thinking of what
to say. We could not see each other's expressions, not in the dark.
There was just our voices, and the distant murmur of the fire, and a
few isolated plinks as burnt stems dropped into the water.

"Who do you think I am?"

"Shorty thought you might be the old emperor, but I don't
know … The Tigara came to speak to you."

"And so?"

"I always thought you were a myth," he said in a lower voice.
"Coming out of nowhere to spark adventure …"

He made noises indicative of doubt, shifting a bit on the boards
and making the bicycle jangle softly as he knocked against the
chain. I waited.

"My granny always said you'd come—if you came—inexplicably."

I was not at all certain if he was speaking of Fitzroy Angursell
or Crow or some other figure out of his people's legendary. I
smiled, unseen, into the dark. "Your granny sounds a wise
woman."

"Come inexplicably, do something wild and joyous and strange,
and leave even more inexplicably, with only a song and the world
upended to show you've passed by."

I could not help but be wholly delighted with being given this
reputation, whether or not it was in fact mine. "I shall do my best,"
I promised solemnly.

Off in the distance, a shining gold length of the Tigara arced out
of the burning grasses and twisted sinuously, even sybaritically, in
the air. Wat saw it as well, for he chuckled weakly and lay down
next to the softly snoring Hank.

"Oh, you've started well, at least," he said with a yawn, and then, more quietly, "Thank you," almost to himself. I noticed then that there were tear tracks reflecting the flames on his face, and did not do anything so crass as to respond to his words.

I did not know how he and Hank and Shorty had come to be the ones who walked into the Fens in the dark of the Moon one night, believing that they would not come back, but I saluted their courage.

Dawn came dressed in silver-grey like one of the Ouranatha.

I had moved a little away from the three men sleeping next to the bicycle, and was playing the harp quietly as I folded the magic back into quiescence.

There remained a few smouldering tussocks, but most of what I could see was black and grey: black water, blackened rootstocks, and grey smoke rising. Ashes spiralled by. After an attack of sneezes mercifully unwitnessed by anyone, I kept the ashes away along with the mosquitos still buzzing despite the night's fire.

I walked to the end of the boardwalk. The Tigara was just visible below the water, gleaming gold and bronze under the surface. The black mud was drifting back over the shining coils, and soon would hide the ancient being entirely.

Over in the East, I could see the sun rising over the sea, visible now that the tall grasses were gone but red from the smoke. A distant oblong shape resolved itself into a building, probably the River-Horse Inn; it was much farther away than I had thought last night. I would have been sore and hungry by the time I'd reached it, if indeed I did through the midst of the Fens when I was following the lights and not my own magic.

I am not, after all, actually immortal.

I took a deep, pleased breath. The air was scented not of ashes but of orange-blossoms.

I felt I made a very satisfying picture: a tall black-skinned man, regal of bearing, with the white tunic, and the scarlet silk mantle, and a golden harp in his hands, all against the backdrop of the black water and the rising smoke and the silvery-grey dawn.

The magic was finished, the Fen spirits back in their slumbers, the Tigara down below the mud in its fresh new skin. The wind blew from the East, off the still-distant ocean, though high above me a few clouds, catching the rising sun so they glowed peach and lavender, were moving in the other direction. I turned around to ensure the fire didn't spread out of bounds, satisfied with the night's adventure, and saw bearing down on me across the Fens a ship.

For a moment I stood there awestruck and amazed at the sight, mind dizzyingly full of strange possibilities and fulsome improbabilities. The wooden ship was narrow, the sides blue and green, the central keel a cheerful orange rising up to form a figurehead in the shape of a white swan. Two masts carried ranks of triangular white sails aloft against the silver sky.

It was not in the water; it was skimming the Fens like a low-flying bird.

Faint calls came down the wind as figures moved about the rigging and two came to the side facing me. The ship heeled over to my right and lifted a bare few feet higher off the marshes, slowing as it turned, always keeping me at the centre. It came to a near-halt over the circular lake in which the Tigara dwelled, a masterpiece of sailing I applauded. I have been on the sky ships any number of times, and never had I seen one sailed so finely so close to the ground.

One of the figures at the railing nearest me lifted a hand to wave. "Ahoy the ground!"

I waved back. "Ahoy the ship!"

"All right down there?"

The question was honest; the figure's companion was holding

an item I was fairly sure was a rolled-up rope ladder. I was touched by this concern, and mindful also of Wat's night-time confession of his granny's stories. I had no particular desire to leave the swamps afoot—there was no way I would be getting back on that bicycle if there were any other options to be had—so I waved at them in what they easily interpreted as a request for assistance.

They could not halt the ship entirely, of course. By the time the rope ladder had unrolled to the point where it was accessible, they had circled around almost to the end of the boardwalk. I stowed my harp with careful haste in my replacement bag and tripped lightly to the ladder.

It was harder to climb than I had anticipated. The ship's deck was perhaps twenty feet above the boardwalk, and the rope ladder was unattached to anything but the railing at the top. It swung against the side of the ship under my weight, the movement exacerbated as the vessel just kissed the heavy black water and lifted again.

"I really must work on my upper body strength," I muttered as I reached the top of the railing and nearly fell over it in my haste to be aboard. One of the two women waiting there laughed. The other made as if to assist me upright, but I waved her away instinctively. I used to be quite a tactile person, but learned otherwise as emperor and lord magus; touching the Imperial Person without proper ritual cleansing was taboo on pain of death.

"Ah, thank you," I said when I had managed to rearrange the silk mantle and my bag to their approximate proper locations and ensured the harp had not suffered by being stuffed into the bag, pulling it out again until I found the case.

The older of the two, a no-nonsense-looking woman of around fifty dressed in undyed linen tunic and trousers with a richly dyed orange silk robe overtop (by which I deduced she was probably the ship's captain), gave me a thorough once-over. She raised her eyebrows at the end, but jerked her head over the side instead of commenting directly. "What about the others down below? They all right?"

I smiled at her. "Sleeping off an excess of excellent wine, that's all. They're locals to the area, and will have a story to take home with them."

"Seeing as the Fens were lit on fire around them last night, I daresay they will," the captain said. "One moment—sir." She turned and called a series of commands, which inspired a flurry of activity amongst the ropes and rigging. A few seconds later the ship gave a shudder and angled over sharply—I grabbed the railing to catch my balance, to the other woman's silent amusement; she stood easily upright—before the upper sails caught the wind and whoever was on the tiller angled the keel just so, and the ship lifted up like a gull into the air.

"Now then," the captain said, turning back to me.

I liked her voice, which was low and a little hoarse. She was handsome, her face full of character. She had light brown skin and dark and exuberant hair.

She saw me looking at it and lifted her hand a trifle self-consciously. "Do I have something in my hair?"

I laughed. "No, no! I was merely reflecting that mine used to be as wonderfully wild as yours is."

"A long time ago, I'm guessing," she said, with a meaningful nod towards my bald pate.

"It was, yes," I agreed, sighing extravagantly. "Well before the Fall, in fact."

I have a private theory that the aristocratic fashion for shaving the head bald originated with an ancestor of mine who did not like the way his head was balding naturally, but have never found a source for this asseveration. I also have no idea whether I personally have a tendency towards baldness nor what pattern of alopecia or silvering I might expect to discover when my hair does grow out, since it has been shaved—or to be more accurate, depilated with a special cream—since my thirty-second year.

The captain's eyebrow rose again. "Before the Emperor Artorin's time, I take it?"

I winked at her and shifted the harp slightly, so the strings chimed softly. "Just so."

"I take it," the captain said after a moment's consideration, "that I would probably regret asking you your name?"

"I do try hard to ensure that people do not *regret* meeting me," I returned, "though on the other hand, there is such a thing as plausible deniability."

She made an amused, agreeing gesture. "We do not, in the main, take on passengers."

"I could trade songs for my supper; and you need not put my name on the manifest."

"The officials in Tsilo may insist otherwise."

I shrugged. "I'm sure I will think of something before we get there. I used to be reckoned quite accomplished at improvisation."

The captain bit back a short laugh. "Is that so? Well, Laura, it looks as if we have a guest. Give him a berth and whatnot and we'll have breakfast at eight bells."

Laura regarded me with a deep suspicion. I grinned at her and the captain snorted, which pleased me enormously. Laura sighed.

There were only two dozen or so of the sky ships, as the floating pines that provide buoyancy rarely grow large enough to form the keels of anything much bigger than a small dinghy. The floating pines themselves were a strange natural response to the odd magic of the Fall. Discovering how to harness their buoyancy had made wealthy the princes of Amboloyo (where the pines grow) and Southern Dair (where the wizard-engineers who had designed the ships came from).

Each of the seventeen princes of Zunidh had one, and the

Ouranatha and the Imperial Guard each had three for their use, and one was the flagship reserved for mine. The remaining four or five were given over to government business, primarily the swift passage of parcels and other material goods. This one's white sails and swan figurehead indicated it was commonly used for the post: I well remembered Kip's glee at instituting a worldwide competition for the aesthetic scheme of his new institution.

I had come aboard near the middle of the ship. The doubting Laura rolled up the rope ladder and handed it off to a passing sailor to deal with. The sailor asked her a question, which she answered in a moderately brisk sort of voice. I took the opportunity to look over the side.

We had already left behind the blackened Fens, still partially obscured with smoke, and were now over the mouth of the River Dwahaii and the commercial harbour of Port Izharou. We must have been five or six hundred feet up and still rising, heading slightly north of east, so the bulk of the sails obscured the direct light of the sun. Tsilo is the second largest city in the province of Amboloyo, located on the most northerly inhabited island of Zunidh, so I presumed our direction was across the Eastern Ocean and over the northern portion of the continent of Kavanduru.

Farther west the sun caught the golden domes of the Palace of Stars and the white city around it, and yet farther back the Grey Mountains were all pale stone outcroppings and dark green jungle. Waterfalls, thin and intermittent as they are in the dry season, flashed as the ship moved out over the Eastern Ocean.

I turned to Laura, who was waiting almost patiently, with a broad smile. "I don't suppose there's any chance of a bath, is there?"

She gave me an incredulous stare and then started to laugh almost despite herself. "By the Emperor," she said, "you certainly did your research!"

She clearly thought I was either deliberately tricking them or entirely mad. I smiled, not in a way calculated to reassure her. "I do try."

～

Laura led me to a hatch in the prow of the ship, which opened on a short ladder descending to a corridor that mostly led back towards the stern but had three doors forward. One seemed to be the galley, from the sounds and smells drifting out of the half-closed door. I hadn't any time to investigate this intriguing place, for Laura was opening the door to what she called the head but I would call the privy (if I ever called it anything at all; I had all sorts of code phrases to indicate to my guards I wished to visit). Private indeed it was, being barely two feet wide.

Next to the privy was an equally narrow closet whose most obvious features were a bamboo pipe sticking out of the ceiling, brass handles on one wall, and a grooved wooden floor sloping towards an opening that appeared to lead right through the side of the ship. I regarded the space politely.

"You've never been in one before?" Laura asked, then answered her own question. "Of course you haven't. This is a water closet."

She indicated one of the handles sticking out of the wall beside the door. "Pull the lower one to open a trickle. Here."

I stepped into the space to try it and get away from her close proximity. She passed me a shallow wooden bowl and a sponge from somewhere. Tugging on the handle released a thin stream of water, which splashed over my feet onto the floor and ran off to the opening. I watched this, pleased, and Laura grabbed the bowl back out of my hand and deftly caught the water before turning off the handle.

"When you're done with the sponge bath, pull the other handle for an overhead sluice. Do you need a towel?"

I was fairly certain Conju, my chief attendant, had packed me several, but before I could say anything she'd turned around again with one in her hands. This time I saw the open door of a cupboard in the hall, presumably the storage for the water closet.

"Soap, too, I suppose," she muttered, putting a small white patty on top of the towel. "Don't use too much water—there's not an unlimited supply, and this is a five-day run out and back. Leave the towel in here when you're done and come back on deck."

I took the towel with the hand that wasn't holding the half-full basin. "Thank you."

She gave me a shake of her head that made her long braids swing and hastened off into the galley to speak to whoever was in there.

She must be the second in command, I mused, with that sort of practiced and practical efficiency.

I shut the door, which latched into place with a pair of brass hooks. The water closet was narrow and not much deeper than it was wide, with the far wall curved with the side of the ship. It was quite high-ceilinged, however, with an open window letting in light and air above even my head. A brass grille prevented anything large from coming in or out.

There were hooks—brass again—on the inside of the door. One for the towel, one for my bag, and one for my clothes, I presumed. Surely such a well-appointed closet would have somewhere cunning for me to set the basin down—and there it was, a little wooden rack that folded out of the wall next to the handles, just the right size for the basin and the sponge. There was even a little ceramic cup for the soap.

The closet had enough elbow room that I could take off my tunic and fold it and the silk mantle into the bag without banging my extremities more than once. I hit the door with my elbow and was glad for the hooks, for I was fairly sure I would have popped the latch otherwise. I pressed the door back into place and surveyed the grey footprints I had left all over the floor. In the light of day I could see that I was thoroughly coated in dried mud that made my skin seem about eight shades lighter and several tones warmer brown than in truth.

I dipped the sponge into the water already in the basin and daubed at my forearm, which did nothing but streak the mud, and looked thoughtfully up at the pipe in the ceiling before reminding myself that I was an unexpected guest and it behoved me to follow their instructions about water usage.

Besides, I was on an adventure. I may be accustomed *now* to bathing in what amounts to a swimming pool, but there was a time when a sponge bath would have seemed a luxury.

A lukewarm sponge bath after a night spent coated in dried mud might not have been luxurious, but it felt splendid. I was particularly pleased by the douse of sun-warmed water at the end.

I might have been a little enthusiastic with that, actually, as the towel was perhaps a bit damp when I came to dry off. There are some benefits to being older and more experienced: the bag's enchantments had thankfully kept all its contents safe. As I decided what to wear next I reflected that I had not been all that sympathetic to Conju's entreaties that I place *all possible* magical protections on the bag.

Despite agreeing with the practical suggestion, I had protested that surely I wouldn't need them, mostly to keep Conju (of all my household, the most nervous about this excursion; and that was without knowing me for Fitzroy Angursell) from fretting himself to distraction. And yet here I was, not even a full day since leaving the Palace, and the bag had already been subjected to tomb dust, swamp mud, being spattered by a cooked fish, and both fire *and* water.

I could hardly wait for what would come next—though of course I was currently most looking forward to breakfast.

Bearing in mind that the temperature several thousand feet up would be much cooler than the Equator at sea level, I selected a fine woollen robe to go over a fresh white linen tunic. I debated about socks, but left them off for now on the thought that I couldn't recall the last time I'd had cold feet.

The robe was a wonderful apricot colour, embroidered all along the hems with delicately dawn-tinted clouds. It was north-Voonran in style and origin, falling to my calves and buttoning up the front with many small amber toggles into green silk cord loops. I was glad of the privacy as I did up the buttons, for I missed the proper sequence twice before I got them satisfactorily aligned.

It's amazing how little of any practical activity one does as an emperor. Sometimes I wondered if I would forget how to use my hands for anything but signing my name.

Once dressed and invigorated, I visited the privy (also brass and bamboo and the reddish wood), and then made my way up the short ladder and out into the bright, refreshingly cool air on deck.

A quick peek over the railing showed us to be well out over the ocean. The coast of Eastern Dair was a dim brownish line in the distance, with a pale splotch that must have been Solaara and a darker green line for the Grey Mountains behind. A few white clouds were piling themselves up over the mountains, the only ones to be seen except for high feathery clouds that betokened good weather ahead.

A couple of gulls were soaring beside us. I met one's savage golden eye as it passed, and laughed aloud when it tilted its wings away from me to take up a station further down the ship. I've always liked gulls, fierce scavengers that they are. They would have been a better emblem for the emperors than the bee Yr the Conqueror chose.

I was hungry, and didn't dawdle to investigate as I made my way aft. I've flown on sky ships reasonably often, once or twice a year: it is such a production to go anywhere with the entourage expected of me. Only once have I travelled without a full retinue, on my single true holiday, which Kip organized for me in his home-land of the Vangavaye-ve on the other side of the world. And even then I spent that journey, like all the rest, in my cabin.

A young sailor, almost as black-skinned as myself, slid down the central mast as I passed amidships. He saluted me cheerfully.

"Hallo," I returned. "Are you to guide me somewhere, or just curious?"

He grinned happily. "Mostly curious, sir! But come with me, I'll show you to the captain's table."

He wasn't much more than a boy, surely fifteen at the most, and wore his hair in short braids with wooden beads at the ends. Potentially a scion of the upper nobility trying to pass himself off as less posh than he was, though he must be a prodigy with accents for that to be the case, or a scion of one of the darker-skinned tribes trying a new life. He wouldn't be Tkinele, as he had no ritual scars on his arms or face, but he might have been Choksoi or even Damaran. I considered his broad features and wide nose and the geometric lines carved on the wooden beads.

"Choksoi?" I guessed.

"Dobu, but close enough."

Dobu was the next island over, so I was well pleased.

"Golly, but you're darker than I thought—from the songs, I mean. Oh—Cap'n said we weren't to ask for names."

He sound very disappointed, which made me chuckle.

"That doesn't mean I can't tell a story or two—anyone might know them, you know."

"But you *do* know them, personally, don't you?"

"Depends on the story, of course."

"Can you tell us the one about going to the Moon's country?" he asked eagerly. "Is that one really true?"

I considered how to answer that. "I'm not sure what version you might have heard, but if the captain doesn't object I can tell *my* version later—and that one will be as true as you can believe."

"Golly," he said again. "I never thought I'd ever get to meet *you*! Are you—are the rest of the Red Company—oh, I'm not supposed to ask!"

That was nearly a wail of anguish. I grinned at him. "I'm on a quest at the moment, and indeed I do hope to meet up with old friends of mine. I won't say their names, as I'm sure you've heard them, too."

Damian Raskae. Pharia Cloudbringer. Jullanar of the Sea.

Pali Avramapul. Her sister Sardeet Avramapul. Gadarved the Tall.

Faleron the Blue. Ayasha e'Oroto-o. Masseo Umrit.

And me.

"Have I ever," he breathed, then jumped when a bell rang vigorously from somewhere all too close by. "Oh! This way, sir, the captain's waiting."

He was proud of the ship, it was obvious, and though he didn't waste any more time, he did point out various features of interest to him as we traversed the length of the ship to reach the rear cabins.

He knocked on the door of one and said, "Your guest, cap'n," with another salute, this one rather more crisp.

The captain waved him off and welcomed me into the cabin, which was not large but was as well-appointed (and as predominantly brass and wood) as the water closet. Two large windows took up most of the rear wall, and well-latched built-in cupboards and chests of drawers ran around the other walls. Maps showing the eastern and western hemispheres of Zunidh, with the Lights marked in silver ink, were the main decoration.

There was a large table set for four in the middle of the room. The captain sat at the head, Laura to her right, and a man of similar enough feature and colouring to be a close relation of the captain's to her left. The man regarded me with open skepticism; but as I assessed his mood I could see a suppressed desire that I be exactly who they suspected in his eyes.

I gave them my best, least imperial smile, wide and frank and merry, and thanked them fulsomely for their hospitality even as I seated myself at the last place.

"Welcome to the *Northern Joy*," the captain said. "I'm Captain

Audmon, and Laura Mwalasa is my second. This is my brother, the postmaster."

Postmaster Audmon frowned at me. "And you, I am to understand, are …?"

"I've been called any number of things over the years, some of them well deserved and many much appreciated," I replied cheerfully. "I do answer to extravagant titles but the name Tor is quite acceptable and not entirely inapt."

"You do have a silver tongue, I suppose," he admitted begrudgingly.

"Oh, not silver! Gold, surely, at the least."

My late cousin Shallyr was called the Silvertongue, and having met him on several occasions I had no wish to be compared to him. For all my faults—and I am aware I do have some—at least the majority of my criminal offences were against silly and unjust laws, and I am not of such brutal insanity that someone felt the need to murder me to prevent me from acceding to the throne. Quite the opposite, in fact.

I leaned forward earnestly. "I've never had roses and diamonds fall from my mouth, which is just as well, as, while fragrant, it did seem most uncomfortable, the time I saw it; nor have I been afflicted with toads and snakes either, which would be more useful to many communities but even less pleasant than the rocks and the thorns."

"I—" The Postmaster started to speak, then stopped with a puzzled countenance. After a moment he went on more slowly, as if sounding out each syllable with the greatest of care. "I have no idea what you're talking about."

Laura made an abortive gesture by her head that clearly indicated she thought me cuckoo-mad, while the captain's lips were twitching again as she tried to keep from laughing.

I smiled winsomely at the Postmaster. "Admitting one's ignorance is the first step along the road to wisdom, or at least to better knowledge. Oh, is that breakfast? I give you thanks," I added to the youngish man who had come in with a tray containing bowls of a rice dish, possibly the congee of which I have heard tell. (It is not a dish served at my table.) He set them down before us and offered coffee, which I eagerly accepted.

"Surely you don't need the buzz," the Postmaster drawled.

"I like the flavour. Also I was awake all night. It was splendidly invigorating to experience the douse."

"You do clean up well," the captain said. "You're ... darker than I'd thought."

Pigeon-holing by appearances is one of humanity's greatest joys. I shrugged as magnificently as I could. "I fell into the Fens."

Laura shuddered, but she had a Western Dairese accent and so it was not because of the Fen spirits. "Did you have any problems with leeches?"

"You are a woman of exquisite sensibilities," I told her gravely. "I did; but fortunately I learned that fire dissuades them."

"Whence the ... conflagration?" the Postmaster asked with a certain degree of snark.

"No, no, that was requested by one of the Ancients of Days." Mirth bubbled in the captain's eyes. I turned to her. "You can hardly blame a poet for not putting one's most distinguishing physical features into songs meant for general dissemination. One might occasionally wish to be discreet."

At least, I presumed that if I had not been wearing what amounted to the costume of Fitzroy Angursell from the songs they would have been substantially less likely to come up with the idea on their own.

The Postmaster affected amazement. "Really?"

I was beginning to like him, but the captain seemed to feel trouble was brewing, for she passed her brother a bowl of sugar without being asked and prompted me with the words, "So, about these diamonds and snakes?"

"It's a convoluted and fabulous tale," I said, settling into my seat and into careful assessment of my audience, who were close to rapt.

"I find them often the best kind, especially when they are also true, as is this one. You see, once when I was younger I travelled with some friends—you will understand if I do not name them—to a country on the edge of Faery, and along the way we encountered this boy trying to sell his mother's cow, which we needed for our own purposes, and so bargained with him to sell it to us for a handful of magic beans ..."

5

IN WHICH I AM AIDED AND ABETTED

a fter breakfast my hosts had to return to their duties; or at least Laura and the Postmaster did, looking as if they didn't know to what degree they should consider my tale a complete fabrication. The captain told me she felt well repaid for her decision to bring me aboard already, so that was all right.

I expressed interest in the ship, so the captain showed me around practically every inch. I'd never given so thorough an inspection in my own official capacity, not even when the first of the sky ships was built and I helped launch her maiden flight.

Captain Audmon loved the *Northern Joy* and her work and was at least fond of most of her sailors. For their part they appeared happy enough, even the ones engaged in the tedious jobs of polishing the many brass fittings or washing the decks.

"It's a privilege to sail her," Captain Audmon explained when I commented on this. "We always have far more applicants than places for them. Who doesn't want to fly?"

"I've always wished I could," I agreed, though I knew at least one person sufficiently terrified of heights to prefer staying well away from the ships. Well, two, unless Jullanar had overcome her fears in the time since I had last seen her.

"You're a wizard, aren't you?"

I made a noncommittal gesture with my hands. "A wild mage, rather, and generally good with weather in particular, but I haven't figured out the knack. Not to say I never will, of course. I keep working on it."

The captain looked at me for a long, surprisingly serious moment. I regarded her equally seriously, enjoying the opportunity to look my fill on someone. I was careful not to meet her eyes full-on—my level of magic makes that a chancy proposition—but it was lovely to see, and be seen.

"I envy your … verve," she said at last.

"Verve is an excellent word," I agreed.

"No, I mean … You're not *young*, are you?"

Everyone seemed dead-set on reminding me of this lately. "It's not such a terrible thing," I complained. "I'm sure I would have been horribly stiff after riding a bicycle for two hours when I was thirty, too."

Captain Audmon shook her head and leaned back against the railing so her hair bounced in the wind. I watched it enviously. She lifted her hand again. "Do you really like my hair that much? No one else does! My brother thinks it's unprofessional."

"How absurd of him."

She laughed. "He can be. Have you any siblings?—I'm sorry, that was indiscreet."

"I have a sister, but we're not close. She's younger than I, and we were raised separately."

The captain's eyes were on a pair of gulls flying next to the ship, wingtips nearly touching. "What happened to you, really?"

I stepped back so I could look out past her. We'd moved round to the north side of the ship by this point of the tour, so the sun was behind the sails and our shadow visible on the silvered-blue surface of the sea, far below us. The air was bright and cool and smelled like very distant mountains.

"What happened?" I murmured at length. The air caressed my head and made the captain's kinked curls quiver, and fluttered my robes against my calves. "You will understand that the full tale will have to wait until I have told certain of my friends first."

"Of course," Captain Audmon said at once. "I apologize if I am out of line."

I dismissed this with an airy gesture. "Your curiosity is perfectly natural. For almost a decade my friends and I travelled widely and did many great and remarkable things, and were subjects of many rather popular songs. And then one day—"

I paused. Captain Audmon gave me a sidelong glance, half-doubtful and half-wistful. Her voice was equally ambivalent. "They ... you ... stopped. And no one ever heard tell anything more about any of you."

I was sorry that my own understanding that my friends had gone to ground as thoroughly as myself was not discredited. Well, I would find out what had happened to them one way or another.

In some ways it was a relief to know that the intelligence-gathering operations of my empire had not been so ineffectual.

Speaking of which, I was probably being overly indiscreet.

I considered her impulse to immediate hospitality. The captains of the sky ships were technically part of what remained of the Imperial Army, and though they had a good deal of independence, as far as I was aware this did not usually extend to collecting unofficial passengers who were not-so-secretly notorious outlaws. I owed her an explanation, I decided, and it was my practice to give one that would be more marvellous the more she understood of what I meant.

"The short answer is that a curse on my family caught up with me," I said therefore.

The captain's eyes widened most gratifyingly.

"I have spent the time since subject to a grievous enchantment which I have only recently begun to lift."

"Oh," she said faintly.

I grinned at her, and made her a solemn and grand promise. "History is being reshaped even as we speak by the quest I am undertaking. You will look back on this encounter a year from now and marvel that you had your part to play in the great narrative."

Captain Audmon laughed and called on Laura to show me to a hammock.

I spent the day lounging on a bed with bars along its side, like a child's crib. I was fully game to trying the hammock, but after watching me try unsuccessfully to clamber into it for several minutes Laura couldn't take it any longer and took me to one of the guest cabins. It was, unsurprisingly, small and made of wood and brass, and quite pleasant.

The bed was probably better for my back than the hammock would have been.

People often think the life of upper royalty is one of endless leisure and obscene consumption. While I can't deny the great wealth at my command—a world has quite literally given me tithes of the best of all things produced for a thousand years—leisure is as precious a commodity to me as to any of my subjects. More so, I sometimes think, for even Kip, extravagantly overworked as he unfortunately is, has annual holidays and most evenings for himself. My days are regulated to the quarter-hour from dawn till midnight.

Laying about on a bed during the day is, in short, not something I have often done apart from the period I was recuperating from a heart attack. And since I do not have outdoor windows in my bedroom (for reasons of ancient custom regarding the security of the emperors of Astandalas, not personal preference), lounging on a bed in the daylight felt deliciously scandalous and just that perfect touch debauched.

I slept for a while, to make up for the sleepless night and the busy day yesterday, then read one of the novels I had brought with me, a humorous mystery I thoroughly enjoyed. I dozed after that, daydreaming of new poems while letting my magic relax and match resonance with the ship.

The sky ships are able to fly because of the cunning mixture of shipbuilding techniques and aeronautical magic developed by the guild of wizards based in Southern Dair, but their great speed in crossing oceans is possible due to magic I had wrought for a different purpose entirely.

The Lights were intended to corral the unruly and chaotic magic caused by the Fall of Astandalas into a kind of orderliness, acting as linchpins for a network of enchantments I had cast with great effort over many years. Each Light—and there were several dozen around the world—represented years' worth of calculations and careful ritual preparations.

That sort of magic is not my natural inclination, and it was a slow, difficult grind to effect. It was my responsibility as Lord of Zunidh to do *something*, and I was the only one of sufficient power and imagination to create it. Like the work on the Fens, I was proud of the result.

By the time I had finished the anchors, the Lights, the magic had stabilized enough for wizards to begin rebuilding according to the tenets developed in Astandalan days, and the weird fluctuations in time had mostly normalized. It is rarely the case nowadays that someone leaves his home village and returns six months later to find that centuries have gone by, and even rarer that the opposite happens, which I believe is a relief to everyone.

Events inside the Palace still seemed to occupy as much time as seemed necessary (to whom? it wasn't me) without much heed paid to what the outside world was experiencing. I didn't myself much notice the effect, but Kip, whose family lives on the other side of the world, occasionally mentioned that he was surprised by the intervals between annual festivals and so on, and wondered if he'd missed one somewhere along the line.

Kip had survived the Fall in the Palace, and was one of those who had spent an indeterminate period of time travelling home, in a small boat he had built himself to sail across the entire width of the Wide Seas, to find that barely a year or two had passed there.

Perhaps it is to *his* idea of how much time things ought to take that the Palace clock runs. He may not be a wizard of any form but his mind shapes the world even so.

It was, of course, Kip who had realized the Lights represented far more than a stable network of magical nodes, and he had set wizards and engineers and artists and all sorts of seemingly unrelated trades to investigating the possibilities. Eventually it became clear that people could use the Lights to improve certain forms of communication and transport. Anything larger than a letter needs to go by ordinary physical means, but letters themselves could be ported from one Light to the next without great difficulty.

And the sky ships could use the connections between the Lights to boost their speed. Between the leylines connecting the Lights the ships could go only at the speed of the wind in their sails, but following the leylines from Light to Light they could reach incredible speeds. From Solaara to Tsilo along the line of Lights including Copper Eyot, Gadora, and Boloyo City would take a day and half, while a sea-borne clipper might take three months to cover the same distance.

Of course, there only those two dozen or so sky ships, whereas there are as many clippers as the shipwrights of the world choose to make.

So I lay there dreaming the day away, resting and relaxing, clean and content and aware of the movement humming in the wood and brass and air all around me. I should not like to spend every day doing that, but it made for a pleasant change.

In the late afternoon I emerged to see what I might find on deck.

We had passed over Copper Eyot sometime earlier in the day. I had felt the change in magic, like someone handing us off to another to carry onwards.

And didn't that remind me, oddly, of my youth, when I woke three days after my sixteenth birthday from a dream of being passed hand to hand across the Empire to find myself exiled to a tower at the far edge of Colhélhé, there to stay.

I had not stayed there, though everyone who was concerned with the matter thought I had. When the magic in the Silver Forest was stirred up by the death of Shallyr Silvertongue within twelve hours of that of the emperor his father, it scattered the rest of the Red Company for good and sent me posthaste back to my lonely tower.

That was a mad journey I had never described to anyone: three days of wild magic on a horse made more of wind than flesh and bone, thundering across the breadth of the Empire with the magic of Astandalas bearing down upon me. By the time I reached the door it caught me, and for a dozen years on the throne and a hundred more in an enchanted sleep after the Fall I wrought no further magic of my own at all, and almost no poetry either.

But no matter that. I went up on deck, harp in hand, and found that the sun was sinking behind us and the continent of Kavanduru filled the horizon to the east. We were still over the ocean, or rather the vast aquamarine-coloured shallows known as the Lissurian Sea. There were low islands full of mangroves and endless mazes of reefs, interspersed with mudflats host to choking masses of seagrass. Manatees grazed there, and endless schools of fish, and strange ancient sea-going lizards the size of whales.

People lived around the edges, and a few tribes deeper into the maze, but everything here was marginal, and as far as I knew few loved it. Most had moved north, to work in the floating castles of the Galagar Coast or the mines and cities of northern Amboloyo proper.

It was quite fascinating to look over the side of the ship at the patterns made by the reefs and islands and mats of seaweed. A yellow-dun line was thickening ahead of us: the sparsely inhabited belt of land between the Lissurian Sea and the desert and savannah of southern Amboloyo. Once there had been an entire subcontinent south of here, full of cities and farmland—Kavanor, the heart of Astandalan Zunidh—but it had collapsed into the sea in the Fall, and left this part of the world always strangely desolate.

The Dobu boy appeared before I was able to work myself into melancholy. His grin hadn't faded in the course of the day. I asked him what he'd spent his time doing, and was regaled with an account of acrobatics in the high rigging. He seemed utterly fearless, and shrugged off any hint of concern he might fall.

"We wear ropes around our waist when the wind picks up," he offered.

I am usually considered somewhat reckless with respect to physical danger, but then again I am a powerful wild mage, and even if I can't fly I could very likely catch myself before hitting the ground. The boy showed no evidence whatsoever of having any degree of magical ability. I admired his nonchalance.

"You've got your harp," he said meaningfully.

"This is true," I replied, smiling at his eagerness. "Should I talk to the captain first, do you think?"

"She'll be busy with the ship's wizard as we come up over the land."

"By which you mean, no." I considered the fact that Captain Audmon had made no effort to dissuade me from performing. "Is there a good place where most of the crew can hear me but I won't disturb anyone at their work?"

His radiant smile in answer was balm to the soul. While it is true that there are those who worship me, it had been a long time since I saw someone light up with anticipation because of my very own skill.

The boy led me to a spot at the base of the central mast. He, or someone, appeared to have already been planning this, for there was a stout crate set there with a comfortable cushion on top, and a glass bottle of water with a cork in the top to keep it from spilling. I thanked him for his thoughtfulness, which made him scuff at the floor and smirk self-consciously, then settled myself down on the cushion.

I tuned the strings and played a few passages to warm up, which attracted an audience of sailors. Some sat cross-legged on the deck in front of me, while others leaned up against the railings or various giant coils of rope. Their expressions ranged from anticipatory to deeply skeptical.

I smiled around the grouping and decided to say nothing by way of an introduction. Most of the sailors I could see were much younger than I, in their forties at most. That meant that even if they'd been born before the Fall they had grown up with songs and stories of the Red Company as their common vernacular. We had been great even in our own day, and the legend had only grown in the years since.

A discreet small magic amplified the harp so that the sound of the wind did not drown it out. I set the harp on my knee and cracked my knuckles while I mentally prepared the sequence of songs I intended to play.

It's all about the performance, really. I was glad I'd been practicing.

I played until the sun started to go down, the entire sky flushing with a clear pink light. We were well over the savannah of southern Amboloyo at this point, and the shadows of acacia trees and baobabs and herds of various animals—giraffes, elephants, wilde-beest—were long across the earth.

My audience had fluctuated as their duties recalled some and permitted others to listen. From their expressions I thought they had found my playing good entertainment, which was pleasing. I have only performed in public a few times since that night in the Silver Forest, most of those when I was on that singular holiday to the Vangavaye-ve which Kip had contrived for me.

The Islanders had not expected anything other than a musician, and though critical—Kip says that Wide Sea Islanders hold that the Vangavaye-ve is the home of music, and indeed I have rarely met a population containing so many so skilled in the art—they had not been *skeptical*. They hadn't been judging my performance against however many years of legend-building the sailors had expe-rienced.

I may not have played my harp much in the intervening years, but no one can deny that I have been performing, and performing well. A court of fawning courtiers is easier in some ways to manage than an audience of skeptical sailors, but not by much.

A bell rang from the prow of the ship, three bells chiming out. I stopped playing to take a drink, and the Dobu boy appeared out of the crowd. "That's first call for supper," he informed me.

"I'll stop then for now," I said, rubbing my hands briefly. An hour's near-continuous playing (I could not resist a *few* intercalated stories) was more than enough to begin with.

"The captain'll want to hear you after," he said darkly.

I smiled at him. "And did you think, this time yesterday, that you would have anyone performing for you today?"

He shrugged. "Some of the men have a little band, and others dance. They're not as good as you."

"I'm sure they're significantly more accomplished dancers."

He laughed, as did a couple of the men who were lingering close to hear what was said. It was true: I am a great connoisseur of dancing, as I have spent an absurd amount of time watching it from the vantage point of a throne, but I do not myself practice the art.

As if the comment were a signal, I was surrounded by sailors asking questions. Most were shy and a few were eager. All were careful not to use any names, though the questions were specific enough that there was no doubt they took me for Fitzroy Angursell in truth. I answered the questions that had to do with actual adventures, ruefully acknowledged that the story about the Dragon of Brystan was made up, and smiled and refused to answer any questions about what I'd been doing since the day the Red Company dissolved.

This went on while the air cooled and the sky darkened and the first few stars came out. I leaned against the mast, the air moving gently on my skin, and willed myself to stay calm and answer the questions politely. These were my people, in more ways than one. I couldn't—

I couldn't but be glad when the dour Laura pushed through the crowd, took one look at me, and said, "Right then, story-time's over. Come along, sir guest, the captain wants to see you."

I managed a brilliant smile for my audience and followed her to the stern of the ship and the same cabin where we'd breakfasted. Laura didn't say anything else, but when we were away from the sailors I said quietly, "Thank you. I was starting to feel a bit overwhelmed."

"Not used to so many people?"

There were so many ways to answer that. Of course I was used to people—I was *never* left alone. But they did not press; all conversations, save those begun by Kip in these latter years, were begun and guided and ended by me.

"Not exactly."

Her voice was marginally more welcoming. "The captain has invited you to dine at her table once again."

"Wonderful," I said, aware that I was more than a little peckish.

The meal set before us was hearty and while not court-refined, certainly not common fare either. "Your cook is skilled," I said after tasting a delectable lemon-cream sauce over fresh steamed vegetables. "This is delicious."

The captain smiled; her brother the postmaster, once again joining us, looked as if he were trying to find the trap in the compliment. I gave him a serene smile, remembering only at the last minute to edge it towards slyness.

He cocked his head, eyes flickering to something behind my back. "You look remarkably like the Lord Emperor," he said.

I twisted around to look at the state portrait I had missed seeing earlier on the wall. Well, at least it was slightly out-of-date. "Don't I!" I agreed cheerfully.

Postmaster Audmon furrowed his brow. I waited him out; at last he said, "And so?"

I feigned—quite obviously—ignorance. "And so? I'm never sure what I'm supposed to say in response to things like that. I can hardly deny the resemblance."

I could see him trying, and rejecting, various comments. He had not immediately jumped to the true conclusion, *This is actually the Lord Emperor in disguise!* but since he hadn't, this left a mystery. It was fairly clear he was trying to remember the genealogical charts of the imperial lineages he would have learned at school. Laura, for her part, had a darkly satisfied look in her eyes that made me think she'd written me off as someone's eccentric-to-mad relative, escaped from his minders.

Which wasn't *entirely* untrue.

Captain Audmon's eyes were crinkled with what I took to be deep-seated enjoyment in a sibling's discomfiture. I do not have that relationship with my own sister, but I have seen it in others.

The postmaster finally asked the obvious question. "Are you *related?*"

"I've often imagined so," I replied easily. "Even emperors must have relations who didn't make it into the history books, don't you think?"

"Or who do so under other names," said Captain Audmon.

"Very true."

Postmaster Audmon chewed at his lip, but could not come up with a response he liked better than my suggestion.

Laura gave me a more decidedly judgmental glare, to which I could only respond with a guileless expression.

"My friends used to hold coins up to my profile to check whether they were genuine or not. We often came across ancient hoards in our adventures, you see, and it wasn't until quite recently that magical safeguards against forgery were instituted, whereas apparently the nose has persisted across millennia."

I tapped mine even as he stared at me in total befuddlement.

Laura gave a resentful glance at the captain, who nodded in apparently-unwelcome encouragement. Laura gritted her teeth and said, "I was wondering if you could tell us a story after supper."

Laura, I suspected, thought she was being set up as a fool, and did not appreciate it.

"Any particular one?"

The question hung there, with all of its possible treasonous connotations. The postmaster and Laura both looked down, obviously recusing themselves from decision. The captain's eyes were twinkling as she said, "You seem well acquainted with the legends of late Astandalas. Do you happen to know the one about the time the Red Company attended a party at the Palace?"

That was an *interesting* choice. "Oh?" I said, smiling ironically at her, and reached for my harp. "This—or rather *That* Party?" I strummed a few bars of one of the most egregiously criminal songs of my entire repertoire, if also (I still maintain) one of the funniest; though perhaps I only think so because it skewered the entirety of my living relations at the time. "You mean the one where they were said to have stolen six bottles of Faery wine, a sturgeon, and the Diamond of Gaesion?"

"And one lady's maidenhead," Laura said, disapprovingly.

"I'm afraid I don't know much about that," I replied honestly.

"It is an excellent refrain, however."

I played the refrain, and refrained from telling her that my attention had been focused on the diamond—which to my surprise I had recognized as a stone I had seen in my childhood home, and which I had experimented upon with what I had thought at the time was make-believe magic—and so I had not paid much attention to what the others were getting up to in the shadows.

Well, what Faleron was getting up to in the shadows. Damian was happily married to Pharia, Gadarved was uninterested in maidens, and Masseo was under some sort of vow of celibacy he never explained. And I, of course, was otherwise occupied.

Laura, oddly, appeared utterly devastated. "You mean you *lied*?"

"Goodness no," I said. "Every word I've told you has been the truth. As for the song that was written, as you know, by Fitzroy Angursell: haven't you ever *listened* to the words?"

She did that time, at any rate.

I finished the story around midnight, when the Moon—a thin crescent this time of the month—had long since set. The captain, in a move of unexpected generosity possibly inspired by Laura's response to really and truly paying attention to *That Party*, had suggested I tell the next story, about hunting the White Stag, from my position amidships again, so the sailors could hear.

She was not, I took it, an aristocrat born, not with that consideration for her common sailors. Kip has spent many years chipping away at their bedrock assumption that they are all that matters, but it remains intransigent.

I had just concluded with our—or rather, the Red Company's, for I was just about discreet enough to remember to tell it in the third person rather than the first—return to the mortal worlds after our visit to the Moon's country when a sailor slid down the mainmast from the crow's nest lookout at the very top. He approached Laura, who was seated quite near me, so I could hear what he said.

"We're coming up over the sky forest," he said, followed by a string of unintelligible technical details I was glad to disregard.

The sky forest! I'd only seen it once, on a state visit to Amboloyo, when the trees were close enough to Boloyo City to permit an excursion. Usually the winds and their own mysterious processes keep them over the savannah and true desert of southern Amboloyo, blocked by various mountain and hill chains from drifting too far. No one lived in those regions bar a few hunter-gathering tribes and isolated hermits, and there had been no need to anchor the magic with one of the Lights.

The rips and tears caused by the destruction of Kavanor were slowly mending on their own, but overall both the geography and the magic of Kavanduru were wilder than in the rest of Zunidh. The so-called Prince of Kavanduru was actually prince over an island city-state that was all that was left of Kavanor, whose continuation as a province was largely due to the fishing industry centred there and Kip's and my desire to prevent the Prince of Amboloyo from fulfilling his ambition to rule half the world, or at least his whole continent.

"Will I be able to see the forest?" I asked Laura once she had turned from the sailor on watch. "I've always wanted to see the wild trees."

She rolled her eyes, whites visible even in the soft light from the lanterns hung on a few posts and beams around the ship, and directed me to follow her to the prow of the ship and the look-out there.

The captain (who had listened to most of my tale at the back of the crowd, where she was given polite berth by her sailors) was already there, peering through a fine brass telescope into the night. "I see them," she said, nodding, then carefully backed away from the telescope to let Laura look through it without jostling it from its orientation.

In the light from the lantern hanging above us from the beak of the swan figurehead, her face was intent and professional. I stepped aside, not wishing to interfere with her work, but she merely called out, "Sala!"

"Here, captain," a contralto voice said out of the shadows, and a plump man emerged. He wore a severely cut robe in blue-black silk, with a grey silk mantle over his shoulders. I retreated back yet another step, and made certain my magic was tightly furled. I'd never met this wizard before, but those who were trained by the Western College of Wizards in Mgunai, as his garments indicated, were often very skilled at identifying magical signatures. Most of them worked with police forces as part of forensic units as a result.

I was glad he had not joined us for meals at the captain's table, which his rank usually would permit him.

He nodded at me but gave no indication he'd noticed anything odd. Laura moved over the way so that he could look through the telescope next.

"It looks like the whole forest," he commented. "I'm sorry, Captain, I think we'll have to make a detour to avoid them. Their magic will interfere with the ship if we try to go over."

Captain Audmon tsked, then jerked her head at Laura. "Call up the sailors to their stations. All hands."

Laura nodded and hastened off, the wizard following after a brief further technical exchange with the captain. She turned to the telescope again, searching the horizon and orienting herself on the stars if I comprehended her motions correctly. I looked down and out at the trees we were approaching with considerable speed, and an idea sparked.

Leaving the heading so dramatically would mean the ship would fall away from the leyline connecting the Lights and would have to sail under her own power until she was able to reach the next, probably that at Boloyo City if I hadn't mistaken our location entirely. That would be at least another three days of sailing before they could re-stock and return to their Tsilo-bound route.

I had no particular desire to go to Boloyo City, or indeed Tsilo, whereas I knew there were definitely passages out of the world in the mountains to the east. And I had always wanted the opportunity to observe the flying pines more closely.

I had my bag with me, of course, as I had not forgotten the first rule of adventuring: always be prepared to seize an opportunity that presents itself. Well, here was an opportunity, and let it not be said that I wasn't prepared to seize it!

The captain sighed and stood from the telescope. She jumped when she saw me behind her, and laughed with a slight strain in her voice. "Oh! There you are."

I gave her a short bow. "I wish to thank you for your hospitality, Captain Audmon. It was a great pleasure to meet you."

She blinked at me, her pale face a blur in the lantern-light. "Ah, are you planning on going somewhere?"

"I have always been most curious about the sky forest," I said, waving in its direction. The nearest trees were still a fair distance away, and though I could hear whistles and calls indicative of the sailors attending to the rigging, the ship hadn't yet turned. "I shall therefore take my leave and continue on my way in that direction."

Captain Audmon opened her mouth, closed it, opened it again, and said, "I thought you said you couldn't fly?"

I grinned at her, knowing she wouldn't be able to see much besides the light reflecting off my teeth. "It seems as if it's an opportune time to try out my next idea."

And with that I bowed again, made sure the strap of my bag was securely over my shoulder and across my chest, and climbed up the short ladder that led to the swan figurehead, presumably for the convenience of whoever was supposed to tend the lantern. Sala, perhaps, or another minor wizard amongst the crew.

Once up there I balanced myself carefully with my feet between the outstretched wings of the bird. The trees were still a bit too far away for the idea I had in mind. I looked back down the length of the ship.

The captain stood at the prow lookout with her hand on the telescope, though her eyes were on me. Various sailors were aloft, their hands on ropes and pulleys and other miscellaneous nautical gear. Most of them were attending to their work, but those closest were watching. One was the Dobu boy, who was visible in a spot of light as a black figure high up on the foremast, leaning out at what struck me as a dangerous angle.

Far to the rear Laura and Sala the wizard stood at the wheel that worked the vertical and horizontal tillers. I could see them in the circle of light made by the wizard to illuminate their work, but I doubted they could clearly distinguish me in my pale robes against the white-painted shape of the swan. I hoped I was not about to destroy the garments, which I quite liked.

A bugle sang out a clear pattern, and there was suddenly movement in the sails as the sailors remembered their duties and attended to them. The captain had picked up a white flag, luminous in the dark, and was gesturing vigorously with it to the bugler who stood (I could now see) on the deck just below her.

The sails shifted and the angle of the ship changed. I put one hand on the highest curve of the swan's right wing to maintain my balance. The land below was dark; no fires or lights burned in that wild savannah. The stars above were brilliant but obscured here and there by filmy clouds. Enough light came through the haze to silver the outer branches of the flying pines; tiny sparkles of fireflies added to the effect.

The magic of the trees was intoxicating even at this distance, wild and full of air and fire. They were below us by a hundred or so feet, and over another two or three. I took a deep breath, flooding my system with the wild scent of the distant mountains and the resin and ozone of the trees.

The ship tilted, slanted, slowed. Just as the prow started to sweep to the left, the north, in its curve, I slid my feet out along the swan's neck and gathered my magic to me and—leaped.

IN WHICH I FAIL TO FLY

I have tried to fly on four deliberate occasions, and once by accident.

The accident came first, as these things tend to do.

As the second, back-up heir of the empire, I occupied a strange liminal position called the Marwn. The Marwn, it was acknowledged, was of the imperial bloodline and of theoretical right to the throne, just in the case the worst should happen and the primary succession fail. In the two thousand years since the institution of the position, after the mysterious disappearance of Aurelius Magnus without a clear line of succession, the Marwn had never been recalled to court, and by my day all of my identity that was written into the history books was the short note that amongst the members of the Imperial family there was also *The Marwn, in exile.*

There was not even an indication of exactly how I was connected to the Emperor. If I had lived and died in the Tower of Harbut Zalarin as planned, that would have been my sole contribution to written history, despite occupying what was arguably the second-most important position, magically, after the emperor.

The magic of the Empire, which bound five worlds together in its might and complexity, required safeguards. There always had to be someone in the centre, a person whose very being was given solely to the task of being the linchpin.

(The literal Linchpin, safely stowed in my bag, was used in the coronation ceremonies and otherwise formed part of the formal regalia of the emperors.)

Schooled magic worked by pairs and opposites, balanced by complex rituals and ceremonies. And so there was the openly acknowledged centre, the Emperor who was called the Heart of the Universe, cynosure of all eyes; and there was the Marwn, nameless and hidden, bound by crippling magic never to utter and barely to imagine a word of any other identity.

I had tried many times and many ways to tell my friends who I was, but even the existence of the position of Marwn was a state secret, and I could not.

And since I had not bound anyone to that position when I came to the throne, it is quite possible it was entirely my fault that the Empire did *not* hold, in the end, and collapsed as utterly as it did.

The Marwn before me had been the youngest sister of the Empress Anyoë, whose name the history books do not record but which I eventually was able to find out, buried deep in the sealed records of the Ouranatha, was Inyara. She lived and died the Marwn, in a place I never did find, probably as remote as the tower to which I was sent at the very farthest edge of Colhélhé. There was no record that her sisters remembered her except one note, terrible in its very brevity, from my father's mother Inera to her remaining sister Anastasia, stating without salutation or conclusion:

In a repeat of history, my grandson's name is now erased in service to the Empire.

It was Astandalan court custom not to announce the existence of any children outside the immediate family until they were nine, so it wasn't as if anyone else knew I existed.

In my case, I was nephew and first cousin to Eritanyr and his son Shallyr, eldest child of the Princess Lamissa and the Grand

Duke of Damara. By rights I ought to have been one of the great landowners of the empire, Grand Duke after my father, a powerful political figure in my own right if always subordinate to the Emperor. I ought to have been educated to power and prestige; sometimes I wonder what I might have been had that happened.

My father was too powerful, in the days of the Emperor Eritanyr, and too popular. My cousin Shallyr was seven when I was born, and already (as I learned from reading the private records after I came to the throne) showing his inclinations towards disturbing and dangerous lunacy.

It was, I understand, a political manoeuvre. I was born: healthy, of the imperial lineage on both sides (my father's mother was Inera, the third sister of Anyoë; my mother Anyoë's daughter), son of a more popular man than the emperor himself. And I had the golden eyes of the ancient emperors, sign of the magic it would turn out I possessed, but long before then a dangerous potential rallying-point for the disaffected.

With a month of my birth I was made the Marwn, supposedly an honour.

My name was stripped from me, taken into the possession of the Emperor and the chief wizard of the Ouranatha, and I was sent to be raised in isolation under the ever-increasing bindings required by the position.

By the time I was sixteen I knew the basics of Schooled wizardry, through I showed no great skill at it; I could read and write and speak nine languages; I was well-educated in all the lands and peoples and politics of the Empire; and I had seen my parents for a quarter-hour each year, when they came to fulfil some of the ritual duties required by their position. I did not know I had a sister; I had seen a total of fourteen people in my entire life; and it was not until I was eighteen that I even realized I didn't have a name.

Two days after my sixteenth birthday I had that dream of being passed hand-to-hand across the width of the Empire, and woke up

in a tower on the edge of the Abyss. It was enchanted with everything I should require for the rest of my life, assuming one does not
require human company, of course.

The only mistake anyone had made—and I don't see how
anyone could have known by what evidence I gave them as a boy
—was failing to recognize the nature and degree of my wild magic.
Magic no longer ran in the imperial lineage; it had been seventeen
or eighteen generations since the last time anyone had had more
than a drop of power, and that had been fully subsumed by
Schooled wizardry.

No one could have thought, even with the colour of my eyes,
that I would have magic like my first ancestors, the ones who
conquered worlds.

The only magic I had performed as a young boy had been in
secret, and had been, I had long thought, no more than make-
believe. I had read in a poem of someone who had enchanted a
stone with all that was heavy about himself, so that he might be
able to fly.

I had made up my own ceremony of enchantment, imitating the
Schooled magic I knew and could not perform. I had not really
understood then what was meant by *all that was heavy*, for the
enchantments on my person precluded most negative emotions—
they did not want me disaffected, after all—and so I had tried
instead to bind my life to the stone (the diamond later called the
Star of the North, the Diamond of Gaesion, which had been as yet
uncut and had not looked like one to my inexperienced eyes)
following a folk tale of Northern Damara I barely remembered my
nurse telling me as a very young boy.

I never learned to fly, but I did survive the Fall of Astandalas.

They sent me to the Tower of Harbut Zalarin, the greatest mage
of pre-Astandalan Zunidh. Only Aurelius Magnus, forty-seventh
Emperor of Astandalas, looms larger in the histories of magic. He
had probably been the last to study in that tower. No one without
the right would have been able to open their books and read what

was written within them: but I am Harbut Zalarin's descendant through nearly a hundred generations, and Aurelius Magnus's through fifty, and despite everything that blood runs true.

It took me two years to learn enough wild magic to break my bindings.

I made my wonderful Bag of Unusual Capacity, recalcitrant in returning items as it might have been, and took with me the books and harp and clothes and food I thought might be necessary. My only exposure to anything of such practical matter being epic poetry, my choice of gear was somewhat eclectic; but as I wanted to become a bard out of an epic, they proved mostly useful in the end. I left the tower, never intending to return, and set out in a fine blue velvet cloak in a random direction *away*.

Not even half an hour later I tripped over a stone and fell head-first out of that world and into another.

It was my first experience of anything resembling flight, tumbling down several hundred feet out of thin air towards a river. It was exhilarating, though I couldn't really do anything besides hold onto my bag and the cloak and fall head over heels in love with existence.

I landed in a small boat being rowed across the river by two people who would become my first and staunchest friends, and just like that the history of the Nine Worlds shifted.

I have tried to fly three times.

Each time I have failed, but never so severely as to lose my life. This fourth time was no exception.

I tried to gather the wind under me, and while the air cooperated, my essential corporeal nature did not, and I sank like a piece of cloth thrown into a pond. That is to say, I fell, but slowly, with enough resistance that I could more or less guide my direction.

Of course I could work with things like sails or artificial wings or gliders; but that's not *flying*. We've all had the dreams: you know exactly what I mean.

I fell slowly, at an angle, missed the topmost trees by several feet each time, and finally managed to fold myself over the stout branch of one near the bottom of the forest.

It took me a few minutes to catch my breath.

Eventually I determined that I hadn't cracked my ribs nor dropped my bag, remembered after a moment that I hadn't been wearing sandals and therefore hadn't lost them, and then faced the joyous discovery that I am, as people keep telling me, no longer young, and even if I have kept reasonably fit by means of swimming and pacing, my upper body strength remains limited.

We shall draw a discreet veil over my efforts to move from folded over the branch to sitting securely on it at the fork of the tree. Suffice it to say that my beautiful apricot robes did not appreciate this, and neither did my shoulders nor the palms of my hands.

By the time I had caught my breath a second time, wiped my face with a handkerchief I found in the bag, and was able to look around, the sky ship was nearly invisible in the distance. I only found it because of the peculiar arrangement of lights, too close together and too low down to be stars.

I confess that the thought of the likely reactions to my grand exits of the past two nights—one from the Fens, the other from the ship—pleased me greatly. Anyone who had doubts that I truly was Fitzroy Angursell might well still prefer to believe me a madman instead; but at least they could hardly deny that I was a madman with *style*.

So much for the *Northern Joy*. I dismissed the ship and her sailors from my mind and focused instead on my immediate surroundings.

My first thought was how very dark it was. The trees loomed bright in my mind's eye, their magic loud and strong, a rushing river. But the actual forest was nearly silent and nearly dark. The firefly sparkles were hardly brighter in close proximity than they had been from the ship, and clustered in the highest trees above me, and the starlight still only illuminated the edges of branches of the topmost ranks.

The trees moved at the speed of the wind, and were almost utterly silent. As my heartbeat stilled and my breath quieted I began to hear the very soft, very gentle whisper of air through the long drooping needles.

I leaned my head against the craggy bark of the trunk beside me. It was mossy, which seemed odd given the trees' location floating above a hot and dry savannah. The tree was old and slow and crooked of branch. My magic touched it and was welcomed by the deep life, the fire in the sap greeting mine.

I fell asleep.

I woke at dawn when a crow cawed in my ear, and nearly fell out of the tree.

After flailing in a most undignified fashion—though one might argue that anything I do is by definition dignified, in practice this is not the case—I managed to right myself and secure my position once more. With my legs wrapped around one branch and my hand clasping another tightly, I felt ready to take on the morning.

The crow watched me derisively from the next branch over. I regarded it with interest. It had been a long time since I was so close to a bird, and I'm not sure if I'd ever been so close to a crow in particular. It was a very handsome specimen, with glossy black feathers and bright eyes.

"Good morning," I said to it. "I thank you for the wake-up call."

The crow tilted its head to regard me with one eye and then the other. Crows and all their relations tend to be terrifyingly intelligent birds even without the influence of magic. This one was a wild bird living in a savannah far from human habitation and thus out of the likely influence of deliberate or accidental human magic; but

I had not needed to encounter the Tigara to know that there were many other forms and beings of magic in existence.

The crow pecked at something on the branch, preened itself briefly, and then flew off towards the east.

This seemed as good advice as any I was likely to receive this morning. I began with digging in my bag for something to eat, and when I had a box of vegetable pastries to hand, settled myself against the trunk more comfortably and looked around.

The sky was bright and the light a rich gold, but the land below was still dun and grey, as the sun was rising behind the mountainous spine of central Kavanduru.

We were much closer to the mountains than I had anticipated. I could see individual peaks clearly, and guessed that if I were more familiar with what they looked like I could probably have determined my exact location. I couldn't see the sharp pinnacle of Mt Damar in the north, which I knew from occasional visits to my sister stood up in obvious isolation, nor could I see any evidence of the long inlet of the sea that came in up what had once been the Jurushir Valley of Kavanor in the south.

That put me squarely in the middle of the mountain chain. The only potential concern with that is that there is a religious house somewhere there, whose mother superior is the wizard I had tasked with ensuring the overall stability of magic while I was away. She would know the touch of my magic instantly, and I was fairly certain she was likely to be in residence at the moment.

I peered at the mountains for the distinctive triple peaks of Ousanadh, upon which the Abbey was built, and eventually picked out two possible contenders. One was safely to the south, the other was more or less directly where the wind was taking us.

I thought through that while nibbling a second pastry. No magic beyond the smallest actions.

It's like constraining one's poetic vision to a specific, intricate form. There was a period when I was fond of sonnets.

The sky forest appeared to be composed of only one sort of tree, long-needled pines. Most of the trees I could see had fantastically curved and twisted trunks and branches, with many forks and snaking ramifications.

I seemed to recall someone telling me once that trees that grow close together, as in a dense forest stand, grow straight and tall (and useful to carpenters) to reach the light, while those that have space and air and light all around them grow wide and comfortably branched.

It might have been Kip, come to think of it, who told me that. It's the sort of random fact of economic significance he would know and feel inclined to share.

The sky forest was more like a school of fish than any terrestrial boskage. The trees were for the most part well spaced out, a few yards between each and its neighbour. Light filtered down between them as well as through their branches. I could see scattered clumps where two or three trees were enmeshed together at branch or root, though whether because they had always grown that way or because of some windstorm entangling them I couldn't tell.

It was immediately clear why the long straight trunks required for the sky ships were so limited in number. I knew this bothered Kip, who decried the essential elitism involved in having some-thing so self-evidently beneficial available to so few. (Indeed, I do not disagree with his principles, which is one reason why the postal service has the ships it does.) Nonetheless, I could not but rejoice in the wild individuality of growth that made those ships so rare. If laminating or joining the logs worked, this forest would likely be nowhere near so extensive or so beautiful.

Some trees were crowned with sunlight, others with shadow, but all were full of insects and birds. The air was so full of sound I had hardly noticed at first, though now I did it was all chirps and warbles and twitters and trills and chuckling sorts of calls.

I could see no other crows nearby, although there were a few dark shapes further off. Close to me were all sorts of little birds: plump pink and black and white ones, others smart yellow and black as if they were in Imperial livery; some with fat conical beaks and others with bills that crossed at the tip and yet others with slender arched beaks to winkle into crevices. There were woodpeckers with ivory plumage and a splendid dusky-blue jay with a fine silver crest.

It was all rather like the experience of walking through the marketplaces of Solaara as I made my way from the Palace to the Necropolis. I watched a pair of woodpeckers follow each other in a spiral up the trunk of a tree a couple over from mine, their stout beaks hammering into the wood with resounding clunks. It was much easier to watch from my seat than it had been to walk through those crowds.

The perch I had found last night was near the middle of my tree. After finishing my breakfast I returned the half-full box to my bag and brushed off my hands with a grimace at the scrape on one palm from my inelegant landing. Then I considered the disposition of branches on my tree.

Up first, I decided. The main trunk forked not far above my head. The crotch formed a reasonable platform on which to balance as I surveyed the scene.

The trees looked rather like I expected any pine tree might if you could remove it, roots intact, from the ground and display it in midair without the concealment of the soil. Each tree's root system hung down below its trunk like a rustic chandelier. The roots had bark close to the trunk, as if they were nothing more than inverted branches; as the roots extended down and out the bark dwindled, until the lowest and thinnest roots were a pale golden-brown.

They looked a little sticky, I thought, gazing up at the roots of the tree above. Some acrobatic little birds in natty blue and yellow plumage certainly found whatever was caught in the finest rootlets very interesting.

While I confess I was curious about the ecology of the sky forest —I had had no idea there was what amounted to an entire ecosystem up here, with ferns and fungus and other epiphytes growing along the wider branches—and some distant memories of northern travels suggested the birds were not quite tropical despite their bright colours—my main interest was what would happen as we approached the mountains.

I daresay a full day and a night was not long to wait to find out, but I had not spent a day and a night alone for as long as I could remember. It was possible, I mulled in the mid-afternoon (long after I had gotten bored with my observations, my book, and the leftover vegetable pastries), that I had not been along for so long since those long-ago days in my tower of exile. And I left that at eighteen.

I clambered up and down the tree until I determined that it would be foolhardy in the extreme to try to jump to another. Foolish I can certainly be, and foolhardy too, but as I had neither cause nor audience I was able to resist the temptation. Being higher would hardly assist me, and my tree was already one of the lowest in the forest.

Instead I wedged myself in the crotch of the tree and watched the world go by below me. This would have been more entertaining had I not spent far too long on a throne doing so already.

As the sun set over the now-invisible ocean in the west, the motion of the trees slowed imperceptibly. I tensed in readiness when I noticed, unsure what might happen, but nothing did. The trees slowed, reached a new equilibrium, and continued their steady eastbound drift towards what I was increasingly sure was Mount Ousanadh.

The sun went down in orange and red glory. The birds disappeared into their nighttime roosts, leaving only a couple at the top of the higher trees to serenade the sunset. The air grew cooler, and I spent some time examining various items of clothing before deciding not to damage anything else and merely added a pair of green leggings to go with my apricot robes.

As the sky darkened and both stars and fireflies began to glimmer I added socks. I hadn't worn those since the days in Astandalas, either.

It was quite amazing how hard it was to be on my own. I had not thought myself so dependent on company, when I yearned for solitude and privacy.

It was a restless sleep I had that night, and I played my harp for the trees through many watches.

~

The crow woke me again at dawn.

This time I wondered how the morning chorus had not woken me first, but no matter that. I saluted the crow joyously and stretched out kinks from the awkward poses of the night. The mountains were close ahead: the air smelled of snow, cold and clear and exhilarating. I sneezed as the sun infused the sky with lambent gold. The very breaths I took were full of promise.

"Something marvellous is about to happen," I informed the crow, which did not seem particularly impressed.

I rubbed my hands over my scalp, but I'd played a little too much over the past few days. My fingertips were raw and sore as a result, and I couldn't tell if I had any hair growth starting or not.

"It's the third morning of my adventure," I told the crow. It cawed; I chose to take it as encouragement. "You're quite right, good sir: it's time for breakfast."

I pulled out an orange from my bag. I peeled it slowly, inhaling the sharp scent as I broke the skin with my thumbnail, and took a great deal of care to remove every bit of the pith.

Down below my dangling feet in their green leggings and grey socks the savannah had given way to rocky canyons. The climate here had shifted dramatically after the Fall and subsidence of Kavanor; there had been many earthquakes and a significant rearrangement of wind and precipitation patterns. Not to mention the chaotic magic that had created the sky forest, and much else.

What had been a thriving forest had dried up to savannah and desert. It was beautiful in its way, all striking pale-grey cliffs and tumbling boulder fields. I was sorry for the people who had been forced to flee, but that had happened long ago as the world reckoned those things, in the days when I was neither emperor nor renegade but had been merely a man lying in an enchanted coma, and the land had become its own place again.

I like the cultivated regions—I deeply enjoy cities—but there is something about the true Wild that speaks to my soul.

The mountain range curved here, forming a convex bight. On the maps it was marked as *desolate*, with the ruins of a few lost cities here and there. The serried ranges bisecting the continent thinned here to only one. That barricade was formed by the highest mountains in the world, massive, glacier-crowned, sacred; with desolation on the western side no one bothered much with crossing.

The only people who did were occasional hermits from the religious houses scattered on the eastern shoulders of the mountains. The sky forest was low enough now that the mountains rose above us, silhouetted against the rising sun. I squinted against the light and could just make out the triple peak of Ousanadh, the tallest in the world.

On the other side of Ousanadh were the fertile plateaus of central Damara. Somewhere very close to here was the Abbey of the Mother of the Mountains. She knew me too well, both my magic and my appearance: it would be a very difficult bluff. A month from now, or three, I could probably pull it off, but three days out from the Palace?

I turned to the orange in my hand while I watched the mountains loom ever larger. I savoured every bite. Due to various taboos, it was the first piece of raw fruit I had eaten in decades. You can imagine how delicious I found it.

It was probably just as well I (or rather Conju) had stocked my comestibles based on their relative durability. If I'd had any of the other fruits I'd dreamed of over the years available, I should have gorged myself most intemperately. My digestion would probably have greatly regretted it, and I might have missed out on a splendid opportunity.

As it was, I finished my orange, amused myself by breaking up the orange peel into small bits I then dropped between the branches and roots below me, and was witness to an extraordinary thing.

The steady west wind was pushing the flying pines almost directly towards Ousanadh. Below us—still dim grey in the shadows of the mountain—the land was rising into an ever-narrowing valley between two great spurs. We were aimed just to the south of the northernmost shoulder of Ousanadh.

As the land rose, the flying pines slowed and bunched together. I looked down and out and up, and could see no cluster of trees against the mountainside, nor floating over the triple peaks. I peered up but couldn't see through the masses of trees above me where they went.

I clambered down to the lowest branches and found a place to balance while I leaned out, a little precariously. Even though I knew we had slowed, the closer the ground came the swifter it seemed to be moving. A glint of water was there then gone; the great grey boulders were omnipresent.

I wrapped my arm around a branch and leaned out as far as I could. The trees were *moving*.

Not simply at the mercy of the wind, though that, too. As the leading trees swept up the valley, they came to a great cliff. A river thrust a waterfall over the lip of the cliff, though the wind caught it so none of the water seemed to reach the valley floor. Instead a veil was cast out over the fall, scattering water droplets in a fine white mist around us.

As the trees were swept by the wind into the mist, the pines closed their branches, furling them like an umbrella or a dancer making a spin. And like a dancer, the tree would start to spin, faster and faster, and then rise suddenly up out of the mist and over the headwall before opening its branches wide to catch an upper wind blowing westward.

This seemed almost more impossible than the very existence of the flying pines in the first place. I watched in delighted amazement as each tree entered the mist, only to pop up again a moment later like a cork, spread out much wider than the forest had been as it moved east, and drifted off at a gentle pace back westward.

As my tree made its way towards the waterfall it occurred to me that I did not want to float back west again with it.

I was going to have to jump.

I secured my bag and climbed down as low as I could safely get in the root system. The pale golden-brown rootlets were tacky rather than sticky, and seemed to have collected dust and yellow pollen and small insects and seeds. I positioned myself so I could have a relatively clear drop, gathered my magic as discreetly as I could manage, and waited.

This was not a time to attempt to fly. I was too close to the Abbey. I could only mitigate my landing so I didn't break anything important.

My tree slowed. The constant flood of magic changed pitch with an abrupt jolt, lightning shocking through the background fire. A few drops of water landed on me, like a priest's benediction.

I felt galvanized almost to youth: the tree folded its branches and popped up.

On the other side of the valley wall was a tarn. It was blue and pink and white and sunshine yellow, all suddenly *there* below me.

I pushed myself off my perch and dropped like a stone into the middle of an expanding arc of flower petals.

7

IN WHICH I ANSWER PRAYERS

The water was very cold.

I plunged down in a blur of bright colours, hit the water with a painful shock, and submerged to the point where my feet thumped against the rocky basin. I thrust back up with an automatic response, and resurfaced in a great spout of water and air.

After a few moment spent shaking the water out of my eyes and mouth, I struck out for the shore.

Once on shore I assessed the situation. I was soaking wet and had lost one sock. The air was thin and cool; in the shadow of the mountain, it was cold.

A person in a white robe sat on a yellow boat in the middle of the tarn.

"One moment!" I called, and hastened off behind a convenient large boulder to strip off my wet clothes and find something warm and dry to change into.

I was fighting with the leggings when it occurred to me that this was an unaccustomed modesty. Usually I have at least three and sometimes more attendants present; most of my court costumes require considerable assistance to don and doff. The idea of privacy was desirable but long-forgotten, even foreign.

On the sky ship I had been grateful for privacy when I struggled with the buttons of the apricot robes, as there were no familiar attendants but only strangers around.

That was it. I didn't *know* whoever it was in the boat.

I eventually got the clinging wet garments off and found one of the towels Conju had indeed packed for me. The air was brisk and I did not linger long on choosing what to change into after I had rubbed myself dry. Blue leggings this time, another white linen tunic (this one a bit shorter, only to my knees instead of my calves, and with sleeves down to my wrist), and a fitted coat in a splendid midnight-blue velvet spangled with silver stars. This went down to my knees and had short stuffed protuberances at each shoulder, along with magnificent silver and moonstone buttons. I had no idea at all where it came from or when it had been in style, but I loved it.

In deference to the rocky terrain, I found a pair of tall boots in supple black leather. As far as Conju knew I had never worn boots, but he'd indulged my love of odd costumes by providing my cobbler with examples from various personal and public collections in Solaara. I knew of at least seven pairs of footwear in the luggage, and hoped there were more to discover as my quest went on.

I found a hat to match the coat, a floppy blue velvet tam that was much more comfortable than the one I'd lost in the Fens, and which I believed would be much warmer. Gloves were not quite necessary, but I did take the time to ensure my signet ring was turned inward.

Fortunately no one on the sky ship seemed to have noticed that I wore the Imperial Seal. The sun-in-glory insignia was unmistakable, but the ring itself was much less grand than people expected. It was engraved gold, with no diamonds or other precious stones or metals, and not as large as later seals and signets had come to be.

It was said to have been Yr the Conqueror's own ring, passed hand to hand over the course of one hundred emperors. The magic in it was inward-turned and subtle, unforgeable and unmistakable. What was sealed with that ring stayed bound.

It had not seemed a good idea to leave it behind; you never knew what I might need on a quest.

I could add a deep submersion to the indignities suffered by my poor replacement bag. I really would have to remember to thank Conju for insisting on the protections.

All that sorted, and more or less warmed up, I got up from the stone on which I'd been sitting while remembering how to put on tall boots and went back to the shore of the tarn to see what ritual or ceremony I'd interrupted. Before I quite reached it I tripped on a long, stout stick just perfect for a walking staff. I picked it up, pleased to discover it was just the right height for me, and used a very small bit of magic to smooth the rough bark at one end. Surely no one would be able to notice *that* over the firecracker pulses of the trees bobbing up over the mist of the waterfall and gliding back westwards.

The pink flowers were spreading out across the small lake. It *was* small, probably no more than a hundred or a hundred and fifty feet across. I knew it wasn't particularly deep, as I'd touched bottom on landing. The mountains stood up in a semi-circle around us; on the open side the sky forest had finished its turn through the mist and the trees were now small specks dispersed across the air to the west.

The yellow boat was being rowed to shore by a young woman in a simple white dress. She had black hair done up in long cornrow braids; her colouring was a little lighter and a little warmer in tone than mine, but she was still very dark.

The long braids along with her broad features suggested she was not of the aristocracy born. As she came closer I saw her dress was belted with a pale green rope girdle, and she wore straw sandals on her feet.

An acolyte of the Abbey, then, perhaps a novice or a postulant, but not a full-vowed nun. I smiled at her. "Good morning!"

She shipped her oars as the prow of the boat ran up on a little gravel shingle in front of me. "Good morning," she replied after a moment, taking in my appearance.

The floor of her boat was taken up with several shallow baskets. A few pink petals caught in the wicker indicated they'd been used to convey the petals out. I gestured at the water. "May I ask what the purpose of the flowers is? An offering?"

She considered, tilting her head to the side. "I was praying for assistance," she said slowly.

I gave her a semi-courtly bow, just remembering to catch my hat before it fell off. I straightened and smiled brilliantly. "Well, here I am! What can I do for you?"

Marilda, as was the young woman's name, didn't know what to make of me.

"I was praying to the emperor," she said earnestly.

This is the problem with an official state religion. I'm not a very effective deity, I'm afraid. But what could I do but try?

"You can disburden yourself of your concern, at least. I cannot promise I can entirely solve it, but I can listen and perhaps offer you some advice."

Marilda appeared to be a serious young woman, prone to considering her words before speaking. She considered my offer for some time.

I watched the ripples from my arrival and her rowing subside and the pink flowers gather along the edges of the tarn.

Three days after leaving the Palace and here I was, already halfway across a different continent having adventures and assisting maidens in distress. It was all most satisfactory.

I stored up mental images of Ousanadh from this side—not a view I'd seen before—and the feel of the place, the clarity of the air, the vividness of the colours. I would write a poem about this, the trees, the mountains, the young woman, the tarn.

"I wish to leave the convent and marry," Marilda blurted suddenly, recalling me from daydreaming of musical progressions and rhymes for *mountain* that were not *fountain*.

"Oh?" I said in encouragement. "Have you taken your vows?"

"No, but the Mother Superior is away and I ..." She looked away, one hand stealing to her waist. "I do not wish to wait for her return to give permission."

The Mother Superior's absence was a relief to me, personally, but I could see why it was a trial to Marilda. "It's known to happen," I said with as much empathy as I could muster. "Though not perhaps when you're a postulant nun."

She looked wounded, her dark eyes large and pained. "I didn't want to be one, but I didn't think ... my parents couldn't afford a dowry, but I have a gift of magic and the Mother Superior said she'd take me for training ..."

I examined her magical aura as best I could without being obvious or going into a full trance. Her power lay in well-trained coils about her centre, the pattern one exceedingly familiar to me as a part of the branch of Schooled wizardry practiced by most of Kavanduru's wizards and a few of those trained in Eastern Dair as well. She was no wild mage, nor of great power: instead, exactly the sort of wizard any small community would want.

"Have you begun to focus your training yet?"

"My teacher suggested I might do well with healing. I want to work with animals."

"Animal healers are always in great demand," I pointed out.

"My ... my beau is a journeyman carpenter. We were hoping to marry later, once he had his mastery, but then ..."

I regarded her with some perplexity. "I'm afraid I don't quite see the problem, miss."

"Marilda. You still need something to live off of! And with a baby I won't be able to work. My parents won't help, and *he's* an orphan. He has a sister, that's it."

"That is unfortunate, but why don't you apply for the annual stipend? Surely that will solve most of your concerns. With the two of you each receiving it, you should be able to find somewhere to live and support yourself while the baby is young and your beau finishes his apprenticeship."

She stared at me. I stared back.

"But ..."

I raised my eyebrow. She bit her lip. I waited.

"I didn't think about that," she said in a small voice. "I don't know anyone who's applied for it."

"It's not hard," I assured her blithely. Not that I had ever personally applied, of course—though thanks to Kip's absolute and much-derided insistence that it not be attached to income even I in my proper persona would theoretically be eligible—but I knew for a fact that it was designed to be easily accessible. I thought back to the many, many conversations I'd had with Kip on the subject, and the nine-hundred-page Plan I'd dutifully read.

"I believe you need some indication of who you are and where you live. If the Mother Superior is away surely whoever is in charge of postulants can supply you with a letter, or you can begin with your beau's and get yours once you've settled in."

Marilda considered this carefully. She placed both hands on her stomach, which was still fairly flat (she was not particularly svelte in figure), and seemed to commune with herself and her unborn child. I reached out and held the prow of the boat so it didn't slide back into the water, and watched a large white-tailed eagle come soaring over the shoulder of the middle peak and circle lazily above us.

"You *are* the answer to my prayers," she exclaimed. "Please, sir, will you come with me to meet my beau and tell him the good news? He's in the village on the other side of the mountain, just down from the Abbey."

I smiled at her. "I'd be delighted."

Marilda's beau was a strapping young man called Daro, handsome in a rather bovine manner. We found him alone in his master's workshop, engaged in patiently turning the legs of a chair on a lathe. It had started raining as we arrived in the village, an intense spring shower, and Marilda had insisted I come inside out of the wet while she talked to Daro. I tried to hover unobtrusively in a corner and not listen in on their conversation.

I enjoyed the opportunity to look around the workshop. It appeared to focus on useful, ordinary furniture, made sturdily and well without much in the way of sculptural pretensions or ornamentation. Tables and chairs, benches and boxes. Old Damara is sitting country, not squatting, at least amongst the general populace. My sister, the Grand Duchess, still prefers to recline on couches in the old Astandalan fashion, and the regional nobility follow her example.

I'm more of a sitter, myself, by preference. I was glad to get rid of the eating couches after the Fall.

"And so I went to the sacred lake to pray for guidance, and he appeared out of nowhere to help me! It was like a miracle, Daro! We are to go to the—" She turned to me, frowning slightly. "Where *do* we go, sir?"

I could wish I had listened better to Kip's more detailed explanations.

"I believe we need to find the nearest offices of the Department of the Public Weal."

If that wasn't quite correct, the officials would know where we should go, at any rate.

"I think we go to the post office at the river station," Daro said at length. "They do all the government work hereabouts."

"You'll come help us, won't you, sir?" Marilda asked me,

anxious and pleading. "Neither of us are very good with official paperwork, are we, Daro?"

Daro shook his head solemnly. "My sister helped me with the apprenticeship contract. She's an apprentice blacksmith, nearly finished," he added proudly. "Down the river a ways, just past the station. She's really good. She'll be pleased to hear we're marrying. She knew we didn't like to wait."

Marilda took Daro's hand. "Oh, Daro, what shall we do? Whatever am I to tell my parents?"

People who sent their daughter to a convent because they couldn't afford a dowry were unlikely to rejoice in an illegitimate child.

The lovers pondered. I examined a shelf of unidentifiable woodworking tools and wondered about the possibility of breakfast. Such healthy, hearty young people who had been up and working since dawn had probably long since eaten.

My orange seemed a long time ago.

"We must marry as soon as possible," Daro declared.

Marilda beamed at the thought, then turned to me with another wash of anxiety. "How can we? My parents don't like Daro and I don't like their priest. And he might not marry us, anyway ... Daro's Iyesani, he's of a different faith."

Ah.

"The Mother Superior does most weddings around here, Master Joff says," Daro offered.

Marilda shook her head. "She's away for a month or more, the postulant mistress said so."

It gladdened my heart that I truly didn't need to concern myself where the Mother Superior might have gone. Kip was seeing to the government of the world, I had prepared the magical side of things as best I could for my absence, and would probably have noticed anything untoward happening in the few days since I left. The Mother Superior might well be simply off visiting friends or relatives elsewhere. Even abbesses have them.

"So please, sir, how can we marry?"

Now, while I may not be the repository of useful facts concerning the hidden economic qualities of random things that Kip is, I do have a knack for some things other than poetry and wild magic. As emperor and lord magus I spent a good deal of time working on legal matters, and have over the years collected a wide knowledge of strange and wonderful legal practices from various parts of my (former) empire.

I find marriage laws particularly intriguing; there are some wondrously bizarre ones out there.

"I happen to know," I said therefore, "that you can legally marry in Old Damara by reciting your solemn pledges over an anvil in the presence of the blacksmith and two other witnesses."

They both looked at me askance. I was not particularly worried they would recognize me. Even if they did, Marilda had literally been praying to me when I showed up. It wouldn't help with my eventual project to cease being considered a deity by my populace, but it wouldn't harm my immediate quest either.

"So we could ask my sister's master," Daro confirmed slowly.

"Exactly."

He frowned. Before he could formulate his next sentence the workshop door opened and an older man stumped in. He rather resembled Marilda in colouring, though he wore his greying hair in a short cut. From Daro's immediate deferential bearing as well as his own indefinable air of competence I deduced this was the master carpenter.

"What's all this, then?" he asked, surveying Daro, hand in hand with Marilda, and me in my wonderful midnight-blue velvet coat.

Daro and Marilda explained the situation and my proposed solutions. The carpenter listened carefully, betraying no emotion.

"Well," he said when they had stumbled to a more or less coherent end, "there's a three-week holiday starting tomorrow for government folk, so if you want to get your stipend you'd best be about it today."

"But the chair, sir," replied Daro.

The carpenter grimaced tightly, though his eyes were warm. "Never mind the chair for now. You can finish it next week after you and your bride sort yourselves out. Do you have your things from the Abbey, Miss Marilda?"

She shook her head mutely.

The carpenter looked at me. I didn't have all that much experience with families, but I could see a certain fatherliness in him as he put a hand on Daro's broad shoulder, reaching up to do so. "You're helping them?"

There was not quite a threat there. I agreed complacently. He nodded in satisfaction and with a bare hint of surmise. Marilda hadn't given any explanation for my arrival besides *he arrived after I prayed to the Emperor*, but that was probably enough.

"Best if you go with them to explain to the postulant mistress. I'll round up the boys for a do tonight. My good wife will help Marilda get ready for the night and see a room is readied. Best go to Master Smith down the river, he's a good man, knows Daro from his sister, and he'll do them right."

This seemed eminently reasonable. Daro removed his leather apron and hung it carefully on a hook by the door, then opened it for Marilda.

I was last out. The carpenter held me back with an outstretched hand and a questioning expression. I waited.

"Should I ask who you are, sir?" he asked. Though his seamed features did not really show fine emotion, his eyes were conflicted with hope and worry and awe.

I considered, then gave him a quick grin. "Probably not. I promise you by the Sun and the Moon and the One Above that I mean only good to those who have asked my assistance."

That was a binding oath; but it was not the first I have made to my people.

And the right sort of mischief can bring *such* results.

8

IN WHICH I IMPERSONATE ANOTHER OF MY ANCESTORS

*M*arilda had led me through a (firmly terrestrial) pine
forest upon leaving the immediate environs of the
tarn, and once we were in the village my attention was occupied
with examining the local architectural features, which included
fantastic wooden gargoyles at what seemed like every corner.

On our way up to the Abbey we started up a much more well-
used path that led across a grassy valley towards what seemed to
be a switchback stair cut out of the rock face. High above the valley
and the village below was the great Motherhouse of the Mountains,
all stone and widely outflung gilded tile roofs.

I had visited it twice before, when the current and former
Abbesses were inducted into their positions. On those occasions I
had come by sky ship, to a platform even higher up the mountain,
and spent perhaps a total of eight minutes outside. If I tipped my
head back far enough I could just see the horizontal line of the platform against the brightly-lit stone of the cliff face.

The Abbey was magnificent, brooding over the valley from its
perch halfway up the central peak of Ousanadh. The air up here
was thin and rarified; I felt slightly breathless from the altitude. I'd

never had altitude sickness before, but then again it had been a long time since I *climbed* so high.

We stopped at a particularly scenic point for Marilda and Daro to coo at one another and for me to catch my breath. I appreciated the thoughtfulness.

We were north of the Equator by a goodly distance now, so the sun was nearly directly in our face, if just high enough to permit a view. The light cast great shadows across the valley below us, silhouetting the mountains to the east and the hills to the north. The central plateaus of Old Damara were high and wide, broken by the ranges.

Cattle country, and sheep a bit farther north. Wheat up here, though a few hundred feet lower it was wet enough and warm enough for rice cultivation, in terraces running down in ledges from the grazing lands down to the rivers far below.

The gorge of the Qavaliun River, one of whose headwaters began on Ousanadh, was emitting great plumes of mist to the south. It wound through the plateaus in deep slashes before falling down a series of waterfalls into the jungles southeast of here. That had always been uninhabited land, and remained so. The jungles of Xiputl are dangerous, but not like the Qavaliun basin.

I turned to Daro and Marilda, who were standing close beside each other watching me regard the scenery.

"Do any of the trees from the sky forest ever come across to this side?" I asked Marilda.

She blinked at me. "The sky forest?"

"That's the flying trees, right?" Daro asked. "Never seen them, me."

Marilda's expression cleared. "They're in Amboloyo, aren't they? That's what the Postulant Mistress said."

It was my turn to blink. "Amboloyo is the other side of the mountain."

Daro said comfortably, "Never been there, me."

"Nor I," added Marilda, and shivered as if at the thought. "Come, sir, we're almost there."

I crossed the few steps necessary to rejoin their sides, pondering their words. "What about the tarn where I … met you?"

She laughed, turning her bright eyes on Daro, and took a path that led us up to the switchback staircase. Small trees with short spiky needles and aromatic blue berries grew in cracks in the rock, and tufts of glaucous-leaved flowers with pompom pink and purple and white flowers and a faint, agreeable, clove-scent. It was all very pretty, what with the clarity of the air and the increasing drop on our left.

"The sacred lake is neither of this world nor of the divine lands," she said in a recitative voice. "It is water between mountain and air, surrounded by mist, where the gods are close, and may directly respond to those who are worthy of their regard."

Her expression, when she looked sidelong at me, made it clear she had indeed taken me for a directly responding minor deity.

"Ah," I said, and left the puzzle at that. I had seen no mist beyond that cast up by the waterfall; but if not actually a deity, I did have power and a magic connected to that of the world by many ancient obligations and ceremonies.

We stopped to rest several more times on the ascent. Marilda didn't seem to find this strange, making the off-hand comment that almost no one could go up in one go. I was somewhat glad to see both she and Daro needed breaks as well, at least to affirm their commitment and discuss in low voices their sudden shared future. I climb up and down the stairs of the Palace on occasion, but hardly every day or even every week.

Eventually we made it up to the rocky forecourt of the monastery. There was a huge horizontal bell or gong there, the sort made out of a cylindrical section of tree-trunk with a slit in it. I regarded the padded mallet beside it.

"No, we don't need to ring," Marilda said. "Surely you don't think *you* need to, sir?"

"Courtesy," I replied gravely, "is always appreciated."

She seemed struck by this trite comment. "So true! Perhaps you might wait just inside the forecourt, then, sir? There is a bench and a fountain there for your refreshment. Men are not supposed to enter the Abbey proper, you know. I won't be long."

We agreed, and she led us inside a small door inset in the large ones, which let us into a flagged courtyard. She ran off lightly, quite as if she hadn't just climbed halfway up a mountain. I was glad for the cup of water Daro fished out with the dipper from the well for me (it was my own cup; I may not be subject to the taboos at present but I thought the supplied dish rather unhygienic in appearance), and to sit on the bench looking at the multitude of gargoyles carved on the inner beams and corner posts of the buildings before us.

There were a handful of nuns and acolytes around. Two acolytes were sweeping the courtyard, sending giggling looks over at us. An elderly nun sat in the sun on a bench a few yards away from ours, seemingly half-asleep. After a few minutes another nun, this one middle-aged and remarkably short, came bustling up to us from the door Marilda had gone through with a plate of sweet buns. She offered them to the elderly nun (not so asleep as all that, as she proved by taking two without opening her eyes) and then hastened over to us.

"So you're taking Marilda away to be married," she began, her eyes on Daro. She had a gorgeous voice, rich and resonant and medium-toned, like a violoncello. I listened in admiration even as I ate a bun in neat but quick bites. Then she caught sight of me and stopped in utter shock.

I hadn't furled my magic as tightly as when I thought the Mother Superior was going to be present, because it's uncomfortable to keep it that suppressed. It was at its usual degree of extension, hardly to be noticed except by those of great sensitivity.

It was, alas, quite clear that this nun was a person of such nicety of sense.

She stared at me, mouth open, then made as if to fall on her face. It is a motion I am very familiar with.

I lifted my hand in a gesture to forestall her. "Good morning, Sister," I said, pleasantly if not quite with full Imperial dignity. "Marilda asked me for my assistance, and so I am here. Not officially, you understand."

The nun closed her mouth with a snap. She was round-faced and broad-nosed, her brown skin a touch sallow and her eyes heavy-lidded and angular.

"Of course," she said, recovering. Her voice really was astonishingly beautiful. I hoped she read the sacred texts out loud to the others.

"I trust it will not be a difficulty to release her from her position here?"

The nun kept her eyes down, focused on my toes in their black leather boots. Her hands found a position folded inside her sleeves; she wore the double-layered woollen habit of the Mountain Abbey, the inner a pale brown and the outer a deeper terracotta, with wide sleeves embroidered with simple bands in green and blue.

"Certainly not ... sir ... She had not taken her formal vows. She will be permitted to continue her training, if she so wishes, as a married laywoman."

"That is good to hear," I said agreeably, taking another two buns and then looking for a cloth to wrap them in before placing in my bag. Daro was looking from the nun to me with a ponderous confusion. The nun herself did not seem to know what to do with herself. After an awkward silence (at least on her part) she started murmuring prayers inaudibly under her breath, hand stealing to a rosary with three gold beads mixed in with a length of wooden ones.

That had some significance, I was sure, but didn't know what. The Abbey of the Mountains belonged to the Cirithian religion, which was fairly eclectic and involved a very complicated and hierarchically structured heaven of innumerable deities. The pantheon naturally included various emperors (though not *all* of them were considered of the upper tiers, a fact of which I approved), mixed in with various nature deities and other creatures of magic and myth.

I politely ignored the nun's praying and regarded the courtyard. It was not regular in shape, being formed out of the space between three buildings, some outcroppings of stone, and the wall through which we had entered, all flagged with a pale tan stone (apparently very dirty, from the slow, thorough sweeping the two acolytes were doing) interrupted only by the benches around the walls and a fountain with a small shrine set into the wall beside it, a little to our left.

The nun was still praying. Daro was watching the entrance of the main building with placid patience. The old nun, having eaten her buns, seemed to have fallen asleep again. The two acolytes continued to sweep the same patch of flagstones. I walked over to the fountain.

The water came out of a spout of bronze worked into the shape of a crane, its wings extended in an arch over the basin, which was stone. I washed the crumbs and red bean paste from my hands. The water fell at my feet and ran down between the flagstones to a grate of dark metal.

The fountain shrine was to an emperor, but when I looked at it more closely—I haven't actually investigated many at close range—I was fairly sure it wasn't intended to be me. Images depicting me distinguished me from my ancestors—even if I hadn't actually resembled them, the history of state iconography would have insisted on it—by showing me holding a hectohedron, a hundred-sided figure, in my right hand, the five-flowered sceptre in my left, and over my shoulders a mantle in the orange and blue of Zuni formal regalia. Often there was some other reference to my being the hundredth Emperor of Astandalas in the background, or a tiger to represent my lordship of Zunidh.

The Emperor in this shrine was wearing a long garment in a striking midnight-blue, all spangled with stars. He had white wings on his sandals and held in one hand a traveller's staff, in the other a crystal sphere with a light like a sun in it.

I shifted my walking staff from one hand to the other. I confess I felt perhaps the smallest bit self-conscious.

I know; I was tired. Usually I don't have much difficulty in presenting a serene benevolence to those who fall at my feet.

The nun with the beautiful voice was still praying. I dipped my cup into the water coming out of the bronze crane's beak and sipped it until I felt my equanimity was prepared for any response. Marilda's response to my arrival was starting to make somewhat more sense.

No one surely *expected* me—Artorin Damara, that is—to actually answer prayers. (I remain unconvinced that the state religion is anything more than lip service for anyone but a very few.)

But Aurelius Magnus, who was stolen away two thousand years before my birth by the Sun for his beauty and his magic and his power?

Not that I am particularly handsome, except insofar as wealth and nourishment and custom supply a veneer of it, but I do have the magic and power.

Daro's placidity slid from his face in favour of shy eagerness when he saw that Marilda was crossing the courtyard towards us. She paused to say something to the two acolytes sweeping the flags, whose responding giggles were audible, then tripped lightly to us. She had changed into the loose trousers and long tunic commonly worn in Central Damara, in soft sage-green and umber.

Daro immediately took her bag and smiled reverently at her. "This is happening, isn't it?" he said.

Marilda's eyes were bright as she nodded. She looked at the nun. "Sister—"

"Go in peace," the nun said, lifting her eyes to look at her with a fond expression. "Return once you have wed and we shall speak of your further training."

"Oh, Sister," Marilda said, her heart in her voice. She dropped to her knees, Daro following a moment after. "Will you bless us?"

The nun gave me a quick, questioning glance, to which I nodded gravely, then laid her hands on their heads. "Go in peace," she said again, "and walk with joy into your new life together. Do not forget the prayers you have learned here, child, and return when you need your spirit to be refreshed."

"How could I forget?" Marilda replied, twisting to look up at me with something like adoration in her face.

The nun removed her hands and also looked at me, her eyes not questioning, but utterly sincere. I cleared my throat.

I do know what a living god is supposed to do, at any rate.

"May the blessings of the Sun and the Moon and the One Above shine on you through the day and the night," I said, in the round, rolling tones of a benediction, letting my magic unfurl briefly to arc over them with its fire-warmth.

I did not touch them physically; I never did.

Both Marilda's and Daro's eyes were brilliant with tears as they stood up and Daro shouldered Marilda's bag. The nun lifted her right hand to her lips and flicked it out towards me, in a gesture of respect and reverence that was very old and not quite that commonly given to me. I inclined my head in acknowledgment, then paused when it seemed as if she had a question for me.

"Please, sir," she asked in a low, quick voice.

"Sister?"

She wavered, but went forward bravely. "This Abbey was built where you were said to have attained your apotheosis? Is that —*true*?"

Of all the multitude of gods in the Cirithian religion I had to imitate *theirs*!

I smiled at her, letting my magic grow just that touch more expansive, though I was careful not to meet her eyes. There was no way I would lie about something like that. "Sister, I cannot speak of the great mysteries, but I can say that there is nothing I find displeasing about this abbey's location. Except perhaps the stairs up!"

She laughed, visibly flustered, and I gave her a formal benediction, as I did at certain ceremonies in my proper persona, and departed down the multitude of steps after Marilda and Daro.

My knees and thighs were protesting their distinct lack of divine strength by the time we reached the village again. We did not stop except for Daro to duck his head into his master's workshop and inform him that we were now on our way to the river station. I took the opportunity to eat another of the buns, though Marilda professed herself not at all hungry when I offered her one.

The walk to the river station was pretty. The road was beaten earth and well-used. It took us first through a field, green grass with white hump-backed gaur cattle in the distance, and then into a forest of pines and some sort of tall leathery-leaved shrub with round heads of pale lemon-yellow flowers. They had a pleasant fragrance (not at all citrusy) and were well worked by bees and other insects.

Daro and Marilda walked hand in hand, talking about where they should look for a home and what they would need for it and all those sorts of practical questions I had never once had cause to consider. I walked along behind them, grateful for the richer air, looking at the shrubs and listening to birds singing overhead, and contemplated what I should do after I had seen them safely wed.

Somewhere downriver from here there was a way to cross from Zunidh to Alinor. Long ago, when I was still fairly new to my lordship, I had marked the gate with a pair of standing stones, for the convenience of those who had occasion to travel between the worlds.

As the gate was quite far down into the lower gorge system, it was decidedly inconvenient for everyone; there was another such passageway, more intermittent in accessibility but much more usefully located close to Boloyo City. That was the way merchants and ambassadors travelled, as the route (even if only open at certain times of day and season) was clearly marked and led to a known destination.

This one I had marked and thereafter left alone. As far as I knew no one much went through it in either direction, and I had never heard any indication of where exactly on Alinor it might lead. I only knew it went to Alinor because that was the dominant feel of the magic brushing up against Zunidh's. There could well be a full Borderwood and all that *that* entailed there as well.

Well, we were going to a river station. Surely I'd be able to find a boat or some other means for travelling downriver as far as river traffic permitted. And after that—well, who knew? Something would happen. It always did.

We passed out of the yellow-flowered shrubs and into a flowery meadow. It was spring up here in the high mountains: the meadow was moist, even boggy in spots, and daubed in broad, bright swaths of short recurved pink and white dogtooth lilies with glossy green leaves, and even bigger patches of giant yellow cowslips and some sort of candelabra primula in hot pink and orange. It was all very fetching.

"We're almost there," Daro said, glancing back at me with an encouraging smile. I smiled back at him and continued to thrust the walking staff down with great enthusiasm. The One Above only knows what they thought of me, but that has never bothered me overmuch. People will persist in ascribing divinity to human beings despite the sure and certain knowledge that no one is perfect. I could only do my best.

Only a few minutes later we were across the meadow and into another forest. The path led steadily downhill (I was grateful for the staff), winding between huge droopy-branched conifers that were not pines, given the short, dark green tufts of their needles. There were more broad-leaved trees mixed in with them, some I recognized as magnolias, a few in flower. There had been a garden visible from my window in Astandalas with a huge magnolia tree in it, white-flowered and with leaves russeted beneath their glossy surfaces.

I hadn't thought about that tree for years. It had been a solace to me, in those days when strict custom and overwhelming magic kept me inside and well away from any possible touch of sunlight or moonlight on my skin.

Long ago, the stories say, Aurelius Magnus was stolen away by the Sun for his magic and his beauty and his moral rectitude. I quirked my lips, amusement lifting the cloud of melancholy that had settled over me at the memory of that beautiful, ancient tree. Long ago, but not far away, at least not according to the Abbey of the Mountains!

On the edge of that belt of trees was a stand of glorious blue poppies, waist-high to me, their silken petals translucent and quivering in the slight breeze. I stopped to regard them in awe. "What a divine colour!" I exclaimed aloud.

Marilda considered this with a puzzled air, then smiled enthusiastically. "Yes, sir!"

Well, I try.

After the poppies in their magnificence the rest of the walk to the river was mundane: merely tussocky grass, a few wooden structures of no particular architectural interest, and a couple of dun mules in a paddock standing nose-to-tail so one could keep flies off the other.

The post office was also a wooden building of little architectural interest, save for the large white swan in flight painted in exuberant strokes on the otherwise plain siding. I regarded that with some bemusement.

"Chazo from the village is a painter, like," Daro said. "Isn't he good!"

"It's delightful," I said. There was a certain naivety to the execution, but the idea was admirable and the effect most agreeable.

It was a very quiet place, just before noon on the day before the government folks took a holiday. A single older man—older than me, even—sat on a stool behind the counter, reading a book. He set it down after finishing his paragraph when we came in and set a bell tinkling over the door, and surveyed us with as imperturbably pleasant an expression as Master Joff the Carpenter.

"Hmm," he said when he saw me.

He was Amboloyan or Ystharian, pale-skinned and with straight white hair cut short. His eyes were a bright, twinkling blue, protuberant in his face. He had pink cheeks and a bulbous nose and the wrinkles of someone who had relaxed away from previous stress. I was inclined to like him on sight.

I should perhaps state that I don't actually like *everyone* on sight, but most people are so intriguing it is hard not to find them appealing. It may be the poet in me, or perhaps the youth who had only met sixteen people before his eighteenth birthday, or the folk hero who travelled far and wide talking with everybody. Or perhaps it's just that I meet very interesting people.

I'm sure that's it. Nothing to do with most of a lifetime kept rigidly and rigorously apart from any normal interactions.

Marilda was already deep into an explanation about her and Daro's sudden decision to get the annual stipend. The post officer listened thoughtfully.

"So we were wondering what we needed, sir," Marilda said anxiously. "We know you're on holiday starting tomorrow ..."

"Oh, don't you worry about that," the post officer said, waving it off. "We've got all afternoon to sort you out, and you can still get married before sunset."

I lifted my eyebrow at that; it was a nicety I hadn't previous mentioned to my lovebirds.

"I used to be a lawyer down in the big town," the post officer said, glancing towards me, even as he pulled out several ledgers and a locked strongbox from beneath his counter. I leaned along it farther on from Daro, where I could watch the proceedings without getting in the way.

The post office was a curious building. It was not large, and most of it was occupied by a large wooden counter set above what seemed to be shelves on the inner side. The back wall was windowless, with a door to one side, and was occupied by a large set of pigeonholes.

"I take all the mail for the villages roundabouts," he explained. "We keep it until someone comes to collect it. Some of the villages in the gorges are remote, you know."

"I can imagine."

"We send the outgoing mail on the barge to the big town, Cozorka, where it gets taken across the canals to Ffilano and the Light system by the Grand Duchess's Summer Palace. All told, takes about a week extra to reach us, which ain't bad. Not like it used to be after the Fall!"

There's much to be said for having someone from the far hinterlands—and the Vangavaye-ve is *very* far—as the head of the world's government. Their priorities are never quite the same as other people's. Kip had entirely reworked the post system several times (the last after the development of the sky ships) after some letter from his family had taken eight months to arrive.

"Here we are, then," the post officer said, pulling out a pen that throbbed with magic in my vision. I blinked away from it; he laughed shortly. "You're a wizard, then, of course? Sorry, it does take those as aren't used to it a bit funny."

"Mm," I managed, imagining a veil coming down between me and the enchanted object. Not something I like doing if I can avoid it, but there's just something about things enchanted in full Schooled wizardry that gives me an immediate pounding headache.

Well, I know what it is: the fundamental antipathy between wild magic and Schooled. Though knowing that doesn't help much.

"What you need, see," the post officer said to Marilda and Daro, "is to sign your legal name and where you're from in this ledger, using this pen. It's enchanted, as your friend saw, with a powerful great magic to make sure you're who you say you are and that you haven't already drawn your allotment this month."

"What does it do if you're cheating?" Marilda asked nervously, staring at it with a combination of repugnance and curiosity.

"Won't sign, first of all, and second of all, it tells me to alert the local constables so they can give you a fine."

This was a splendid piece of magic; one I could never have done. I retreated another step as Marilda took courage and signed her name and that of her village with small, neat lettering. The magic flared, connecting to a network pinned to the one I had created with the Lights. I held my breath unconsciously until it subsided again.

You cannot imagine how difficult it was to ensure the Lights were accessible to Schooled wizards as well as myself. The hybrid form of magic I created as Lord of Zunidh was not impossible, obviously, but it wasn't something I *enjoyed*. The puzzling out how to do it was engrossing, and the satisfaction I took in finishing works certainly real, but the *act*? Drudgery. And that is not a word one should associate with magic.

Daro signed his name next, with concentration akin to that with which he'd attended his lathe. He beamed when the ink flowed without hesitation. I braced myself for the next flash of magic, and caught my breath a little more quickly this time. The post officer looked very curious.

"Right then," he said, and used a key to unlock his strongbox. He took out two prepared bags and handed one to each of them. "There you are."

Marilda looked inside her bag and then up at him with utter amazement on her face, equal to when she'd seen me arrive. "That's it?"

The post officer smiled at her. "That's it. Enjoy your marriage, children, and come back again in a month if you'd like another lot."

"We don't have to do anything else?" Daro asked slowly.

The post officer shook his head. "No. Do your best to use it well, and make good tithes to the Lord Emperor with what you're able to accomplish because of it!"

Their eyes were wide. Marilda turned to me. "Sir—how—how can I thank you?"

"It's not me you should thank," I replied, thinking of how hard Kip had worked to make this a reality. I had done so little besides encourage him. (And read his nine-hundred-page Plan.)

"Still—"

"Look," Daro interrupted; he had gone to the window so he could see inside his bag in the light streaming in. "My sister's outside—let's tell her the news!"

"Go," I said to Marilda. "I'll follow."

The two dashed out, leaving me with the post officer. He hadn't put his ledger away; on the contrary, he offered me the pen.

I looked up at him, meeting his eyes before realizing what I was doing. My magic was tightly furled after the impact of the Schooled wizardry, but still. It was astonishing how quickly I could fall away from long-instilled habits.

"I believe you're eligible, too," he said quietly.

"Really?" I said in astonishment, trying not to laugh. And who did *he* think I was?

He chuckled and set the pen down in the crease formed by the open pages of the book. "Are you not a Zuni citizen?"

"Technically, I suppose so. I would certainly meet the residency requirements. But I don't *need* it."

"And so?" He settled himself comfortably on his stool. "Look, sir, I don't rightly know who you are, and I surely don't need to know. But if you're a citizen of this world, you are eligible to receive the stipend. And who knows? A little extra cash never hurt anyone."

Kip had argued *so hard* that it had to be equal across all ranks of society, all ages, all sexes and genders and races and incomes and whatnot. Anyone over the age of sixteen was eligible: *anyone*. No one knew, he had said, what went on behind closed doors; for whom this stipend might be the difference between life and death.

"I'm travelling."

"I can see that," the post officer replied, unmoved. "Let me tell you what I see, sir: a man who has fulfilled every one of society's expectations for him. He has left his position, very recently I would guess, and is now looking to find out who he truly is."

I daresay I looked flabbergasted. It sometimes happens.

He chuckled again. "No, I don't know who you are. Someone of high birth, I'm guessing. Probably not who *they* think you are, eh?"

"Probably not," I agreed, smiling wryly.

"I doubt you're who *you* think you are, just now, either. Give it some time. Go see the world. Find the old friends you've lost touch with. See the places you knew as a youth. Find out something ... magnificent."

My hands were sweaty on the wooden walking stick. "You're most perspicacious."

"Also discreet, don't worry. I was a lawyer, you see. A big man, in the town. Came up here to get away from it all when I retired, after my husband died ... I couldn't handle the quiet. This job came open so I applied, and you know what? It's amazing what you learn, helping people with their letters and their stipend. It's changed the world, this," he said, thumping the ledger with the palm of his hand. "I'm not sure anyone can know how much."

I wasn't sure even Kip did, though in his heart of hearts he must have hoped for so much. His nine-hundred-page Plan had had much to do with the logistics and the principles behind the stipend, and less to do with what he thought would be the results in any form except the most banally economic.

Or perhaps he did. Kip is an artist of the government; he makes the banally economic the clay of his work.

The world gives me a tithe of their creations, financial, artistic, material, and so on. I accept that as I must, as every emperor before me did, as my due.

This, this offer was not for my position, not for any good I might do, not for my authority or my dignity or my symbolic position as mediator between the human and the divine or as centre of the order of the world. This was for *me,* and me alone.

I had not understood how humbling it was to take what was freely offered.

I swallowed. "I'm planning on going to the gorges and away from the world …"

To my surprise the post officer smiled brightly and reached under the counter for another, smaller strongbox. "Alinor or Ysthar? We've had a few travellers over the years come out of the gorges. I can't bear not to help them, so I exchange their money for them even though I never knew what to do with the foreign coins. One day, I said to myself, one day someone is going to be going the other way and I can pass it on."

He opened the box and set out several bags and a thin bundle of brightly coloured paper. "Isn't this strange?" he said, pointing at it. "That's the new Ystharian money. Got it off a fellow two or three years ago. So odd. I guess that must be their queen … The Alinorel stuff is more familiar. Still has our Lord Emperor on it, most of it."

"Ah," I said, and considered the book he pushed towards me, and the pen.

"Do you mind if I try something first?" I asked. "It may not write; but I shouldn't like to alert the constables unnecessarily."

His eyebrows twitched with curiosity. "Go ahead."

Kip had arranged such papers as I might need under a not-quite-false name, but I wasn't sure if he would have thought of this. I began to write *Tor,* but the ink did not flow.

It made me, I confess, inordinately pleased that Kip had missed that one small detail.

"And your real name?" the post officer said, smiling mischievously. "No one else sees these books, I promise you."

I hesitated, but if it *did* accept Fitzroy Angursell … ?

And if it didn't?

To my shame, I was not brave enough to test the magic.

"I am trusting in your discretion," I said, and even as he nodded, I wrote *Artorin Damara of Solaara*.

This time I did not flinch as the magic connected.

He passed me the small coin-bags and the bundle of bright paper, strangely thick and slippery to the touch. And then he turned the book around, glanced down at the name out of habit, and halted in shock.

Whatever identity he'd thought for me it had clearly not been *that*.

"*Oh*," he said, in a very quiet exclamation.

"You were reasonably correct in your assessment," I said blandly, "though I am not, at the moment, fully retired."

9

IN WHICH I STARTLE A SMITH

*D*aro's sister, Kenna, looked very like him, being also tall, broad-shouldered, and of similar colouring and features. Her eyes were sharper and very alive. She regarded my outfit with skepticism edging into outright suspicion; I smiled back at her. From what I had seen of the local inhabitants, who all seemed to wear earth-toned cotton and wool garments (and Kenna, in soft ochre and sage green, was no exception), my star-spangled midnight blue velvet was utterly outrageous.

Kenna wore her hair up in spiral braids anchored with polished steel jewelry. I regarded the ornaments with minor envy. It is possible I have in my ostensible possession tithes of the greatest art of Zunidh; but I have never been crafty with my hands.

"So you're the answer to Marilda's prayers?"

"More of a facilitator, I think," I replied demurely, ignoring her tone. "I like your hair ornaments. Did you design them yourself? I presume you made them—Daro said you were a blacksmith."

"An *apprentice* blacksmith," she said, though one hand went up to touch an ornament, a flower made of one cunningly twisted piece of steel. "And yes."

"They're beautiful."

"Mmph," she said, pretending to be unimpressed by the compliment.

I regarded her with some amusement. "Would you like us to invite the post officer along as a witness? He was formerly a lawyer, he told me, and knows the marriage law I mentioned to Daro and Marilda."

This reasonable suggestion seemed, if anything, to increase Kenna's suspicion. Nevertheless, she went into the post office, opening and shutting the door behind her with decisive thrusts. I wandered down the path a few steps. Past the post office was another building with a wall mural, this one an array of clouds with a flight of cranes coming in and out of them. I suspected it was slightly later in date than the post office swan, as the lines were surer and the colours cleaner.

The sound of a door opening returned my attention to the post office. Kenna had been successful in her request; no doubt the post officer was curious. He shut but did not lock the door behind him, then hung a slate on a hook beside the door.

If it came to that, I was curious. I walked back close enough to read the slate: *Gone to see Master Smith.*

"Do you not need to lock the door?" I asked, mindful of the strongboxes full of stipend bags.

The post officer appeared to have spent the intervening few minutes hyperventilating, but managed to utter an answer in relatively unstrained tones. "No, s-sir, everything precious is in the back room, which is locked and protected, and people still need to be able to collect their mail. It's an offence to tamper with the post, you know," he added solemnly.

"I do know," I replied, laughing aloud at the thought of Kip's earnestness.

(The Postal Plan was only three hundred and twenty pages, but I had read that, too. The things I do for my people!)

The post officer tried not to look either scandalized or delighted

121

at my laughter, and succeeded only in appearing mildly constipated.

Kenna gave me another suspicious glare, then tripped up to her brother and soon-to-be sister-in-law and took their arms in hers. I settled in at a reasonable pace behind them, my staff thumping pleasingly on the beaten earth of the path. The post officer came up on my left. He had a slight limp but did not seem particularly fussed about it. Mind you, he was fairly obviously focused on not starting to hyperventilate again, so perhaps that was sufficient distraction.

"One of my legs is shorter than the other, s-sir," he explained without prompting.

I nodded in agreement, then decided that if I wanted a conversation, I was going to have to do more than that. "Now, you know *a* name for me; may I have yours?"

He stammered silently for a moment, then said, with almost painful sincerity, "Aelian Izucar at your service, sir!"

"I am at yours," I returned, inclining my head politely, quite as if I had not just upended his day. "Thank you for the company."

He took a deep breath, rallied, and was more or less the former lawyer, respected in his community. "Yes, sir, a clever blow. Kenna was entirely certain it was all a joke on her brother."

"I am not beyond a certain degree of mischief, but I hope I am not so cruel as that."

He seemed to want to say something appropriate to that, but to my pleasure refrained. "Ah, she's a protective older sister, and Daro, while a splendid man, is not the swiftest of thought."

"Swiftness of thought can be overrated," I murmured, as we went past another windowless building—a warehouse?—decorated with a fine stylized tiger and an iconographically clear depiction of me. I raised an eyebrow at the deftness with which the artist had suggested a hectohedron without actually drawing all hundred sides. "Your wall-artist appears to be improving in his art," I said, nodding at the painting.

Aelian snorted involuntarily, then went on hastily. "There's someone who was lost before the stipend. His mother's joy, and his father's despair. Chazo is the youngest son of a farmer with no land to spare—but what a gift at seeing the world! He's only twenty, you know, sir. This is his latest."

"Your village seems well-supplied with artisans."

"Three years of the stipend and things are changing already," the post officer said, gesturing around. "There's an ease to people that wasn't there before. This was never a rich land: too high and too remote. The Abbey was the only thing that ever brought anyone here, or bought surplus food. I hope I live to see a generation grow up who never knew that niggling want. I think the world will be a far finer place for it."

"I agree," I said quietly. Aelian appeared to remember who I was, and stared resolutely straight ahead.

We reached the river-bank and turned to follow its stream to the left. The young folk had drawn ahead of us. I was glad to see that Kenna was laughing and joking with them now: ribbing her brother, if I could read their gestures properly.

"How far is it to the smithy?" I asked.

"Not far … a quarter-hour's walk, maybe. Master Smith is a bit of a recluse. He's not from the neighbourhood originally, you see. Came years and years ago—a question for the Mother Abbess, I've heard, and never left."

I looked around. The river beside us was young, shallow and turbulent over rocks, milky aqua in colouring from the silt. Away across from us were meadows framed by forests, and behind them the high peaks of the next range over, the Zilifiri Mountains on the other side of the gorge system. There was not much agriculture on that side. Our side was mixed woods and small fields, many showing the young growth of grains against their dark soil, or pastures for short, stocky horses and the hump-backed cattle.

Three-headed Ousanadh was behind us, tall and glorious with the sun on its glaciers and the blue sky behind. More mountains marched northward, though the trees in the near foreground prevented an extensive view.

"It's a beautiful place," I said. "I can see why someone might choose to stay."

"Especially someone seeking a bit of solitude," the post officer suggested. I cocked an eye at him, remembering what he'd told me of his history. He grinned and shook his head. "Master Smith doesn't get many letters from outside the region. There's some as wonder what his true name is, I can tell you; but that the Mother Abbess gave him welcome is enough for me."

That piqued my curiosity, as it was undoubtedly intended to do. I said nothing, however, though I did amuse myself by contemplating the various reasons Master Smith might have for his anonymity. A criminal past, while likely, was boring: how much more delightful to imagine him a weary sojourner finding peace in this high and pleasant land, perhaps one of the ancient smiths cursed by the gods for forging weapons great enough even to assail the heights of heaven.

This naturally led me onto thoughts of famous blades, past and present—Aishur! Anorianas! Adamai! and many others not starting with a—and from there on to the question of the Three Mirrors of Harbut Zalarin.

My studies into such esoteric lore have not been as deep as you might expect, partly because there was a lengthy period of time in which I used my spare hours in a hobby of learning spells of unlocking (for no particular reason, I assure you; except possibly something at a deep metaphorical level that I certainly never once thought of), and partly because the Imperial Archives, famed though they rightly are, have little of pre-Astandalan history in them.

Indeed, most of my findings had come about as a result of looking into questions of the succession of the lords magi of Zunidh. A scholar (one of Kip's multitude of cousins, in fact) had informed me that there was a ritual to inaugurate a quest to find an heir. I could not resist such a legitimate excuse to do what I had been wanting to do for half my life, and immediately delved into what was necessary for me to leave my throne and my palace and set off on adventure.

In several of the ancient sagas I had found mention of the mirrors. In the oldest scrolls in the Archives I had found out that there were three, left by Harbut Zalarin to his children, and that Yr the Conqueror had been buried with his. As for the other two, they had been lost to time. Damar the Bold had ended up a hermit on a remote islet of Colhélhé, and Lazunar the Fair was said to have woven a cloak for herself that hid her from all sight, which she came to wear more and more frequently until at last she disappeared for good.

Lazunar had presumably been the inheritor of her father's magic, though Damar the Bold had had some power of his own: enough that it was said he had laid a great curse on his brother's line, that for ninety and nine generations they would gain exactly what they wanted, no less and and no more.

A small river coming down from the north face of Ousanadh joined the larger stream to our right. The river-side road crossed it on a bridge with supports carved into gargoyles. It appeared that Chazo the Muralist had been busy here as well, for there were panels between the support posts, acting as a kind of railing for the crossing, which were painted with another series of cranes, these ones standing in various poses and attitudes.

"Is there some significance to the cranes?" I asked the post officer.

"They spend much of the winter here, and are beloved visitors, sir. The old country tradition is that they bring the souls of our dead to visit us, so that we are protected through the cold and wet season."

I trailed my hand along the panel, just above the powderpuff crest of an elegant grey and white bird. And by whom should I hope to be visited? I did not know if any of my old friends were dead, and though so many had been lost in the Fall of Astandalas, and in the years since, my grief had been general. In my years as Emperor, I had had courtiers and attendants and servants and guards by the score; but none had ever touched me, or looked me in the eye, or called me by anything like my name; and I had hardly known any of theirs.

"A lovely idea," I said at last, wishing silently for reassurance that I had not lost all ability to—what?

There are those I would grieve deeply if I lost them, even in that Palace on the other side of the Eastern Ocean. Kip, for one, and many of my guards, and Conju who had been so endearingly worried for how I would cope away from my household, and ... and there are a few others. I smiled more brightly and looked at what confronted us now.

There was a small stone-walled house on the other side of the river, snug against a low bank. The river fell over the bank, turning a waterwheel. Something about its design struck me, but I let it sit there without worrying. The niceties of millstream mechanics are hardly matters I have studied. No doubt I had seen something similar, once upon a time, in my travels.

"Is this the smithy?" I asked my helpful companion. "Or a mill?"

"Aye, sir," Aelian said. "Till he apprenticed Kenna Master Smith had no assistant, and the water-wheel lights his bellows for him. He has a small grist-mill set up in one of the buildings, for bread-flour, which is a help. All the grain used to have to go down to Stasrick for milling, and even with the lock it's an overnight journey."

The mill, smithy, and cottage were a pleasing conglomeration of buildings. Nothing big—I could well believe it held no more than a single family, or indeed a single man and possibly his apprentice—but having that organic quality indicative of being added to as necessary, using close-to-hand materials. A few russet-and-green chickens pecked around the well-trodden earth between the riverside path and the mill, and some large grey geese with knobs over their beaks hissed at us from behind a low stockade further along.

Kenna, Daro, and Marilda had already gone to the wide-open doors of what I saw, as Aelian and I left the bridge and approached behind them, was the forge proper. Master Smith appeared to have been finishing up his work, if the banked fire and neatly stowed tools was any indication, but still wore his thick leather apron.

Marilda was explaining the situation to him, with joy and earnestness. He listened carefully, one hand hooked into the side of his apron, the other holding a long-handled hammer with a round head that he was bouncing lightly against his thigh. His head was turned away from me, in shadows; I could see short-cropped curly black hair, lightly salted with grey, and what seemed to be a bronze cast to his skin.

The air coming out of the smithy was hot and languid and redolent of iron and fire and singed wood and steam and just a hint of horse. It was so strongly familiar that I had to step back and turn my head so that I could hide my face.

How often had I watched Masseo stand thus, half-smiling at whatever absurdity I was promoting, already planning the practical steps needed to make it come into reality? His forge had so often been makeshift, a stone and a lump of pig-iron and his precious hammers with their strange names, with which he had wrought such mighty things.

Forge us swords out of starlight, Masseo, so we will be able to cut through the shadows, I said once, gesturing at the Dark Forest on the other side of the Moon's bright tower.

Will you make us a goblet that can hold the truth? I had asked on another occasion.

Will you make an axe strong enough and sharp enough for Pharia to cut down a mountain?

Will you make a lock that only we could ever open?

He had not thought, when he first joined us, of ever being able to forge such things. He was only a journeyman blacksmith, and (he claimed) an indifferent one. He could shoe horses and shape nails, forge ploughshares and eating knives and gate-hinges. He had no plans for glory, he said, with a wistful look in his eye. He just wanted to do something wholesome and useful and good.

He had forged us those swords, and that goblet, and the axe, and that lock, and many more things besides, so many of them wholesome and useful and good.

I could hear his voice suddenly clearly in my mind, the nearly-submerged burr of an accent he had never quite lost, the deep baritone undertones that came forth strongly when he could be persuaded to sing, the rumbling laughter that was so rare and so precious when I could tease it forth.

"So," he would say, with that crooked half-smile, "what nonsense have you come up with this time?"

And I would say—I looked up, at a motion in the corner of my eye, as if Aelian were about to touch my arm. I shied away from him with automatic haste, ignoring his embarrassed frown, and looked up into the older, more wrinkled, but still so familiar face of my friend. My breath caught.

"Dear God," said Masseo Umrit of the Red Company, dropping his hammer.

"Oh, we're not supposed to *say* that!" cried Marilda.

II

THE LAST FREE CITY OF ZUNIDH

10

IN WHICH I TRY TO CLARIFY THIS MATTER OF IMPERSONATION

"*H*ello," I said, smiling at him.

He stared.

I bent down and picked up the hammer, running my fingers down the smooth metal of the head and the smoother, well-worn wood of the handle. The air inside the forge was even heavier and headier. I felt nearly overwhelmed with emotion and had to work to keep my magic controlled.

"Is this a ball peen?" I asked, handing it back to him handle-first.

"Cross peen," he corrected automatically, accepting it. "How … Do I even want to know?"

"Probably," I replied. "But that can wait for later. First off, we're here to witness the wedding of Marilda and Daro. Once that's sorted I'm sure we will have the opportunity to … chat."

"Chat."

"It's also the name of a small bird, did you know?"

He tapped the cross peen hammer against his thigh, face unyielding. I myself was endeavouring resolutely not to start

131

131

weeping in joyous reunion, so I quite understood the stiffness of expression. "And then what?" he enquired, slowly.

I heard the unspoken, *So, what nonsense are you about now?* and answered him the way I always had, with my most brilliant, probably slightly mad, madcap smile. "I've an adventure in hand which I think you would be most excellently well suited for, Master Smith."

One of the others gasped very faintly, but I didn't look away from Masseo. He gave me a flat, disapproving look. "I heard no horses."

"South into the gorges is my first direction."

Masseo tapped the hammer a little more heavily. I hoped he wouldn't bruise himself with this access of emotion. "I'm a small village blacksmith."

"And you never know when I might not need a man who can shoe the West Wind or forge a sword out of sunlight or a chain strong enough to hold a kraken."

I could see in his face the reluctant curiosity as to whether these were literal requirements. They might have been, on other occasions.

"I am the only smith for miles around," he said, which was far weaker than the words he had first used to reject my offer, long ago when both of us were young.

I was glad I did not have to pretend not to be delighted with this. I grinned. "It's fortunate, or perhaps fortuitous, then, that you had the foresight to train a successor."

"I'm an *apprentice*," Kenna said faintly.

"No one who could design and forge steel with the delicacy of her hair ornaments is a mere apprentice."

At that Masseo did crack a smile, which he directed towards Kenna with a definitely paternal pride. With his eyes removed from me I took a deep breath, hoping I wouldn't cough from the smoke and dust in the air. It was a most neat and tidy forge; but it was still a forge.

The four locals were regarding our interaction with varying expressions of puzzlement. I swept my gaze over them and returned to Masseo, who shifted to stand foursquare before me, face again stern after his momentary softness. The steady tap of the cross peen hammer never faltered. I didn't watch our audience's reaction closely, but nor did I cry out "Masseo!" and fall upon him as my heart yearned to do.

"It's not done, around here, for a young woman to live alone."

If there had been any doubt in my mind—not that there *was*—this shift to hypothetical reactions to his departure put it to rest.

I raised an eyebrow at him. "Fortunately, or perhaps fortuitously, I happen to know a young couple, very soon to be married, who are in need of a house for themselves and their future child. Even more fortunately, or—"

"Yes, yes, perhaps fortuitously. Get on with it."

I suppressed a most undignified snort of amusement. "The young man is the brother of your apprentice blacksmith. Journeywoman, I do apologize."

I glanced sidelong at her to see that Kenna was regarding me with furious confusion.

Masseo grunted, the sound so doubly familiar that I nearly started.—Who *else* sounded just like that?

"You," he said firmly, "are utterly impossible."

My heart was so full my magic was surely welling up into noticeable power. I could already begin to imagine the poem I would write about this meeting, this first true step towards the reunion (reunification?) of the Red Company.

"Bah," said Masseo, lifting the hammer from its steady tapping and setting it on a rack next to its fellows. I followed the movement with my gaze, and Masseo, proving he had not forgotten my essential nature, tapped the one next to it. "This is the ball peen. Note the spherical, even ball-shaped, head."

"Ah," I replied gravely.

The others looked entirely baffled.

The marriage ceremony, as befit something so ancient, was very simple. Marilda and Daro faced each other across the anvil, hands outstretched to clasp each other's above it.

Kenna stood behind her brother, and Aelian behind Marilda. Masseo stood at the flat end of the anvil, and I faced him from the god's place at the point. He raised his eyebrows but said nothing when I took position there. Aelian frowned thoughtfully.

He nearly had enough evidence to figure out the truth, I thought, but I was too overjoyed at finding Masseo so unexpectedly, so serendipitously—so *fortuitously*, even—to mind overmuch. Who was he going to tell? And who would believe him if he did?

"I pledge myself to you," Marilda said to Daro. "To honour and to love, to cherish and to aid, wherever our roads take us."

"I pledge myself to you," said Daro to Marilda, his honest face shining and focused. "To honour and to love, to cherish and to aid, wherever our roads take us."

"So I witness," said Kenna, her eyes soft.

"So I witness," said Aelian, with all the solemnity of a lawyer.

I gave a full formal benediction, which took as long as the rest of the ceremony together.

The wedding over, Masseo took us into his kitchen, where he (not being one for alcoholic drink) made a celebratory pot of tea. I watched him move around the homely little space with delight.

I've always found kitchens fascinating, windows onto a realm at once alien and utterly familiar. I recognize what comes *out* of a kitchen, and most (certainly not all!) of what goes *in*; but how the basket of eggs is turned into, say, meringue is a great mystery to me.

Masseo's kitchen had white-plastered walls and dark slate

floors. The ceiling was also white plaster between dark wooden beams, crooked with age or design. There was a large wooden table in the middle, six chairs set around it. I wondered why he had six, when he lived alone. It was nice to think him so sociable, when I had always thought of him as grim.

Of course, anyone might present a certain dourness when faced with Sardeet's prattle and my own—I can admit it!—relentless love of talk.

On one wall was a window with a slate sill, a slate trough (or a sink?) below it, bronze taps coming out of the wall for water and a pipe underneath to take it away. Several wooden cupboards, one enchanted to keep cold, and a set of shelves containing copper pots, sturdy but not unattractive grey stoneware (plates of different sizes, bowls, mugs), squat handblown glasses, and a few more aesthetically impressive serving dishes in wood and ceramic.

Opposite the window was a great stone chimney with a glassed-in hearth and several doors set into the stonework. (For baking, perhaps?) Next to the chimney in the corner was an ironwork stove enchanted to heat on demand. There was a small fire burning in the hearth but Masseo put the kettle on the stove. That sort of domestic enchantment, useful and usable by those without their own gifts at magic, was another feat of Schooled wizardry I could not hope to match. Fortunately it was far less dramatic than the annual stipend pen and though I noticed the magic it did not cause any pain.

The only colour in the room came from the copper pans and kettle and green and orange cloths draped over a kind of wooden ladder leaning against the wall next to the sink. There was also a small pot of some sort of plant on the windowsill over the sink. It looked like jade beads on strings. I actually reached out with my magic to determine that it was a living plant before internally reproving myself. Unlike myself, Masseo was unlikely to want a sculpture of a plant made out of jade.

I didn't have much to compare it to, but I thought it a pleasing room. Plain and practical though it might be, everything was cared-for and carefully situated. Wood and copper alike had the rich patinas of long and frequent polishing. Masseo filled the kettle at the sink and set it on the stove. Kenna brought mugs and little plates from the shelves, and Masseo disappeared to another room and returned with a teapot that I was sure I recognized from one of our adventures.

It was silver, round-bellied and curved of spout. The lines of the pot were satisfying and the engraving subtle, all leaves and little birds. There was one small rabbit in amongst the foliage, if I recalled correctly, the maker's mark.

We had spent a long and tiring but happy day in the Great Bazaar of Yedoen, on the Isle of Ekkrai in eastern Colhélhé. It was one of the greatest and oldest cities in that part of that world, a trading centre since long before the coming of the Empire. The locals boasted that you could find things from every world there, even half-mythical (to those from within the Empire) Kaphyrn and Eahh.

We had taken that as a challenge, and had a delightful day exploring the Bazaar as a result. Showing off our treasures that evening had been almost as much fun. We had managed to find something from each world: the book from Eahh that Pharia had found, written in Tanteyr lettering, had seen us off on a new adventure.

Gadarved in particular had loved the place, I recalled. If serendipity failed—and given that three days into my quest I had stumbled on Masseo, I did not really expect it to—we could search Yedoen to see if he had decided to make a life there.

I accepted a mug absently, breathing in the smokey rich aroma of the tea. Caravan tea, exactly as we had made it so many evenings over the fire, back when tea and travel between worlds were both easily accessible.

But Masseo had tea here, despite the expense of importing it from Ysthar; and I knew a route out of the world to another, and he had never lost or abandoned this teapot. I hoped the mug hid my expression. It was unaccountably hard to keep my face calm. At court I could hold my expression unmoved though my heart was laughing with mirth or crying out with fury—

Masseo sat down at the opposite end of the table to me. For a moment our eyes met. He held up his cup in a toast, and I nearly lost my composure entirely.

Fortunately Marilda came to the rescue. "Master Smith," she said politely, "Sayo Aelian, and, er, *sir*," (that was me, her adoring glance obviating any insult or complaint about precedence), "Master Joff said he would provide a supper for us today, and we, Daro and I, would be honoured if you all were to join us."

The others murmured their gratitude. I hesitated a moment before agreeing outright, for I wanted—oh, beyond anything!—to talk privately with Masseo. I was conscious of a great need to apologize to him, and of the difficult explanation before me, and I did not know what to say.

Fortunately, or perhaps fortuitously, he did. He said, "Thank you to you both. Now—to our unexpected visitor—"

Everyone looked at me, as if their heads were drawn on a string in my direction. I set down my mug, wrapping my hands loosely around its lingering warmth, and smiled in what I hoped was not too fatuous a manner. "Yes?"

Masseo grunted, but I thought there might be a smile hidden in his eyes. "Do you intend us to leave today? Or is tomorrow acceptable?"

Kenna said, "Master Smith—" in a sharp voice.

My heart lifted. "Tomorrow is indeed quite acceptable, Master Smith. I take it you will accept my invitation?"

"Your arguments were most persuasive," he retuned, straight-faced. "My apprentice is ready to be tested, and if she agrees to the sharing of the cottage and its garden and so on with her brother and his new wife, I see no reason why I should not go with you save the fact that it has been long and long since I forged aught but shovels and ploughshares."

"If it comes to that," I replied, "it has been long and long since I last set out on a quest seeking adventure." I turned to the young folk and the silent Aelian, who all seemed astonished that they were witnessing this conversation. "What say you?"

They said yes, of course, and Aelian the former lawyer oversaw the drawing-up of a simple agreement regarding the tenancy of the cottage for the next year and a day.

"If I'm not back by then," Masseo said, "I'll not be needing the cottage thereafter, for one reason or another." And he added a line stating the cottage was to go to Kenna upon her mastery if he had not returned before.

Eventually the tea was finished and the arrangements settled and the young folk and the post officer left for the village and the celebration awaiting them. I watched them go from the doorway, Marilda and Daro arm-in-arm behind Kenna who was talking earnestly with Aelian, and thought with satisfaction that this had been a good day's work.

"Although I'm not sure I entirely understand the haste," I murmured, reflecting on how quickly everything had happened. I was motivated to finish things with dispatch, of course, for without discovering Masseo I had not wanted to linger so close to where the Mother of the Mountains might return unexpectedly early, but there was no legal requirement for them to marry immediately. Even the 'before sunset' clause in the ancient marriage law was only intended to ensure the ceremony was performed in the clear light of day.

Masseo snorted. "It's one thing to fool around, and round here that's not well accepted even if you're not a postulant nun. Pregnant out of wedlock? She'd be shunned if she didn't remedy it immediately, and him if he didn't honour his deed. Her parents are not known to be understanding. It is very fortunate—"

He paused, and finally grinned at me. "No, I'm not saying it! They'll both have a far better time of it that you were here, irritating as it is to admit it. One thing to have an anvil-marriage and another to have the local deity show up out of the blue to bless it in person."

And that landed me squarely in the awkward conversation. "Masseo—"

He gave me a quietly mocking, "Fitzroy," in return.

It had been, I dare say, about equally as long for either of us since we were last addressed by those names.

"Come in," he said, beckoning me back through the door and once more into the kitchen. "Have another cup of tea, and a cake, and tell me a lie to explain away Marilda's theory that you're Aurelius Magnus returned."

I sat down again at the table. You may laugh, but though I'd thought many times how I would explain things to my friends—of *course* I have spent many hours imagining such conversations—I had not expected this one so soon.

Nor for Masseo to sound like the Tigara identifying me as Crow. "I'm not," I said, a little hopelessly.

Masseo refilled the kettle and set it on the stove. He settled into the chair opposite me and regarded me with a disquieting expression that said *if you say so* far louder than words.

The silver teapot sat on the homely table, somehow not out of place despite its exquisite beauty. Everything else in the room was as well-made, if simpler in craft. I picked up the pot and turned it around, looking for the little rabbit tucked into the vines. I found it by the base of the handle, just the size of the pad of my thumb. "This is the teapot you found in the Great Bazaar of Yedoen, isn't it?"

"And if I had any doubts who you were, that would settle them," he said, and smiled. All his face crinkled with the expression. I gripped the teapot till my fingers strained.

Why was this so hard to say? Being forthright is—well, is that not the problem? Fitzroy had no problem being forthright; Artorin Damara was of necessity anything but. Explaining that one was in fact the other was apparently beyond either.

The kettle sang, and Masseo tugged the teapot gently out of my hands so he could rinse it out and replenish the tea leaves. He filled it with boiling water and set it down again between us before retaking his seat. I felt unduly shaken.

"Masseo," I said intently, "I want to hear all about your life, but first I must tell you—I must say I'm sorry—I'm so sorry for leaving so suddenly and without any explanation and with the magic of the Silver Forest all roused against you—"

The full weight of that abandonment seemed to crash over my mind, as I had never let it before. I stumbled out of my chair and knelt beside him, bumping the table with my shoulder. I looked up in anguish. "Masseo, I am so sorry!"

He reached out to steady the teapot, then behind him for one of the orange cloths to wipe up a splash. Then he reached out and gripped my sleeve-clad arm under the elbow and heaved me up. "Have you ever actually made an apology before?" he asked, apparently sincerely.

"Er ... one or two," I stammered, only able to think of one.

Surely I'd apologized more than once in a thousand years?

Officially divine emperors are not required to, whether or not their empire is still technically in existence. I had apologized, deeply and sincerely, to one of my household, and nearly over-whelmed him entirely.

"Sit down," he said plainly, and I sat in my chair, embarrassed and uncertain and hating the unaccustomed emotions.

"Fitzroy," he said seriously then, as I watched the steam rising from the spout of the teapot and admired the splash of soft orange from the old cotton kitchen-towel. "Look at me."

I did, recalling once again as I did how for almost that entire thousand years the only person who ever met my eyes was Kip.

(How he and Masseo would like each other! Oh, so I hoped so dearly!)

"You *are* emotional today, aren't you? It amazes me. Fitzroy, you came into my life like the incarnation of chaos and I always expected that one day you would leave it as precipitously and as much in a jumble. Between those two moments my life changed—*I* changed—so much and so much for the better. Never apologize for being who you are!"

His expression said that he clearly *did* think I might well be the incarnation of Aurelius Magnus if I wasn't actually a trickster god.

"Masseo," I said, endeavouring to convey my utter sincerity.

"Yes, Fitzroy?"

His lips were twitching, but at my expression he forced himself to be serious and attentive. I regarded him doubtfully, but apart from the encounters of the past few days—which probably didn't really count, given how exhilarated I was on my freedom from the Palace—all of my interactions were with people who either found it a sacred duty to attend to me, or who found it politically expedient to pretend it was.

I really wasn't sure how I was supposed to respond to his half-serious, half-amused expression, so I went on with deliberately admitting one of the greatest secrets of my life.

"My real name, or at least my legal one, is Artorin Damara."

Masseo regarded me. His lips were pressed tightly together now, and when he spoke his voice came out strangled.

"As in the Last Emperor of Astandalas?"

I braced myself. "Yes."

He said, slowly, tightly, "Do you mean that when you invited us to come gallivanting around the Nine Worlds with you and raise merry hell in the Empire, you were actually the Emperor's nephew and second in line to the throne?"

I nodded, my heart high in my throat. Only one other person had explicitly made this connection, seen both Fitzroy and Emperor, and she had been decidedly unimpressed.

To be fair, every other time I'd seen Pali after an absence I'd asked her to marry me, but that recurrent daydream had been far from my mind when I'd granted a private audience to a noted scholar of Late Astandalan History from the Alinorel University of Stoneybridge and discovered that said scholar was none other than Pali Avramapul of the Red Company.

I had no idea whether she'd expected Artorin Damara to be Fitzroy Angursell or whether it was as much of a surprise to her, but she had not been pleased with the reality.

I returned my attention to Masseo, wary of his silence and his response once he'd assimilated this new knowledge. His eyes were glimmering, and as I cautiously met his glance with mine his composure broke.

Not into high temper, as Pali had, but into laughter.

Great gulping belly-shaking whoops of laughter, loud and joyous and suddenly familiar as a long-forgotten dream. He laughed until his eyes were streaming and his throat was hoarse.

I confess I was nonplussed.

When at last he subsided, into titters that erupted at increasing intervals, I felt perhaps a little miffed. Had I not been clear in my apology?

"Oh Fitzroy," he managed at last, "you nearly had me there for a moment. You *do* look enough like him to fool the eye, although the gods know we never found an emperor you *didn't*! Ah, suit yourself! You wouldn't be you if you weren't claiming some transcendent absurdity."

"I'm serious," I insisted.

He laughed again, not quite as dramatically. "You always are! Do you often answer prayers, or was Marilda's a special case?"

"That's an unanswerable question," I replied, meaning that I could hardly know what prayers my actions might unwittingly answer, but before I said that Masseo went on.

"Divine mysteries, no doubt?"

I sighed. "No doubt."

"Do you know, you being one of the apotheosized emperors of Astandalas explains *so much* about you. Was it very strange to return to mortal life?"

I gave in. "Yes, it was, actually."

"Ah, I needed that laugh," he said. "Where are we going, by the way? I'll need to pack a few things before we leave."

Of all the possible reactions to my revelation of identity I had never imagined this one.

Still—there would be plenty of time later to insist on it, surely.

I might have been inclined to be cagey about our destination in other circumstances, but felt rattled and that I owed it to him to be more direct than that. I was grateful for the warm familiarity of the tea in my hands.

"Alinor first. I've learned Pali is a professor at the University of Stoneybridge, so I thought I'd head there."

And gods, that sounded as boring as anything, didn't it? Not to mention carefully avoiding any mention of *how* I'd learned that.

I hesitated, then added reluctantly, "She came to do some research in the Imperial Archives, and … that's how I know."

Masseo gave me an intense scrutiny. "Goodness, you were all worried about how I'd react, weren't you? What happened to the riddles and the enigmas and the invocation of grand mysteries and ancient legends? You can't be *that* out of practice with them!"

He sounded disappointed. I frowned at him, noting absently that this had no effect whatsoever (and my frown has caused great men to quake with fear and shame!).

He waited, eyes as eager as Gus at the Nec's, or Postmaster Audmon's, or even the Tigara's.

"I'm looking for an heir," I said, which was the truth.

"And? I know you, Fitzroy, you're never only looking for one thing. Obviously we're *really* looking for everyone else, but I'm sure you have another object in mind."

Surely an heir was sufficient? A thousand and twelve years of people complaining about unclear lines of succession had suggested as much.

—But it was true I'd given myself a more concrete item to search for.

I rallied myself with a smile such as I'd given half a dozen strangers across the world this week. "Very well, then, we're ostensibly looking for the three mirrors of Harbut Zalarin, the father of Yr the Conqueror. One is entombed with Yr, but the other two have been lost for ages untold."

"What do they do?" Masseo asked with a certain curiosity.

"When they are brought together with Zalarin's golden key they are supposed to reveal how to unlock any heart."

Masseo reached out and patted my hand. "That's better. Don't worry so much about Pali, I'm sure she was angry with relief and because she'd been nearly ready to say *yes* when you disappeared, and she wasn't one to get over that easily."

I stared at him, nonplussed. He grinned at me—Masseo did!— and released my hand. "You know—speaking of the Great Bazaar of Yedoen—I am reminded of the mirror Jullanar traded her copy of *Aurora* for there. Do you remember? It was the first time I'd ever seen you actually angry."

"Of course I was upset. It was the very first copy," I said stiffly, sitting back, the echo of that ancient fury and hurt rising up.

How embarrassed I had been when she eventually told me that she'd given away a second copy and just told the man it was the first.

Masseo snickered. "She got you good and well, didn't she? She was the only one who ever could."

11

IN WHICH THERE ARE NOT ENOUGH STRAWBERRIES

*W*hen I had packed for my quest—

Well, let me rephrase that. Conju, my chief attendant, had done most of the packing of items such as clothes, food, and what he felt were practical necessities.

I had been responsible for all the *important* items, to wit the books, instruments, and oddments rosy memory made essential. The harp and the boots and the great sweeping scarlet silk mantle: really, what else does one need?

(The boxes of comestibles were obviously pleasing. One cannot expect ancient originary deities to throw charred fish at one in the middle of *every* night. Some nights one might otherwise be too busy sleeping in a tree.)

Masseo's packing method was both methodical and brisk. I trailed after him from room to room as he collected items and conveyed them to the kitchen table.

"How long have you lived here?" I asked after he had placed a wooden box next to a neatly folded stack of clothes and a pair of felted wool slippers in a pleasing shade of dark blue.

"Oh, about fourteen years, I suppose."

He rinsed out the silver teapot and set it on top of the box, along with one of the sturdy mugs and a small copper pot, just the size for two cups of water. I frowned at it. I hadn't thought about cooking utensils.

"Do you have any food? Silly question. You probably have strange cakes and odd fruits and enough spices to outfit a small store."

I smiled reluctantly at this sally. "Don't forget the olives."

"I could never forget the olives," he replied solemnly.

I had once stuffed an extremely large terracotta amphora full of olives into my Bag of Unusual Capacity, and was forever bringing them out whenever anyone complained of hunger.

"Upon reflection, I don't know that we ever finished those olives," I murmured even as a stout canvas sack of something joined the tableau.

"That's not your same bag?" Masseo asked, adding two knives and a whetstone. "It's surely smaller."

I was inordinately pleased that he recognized the annoyance of this. "No, it's a replacement. I lost my old bag when I ... left."

"What did happen?" Masseo asked, examining the items in a drawer with a dissatisfied expression.

I sighed.

"A curse laid on my family came upon me, and I rode my horse across three worlds until it caught me and held me and bound me in its inexorable requirements, and I spent the rest of my life until three days ago under the heaviest guard in the Empire of Astandalas."

Masseo selected an array of cutlery to go with his knives, and added a small wooden box. "Salt," he said, and then: "What *did* constitute the heaviest guard in the Empire of Astandalas?"

And what sort of question was that, if he didn't believe me?

I glanced at him sidelong, but his expression seemed to be one of humouring me in my tall tales; it was a long-forgotten but nevertheless immediately familiar look. I leaned back against the table. "Sixteen guards on short rotation, at minimum two within the room at all times."

I *liked* my guards—I might even go so far as to say I loved some of them, as one loves extended members of one's family—cousins, perhaps—and Ludvic and Rhodin a little more than that—but their relentless presence grew wearying.

I had a small private study which I had fought all the priests and the guards and the servants and the masters of etiquette and so on to make, and keep, my own, and even that I only ever entered for an hour or so a day, and the guards were always on the other side of the wall, beside the only door.

There was one high window in my private study, too high to look out of unless I climbed up onto a table and thence onto a chair I'd put on the table. From there I could lean my arms on the narrow sill and see a wedge of sky and (in Astandalas) that one magnolia tree and (in Solaara) a sliver of the Eastern Ocean.

"Hmm," said Masseo, grimacing as if he were trying not to laugh. "I suppose they were afraid what you might do, left to your own devices."

Left to my own devices I'd become one of the most infamous poets and folk heroes of the Empire, and his friend. "Indeed," I said, with a crooked smile.

The cottage was small, five rooms downstairs and three up. Masseo seemed to have taken the majority of his clothes downstairs; the rest went into a wooden chest which he carried down to a small room under the stairs. That left his bedroom empty but for the bed and its furnishings. The other two were furnished but otherwise plain, ready for visitors or the new occupants.

"Kenna doesn't live here?" I asked as Masseo surveyed his room and nodded in satisfaction, then returned downstairs. Along with the kitchen, a privy, and a workroom he hadn't taken anything from, there was a sort of sitting room or study, with one bookcase along the wall. I had naturally examined this immediately on entering: there were several pattern-books for smithcraft, primarily of gates and hinges; a series of hefty academic tomes on the properties of metals out of Harktree University on Alinor; a few thin books of poetry; and a large selection of novels, most of them either adventures or mysteries.

"That would hardly be appropriate," Masseo said. "She's been living in rooms with her brother, as it happens. The switch here will be more convenient for her if not for him, but I daresay having all the animals to look after as well as the mill will keep them all occupied until the baby comes."

"I saw chickens and geese."

"There's a couple of pigs and a milk-cow out the back, and a fish-pond as well," he informed me. "As well as quite a large garden."

"Somehow I'd never really pictured you as so … rural."

He chuckled. "Oh, Fitzroy, of the many turns my life has taken that is hardly the strangest! Some days I would lie in bed listening to the rooster crow at dawn and think, Did I really once help steal cattle from the pastures of the Sun?"

"We did," I said earnestly, needing the reassurance.

"I'm not sure I can handle this solemn and serious Fitzroy," he said frankly, then turned to me with a serious stare of his own. "But while you are: will your modestly sized new bag of remarkable capacity hold my anvil?"

I had not realized how important a personage the village smith was.

By the time we reached Master Joff's house ("No, not over the workshop, that's not the fashion here, my example notwithstanding"), it was clear most of the village had assembled for the nuptial feast, and also for their smith's departure.

It was also quite clear that his departure in my company and at my invitation—regardless of the equally obvious uncertainty as to who exactly I really was—was the more extraordinary event.

I had my bag, complete with what seemed to be half of Masseo's tools, including his spare anvil, which he'd had to excavate out the storage shed next to his cow byre. "Why do you have a spare anvil?" I'd asked in my innocence.

He regarded me as if my mind had gone wandering. "For when you came back, of course."

There was nothing I could say to that but agree complaisantly to him stuffing it into my bag along with numerous hammers, assorted other tools, and ingots in a variety of sizes and metals, as well as a large sack of charcoal. There was also a large wooden box whose contents he did not detail to me.

"Don't look at me like that," he said as I swung the bag experimentally after the last of the copper ingots went in. "You can't pretend you're actually *carrying* the weight of everything that's in there."

"It has a psychic weight."

He laughed, I might say merrily. I regarded him with some wonder. The Masseo I remembered was always very serious. Grim, even. Certainly not light-hearted.

"Come," he said, reaching out to take my elbow. I skittered back and he let his hand fall with a slightly questioning expression on his face, but I didn't know quite how to explain how I felt about being touched, and he let it go. "You are excellently dressed, as ever, so unless you feel the need to change your garments shall we make our way to the celebration?"

"Let us," I agreed. On the whole I preferred to continue looking like the icon of Aurelius Magnus than put Fitzroy Angursell too much in the minds of the people here. I had, after all, openly told

Aelian the post officer that I was Artorin Damara, legally so by the witness of the enchanted pen.

It was late afternoon by this point, the sun having gone down behind the triple peak of Ousanadh. I followed Masseo not up the river-path but along a smaller trail leading into the woods at an angle up the slope. It brought us out at the village in a very few minutes, hardly enough for me to ask any questions about the locality.

The village seemed rather randomly arranged to my eyes, with no streets or centre. Masseo led me along a lane between small fields, one all full of importantly murmuring white and brown ducks, the other some sort of newly sprouted grain, and through a gate in a stone wall. This, it appeared, encircled the village, though it looked both old and little-maintained.

"They needed the protection back in the Dark Years after the Fall," Masseo said, as we began to weave through alleys between houses "when the Last Emperor was asleep and the magic was wild. The monastery closed itself off, I understand, fighting monsters from out of the Borderlands, and the land down here was full of wild animals and brigands."

I had dreamed of what was afflicting my people during those years, when I was in that enchanted sleep. I had walked in shadows and fear, lost and alone, looking always for my friends of the Red Company—surely we could have fixed the woes of five worlds together!—but though I had sought them long and hard in those dreams full of darkness, all I found were the disasters besetting what had once been my empire.

"They were difficult years for everyone," I said.

"I came here much later. I'd been travelling … I'll tell you about it when we've got the time. We're here now."

'Here' was a two-story house, stone on the ground floor and wood above. As befit a master carpenter's house the wood was well-shaped and richly carved and painted. Protections against evil spirits, I guessed, and for decoration as well. I could feel the tingle of spells carved into the wood and woven into the delicate chains of metal bells and cupped flowers running down each corner.

"Is that your work?" I asked, indicating the rain-catchers.

"Mine and Kenna's," Masseo confirmed, smiling at them. "You approve?"

The magic in them was subtle, guided by runes, so that each drop of water would increase health and thrift and good fortune.

(I remembered studying runes with Masseo, in strange libraries and stranger books in many odd and remote places. He had little direct magic of his own, though long travels in the lands between and beyond the worlds had increased his knowledge and skill.)

"Indeed," I said, my voice a little choked by the memories.

"Come," he said, once again moving to touch my elbow and letting his hand fall when I moved away. A shadow crossed his face but again he said nothing, and I could not.

I set my shoulders and myself for an audience, smiling like a fabled enchanter of old, like Fitzroy Angursell on a quest, like a merry-making Trickster come to earth; and I could not pretend I did not enjoy myself better for the pretence.

After a whirlwind of greetings and exclamations, few of which made sense to me, we determined that most of the initial speeches and toasts had already been made, and that the young newlyweds were holding court, as it were, with their friends in the garden. The interior of the house was devoted to food, drink, and the constellation of activities I set under the heading of Politics.

Masseo was swept off to a discussion involving several other tall, serious, competent-looking men and women—the master crafters of the as-yet-unnamed-to-me village, I guessed—and I waded through many dazed and awed half-conversations until I found myself next to the food in the company of a proud woman of high middle age and stout carriage who found my garments fascinating.

The food was laid out on a table, many plates piled high with all sorts of things: dumplings and little cakes and steamed buns and fruit and sliced meats and mysterious fluffy paste things in pastry cases. I watched for a moment as people took plates from a pile to the left-hand side of the table and drifted along collecting items as they pleased.

It was not at all civilized but looked wonderful.

The woman reached out a hand slowly towards my sleeve. I stepped back as smoothly as I could, turning to pick up a plate.

"Oh, I'm sorry!" she cried, in a voice nearly as high-pitched as Marilda's and with a pleasant fluting timbre and genuine remorse. "The cloth is so splendid I couldn't resist."

"I am unaccustomed to touch," I said, and then handed her a plate, as seemed polite.

Her face clouded and then cleared with wonder. "Of course," she breathed, her eyes wide and soft. Her eyebrows were as carefully shaped as any court lady, and she wore touches of make-up to emphasize her large and lustrous eyes. I particularly liked the thin line of malachite-green on the edge of her eyelids.

I selected an array of comestibles, including three different colours of the mysterious pastes and a little cunningly folded paper cup of strawberries, and made my way over to a corner where I had a good view of the room. The woman followed me.

"I hadn't realized ones such as *you* ate ... ordinary food," she said.

I smiled at her in an entirely deceptive manner, and replied airily. "Naturally, usually I don't. But when one is travelling the mortal worlds incarnate ..."

She thrilled at this suggestion, eyes opening even wider. I ate a few bites of food—I do, as it happens, have plenty of experience eating neatly and unobtrusively while people stare unabashedly at me and my manners—and eventually took the edge of my hunger, which by this point of the day was considerable. I finished with the strawberries and eyed the plate on the table. It was set high and on a beautiful ceramic stand, and there were not many.

"It's early for strawberries," the woman offered. "These must be the first of the season."

This party was not for me, I decided, a little regretfully, and set my plate down on a tray-table along the wall apparently intended for that purpose, as others had already left theirs. The woman followed suit, then hesitated.

Masseo was still deep in earnest discussion with the good artisans. I smiled at the woman still hovering in my vicinity. All people are interesting, if you find out what they are particularly interested in.

Her clothes were finely made and of good cloth. It was the same earth-colours as the other villagers wore, but hers were deeper in saturation, ochre and malachite rather than dun and sage. "What is your craft?" I asked. "Something to do with cloth? Or are you simply a connoisseur?"

She laughed, a high trill that again reminded me more of certain types of court ladies than anything else. Not exactly false, but well-practiced. "Nothing so grand, I'm afraid, sir, though I daresay I know what I like, indeed I do. I own the baths and the laundry—the finest of each for miles around, though I say so myself!"

"Baths? and laundry? The gods' delights! Do tell me about them."

She was delighted to do so, and waxed poetic about the hot springs her grandfather (a carpenter; she was a cousin of Master Joff's) had channelled and her grandmother (a minor earthworker) had shaped. I listened attentively, asking questions.

Eventually she grew comfortable enough to ask me what I liked in a bath. I got the impression that this was something of a private topic; not taboo, perhaps, but not usually spoken of so openly. The high aristocracy of Astandalas had no such quibbles, and I, of course, have not had any privacy. Also my baths are a wonder of the Nine Worlds that almost no one will ever see.

And so I told her about the marble and gold and glazed porcelain, and the many waters, the shaped basins so that the water falling down chimed tunefully, and the scented flowers and multitudes of candles and the soft, warm towels. I spoke of minerals and oils and unguents and perfumes, of soaps and sponges and cool water to drink in the midst of steam.

As I drew to a close I saw Masseo watching me from across the room, a smile on his face as I gestured expansively at the woman. She herself was listening in rapt astonishment, and I could see that she was taking mental notes as I spoke.

If her bath-house was not made rich and splendid in all the many ways she might devise—candles and flowers and warm towels were not beyond ordinary means, surely, though obviously she wouldn't be lining her steam room with tiles made by the greatest ceramic artist of Voonra interlaid with precious gems set in gold—I would be much surprised.

I was a little surprised when I stopped and she said, "Oh, will you come and try mine? I cannot compete with that, of course—" Something in her voice made it clear she was going to try— "but I can give you the best bath you would find from here to the Grand Duchess's summer palace!"

As I certainly wasn't going *there*, I beamed at her. "I should be delighted. Mas—Master Smith and I will be leaving tomorrow, but we need not depart with the dawning."

"I shall have all in readiness by the first hour after," she promised me.

"I thank you," I replied. The words were coming easier, the courtesies and pleasantries in which I had once delighted. Was it only on the sky ship that I had found it so hard to say *please*?

Ah, whatever she gave me would be a better bath than the sponge on board the *Northern Joy*!—and that reminded me. "Stay a moment," I said to the woman, who looked ready to bustle off and rearrange her bathhouse right then. She turned questioningly, and I hesitated, a little embarrassed (and how? How should I be embarrassed for this? *Why?*—Only because Masseo, who knows me, was watching from across the room, a smile on his face?).

"Do you think you could assist me with a small laundering matter? I must confess it is not an activity I am at all accustomed to thinking of."

"Of course not, and of course," she said, an even brighter gleam coming into her eyes.

I recognized the signs of a fanatic about to expound on their topic, and hastily reached into my bag for the apricot robes that had suffered outrageously by landing first on the flying pine and then in the tarn. They were still damp, as I had done nothing more than wring them out before stuffing them into my bag.

The woman took them without further prompting, tutting to herself and turning so she could hold them next to a lamp set on the wall. "What a cloth," she murmured, shaking it out and deftly catching the green hose as they fell out of the folds. "Like it was woven out of sunset clouds."

I smiled mysteriously. Masseo told me later that he had heard before the evening was out that I wore clothing made out of the sky, which everyone agreed was very telling.

The woman bore off my garments with anxious care and a few comments that would probably have reassured Conju. I spoke in pleasant riddles to a number of villagers, some old and some young, including a shrewd-eyed old woman who obviously guessed more of the truth than she felt like saying. I was greatly polite to her, to our mutual amusement, for she knew as well as I did that nothing I said was a lie, even if it were easily misunderstood.

At length I filled (and subsequently emptied) another plate, then made my way over to a table where water, wine, and a thin beer were on offer. After a moment I decided on a glass of the wine, which was not entirely terrible.

I drew closer to the cluster of craft-masters speaking to Masseo, and was beckoned over by Master Joff. Not very much to my surprise I saw that Aelian was included in their group. Along with Master Joff, Masseo, and Aelian, there were half a dozen other men and women, all later middle aged or older, most of them in plain but good clothes.

"I thank you for your hospitality," I said to the carpenter. "May blessings fall like rain on this house and all within it, and your cuts be true when you make them."

That was a blessing out of a very old tale—the *Saga of the Sons of Morning*, in fact—and ran through the folk- and nursery-tales of many peoples of Zunidh. Some of them I had been told as a boy by my nurse, a hundred miles north of here; and some of them had clearly been told down here in the shadow of Ousanadh.

Master Joff said slowly, "And may your path lead you to what you seek."

I smiled at him in delight, for that was the direct line from the *Saga*, and unlikely though it seemed he must have read it (at least in translation) to know to say it. It was the oldest written poetry on Zunidh, treating the earliest days of Kavanor until the early conquests of Yr and his brother Damar the Bold. I was prepared to continue the game of quotations, but Masseo intervened before I could go on.

"Is it your thought still to leave tomorrow?" he asked me. The group was immediately attentive.

"Yes, though not at the first light of dawn, as I have been promised a bath the hour after. Before noon, unless you have any objections?"

Masseo shook his head, a crooked smile on his face. (I am afraid I have never made a secret of my love of bathing.) A woman, grey-haired and pale-skinned like an Amboloyan, stood forth. "You propose to go into the gorges, Master Smith has told us?"

"Yes," I replied. "There is a stone that was set at the mouth of a certain cave to mark the path out of the world, and thus is our direction."

There was a little muttering, and then the Amboloyan woman spoke again. "I am a boatwright, sir, and I willingly give you a craft to bear you downstream, but I must warn you that the gorges on the southern side are little known and have an ill repute. Travellers sometimes come out of them; but no one has gone and returned in many lifetimes here."

Masseo sighed, almost inaudibly, beside me. I gave him a quick, bright smile, and a more reassuring one to his fellows and presumable friends. "And yet I have been in those gorges, and returned, if indeed it was many lifetimes of men in this village since I did so. As for ill repute: perhaps this quest shall be the remedy of it."

Aelian narrowed his eyes and looked pensive, but also confident. Masseo nodded sharply.

"Why our smith?" One of the hitherto-silent masters said suddenly. Those next to him tried to shush him, but he stood forth bravely. "He is not from here, that we know, but he has settled here and been well-loved and well-respected."

I looked at Masseo, who had looked down, his cheeks reddening, and very carefully I laid my hand on his shoulder and gripped it lightly. He glanced up at me, startled. I gave as imperious and magnificent a stare I could to the gathered masters. "This smith is well-loved and well-respected in many places, and I tell you the halls of heaven know his name, though you may not."

We had, after all, stolen cattle from the pastures of the Sun, and dallied in the gardens of the Moon, and sailed across the Sea of Stars in boats borrowed from those who tend the constellations.

At least one or two of the craft-masters had hitherto suspected the identity of their mysterious smith, I could see; all were re-evaluating their interactions with him.

Aelian appeared to be beside himself with curiosity. Probably the only thing more unexpected than Fitzroy Angursell showing up and bearing off their smith (therefore Masseo Umrit) was the Last Emperor of Astandalas doing so.

Masseo himself said, without undue emphasis, "My work here has been no lesser to me."

"Certainly not," I agreed complacently.

12

IN WHICH WE OVERSHOOT OUR DESTINATION

The bath was lovely, and the laundry-woman skilled, for she gave me back my apricot robes and green hose in a condition with which even Conju could have found no fault. I bathed alone, in the hot springs shaped by her grandparents, with candles all around and spring flowers mostly masking the faint sulphur in the air. The towels were warm and fragrant and all in all it was not too poor an imitation of the Imperial Baths, rustic though the wood and stone building might be.

The owner beamed when I told her this. It didn't occur to me to pay her until Masseo asked later (trying not to laugh) whether I had or not, but I did lay on her house and her waters a good word and a munificent blessing, which honestly—if I do say so myself— was a far better return for her night-time labours than any coin I might have given her.

We left at midmorning, taking a small, shallow-drafted boat from the river-station. Half the village was there to see us off. No doubt the departure of their smith was a great excitement. Judging from a few orange prayer-flags, several people had decided to err on the side of visible devotion just in case Marilda was right.

I sat in the prow and Masseo at the stern with the punting-pole and tiller, and we let the current sweep us downstream towards the fork where one stream bent north around the Height of Vultures and the greater turned south into the desolate gorges.

It was a fine day, bright and cool and with the birds singing, and as soon as we were mostly out of earshot I started to sing one of my old songs about starting a quest.

Masseo used to sigh and frown when I did that; but this time he smiled and sang along. When we reached the end he laughed exuberantly and wiped at the corner of his eyes. "Ah, how I've missed this, Fitzroy!"

I felt too full for words—I!

I rearranged myself a little more comfortably on my seat. The wooden boat was long and narrow, with an upturned prow and the middle covered by an arch made of woven bamboo stakes. Masseo sometimes sat, sometimes stood at the rear, a long pole in his hand to fend off rocks.

We went past his old smithy, waving at Kenna and Marilda, who stood on the bank where the millstream entered the main river. Marilda waved a white cloth, and then we were past them, and Masseo guided us quite expertly through a sequence of white-water passages that led us perhaps a mile downstream and several hundred yards closer to the sea-level.

"You've done this before," I observed when we came to what seemed a less tumultuous stretch and the river turned sharply east.

Masseo shipped the pole and wiped some sweat or spray from his face. "Aye, taking goods down to the fairs in the big town. There's a lock to lower us down from the plateau, but we'll not go past the town. I've been wanting to ask the lock-keepers to open the other gate every time," he added, with satisfaction.

After the whitewater stretch another river joined ours, and the combined flood was deep enough to run smooth and fast. We floated along past banks of stone and gravel for the most part, with forest on our left and pasturage and fields on our right.

We talked sometimes, of times longs past and adventures long since fallen into legend, or simply watched the surroundings and enjoyed being in one another's company. Masseo seemed very cheerful, to the point of occasionally whistling. For my part I felt as if we had entered an enchanted moment, and could not bear to break it with words of loneliness and sorrow and questions about what had passed between then and now.

We passed another walled village, this one close to the river's edge, where a bridge sprang over in one arch, high enough for us to pass under without difficulty. A few people were walking or riding the stocky ponies along the bank. They all waved at us, and I waved back enthusiastically, making Masseo shake his head and grin. The sun was bright and the river laughing, and ahead of us the mist rose out of the jungles below the gorges.

The edge of the plateau came suddenly. After the village the fields marched along both sides, new green against black earth, low drystone walls marking out each square plot. Domed structures here and there were dovecots, Masseo informed me, and there seemed to be a lot of ducks and geese around, and occasional thickets of fruit trees just finishing their blossom. The river continued its easterly course.

Ahead of us were the low mountains facing the central barrier range across the width of the Damaran lowlands. Our plateau was among the highest, and the land stepped down from here in a series of broken cliffs and plateaus until on the eastern and northern sides it reached a broad valley, still high above the sea. On the south the plateaus broke into the canyons and flat-topped mountains of the gorge system before sinking down to the steaming jungle in the Qavaliun basin.

From the river I could see the fields and the distant eastern mountains, and a strange sense of absence between them, where the whole floor of the continent had as it were dropped out of sight. There was no obvious marker, besides the wavering line of a stone wall not much higher than those around any of the fields and a few wind-sculpted trees. We swept into a gully that became a human-sculpted cut, and suddenly the current slowed into a broad rectangular pool with a dam at one end and swallows flying over the void.

Masseo punted us over to the right-hand side, where a couple of men were sitting on a bench watching us approach. "Hallo the lock-keeper!" he cried as we came near.

"Hallo the boat!" one of the men called back. "Is that the Master Smith?"

"*The* Master Smith," I murmured, making Masseo blush darkly.

"Aye," he cried, not looking at me, and skilfully brought us to a halt at the wall not far from the dam.

"You've brought a friend with you this time," the man said, jumping down to stand on the top of the siding and grinning down at us. His companion went lightly across the wooden walkway on top of the dam to the other side, where there was a large wheel attached to a post. It was only about twenty feet away, but the dam was high enough I couldn't see over its top. From water level it looked like the top of a pair of gigantic wooden doors.

"Aye," said Masseo, "we're off adventuring. It's time for the gorges at last."

"Strewth," said the lock-keeper, losing his grin. "You can't be serious, man! You know how dangerous it is down there!"

"It's time," Masseo said quietly.

"I *never*. You mean it?"

"I do."

"Strewth," the lock-keeper said again, scratching his head. "I'll —I'll need to get a flag, or a flare, so you can set it off when you want us to open the lower gates on your return—"

"Don't worry," I said blithely, "we won't be coming back this way."

The lock-keeper stared at me. I was wearing the green hose and a different set of robes, in deference to Masseo's practicality (that is: white tunic, and two layers of robes, one cotton in a fine dark purple and the other wool in a bright grey, because it was cold in the shadows on the water), and I grinned up at him not like Aurelius Magnus but like Fitzroy Angursell.

"Well, I never," he said, but Masseo's calm nod seemed to reassure him we were set in our course, for he made no further objections and instead picked up a purple flag to wave to his friend across the way.

The friend was so surprised by this that he came back across the dam to confer. I let Masseo convince them again in favour of reaching into my bag and finding a small present to leave with the men. Not money—Masseo would take care of that if necessary—but what else might be—ah! I closed my hand at last on a small ornamental egg carved out of milky green jade almost the colour of the river.

I tossed this up to the lock-keeper; he caught it reflexively and stared at me. "Good fortune to you and yours!"

"Er, thank you!" he replied, visibly flummoxed. The friend ran back across the dam, muttering something about madmen, and this time when the lock-keeper waved the purple flag the other began to turn the wheel.

Masseo pushed off from the bank and centred us in front of the dam. We waited while mysterious rushes and falls of water were heard, bubbling and glugging and suchlike sounds. It was only ten or so minutes but felt longer, the way that the two men were watching us. Masseo was sober-faced and thoughtful, eyes on the dam, but I could see excitement in the set of his shoulders. I turned to face forward.

At length the man on the far side waved a yellow flag, and the one on our side went into a small hut set at the edge of the bank. Very slowly and with a deep creaking groan, the dam parted and two great leaves folded back into a gate. Masseo pushed off something and then set the pole sideways across the boat as we came to a bobbing halt in the centre of the lock. Ahead of us, over the second wall of the lock, was blue sky and distant mountains and a haze coming up from the lower land.

Very slowly the gates behind us closed. The lock was wedge-shaped, with the narrow point being the gates through which we had entered. One side of the wedge had the pair of wooden doors I'd noticed; the other was tightly laid masonry.

Masseo had turned us so we were facing towards the stone wall. There was a sigh and a soft glugging and the water began to lower.

"I will never cease being amazed at how ingenious locks are," I said as we started to descend.

Masseo laughed. We were already ten or a dozen feet down, and our voices echoed oddly. The air was cool and damp, the stone walls glistening as the water receded.

As we were lowered the artistry of the structure became clear: there were *two* gates facing out, at different heights. One presumably led to the plateau and the 'big town', the other, lower one, to the gorges. We passed a set of square openings in the masonry, their mitred wooden gates thumping into place as our water level passed theirs. Masseo said, "There's a holding pond--really a cistern--so they don't have to empty the lock entirely into the lower waters each time."

It was a very elegant solution to what must have been a complex problem. I rather wished I had seen what the topography looked like before they built the lock. Some fork in the river's course around an outcropping, I guessed. Presumably they hadn't chosen to build a flight of locks because of how all these mountains were sacred, and that would have involved a great deal of blasting.

Down we went. The gate on the left gave way to solid rock, while we came to the top of a scond wooden gate; and still we descended. I looked up, at the wedge of pale sky above us. The swallows were swooping and following us down, chasing after insects invisible to me.

At length, thirty feet below the northern gate, a hundred below the top of the dam, the descent stopped, and with an agonizingly loud screech of little-used hinges the gate to the gorges opened fully. Masseo unshipped his pole and readied himself for the current to take us.

My first glimpse was of bright sunlight reflecting off white stone, and then suddenly an eddy caught us and we were off.

The Qavaliun river system descends from the foot of Ousanadh to the Uncharted Seas south of Old Damara through a great unexplored jungle basin. No one knows exactly what lives in there now, nor ever has. Explorers beg every once in a while for leave (and money) to go exploring, looking for treasures of one sort or another. As far as I knew, only one of them ever came back.

Dimiter Mdang was one of Kip's many (*many*) cousins, and as a Wide Sea Islander he had begun from the sea, and sailed a canoe upriver. He had made it through the maze of reefs and the high waves of the eastern coast, and through the even more convoluted labyrinth of mangroves at the many channels of the river-mouth. He had penetrated upriver as far as a confluence of waters where another great river joined the Qavaliun. He had called that river the Artorin, which was a nice and entirely unnecessary compliment, but it stuck as no one else had ever heard of it before and Dimiter's maps were the only ones anyone had ever made of the area.

He had been forced to turn back when storms rose out of the jungle and an impenetrable wall of rain barred his path. In the little pamphlet he had written, all the account he had ever published, he had said that just before the rain came down he had seen what looked like a fair golden city on a high ridge overlooking the river, up almost at the Wall of the Mountains.

It was, he had written, *almost as if one of the legendary Free Cities from before the coming of the Empire lingered.*

He probably would have gone back to see if he could in fact find this lost city, if a stray comment from someone hadn't sent him haring off to Voonra to perform the first recorded crossing of the Northern Wastes, where he perished from injuries contracted from an angry gryphon on the last day of the traverse.

All that had been before the Fall, when the Palace of Stars was still in Astandalas of Ysthar, long before I knew the odd little book had been written by the cousin of someone who would become one of my greatest friends and one of the greatest statesmen in Zuni history. The jungles of the Qavaliun Basin had been as removed from my thought as my previous life as Fitzroy Angursell. After the Fall I had begun piecing together the magic of the world, and beyond that one excursion to set the stone markers I hadn't given them much thought. There were other impenetrable jungles with known resources and inhabitants to deal with first.

It was very exciting to float down the jade-green river under the high white cliffs with Masseo behind me.

"Perhaps," I said eagerly, looking up at the towering cliffs hemming us in, sunlight in their upper reaches though even just past noon the best we could receive was a bright shade.

"Yes?" said Masseo, pushing leisurely off a large boulder.

I told him the story of Dimiter Mdang. Masseo listened carefully, eyes on the water but attention on me. I kept twisting to look at him and back again to watch where we were going. The huge gates of the lock had shut behind us and quickly disappeared behind bends in the gorge walls.

The water poured smoothly and with a dull, nearly subliminal roar between its walls. The swallows followed us but otherwise the air was cool and fresh and mysteriously scented. Every once in a while streams would come dancing down from the heights, staining the white stone grey. There were plants perched on every improbable ledge, ferns and mosses and strange jewel-coloured hanging flowers visited by swift-moving hummingbirds.

I sent out my magic cautiously, trying to get a sense of where the passage to Alinor might be. It all felt very foreign and nearly inimical. The Qavaliun was a sacred river, and a mighty one—

perhaps the largest in the world—and its weight and strength more than matched mine. I might be Lord of Zunidh, but that was a human title. Such as the Tigara might recognize me, but they did not necessarily *obey*.

There was, needless to say, no hint of my own magic-working, which was a long time ago by the way time had flowed here. I looked up at the towering cliffs, a hundred or a hundred and fifty feet high. They were broken here and there by caves and gullies formed by the incoming streams.

I didn't remember this at all.

We went round a bend and came to a stretch of rough water as the gorge walls opened up in a kind of cauldron. Masseo punted us in to one wall, out of the current, where there was a kind of shingly bay overhung by the cliff. Round mud nests were encrusted all on the ceiling. The swallows dipped in and out, their twittering suddenly very audible.

"Fitzroy," Masseo said finally, "do you have *any* idea of where we're going?"

I lowered my gaze from the swallow nests to his face. He did not look, or indeed sound, resigned. He appeared to be trying not to laugh.

"Yes," I said indignantly, though I had to deflate a moment later as I continued on. "That is, I know that somewhere in here is a pair of standing stones that mark the passage to Alinor."

He covered his face, though not all of his smirk, with his free hand even as he held the pole firm with the other.

"And how, may I ask, did whatever source you're using indicate they should be found?"

I tried to remember pertinent features of the location. I could not quite reconcile my memory of the area with what we were actually experiencing. There had been a great jade-green river coming down a fall over the edge of the plateau—obviously what had been chan-nelled by the lock—and then the meandering river through a cloud forest. The banks had been high, but for the most part not cliffs.

I looked again at the walls, the round belly of the cauldron the river had carved out of the stone. How long did it take a river to carve a gorge system?

On Ysthar it had been thousands of years since the Fall; on Alinor less than a score. On Zunidh it depended very much on the location.

It appeared as if this was one of the regions where the time passed could be measured in centuries at the very least.

"There was a white cliff, and a cave, and … I put them there. I'm sure I'll recognize it when I see it. The magic should be fairly obvious, at least."

He wasn't even trying to hide his smirk now.

"And how," he enquired, "did you reach this locale on that occasion?"

"That is a good question," I said, and stopped. If I recalled correctly we had gone on some sort of barge. Up to the fork from the branch of the river that led to the Grand Duchess's Summer Palace, then down again to the cave where I had yearned to break free from all the responsibilities and hopes that were being thrust on me and go running off into the mystery that was the Border between Zunidh and … wherever.

There had been such a confusion of magic and people and the endless need to *do something* that I had been exhausted and dazed most of the time, barely able to recall the names of my attendants from one day to the next.

After the silence had spooled on a little too long Masseo chuckled with great and inexplicable fondness. "That sort of story, is it? Very well, I presume these stones are yet some distance away?"

"Yes," I said more certainly, relaxing my grip on my magic somewhat. I am attuned most closely to fire, and secondly to air: earth and water are antithetical, though not quite so abrasive as Schooled magic itself. It did mean my magical senses were dulled by their overwhelming proximity, and I could not reach very far.

There was a bright pulse behind us—the Abbey, most likely—and a great wash of undifferentiated power ahead of us, fed by the bright streams of the rivers themselves.

Masseo pushed us back into the current and let it sweep us off downstream. On the other side of the cauldron the river went through several stretches of rough water, not as turbulent as the whitewater passages up on the plateau but, unfamiliar as they were to Masseo, requiring more care to traverse safely. I was kept busy calling out warnings, and he focused on steering our craft, and so it was not until some hours and several miles later that we were able to sit back and think about a drink and a late lunch and a more frank discussion.

Masseo found another bay carved out of the gorge walls, this one with a wider beach, and he pushed us right up out of the water so we could stand and stretch our legs. I made sure the boat wouldn't drift off, remembering a story of Kip's: the first rule of a seafarer's landing is *always secure your boat*.

Second was to find water and food, and third a fire. Kip is from a tropical island of enviable climate, and shelter is usually an easy affair.

We were not camping here, down in the clammy depths of the gorge, but we did have a pleasant enough picnic, sitting on woven rush mats from the bottom of the boat to protect against the cold stones. We finished the last of the vegetable pastries and a couple of the oranges I'd brought from the Palace, along with some pork and cabbage dumplings and sweet red-bean buns from Masseo's village. While we had a whole river-full of water beside us, we kept to the containers we'd filled up above.

Masseo regarded my water bottle, a clever contraption Conju had found somewhere, with minor envy. It was tempered glass set in a canvas bag, with a stout cork stopper held on by wire tension, and while simple in fashioning very lovely to hold and to use. His own water supply was in a stoppered bamboo tube, which explained what the box of them was doing in the boat.

He laughed at my expression. "Hadn't you seen this before? It's the way most people do it, you know."

"We never travelled where there was that much bamboo, did we? I suppose some parts of Colhélhé, but I never paid much attention."

"Yes, you had Jullanar and me for that." He laughed again, and I marvelled again at how light and free and merry he was compared to the dour man I'd known. There had always been some deep kernel of bitter guilt in him, and though there was still a sadness there, it no longer seemed to gall.

"So," he said, stretching out his legs on the shingle with a satisfying rattling noise as his feet pushed the pebbles. "Have you come up with a story for how you found this passageway to Alinor, set up standing stones, and departed again?"

If he had been a stranger, no doubt I could have spun some grand reckoning. I shook my head. "It was a long time ago, and I ... wasn't at my best. I don't remember clearly. I don't think the river had cut the gorges anywhere so deep."

Masseo tilted his head and looked at me with the solemn expression I did remember. It grounded me with its familiarity; I had hardly grown accustomed to the fact that he was so much older than I remembered, as I was so much older than I thought, looking in the mirror. In the mirror I looked like Artorin Damara, Last Emperor of Astandalas and Lord of Zunidh.

"Come," he said suddenly, jumping up. "It's getting cold and damp sitting here. We can talk as we explore downwards. Perhaps something will jog your memory."

"I didn't realize it was so bad," I said, helping to gather up our items and stow them back in my bag or in the bottom of the boat, depending on how well they could take being splashed with water as would inevitably happen. "I don't know why I can't remember clearly ... it's like there's this fog and shadow on my mind ..."

Masseo was looking extremely concerned, and I made a decided effort to shake off the gloom and grin at him, madcap as a fool. "It was early days yet after the Fall. I was—"

He settled himself in the stern with the long pole in his strong hands, and said, "Fitzroy."

I rallied. "Come to think of it, perhaps I was loaned a flying carpet to go over the gorges—do you remember the one Pali and Sardeet's sister Arzu made for us when we went across the Holy Desert of Kaph?"

That had been the journey that forged us into a company rather than simply a loose association of friends and fellow travellers. Masseo let the concern slide and entered happily into reminiscences. We were still laughing at our youthful audacity in going right into a dragon's lair, not after its treasure but after the thief that had gone in before us, when we turned a sharp bend and the gorge walls fell away from us, as did the river.

For a moment my glance was caught by the bright gleam of light catching off—glass—surely that was a reflective surface?—and then the boat tilted and the world fell away from us and Masseo said, "Fitzroy," in a voice that ended with a yelp.

We fell for nine and a half seconds, which truly was *plenty* of time for me to gather my magic and ensure we landed safely.

IN WHICH WE COMMIT TRESPASS

"*I*'m disappointed that you still haven't learned to fly," Masseo said, some while later.

We were lying spread-eagled, head to head. His mouth was right next to my ears, but though he was shouting I could barely hear him over the sound of the river.

I contemplated the likelihood of standing up, then decided that wasn't necessary just at this moment. I was conscious of a comprehensive windedness. At the moment all I could see were whirling flecks of light.

After a few minutes of blinking I pushed myself up, though I nearly fell back again when it turned out I'd injured my right wrist. Cradling it in my lap, I took several deep breaths and wiped my eyes, whose blurriness was not so unaccountable when I realized I was sopping wet.

I was sitting amidst the ruins of our boat on a large flat-topped rock outcropping in the middle of the river. It was a land of sheer cliffs and tumbling greenery. Everywhere I looked were white slashes of water and green trees and pale-grey cliffs. The river was enormously noisy.

Masseo was sitting a few feet away from me, looking about as winded and shocked as I felt. I smiled weakly when he looked at me, then felt the smile fade as I took in the cliff we'd just plunged over.

In other parts of the world, the cascade the Qavaliun River made over the edge of the escarpment would have been a wonder much-visited by those who appreciated such things. The water's roar was so loud it was almost inaudible. I watched a small pebble vibrate and bounce on the rock from the force of the water hitting it, and became conscious of the constant vibration shaking my bones.

"Well," I said, laying back down again, this time with my eyes open at the dizzying height rising far above us, "that was unexpectedly exhilarating. I begin to see why no one ever comes *back* out of the gorges."

Eventually we collected ourselves and took off our wet outer layers. It was much, much warmer down here, and humid, so once I was down to the purple cotton under-robe I left it on. The day's adventures were hardly finished though the sun had gone behind the mountains.

I wiped the water off my lovely new boots before sticking them in my bag to deal with later, replacing them with a pair of leather sandals that tied at the ankle. The laundry-mistress's comments the night before had stuck with me, and I resolved that I would take out the wet items and hang them to dry once we had settled on a place to spend the night.

I assured Masseo that even a thousand-foot fall would not damage his precious spare anvil in my replacement bag. Nor should it have damaged any of the other contents, which were more of a concern to me; I couldn't imagine what would damage the anvil, really.

We also salvaged what we could from the boat, which wasn't very much. The drop had been too unexpected and the power of the water too strong against my mind and body and magic for me to do anything but hold us to a more or less safe landing.

"I do thank you," Masseo said belatedly, after a mildly heated comment that I could at least have landed us on the bank instead of a rock in the middle of the river.

"You're welcome," I replied, a touch snippily, and stalked off to observe what might be visible from the other end of the rock. Nothing much that was different, naturally, except that I discovered a metal ring bolted to the stone.

I called Masseo over. "It's bronze," he said, touching the metal curiously. "Very old. Look, it has markings on it. I don't recognize them, do you?"

I sat down heavily next to him. There was no way I was squatting, not after several hours in a boat and then that fall—or rather, that landing! I touched the ring cautiously with my magic as I examined the carved designs, using my left hand to lift it. My signet ring knocked against the metal, my magic touched something ancient and foreign, and a silent echo ran off along a chain of spells woven into the river and the stone.

"Hmm," I said, feeling the river's natural magic start to shift and stir.

Masseo regarded me cautiously. "Should I be worried?"

I looked back at the carvings. Something about them seemed very distantly familiar ... What had I been looking at ...?

"I think I've run someone's door-bell," I said absently.

It reminded me of the grave-goods in Yr the Conqueror's tomb, that was it. I said as much, to Masseo's patent incredulity.

"And the door-bell?"

Before I could say anything, movement on the southern bank caught our attention. We looked up to see a dozen or so people in long pale garments regarding us.

"I think," I said, smiling, and pushed myself upright to stand free and tall and regal before these strangers, "that we have been found by the Last Free Citizens of Zunidh."

It was just as well, really. Masseo and I undoubtedly would *eventually* have figured out some way across the rushing river on either side of our rocky outcropping, but having assistance on the bank made it much easier.

They fashioned together a sort of bridge made out of lashed poles. I was feeling stiff, and the river was making me feel a bit queasy from its sheer strength of water-borne magic, but I managed to trip lightly enough across to the other side.

Masseo followed me more slowly, shaking his head. "Are you afraid of *nothing*?"

I didn't dignify that with an answer, smiling brightly at our unexpected hosts instead. They looked at Masseo curiously, and then at me with expressions of growing excitement.

There were ten of them, as I saw in a quick overview. They murmured to each other and hung back in little clusters. It was fairly obvious they were no sort of guards or military folk of any sort, though less clear what else we were supposed to make of them.

They wore linen, washed-out straw in colour, in a very simple cut, two rectangular pieces of cloth held together by wooden or copper clasps at the shoulders and braided rope belts at the waist. The tunics, if I could so call them, went down to their knees, and they wore what looked like straw sandals on their feet. None appeared to be much older than thirty or younger than twenty. Their skin was a dark bronze, not far different from Masseo's in tone, and their hair black, straight, and shiny, worn cropped close to their heads. Most had neatly trimmed beards, which were very rare in most other parts of Zunidh.

They were, oddly, all men.

Masseo stood silently beside me. I looked at him, and he shrugged and moved half a step back, giving me the clear responsibility for doing the talking. It was, I dare say, a familiar position.

"Good day," I said in Shaian, though I could not imagine that these folk would speak it. Even now, after thousands of years under Imperial rule, there were people in the hinterlands of Zunidh who still spoke their own languages first and Shaian second or even third; in so isolated a place as this, they would surely have a language that had evolved distinct from any others.

One of the men was nudged forward by his fellows. He looked nervous and—hopeful?

Yes. That was definitely hopeful. I looked at the group, at their body language and their postures. This was a group of youngish men who had most unexpectedly encountered the answer to their prayers. But they seemed strangely reserved even so, as if they could not believe what they saw.

As if they refused to let themselves believe what they saw. Their hope was a thin and watery thing.

I could not but contrast it with my friends of the Red Company in our youth, with Kip in his middle age, with Marilda at the edge of the tarn, whose hope and resolution blazed like beacon-fires. These were poor flickering candles at best. My heart went out to them.

I smiled with my full imperial brilliance at the spokesman. He cleared his throat several times and then said, in the Antique Shaian I knew from long study, "I bid you good day, O Son of the Sun! We have waited long for your returning."

They led us into the trees, along a faint path that looked to have been much wider in the past before it had been swallowed up by the jungle. Ezan, as the spokesman was called, seemed anxious. He told us that his party were students, sent by their master to look on the Great Barrier. The rest of them fell in behind us, apparently uninterested in asking questions. It was all very odd.

The path led more or less along the river-bank, weaving in and out of trees and rocks but always within sound if not quite in sight of the water. Ezan did not set a punishing pace, and I was able to keep up without any loss of dignity due to breathlessness or the like, though I wished soon enough I'd thought to pull my walking stick from the tarn out of my bag.

After about ten minutes we started to descend noticeably, and another ten or fifteen minutes after that Ezan told two of his party to run ahead to 'the arnoi' to tell them what had happened, and led Masseo and I on a branch path that led back towards the river-bank. Masseo asked me in a low voice whether we should be concerned.

I looked at him, and at the cluster of young scholars walking beside and behind us as if were visitors from another world or illusions made out of mist and self-deception. A less warlike group of young men I had seldom encountered.

Masseo looked as if he were about to say something else, then muttered, "*Fitzroy,*" in a low voice and left it at that.

Ezan had listened carefully, with a furrowed brow, to our words. He spoke Antique Shaian fluently, but there were four thousand or so years of sound changes between its heyday and mine, and apart from a few set words—my *good day* had probably been almost intelligible to them—the languages were quite distinct. Even the latest forms of Classical Shaian were hard for most modern speakers to understand without special study.

"We are coming to the Place of Perspective," he said to me. I translated for Masseo, who didn't know Antique Shaian.

"The Place of Perspective?" he enquired, raising his eyebrow.

"The meanings may have shifted," I admitted.

Shifting meanings or not, it was immediately obvious what

Ezan meant when we reached it. We passed through a stand of trees (green and glossy of palmate leaf, and otherwise I knew nothing of what they might be) and out onto a large outcropping of a much darker rock than the white limestone that mostly comprised the gorges. I had to keep my attention down, as it was rough and awkward underfoot, and it wasn't until we reached the far end that I was able to stand still and look around.

Ezan directed our attention upstream first. "The Great Barrier," he said, strangely reproachful.

And a great barrier it was. Looking up the river, which was still a bright jade-green here, hemmed in by its darker green vegetation-covered banks, our attention was commanded by the cataracts of water falling down a sheer white cliff.

The Qavaliun had forked, unnoticed by us in our passage, or else other rivers came down from Ousanadh and the other mountains of the central range and carved out their own gorges, for plunging down the great thousand-foot cliff that extended as far as I could see north and south before disappearing into haze were a hundred streams of water.

High above the deeply cut brow of the cliff was a thin line of dark green, not nearly so bright as the jungle trees, and again above that were the purple and grey smudges that were the triple peaks of Ousanadh and its neighbours. The sun was behind them; I reckoned they would be nearly invisible in most lights.

"We must have descended two and a half thousand feet in an afternoon," Masseo said in quiet awe. "Possibly much more. And half of that in one go."

It was hard to reconcile that barely four or five hours ago we had left his village with the flags waving us on our passage.

"I can entirely understand why no one comes back," I murmured. "We can't be the first to take that plunge."

"I expect we're the first to survive it," Masseo replied dryly.

I turned then, following the current of the river as it thundered past us. It was larger here, still fast, but swollen with the waters of all those other streams that came down the cliff and disappeared into the jungle. If they did not meet here, surely farther downstream they joined the Qavaliun's course.

I did not look so far downstream. My attention was entirely caught by the city before us.

"Mae Irión," Ezan said softly, pride in his voice. "The golden city."

Astandalas had been called the Golden. It had been made largely of a yellow sandstone, and exuberantly planted with yellow roses. In the right season and the right light it had shone luminous as a candle-lantern. I had seen it so on our infrequent visits as the Red Company, and once only as Emperor, on a late-afternoon progress to perform one of the hundred-year rituals of binding.

But even in its heyday, in its height of glory, on an early-summer day when one was dazzled by sunlight and rose-perfume and magic and all the pomp and circumstance of an ancient Empire, Astandalas had had its hidden rival here.

And now Astandalas was gone, and white Solaara had taken its place: a city far more beautiful in all its parts than that ancient and frankly dirty capital had ever been. And yet Mae Irión, unknown to us all, had persisted, still clad in gold and its citizens with it.

There was another set of falls below our vantage-point. The Qavaliun spread out between fingers of rock, paler jade water between the same dark stone as the Place of Perspective, and crashed down perhaps a hundred or two hundred feet into a wide lake before continuing off down a folded valley that already lay hidden in mist.

On the very edge of the cataract a mound rose up, the work of hands and magic (for only magic could counter the degree of erosion the river brought; I did read the reports brought to me). A single road spiralled up from a bridge at the bank to an observatory at the peak. It was lined with houses and other buildings, all built nestling against each other with even their windows lining up agreeably, and every roof and door and window-frame was gilded.

"I wonder who does the polishing?" Masseo muttered.

I reached out my magic cautiously, aware of the influence of the river. There was much magic here, that was the honest truth, different from any I'd ever encountered before. I felt my heart begin to speed up with excitement, and made certain my face and bearing were as serene as for any court appearance.

The knowledge they might have! Four thousand years of discovery and learning, held secret in their hidden jungles behind their high walls—oh, they would not hold it out with open hands, surely, even to me. Perhaps especially not to me. For here I was not and could not be Fitzroy Angursell of the Red Company.

There was a strange heaviness to the air, a net draped across the land with its anchor somewhere in the central tower of the city. It tasted of secrecy and concealment and some lingering unwholesomeness, and I did not like it at all.

I straightened my back and let my magic unfurl just a little more. Ezan shivered and looked around, as if at a breeze passing, but one of his fellows looked on me with wide, astonished eyes. I smiled at him regally and put my thoughts firmly into place as Artorin Damara, Lord of Zunidh and Last Emperor of Astandalas. I could wish I had Kip here, my brilliant diplomat, but his Antique Shaian was limited to a few words, and he was busy on the other side of the world.

Ezan said, "Will you come with us, *khainos*?"

Khainos was the very old word for a sorcerer-king. Evidently some teaching of what the black-skinned, bald-headed men from the west were yet lingered.

I inclined my head formally. "We shall."

And down we went to Mae Irión, whose name was on the list of the last seven cities of Zunidh to fall before the sword of Yr the

Conqueror and his brother Damar the Bold. All I had ever heard of it was a few stanzas in the first written poem.

Mae Irión, queen of cities, said the *Saga of the Sons of Morning.*

Mae Irión, queen of cities,
    too proud to kneel
    she turned her back on the world
    and was gone into the mists

And Yr said to his brother Damar the Bold,
    Thus perish those
    who will not be ours
    Though they learn to beg on their knees
    They will never be ours

And so replied his brother Damar to Yr the bright-eyed:
    Let them be cursed for their pride
    Let our forefather the Sun be pitiless
    Let our foremother the Moon be merciless
    Let their names be forgotten
    So long as our rule is maintained
    Let Mae Irión be lost.

Ai! Mae Irión, queen of cities,
    Where are your gold and your wisdom now?

Neither history nor poetry had any further answer to the question.

We walked down silently along a path of stone flags that had once been very well wrought, but was now falling into disrepair. It sloped gently downhill before breaking into a stair that zigzagged across the face of a hill. Everywhere the jungle was creeping close, sending streamers and branches over the edges of the path and creeping onto the stones. The centre remained open enough that we could pass two abreast without touching the greenery, but only just.

At the bottom of the stair we crossed over a stream by a stone bridge, its balustrade edged with gold leaf now starting to flake off. The design of the stone carvings was odd to my eyes, and looked old, the stone chipped here and moss and tiny plants growing in crevices and shadowy places.

Masseo ran his hand along the railing. I raised my eyebrow at him questioningly, and he said, "You don't need to translate everything for me, but what is the name of this place, did you find out?"

I told him, and recited the passage from the *Saga* in Modern Shaian. He looked around us, face twisted with an expression between curiosity and pity. "The air feels strange here, heavy and sorrowful. That's more than the weight of the humidity, surely, after the high mountains?"

I had been breathing easier, I realized, after the thin atmosphere higher up. But I did know what he meant, and nodded gravely. "There is magic here, ancient and heavy. I do not fully like it."

"Are we to be on our guard, then?"

He spoke very lightly, but his eyes were intent.

"We should always be on our guard to see what happens," I replied, a little reprovingly.

"I see," he replied, something I could not read flickering in his eyes as he met mine.

We passed through a belt of vegetation—there was far too much of it, too many vines and shrubs and trees and ferns and orchids and things tangled together, to call it a copse or thicket—and into an open area. The road was in better condition here, ten feet wide and only crumbling at the edges. Water was channelled through stone rills and stored in square pools everywhere, and stone walls lifted beds of black soil above the ground level.

It was clearly a major food garden for the city, though I didn't recognize much on sight. A stand of broad-leaved plants standing in shallow water were elephant ears, taro, I thought, recognizing them from ornamental varieties with coloured leaves. Another patch of exceedingly spiky waist-high bromeliad-like plants were pineapples, surely, but I couldn't identify much more than that.

The gardens—none were wide enough to really be called *fields*—were being tended by men dressed much as Ezan and his fellows. They saw Masseo and I—in our brown and purple garments and my black skin obviously different from their people—and approached, though not so close I felt personally crowded. They murmured quietly to each other, their faces showing the same mixture of faint excitement and hope as I had seen on Ezan's.

Ezan said nothing to them, but directed us to keep on towards the city. The gardeners fell in behind us, leaving their tools and work without apparent direction or concern. I listened carefully but could only catch a few words here and there. These were slightly disquieting: *Curse* and *khainos* and *at last, at last.*

We came to the bridge before the city, and after a brief pause while Ezan spoke to someone just inside the unguarded gate, we continued up the long spiralling road. It was very like the processional ramp at the centre of the Palace of Stars, which I used on formal occasions to proceed in state from the Imperial Apartments to the Throne Room. I found myself holding my posture and expression as I did on those occasions. There was something about the way that the people of the city came to their windows and doors, silent and watchful, and then joined the throngs behind us.

I could hear occasional calls of *khainos, khainos,* followed by quieter comments to their neighbours. The sorcerer-king, the sorcerer-king. I was conscious of increasing expectation. The weight of the heavy, secretive magic and its sliding, slithering unwholesomeness underscored the situation. The magic was moving, testing bonds and pushing at them. I kept my own powers in readiness.

It had been a long time since I ever had to defend myself with magic, or indeed at all, and I had never been very good at judging when danger had moved from potential to actual. Damian and Pali had used to find it incomprehensible. But then they were the greatest sword-masters in the Nine Worlds.

At last we came to a plaza before the final building on the peak, a tower rising up to a many-windowed observatory at its height. The whole tower was clad in gold leaf. We stopped before the doors, heavy wooden things bound in bronze. They looked very ancient in design—the very oldest sections of the Palace, the inner-most rooms of the Treasury, were similar—but not that old in execution. Centuries old, perhaps, but not millennia.

Ezan said, "We are waiting for the *arnoi* to come."

The *arnoi*, the elders, the chiefs of the city. I inclined my head in acceptance, settled my hands and posture into that I used when greeting great lords of state, and wished I were wearing an outfit other than the purple cotton under-robe. It was finely made and of good material, but hardly imperial. At least it was now merely damp; the humidity in the air had kept it from drying entirely.

The people of the city came first, or their men did. It was very odd, I mused, watching them without letting my attention be apparent on any one thing or person, but I saw no women at all, and no children. Most were men in their twenties and thirties, a scattering of the middle-aged, and then clusters of grey-bearded elders my age and older.

It was a strange demographic distribution. I puzzled over it as the crowds grew thicker, though not much louder. The lack of chil-dren suggested that the women had departed, died, or disappeared approximately twenty years ago, when the youngest now had been babes in arms. Those of middle age now would have been in their twenties and thirties then: young fathers, perhaps, and prime candidates for military service.

It was as if they had staked their entire youth on a hazardous enterprise, and lost.

The wooden doors opened before I could ask Masseo what he thought. I turned my attention to those who came through: three old men, their hair and beards silvery-grey and long, falling straight to their waists. They wore the same pale golden linen tunics as the rest of the people, though the clasps on their shoulders were gold, and they wore gold belts with green jewels set in them. It was mostly their bearing and their expressions that said they were the rulers here.

Their attention was entirely focused on me. The people around us melted away, leaving an open space perhaps a dozen feet around for this historic encounter. I held myself proudly, as if I were greeting one of the other lords magi and not one of my subject princes.

The tallest of the three stepped forward, stopping five or six paces away. He looked intently at my face. I held my magic in readiness but back from overwhelming him. With the doors open behind them I could feel the wry magic emanating from the tower behind; it set my teeth on edge.

And still he regarded me. I retuned his attention calmly, serenely, trying to ensure my bearing said *welcome*. These were a proud folk, to keep to themselves so long and maintain their defences as they had. I had not forgotten Dimiter Mdang's account of the storm that had prevented him from reaching this citadel.

"He is very like," the tall elder said quietly, "and yet not like." He looked at me, and I saw in his eyes pride warring with despair, and even as I waited, power couched but surely apparent around me, I saw something like hope flicker and fade in his eyes.

All this was a very strange lack of greeting. I decided it was time to take control of the encounter, if they were not going to.

"And whom," I enquired, letting my magic rise, "were you expecting?"

He startled, and looked again into my eyes before I could restrain the magic. His eyes widened, and I felt the echoing answer of power, strange and remote though it seemed to me.

"Who *are* you?" he breathed. "You are not Yr, not Damar, and yet … Your magic tastes of theirs, yet foreign. Your face is theirs, and not. Are you their father, the Son of the Sun himself? Was it not enough that your sons cursed us? Have we not paid enough? Have you come then to finish us?"

I confess I was slightly taken aback.

IN WHICH WE LEARN OF A CURSE

*T*he people—the men—of Mae Irión stirred but said nothing out loud. They seemed willing to wait to hear my response. I looked around at them, slowly and magisterially, judging what I saw.

All those apathetic young faces, handsomely bearded as they were; all those older men, weary and resigned.

I touched the heavy, unwholesome magic, which made a net over the citadel and its people. A curse?

Expectant silences are often filled by the most nervous.

Another of the three elders stepped forward. He had a scar on his right cheek, making his face look droopy on that side, as if he'd had a stroke. Nevertheless he spoke clearly and his eyes were bright and hard.

"We acknowledge our crime, our sin against your family," he said, gesturing widely to encompass the entire crowd of silent witnesses. "We were proud in our learning and our knowledge, and wished to be equals, not subjects. Was that so much to ask?

"We were the first to discover how to make glass: was it so

wrong of us to trade that knowledge for your people's skill at bronze?

"We were the first to learn how to pass between this world and the others that lie beyond the mists, lands of mystery and wonder. We did not teach you that you might conquer all our friends and allies. One by one they fell silent and we could find the ways no longer. Was it so strange that we grew angry? You had sent armies against us, and we retaliated in kind."

He stopped there, breathing hard. The third elder stepped forward, putting his hand on the second speaker's arm to comfort and calm him. The third elder looked old, very old, and his shoulders were bowed. I regarded him intently. I could feel his power, strong and resolute despite the way the curse clung to him.

Without going into a full trance I could not fully decipher what I saw, but I could see enough to know that the magic draped over and clinging to him was no outgrowth of his own spirit and work, but a parasite.

My admiration sparked and grew even before he had finished drawing breath, before he had a chance to speak. This man had held the weight of the curse in check by his own magic. He was thin and shrivelled and bowed now in body, but his soul stood strong.

He tottered forward until he could look me in the eye. His eyes were milky blue, and I knew, looking on them, that he did not see me with his physical sight but only by magic. I drew a deep breath, invisible and silent as I had trained so long to be. I did not have to think about remaining imperious in the face of this.

"We admit our crime," the old man said, his voice thin and cracking, breathless and falling away. I gave him my full attention, letting him feel my magic with his own. His felt like stone to me: stone strained almost to crumbling, but yet uncrushed.

"We admit our crime," he said again. His hands were trembling. His skin was loose and liver-spotted, dun rather than the bronze of the rest of his people. The adamant will in him was nearly all that was left.

"We admit our crime," he said a third time, with ritual emphasis. "We sent our young men, the flower of our people, against those ranged against us, and they died. We met with the embassy sent to parley, and we slaughtered them all, all save one. She had something we treasured, and in our madness and our loss we took her to the Rock of Sacrifice and we slew her there, like a beast. We cursed the names of Yr and Damar. For ninety generations and nine, we swore, we would hold our enmity against them and theirs."

His voice had grown stronger as he spoke, the bitterness and gall seeping through the cracks. All around us the men of Mae Irión were silent, their faces downcast, their bodies slack and defeated.

Now the blind elder cackled, a sound without humour. "Ninety generations and nine!" he cried in mockery. "What fine words we spoke, in our pride and anger. We had slain the sister of the beloved of the gods, daughter of the Moon, granddaughter of the Sun. Her brothers' curses fell on us like the floods.

"*You will not join us, and you say you will not be conquered,* Yr said to us at the last parley. *This doom I lay then upon you, that you shall not join us: so long as my empire stands, so will you stand without.* And as his armies grew and his power stretched farther, one by one our allies turned their backs and our friends saw us not, and the walls of the world closed around us. Once we traded wide and far; no longer."

The old man trembled more violently. The scarred second speaker stood forward and took his elbow to steady him. I was conscious of Masseo standing silently beside me as these words were hurled forth. They must have seemed strange accusations to him.

"Then Damar his brother: *You have brought death to our house, slaughtered the daughter of the Moon in the full light of her grandfather the Sun. Let this then be your doom: that as you have slain a daughter of the gods, so shall the daughters of your city die."*

There was a stir then, of grief roused, as the silent men shifted their feet. The young men had bewildered expressions on their faces, loss for something they had never known. The older men were twisted with anger and sorrow entwined; but remorse stood clearest out to me. They had had long to dwell on their crimes and the curse upon them. It said much of the leaders that though there was hate there, it was not directed to me.

Or perhaps that was part of the curse. When I had been fully bound as the Marwn, I had been unable to criticize the Emperor even in my own thoughts. It had taken me several days and numerous books to name the white-hot emotion I experienced after undoing those bindings as *rage*.

The blind elder coughed, a long wheezing hacking cough. I waited, face still, until he had finished and wiped his streaming eyes with the hem of his tunic. His magic brushed once more against mine, seeking consonance or enmity. My fire touched his stone and settled back, content. If it had been a cat it would have been purring despite the sticky ugliness of the curse.

And the curse had not yet been fully delineated. The blind elder went on:

"And the two brothers together: *You have cursed our lines, for ninety generations and nine you have cursed us. Let this then be your doom: that so long as your curse touches us, that you hold your enmity against us, so long shall our hearts be hard to yours. So long shall the borders of our lands be held against yours. Keep what is yours, and trespass no longer."*

He stopped then, swallowing. The tall elder, the one who had spoken first, waited a few moments, and then said: "You are not Yr, nor yet Damar; I remember them well. Yet you resemble them greatly, and the fire in you burns bright, more brightly than I have ever seen before in mortal man, even those beloved of the gods who strode across the face of the world and made it their own. Or all their own but for us, who were never conquered. Have you come to see whether we are ready to submit at last?"

I regarded him steadily. He met my gaze for a moment, before his lips twisted and he looked away, defeat in every line of his body but not in his will. "We are proud, *khainos*, and we will die before we submit. And so we are dying, and soon Mae Irión will be no more than a ruin in the jungle, forgotten by all. We ask you to look in your heart if we have paid enough for our crimes against your family, and let us depart this life in peace, as we may not live together in it."

There was a long silence. I marshalled my words in my mind, thinking again of those few words from the *Saga of the Sons of Morning*.

Mae Irión, Queen of Cities, asking only to die in dignity.

I looked around, meeting the eyes of the silent, despairing citizens. Some of the youngest still had hope, but little enough of that. I could hardly fathom how they found enough optimism to study at all, and my admiration grew in bounds. To plant gardens when your entire people was dying—aye, that was fortitude indeed.

I spoke clearly, in my court voice, widely audible but not shouting, letting my magic resonate gently with the blind elder's, affirming the truth of my words. Those whose affinities were stone found it hard either to lie or be lied to, sturdy and strong as their minds were.

"Yr the Conqueror is long dead, as is Damar his brother," I announced. "Ninety generations and nine did you curse them, and they you."

I looked intently at the three elders, who were regarding me with wary surprise. The vexed question of how many generations descended from Yr I was would have to wait; it was clear that poetic justice was stronger here than any minor discrepancies in the historical records.

"Ninety generations and nine has it been since those days. Yr the Conqueror was first to be styled Emperor of Astandalas, and his dominion reached from the farthest reach of the Wide Seas of this our world of Zunidh across five worlds. We are Artorin Damara, descendent on our father's side in a right line from Damar called the Bold, and on our mother's from Yr the Conqueror. We were hundredth Emperor of Astandalas, and the last."

I paused a moment to let that information settle. No one appeared to know what to do with it. I smiled at them, benevolent and regal, letting my admiration for their strength shine through. "Ninety generations and nine did your enmity stand in secret wounds, for Mae Irión, Queen of Cities, was left no more than a name in the *Saga of the Sons of Morning* by our day. Ninety generations and nine have you been shunned from the bounds of the Empire."

I took a breath. Here we came to it. I must do this carefully: for I could not leave them simply to die, whether in dignity or in despair, not when there was anything I could do to help them. "Hundredth Emperor of Astandalas was I, and last. When the empire fell, I took upon myself the mantle of Lord Magus of Zunidh."

Saavelor was an ancient word, as old as *Khainos*. The Lady of the Peacock Throne should have been known to them. She fought long against Yr before she finally capitulated and went off on a quest for a successor who would be better able to compromise with the new and seemingly inexorably expanding empire.

"I am *Saavelor* Zunidh now," I said in the formal first person, not the imperial plural. I let my magic unfurl fully for the first time in many years. It felt as I imagined stretching out wings might, if I had them, as if I could curl around the whole assembly with my power and bring them warmth and comfort and (I am what I am) the call to adventure. I could see the effect on the apathetic young men and the resigned old men, as fear and hope kindled in their hearts and on their faces.

"I am *Saavelor* Zunidh," I said again. "The Empire is fallen, and the crimes you committed were long ago and long repaid. I do not seek your submission and I do not seek your further punishment. I am *Saavelor* Zunidh, and I have no need to conquer. You are my people, long hidden though you have been, and I will do all I must to see you thrive. Mae Irión is named in the songs as the Queen of Cities, and I would see her so."

I lifted my voice, the magic underlining it so it would be heard in all corners of this tiny beleaguered land: "Mae Irión is the Last Free City of Zunidh, who never was conquered: hear ye all that she shall remain free, and rise again."

The echoes reverberated and the gold leaf seemed to shudder and shine in the aftermath of those words. "Now," I said in a quieter voice to the three astonished elders before me. "I request of you a place to rest for myself and my companion, and food to eat, and then I would consult with you elders and any others of learning and wisdom, that I might be certain to remove every vestige of this curse from upon your people and your city."

The blind elder was the first to speak. Even now his shoulders were straighter and his voice a little stronger, though all my words had done was lighten the curse just slightly, not lift it. "Ah, once we were known for our hospitality," he said mournfully, "but it has been so long since we had any guests we have forgotten all we once knew!"

"You will learn again," I said gently, and set myself to lengthening what had already been a very long day. There was no way I wished to sleep while that curse yet worked upon the citadel.

We were shown to a house a few doors down from the plaza along the spiralling road. The frontage was plain (apart from the gilded window- and door-frames, that is), and the inside similarly austere. The floors were of flagged stone and the walls lime washed, both decorated with little besides a few woven mats. Those on the floor were made of grass or reeds, while those on the walls were wool and silk, in colours that had once been bright but now were a little faded.

Weavings done when there was still trade, and women skilled in the art, I thought. This was the wrong climate for silkworms and I suspected also for sheep or other wool-bearing animals. Their wool had probably come from the high plateaus, when the ways were open. Though who knew what the land was like four thousand years ago.

There were two rooms downstairs, one with low rush-seated backless benches gathered around a bronze brazier. Two chests stood against the wall, and a simple table; there were no other furnishings. The second room was smaller, all stone, with a single wooden table bearing a bronze basin.

"The others will come with hot water soon," our guide assured us.

"And if we should need ..." I made one of the gestures I used with my guards, which seemed to be enough given the context.

Our guide, one of the youngest men in the city, blushed a little but showed us another basin under the table, "if you should have need in the night," and then directed us outside to a small wooden closet built up against the back of the house, where an alley ran parallel to the main ramp.

Inside was a dispiritingly recognizable wooden bench with a hole in it. Hanging on a nail on the wall was an even more dispiriting stick with a sponge on it, whose use I recognized only from travel in very uncivilized lands indeed. Outside the closet was a large clay pot with a lid on it.

"For the one," our guide said, gesturing at it, and inside the closet, "for the other. The ... result is collected and processed for use."

I wondered what exactly one used human waste for, but didn't ask. Masseo might know.

It occurred to me that I hadn't had the chance to speak to him at all. I looked sidelong at him now, but he was merely smiling crookedly and pleasantly, trailing along behind me silently and apparently contentedly.

Back inside, we were led upstairs to a loft that stretched the whole length of the building. It had windows on either side and more of the mats and hangings. A raised platform ran along one wall, with a wooden chest at either side. There were several layers of mats on the platform, and strange wooden shapes like giant spools for thread. Our guide appeared to feel all this was self-explanatory, for he walked passed the platform to a ladder at the far end that led up to a trapdoor in the roof.

I could feel the length and exertions of the day—was it only that morning I had had a splendid bath?—as I climbed up behind him. Like in many hot countries the roof was clearly a much-used living area: we could see down the stepped buildings of the city to many other inhabited spaces. The crowds had dispersed and filtered back into their homes and activities.

"I shall leave you here," our guide said. "Food and water will come soon."

I inclined my head, then recalled that we were the first strangers this young man had ever met, and smiled at him. "Thank you," I said.

"Yes, thank you," Masseo echoed, enunciating carefully.

The young man blushed again and bowed clumsily, or perhaps in a foreign fashion, before clambering down the ladder and out of sight. I took a deep breath and relaxed, then turned to Masseo, who was leaning up against the parapet surrounding the roof and smiling at me.

"Your golden tongue seems to have been successful," he commented. "I was worried for a moment when they started hurling accusations at you. What was the matter? Some long-inherited insult?"

"You could say that."

I looked over the parapet. The golden city—from above the gilded roofs looked like lacework edging to the buildings—was tightly packed together, a true walled citadel on its perch in the middle of the river. The gardens extended in a semi-circle on the southern side of the bank; the northern side looked as if it had once been cleared, but was now being reclaimed by the jungle.

Masseo came to stand beside me. "They are dying, aren't they?"

We had seen such places before in our travels, when some required combination of resources and spirit failed.

"They were cursed," I said, "four thousand years ago or more, by Yr the Conqueror and Damar the Bold. They thought I looked enough like them to be their father, Harbut Zalarin the Son of the Sun. They asked me if they had not paid enough; there are no women because of the curse, and they were shunned by all to do with the Empire."

"You're going to lift it, of course."

I laid my hands on the parapet. Yr's golden ring caught on the stone and chimed. At some point I had twisted it back to its habitual placement, and the inscribed sun-in-glory twinkled in response more to magic than light. The sun was setting behind the mountains, and shadows were falling across the jungle and dulling the river's beauty, if not its omnipresent roar. Mist was already starting to rise downriver.

The unwholesome magic slid over me, seeking purchase. It tasted my magic and recoiled, and I extended my protections more thoroughly over Masseo. He shuddered and looked enquiringly at me.

"We do not fall under the parameters of the curse, but we lie under it tonight," I said by way of explanation. "Come, let us see what food and rest we might take today. Tomorrow I must consult with the elders and see what I need to do."

Masseo didn't move, and after a step I halted, looking back at him.

He met my eyes, familiar solemnity leavened by a touch of the lightness he had gained over the years of our separation. Then he shook his head, smiling, and pushed himself off the parapet.

"What?" I asked, a little sharply.

"Oh, nothing," he said, smiling, as he came up beside me. "I was merely reflecting on how well you hide your majesty, most of the time."

The sponge bath facilities were not nearly so nice as the ones on the sky ship, but we were able to wash our hands, at least, and change into clean dry clothes on my part before we settled in the downstairs room to see what meal we'd been brought. I picked one of the light linen tunics I usually wore underneath my formal robes, with the scarlet silk mantle for comfort. Masseo laughed at me, which was a trifle disconcerting.

The food was strange to both of us, and rather bland: porridge made of an unfamiliar yellow grain, a fruit salsa involving what seemed to be charred pineapples, and some thoroughly well-cooked greens. I was given a boiled egg, which I suspected, from its singularity, was a delicacy.

"No salt," Masseo said after tasting the porridge. He looked expectantly at me, then at my blank stare went to his bag and pulled out his little wooden box. "I'm so used to you having all the spices," he explained.

When I first went on adventures, leaving the Tower of Harbut Zalarin behind, I had taken with me almost everything I could from the enchanted pantry with which the tower had been supplied. A box full of many little drawers had puzzled me mightily but turned out to contain a fortune of spices from across the entire breadth of the Empire. We had never figured out what a few of them were; but they made many an otherwise objectionable meal quite interesting.

"I do apologize," I said. "This curse is weighing on me."

"Ah, is that what it is? Well, you may have some of my salt, if you wish."

I accepted and sprinkled a few grains across the bowl; it did improve things. I wondered how long ago they had stopped being able to trade. I was pretty certain Kip had gone on about the role of salt in health at one point, but couldn't recall why.

"What are you thinking about?"

I looked up at Masseo, who was about halfway through his plate, but had stopped to regard me. I looked down, realizing I had barely eaten more than a few mouthfuls. "The role of salt in human health," I replied honestly, to which he responded with a chuckle.

"Oh, Fitzroy. Only you."

I ate some of the greens, which tasted healthy, and contemplated the strangeness of conversations. There were perhaps three people—no. I could name them. There were three people who regularly initiated conversations with me: Kip, first of all, and Ludvic (Commander in Chief of the Imperial Guard), and Conju, my primary personal attendant.

Conju was an aristocrat born, and deeply, even instinctively conscious of rank and appropriate topics of discussion. Ludvic was by temperament and training taciturn, so his statements were few but striking. Kip, thank heavens, had a tendency to say exactly what he was thinking.

Masseo was still chuckling, spooning up the last of the porridge and setting his spoon down so he could push back a little from the table and stretch out his legs. I watched him, wondering how I had lost that ease. I could portray it, certainly, but I didn't *feel* it.

He yawned, covering his mouth lackadaisically, then grinned at me. "Will you send your lights upstairs, please? I don't think I'll last long tonight."

"It can't be much later than the first hour past sunset," I objected.

He cocked his head at me. "What were you planning on doing, then? I'd love to stay up all night talking to you but I'm not twenty-five, you know. Well, you do know: neither are you! It's been a busy day."

"I was going to start on the curse," I said, indicating the notebook I'd set at the other end of the table when we'd found the food ready for us.

"And are you not tired?"

"Masseo—"

"Fitzroy."

I stopped, astonished and a little affronted. *No one* spoke to me in that tone.

Masseo clearly saw something in my face, for he put his hands up in a gesture of reconciliation. "Fitzroy," he said in a softer voice, less sarcastic and condescending. "I mean no insult to your … dedication. But tell me true: are you not tired?"

I had to pause to consider that seriously, as he waited for a response. As soon as I thought about it I became conscious of a great weariness and a few deep aches from various bruised parts of my anatomy. "I suppose so," I said unwillingly.

Masseo smiled, shaking his head. "And once you were always the first one to complain about feeling sore or tired or blistered or … Fitzroy, my friend, we fell off a thousand-foot cliff today. Even if we didn't land as disastrously as we might have, our boat still shattered beneath us. *I'm* bruised and sore and my arms are tired, and I'm a working blacksmith."

"Oh," I said, taken aback.

How long had it been since anyone called me *friend*? My household attendants were solicitous—too solicitous, often—but it was different.

I could name that person, too. Kip had called me his friend, and he was willing, when no one else was, to take me to task. He had stood up even when I had let my pride speak for me, and castigated him for the impudence; and he had held me afterwards, with a blanket between us to keep the taboos, when I had wept for the failure I was as a human being, who had once been considered a great man and was now deemed only a god.

"I grant the desire to undo this curse as soon as possible—I admire you for it—but I must ask you whether one night more will really make a difference, when they have been four thousand years under it?"

He leaned forward to underscore his intention. "Say the word, tell me that it will, and I will do whatever I can to keep you alert and focused on your task through the night. But if it is not necessary, if another night will not doom them, then … take it. Let yourself rest and come at the problem fresh in the morning. You do not need to solve all the world's ills in one fell swoop."

It had been many years since I had last needed anyone to keep me *alert and focused* through a night's work. My days were organized from dawn to midnight, and if I did not have court of an evening then I often found the time conducive to finishing the work that could not be done in the bright busyness of the day. Being a lord magus was not the same as being an adventuring poet; there was no room for that sort of self-indulgence, for waiting on the Muse.

I touched the magic of the curse, unwholesome and heavy as it was, and restless after the touch of my magic upon it. Such an ancient and powerful working would have developed almost a mind of its own, over the years.

But however unwillingly, I had been lawfully anointed Emperor of Astandalas, hundredth in succession from Yr, and my signet ring seemed to fulfil its storied history, and be recognized by the curse that had been cast by its first owner.

Curses were best overthrown in the light of day, at any rate.

"It can wait till tomorrow," I conceded at last, disappointed in myself for how relieved I was at the decision, and felt weak and pusillanimous in comparison to the stalwart fortitude of the citizens of Mae Irión.

IN WHICH THERE ARE AN AMPLE SUFFICIENCY OF CUSHIONS

*C*onju, justly concerned about the quality of accommodations I might face, and unnecessarily fretful about my likely reactions to them, had ensured that I was well stocked with bedclothes, including an abundance of down pillows. As the sleeping platform was only supplied with light-weight linen sheets above the mats, as well as the mysterious wooden spools, I brought them out of my bag to make something closer to a proper bed.

Masseo laughed at me until he started crying, but he also accepted the pillows, so that was all right.

When I woke the next morning I was quite remarkably stiff, particularly in my torso and my right wrist. It was still dark, and I lay there listening to Masseo's even breathing for a while. It was comforting; I had missed it the night before, when I lay in his guest room. Frustrating as I sometimes found my lack of privacy, I was well accustomed to the guards' constant presence.

I presumed that it was probably about a quarter-hour before dawn, or what was dawn in Solaara. We had gone to bed barely two hours after sunset, which made for a luxuriously long night if I had slept till my usual hour of rising.

I lit a faint light and found my way to my bag, discovering along the way that my thighs had their own complaints about the stairs up and down to the Abbey. Masseo muttered in his sleep and turned over but did not otherwise stir, so I left him alone and went downstairs. Outside in the little court with the privy the night air was soft and moist and scented with something spicy intermingled with the green smell of the vegetation.

The sky was a deep, velvety blue, but the stars were obscured by a high filmy haze. There was a faint greenish light on the eastern horizon. I regarded it thoughtfully, trying to recall how far we were north of the Equator and what that meant for day length. It was spring here, so the days would be longer than the nights, even if only by an hour or two.

As I moved around I felt by degrees marginally less stiff. I was wide awake. I usually sleep six hours or a little less in a night, and despite the fact that it was clearly earlier than I had anticipated there was no way I would be falling asleep again soon.

There was plenty of work with which to occupy myself, at least.

I took my bag to the table where Masseo and I had dined the night before. Someone had come in and removed the dishes (which we had left—Masseo had left—stacked up neatly at one end) and left a jug of water in their place. I poured myself a glass of water, using my own glass, then dug around in my bag until I found a small porcelain teapot and a box of tea.

The small ritual of making tea myself, with my own magic to heat the water, in the quiet solitude of the earliest morning, was strangely liberating. As the fragrant steam rose up I settled down, drawing a soft throw of the lightest, finest wool around my shoulders and pulling the notebook to me. The curse lay quiescent but heavy over the sleeping citadel, a seeping ugliness like a weeping sore.

My mind quieted as I focused on the rhythm of my breathing. In the Palace I meditated most days before bed, as it was the best way to calm down after the excitements of evening court. (Boring I might find it personally, but the lights and the music and the chattering courtiers were physically invigorating even if too-often mentally unstimulating.) It was easy to slip into a light trance.

I turned my attention inward, deeper. This I did not do so often, only when I needed to in the course of a working. To my inner eye my magic was a fire, the flames scarlet and gold and orange and violet. I had long been used to imagining it a campfire, like any one of the hundreds we had lit in the course of our adventures as the Red Company. Sometimes I imagined the shadowy figures of my friends around it, guarding my innermost self from the adulation and perils of the court.

One of the shadows had stepped closer: Masseo, of course, looking young as I remembered him and feeling lighter, calmer, as I knew him now. He was holding his ball peen hammer (I noted the spherical, even ball-shaped end) and an iron bar, the memory of this extraordinary week being held for me.

I tended the fire for a few minutes, adding wood and adjusting the placement of the logs. At length it was burning brightly, the coals glowing, ready (I remembered vaguely) for cooking. The inner image of Masseo nodded in satisfaction, then returned to the shadows, one guard of my mind and heart amongst others.

Not that my heart was located *here*; even in metaphors there was a dark spot in the middle of the campfire where *something* was missing.

I regarded the blank spot, wondering, as I often had, just what it was that I had lost when I was very young and even more foolish.

Soon, I told my silent friends, soon. The three mirrors would show me what I needed to be whole.

I imagined my inner self (much more flexible than the outer

physical reality) sitting cross-legged before the fire, staring into its depths. And then I performed the twist that let my mind turn out of my interior mindscape and look at the magic of the world around me with even greater detail than I could see the physical world with my eyes.

≈

The curse was the most obvious thing.

It draped over and through the region like a monstrous fungal growth, spreading corruption and despair wherever it touched. The strands of malignancy were black and oily to my sight, slithering and hard to focus on. The curse had had enough time to penetrate everything under its definition and seemed to be poised to expand further. Some curses faded once their object was achieved; others, set by a stronger will, twisted and transformed to touch other subjects unless properly removed.

This curse would be the latter, I feared: ones on lands and peoples usually were. Curse an individual and the family would likely also be affected; curse an entire people and the whole region would be blighted, and might remain so for eons. There were places where great magic blessed lands unpeopled for thousands of years, and more, alas, where nothing throve.

I sat very still, not yet acting. I was a passive observer, seeking understanding, not effect. The curse was powerful and hungry for new victims, and it reacted to my presence eagerly. I let the ugly strands slide over me. The golden signet ring of Yr the Conqueror sat on my finger, and I was the anointed Emperor of Astandalas, once centre of a web far more elaborate and extensive than this. This curse was under my dominion, and it *would not touch me*.

The curse challenged, received my response, and slithered away to investigate a bright forge-fire coming near me. *He is under my protection*, I said without words, enclosing Masseo within my magic, safe and secure as an ember tucked into a bed of coals. The curse growled and returned to its own place.

Not for much longer, no indeed.

I followed the lines of the curse with a patience I suspected Masseo would find surprising. I had learned patience in my long tenure as lord magus, learned how to do these slow and subtle and greatly powerful workings. I had not been capable of them as a young man. It was all flashy magic then, bright-burning and quickly extinguished. The period as Emperor of Astandalas, when the ancient ordered magic of the empire held me pinned and bound at its centre, had forced me to learn how to wait.

And yet this curse was yet more ancient. It was centred in something, some object located in the centre of the citadel, in that golden tower that should have held the greatness of Mae Irión. From that anchor it radiated out until it was stopped by the boundaries of the Empire brushing up against it.

I could feel where the noose had tightened just downstream, cutting off the whole of the lower Qavaliun basin in one swoop. That had been Dimiter Mdang's journey of exploration, no doubt, when he re-named a river in honour of the reigning emperor.

All told, there could not be much more than five miles around the citadel that was still *their* land. Each constriction of the net had thickened the curse, increased the malignancy. They had shunned the Empire, and so the Empire had shunned them. And over the years, as Astandalas swallowed worlds and bound them together with magics almost beyond reason or imagination, Mae Irión under its curse of invisibility and isolation had grown nearly detached from its own world.

But yet it was still here; the magic underlaying the curse recognized me as lord magus, as *saavelor*. And why was that?

The thunderous rush of the river answered me. Mae Irión had been beloved of the river, the magic said to me. Earth and water do not fight, not as fire and water do; they partner in the great dance of the elements. The wise ones of this city had loved the great river, from the high cataract to the sea, and as the river's headwaters were firmly a part of Zunidh—that Abbey built above them, whose sorceress-priestesses had long been strong and staunch allies of the Grand Dukes of Damara and their close kinsmen the Emperors—so too was the river below the escarpment.

Yr and Damar had taken that from Mae Irión, too.

The old magic did not *tell* me anything, not that ancient, foreign magic lying near-spent under the weight of the curse. The river rushing down, around, through, past the citadel brought power to the curse, as if it were the waterwheel of some unholy mill. Instead of grain to flour, it ground life to death. All the *time* that Mae Irión should have flourished—all those thousands of years since the days of Yr and Damar, whom the elders here remembered as living men —all those years had been stolen from them to strengthen the curse and the walls enclosing its victims.

It was one of the most beautifully balanced works of magic I had ever seen. I could hardly think that Yr the Conqueror could have been such a wizard to have created it, when he was known as a conqueror, a great warrior. But then again he had conquered worlds, and charisma always partakes of magic though it be the only gift a person might have. And his brother Damar was said to have been learned and wise as well as doughty; and their father was Harbut Zalarin, nearly unmatched in magic.

(And the elders here, seeing me, said my magic shone brighter than that of Damara or of Yr, brightly enough for them to wonder if I were Harbut Zalarin, son of the Sun, himself. And what was I to make of that, but that I had forced my magic to greatness in an alien mode, and now, released at last, it was restless and strong?

I was never going to be able to dwindle back to merely Artorin Damara, lord magus of Zunidh, Last Emperor of Astandalas.)

The forge-fire drew near and settled near me, accompanied by two stones and a small darting creature of some kind. A humming-bird, recalling ones I had seen sipping from flowers here and there in the gorges before the current had caught us.

I had seen enough to make a start on unravelling the curse, at any rate. Now I needed to know how exactly it had taken form, and what that anchor was, so that I might safely remove it and draw Mae Irión as far into the embrace of Zunidh as was desired. I did not think I could blame them if they decided they wished me to loosen their tenuous hold on the world entirely, and let them withdraw into the mists of the Borderlands between worlds.

I turned inward, and smiled at my merry campfire, and at how easy it was to spring up to stand. In my innermost self I was Fitzroy Angursell, young and unafraid and full of poetry. He had not known the name his mother had given him, nor had any fear the weight of the Empire would fall on his head, no matter how angry his comic epics made the authorities.

I blinked and was once more nearly old, and stiff, and the very embodiment of Authority. It reminded me why I didn't go into the deep trance very often.

"Good morning," Masseo said cheerfully. "Another cup of tea?"

I nodded and accepted the cup he passed me. I had forgotten my injured wrist, however, and dropped it. He reached out for my arm with one hand and the cup with the other. I sat back, drawing my arm out of the way, and saw the two stones beside me—the blind elder and the tall one. They were watching me curiously.

One of the difficulties with the deep trance is the length of time it takes to return from it. It is something I do so rarely, and always with such carefully arranged surroundings, that I frankly couldn't remember the last time I had had to interact with people outside of solicitous attendants who knew what I wanted and needed. I couldn't think what I needed, though tea did sound nice.

The tall elder said something about wounds. He was looking at my wrist, so I looked down as well, and was surprised to see it visibly swollen. My fluency in Antique Shaian seemed to have disappeared.

The hummingbird of a person was a young man, perhaps mid-twenties, who was presumably there as the elders' assistant. The tall elder nodded to him and he dashed off out the door.

"How did you hurt your arm?" Masseo asked.

I looked up at his face, unfamiliar again after my vision of him in my interior mindscape. "I think I landed on it after we fell," I managed. The words sounded as if I'd dragged them from out of deep water.

"That was a deep trance," he muttered.

I blinked at him, for surely that was obvious. Time and magic react oddly to one another, one reason why the Fall of Astandalas wreaked such havoc as it did. All those bindings, layered for generations upon generations, intended to create and hold an Empire stretching across five worlds together for thousands of years—and it *had*, Yr's conquest had been nearly ineluctable—with the Emperor at the centre holding the whole.

I still did not fully understand why I had survived its destruction, unless it was that childish game of make-believe with the stone that was truly the Diamond of Gaesion.

The young man came back in with one of the few middle-aged men in the city. He was holding a bag, a square cloth thing with a wide strap that went over the shoulder. The cloth was woven in colourful stripes, reminiscent of the hangings on the walls. An artefact remaining from before the curse, I judged. And if he were a healer, in training or newly released, he would have been kept home from the disastrous campaign that had destroyed his contemporaries, only to fail at saving the women when the curse took them.

He squatted down beside me with the immediate focus of a medical man. I was too abstracted to refuse his touch—Masseo was the only one truly *present*—but my body reacted even if my mind didn't. He felt my pulse's immediate increase and frowned.

He had a gift of magic, small but powerfully focused. He touched my wrist with it, and the spark of an absolutely foreign magic touching mine snapped me fully into myself. It was like a dog's wet nose suddenly pressed to my ear.

I withdrew my arm from his grasp with as much solemn dignity as I could muster, setting my hand to rest in my lap. He looked up at me, dark eyes concerned. "Your heart, *khainos*," he said earnestly. "It is too fast—"

"I am unaccustomed to being touched," I said. "It is not considered appropriate for one in my position."

Shock and then understanding chased themselves across his face, and something like pity. I stared him out, and he looked down, flushing, and dug into his bag for a length of cloth. "Your wrist is merely sprained," he said, and this time added, "You permit? I shall bind it, to give it support, and a sling. Do not use it for a few days and it should heal admirably."

My degree of magic ensured that most such minor injuries did heal admirably, and quickly too. I suffered him to wrap the wrist, which he did securely and deftly, hands surprisingly gentle, but I refused his assistance with the sling. "My friend will tie it for me," I said, gesturing at Masseo, who was watching all this attentively and clearly understood what was necessary.

That done, the healer departed and left me to greet the elders properly.

"I am Tian," the tall elder said, "and he is Bezal. We have come to provide you with what knowledge we can."

His eyes were not so hard as they had been the day before. I regarded him thoughtfully, sipping from the tea Masseo had once again refilled. They had their own cups before them, as well as small, surprisingly sweet cakes. Even if they had had to trade for salt—and perhaps in times gone, they had crystallized their own at the coastline—they still had sugar.

What had changed overnight?

Merely our arrival, and the hope my fine words had brought them?

My fine words and the fact that they had discovered me deep in a trance. Both were magi to some degree; after the deep trance I could feel their banked power, the stones gently resonating with my magic even under the influence of the curse. And the curse was shifting uncertainly. I kept my face and my mind serene, but inwardly I was pleased. Once I had the anchor, I could unravel the whole.

"I have a few questions," I acknowledged, brushing against their solid strength with my warm campfire heat. Both relaxed under the unconscious reassurance, though their faces were drawn with long care and caution. "First: what changes have there been in the curse over time?"

Tian looked at Bezal, who was the one to answer in his thin, whispery voice. "The first blows came hard and fast. First the northern border closed—the roads no longer went anywhere, just around and back. Then the women started to sicken. First no girls were born, and then they sickened and died. Youngest to eldest, as if to mock our hopes for the future. The southern border, gone.

"The west was always hard, because of the Great Barrier, but we had carved a stair up the face of Ayauna, the river-fall that you descended. Then one day it was … not gone, but it did not go anywhere. Men who tried to climb found themselves climbing without end, until they grew dizzy and fell.

"The river-ways lasted longest, for the river was *ours*. Our land was great, wide," he said, chuckling without humour. "From the northern hills to the southern sea, the Great Barrier to the mouths of our fair Urdirión. That was our land, once, before we hazarded all, and lost. When we could no longer pass the edge of the mangroves we knew Yr had conquered all around us. For a while we could still pass through the secret ways between here and those other places, but one by one they, too, were lost. How long?" His voice faded, and he turned blind eyes to Tian. "Was it a year before the haze closed over us?"

"We were wise in the knowledge of the stars," Tian told me. "We did not think, for all we knew the rumours, that we had insulted the children of the Sun. Not until the haze came and hid our friendly stars from us did we give heed to those stories." He sighed heavily. "Their eyes were like yours. Inhuman. We should have understood we were dealing with gods, not men, but though we knew of magic and the passages between worlds we did not imagine that legends stepped down out of the sky."

Every one of my ancestors between Yr the Conqueror (and Damar the Bold) and myself was human, honestly. It was inconceivable that the golden eyes had bred true, and indeed it was impossible to tell—the official iconography of Emperors always painting them with flat gold eyes—if it had between Aurelius Magnus, the last for whom there was incontrovertible evidence, and me.

"A year, yes," the blind elder, Bezal, whispered. "The walls closed in, and stood where they were: a valley full of mourning, too large for us to cultivate as we had, without women and without the promise of new children, but we did not yet know … Not until the terrible storm."

Tian shuddered at the memory of it. Their young assistant had a fearful, anxious expression, as one remembering a horrific childhood memory.

"It was a dark day," Tian said. "There had been a storm not long before, a torrential rain, after which we could no longer find our way past the first confluence south of the city. Two thirds of our land, gone. We had been hoping we might yet find a new way out of the world, one that led somewhere Yr had not conquered, but we could find nothing."

"Never anything," Bezal whispered. "Then the terrible storm. Ten days it stormed, rain and lightning, wind, earthquakes. The river screamed and the earth cried out and the air was tormented. We could do nothing but hold on. It was like the end of all things."

"Like, but the gods were not so merciful," Tian said grimly. "When the storm had passed we found that the jungle had grown in as if overnight. The bridge to the northern bank collapsed in the

211

earthquake, and all that bank was gone wild. Those that landed boats there found monsters; few came back. The south bank we were able to keep longer, but year by year the jungle comes closer as our strength fails and our numbers decrease."

"Not all have been stalwart in their despair," said Bezal.

"Two decades it has been since the terrible storm," Tian went on. "We will not last out a third."

"You will not have to," I responded, fitting this into what I had seen in my trance. It was hardly conceivable, but it appeared that the entirety of the span of the Empire of Astandalas, all four thousand years of it, had been experienced by Mae Irión as one year. The 'terrible storm' that had only strengthened the curse had almost certainly been the form the Fall took here.

I was nearly certain I knew how to deal with this. It only depended on them knowing what the object at the heart of the curse was, and being willing to part with it.

"My second question," I said therefore, "comes out of the knowledge I gained in my meditation. The curse is anchored in an item in your tower—do you know what it might be?"

Bezal worked his mouth and then spat on the floor beside him. Tian looked apologetic in the face of Masseo's visible shock. I would have been proud of my unchanged countenance except that it had been too long since my face was anything but public property for me to even have to think about concealing my personal reaction.

"We know exactly what it is," Bezal said bitterly. "We have tried time and again to get rid of it. Woeful was the day we saw the sister of Yr and of Damar looking in her fair mirror!"

IN WHICH I FIND THE SECOND
MIRROR

They led me to the tower, which was called the Iliath, moving slowly out of deference to the ancient Bezal. He held the arm of the young man, and Tian and I walked behind. Tian spoke to me in a low tone about the mirror.

"We tried to destroy it, but our kilns and forges broke. We tried to lose it in the jungle, but the hunters would find their prey holding it, or it would be in their stomachs when we cut the animals open, and the wild creatures grew fiercer and bolder. There are man-eating tigers on the southern bank now, when before they never came out of the deep jungle. We respected them but were not afraid. They were the special signs of our kinsmen in Mae Osgilian." He looked at me, a question in his eyes.

Mae Osgilian did not warrant even the stanzas that Mae Irión had. It was one of a list of cities conquered by Yr, and had for its reputation in the *Saga of the Sons of Morning* only the epithet *Mae Osgilian, whence came the Tiger of the Western Gate*.

"I'm sorry," I said. "There is little come down to us from those days. I do know that one of the *Saavelor* Zunidh was from there. He was called the Tiger of the Western Gate. I believe he is the reason tigers were chosen as the emblem of Zunidh."

Tigers are surprisingly rare on Zunidh. There had been a sizeable population in Kavanor before it fell into the sea, and it seemed as if the jungle of the Qavaliun Basin might also have some.

Tian nodded, a little blankly. I imagined he found it entirely unfathomable that four thousand years—really five thousand, in these mountains—had passed since their last contact with the outside world. Perhaps they could not yet even begin to imagine rejoining the world, with the curse still heavy upon them.

A few other salient details floated to mind. "He was called Nwo Ya—the *saavelor* I mentioned."

"My sister's son was called Nawoyav," Tian said.

Nwo Ya of Mosgul was how he was listed in the history books. I had found out a few things about him when doing the research before this quest, namely that Mosgul was the modern name for Mae Osgilian and that Nwo Ya had been a shape-shifter, able to take the form of a tiger. It was he who had decided to ally with Yr the Conqueror and bring the wild magic of Zunidh in line with the new emperor's ideas.

"Mosgul is the name of Mae Osgilian now," I told Tian. "It is a large city—two hundred thousand people or so live there. They have a—" there was no word for *university* in Antique Shaian. There was not really a word for *writing*, come to think of it. "They have a place of learning there. I expect some might study this language, which is not what we speak now, and there would be those who would know the history of their city better."

"Thank you," said Tian, more surely.

It occurred to me that if Nwo Ya was indeed this man's nephew —and if I understood the timelines correctly it did not seem implausible, utterly impossible as it was—and he had seen what came of defying Yr the Conqueror, I could understand better why he had sought to make a peaceful alliance. It had always been a bit of a mystery why the resistance to the conquerors collapsed so utterly and so quickly. The Lady of the Peacock Throne went away to find an heir, and found Nwo Ya, and suddenly the invaders were an empire.

I was, I admit, rather curious what would happen after I found my own heir.

Tian took a breath and returned to the less pleasing (but perhaps more straightforward) subject of the cursed mirror.

"We threw the mirror into the river at last, hoping he would bear it away, but it made everything worse," he went on. "The *kiyuna*—the dolphins, I think you call them—went away and would come up to us no more. They were ours, as the tigers were of Mae Osgilian. But no more."

"Perhaps they will return once the curse is lifted," I said gently.

"Perhaps," he said, with little hope.

The tower was a simple edifice, square rooms stacked on top of each other. A stone staircase without a railing led up one side wall. The entry room was as austere as the guest house we'd spent the night in, though the next room up was well-furnished with colourful hangings. Chests stood along the walls, and benches around a table by the window.

"Our meeting room," Tian informed me. "Bezal will wait here for us unless you need him upstairs?"

Bezal was still doddering his way up the first set of stairs, his assistant standing close behind him in case he should fall.

"No, I expect you can explain what I need, or ask the right questions after."

"The true measure of wisdom," Tian agreed, with a glimmer of good humour surfacing.

I had a sudden image of him as a much younger man, silky

brown-black hair tied back in an elaborately plaited queue. He wore knee-length open robes over short culotte-type trousers, both brightly coloured in many stripes, and bore a wooden spear in one hand and a proud, fierce look in his eye.

I blinked, and he was once again ancient, white-haired and stoop-shouldered.

There had to be a great degree of magic concentrated here if I were starting to see visions, especially of the distant past.

I followed Tian up to the next floor. What visions I had received in the past were of the present, if of places far removed geographically, and even those were rare and usually enigmatic.

I stepped off the stairs and found my attention locked immediately on the innocuous bronze mirror Tian was regarding with loathing.

The stories were not consistent as to which of the three mirrors Harbut Zalarin had given to which of his three children. It was possible that Lazunar had been given the one showing the future, and that the strange lack of history—of *pastness*—that the curse had wrought on Mae Irión was of a piece with that. Since they had stolen the mirror all they had had was their past, and no future.

I was suddenly grateful I had decided not to desecrate Yr's sarcophagus in order to steal his mirror.

"There it is," Tian said unnecessarily.

I focused on the immediate concern before me. This was, without a doubt, the central anchor of the curse, and the weak point for those who had the skill and power to break it.

We are not many. The present Lord of Ysthar was the only one I could think might have any greater skill at such disenchantments than myself, and he was even more naturally opposed to Astandalan magic than I. He had come into his power after the Fall, and though he had spent his life repairing the effects of that catastrophic failure of magic, he had never had to fit himself within it.

Assessing the magic in the room—there was too much of it for me to pay any real attention to the physical space—I could see one simple, if not exactly *easy,* way to do the thing.

"Will you willingly, on behalf of your people, return that mirror to me?"

Tian's voice was surprised as he answered. *"Return* it?"

The curse heard my words, in whatever near-intelligent way such great and powerful works of magic can, and heeded his closely in turn. The weight of it thickened the air.

I spoke clearly. "As far as our records say, Lazunar's line died out seven generations after her death. Her descendants were all daughters, and the last married an heir of Damar the Bold. I trace my line ninety generations and nine to Damar on my father's side and to Yr on my mother's. I was the hundredth and last Emperor of Astandalas after Yr. Will you, speaking for Mae Irión, return this mirror to me?"

I forced my eyes to see his expression. Tian looked at the bronze oval, gleaming in the sunlight coming through a window. It seemed incredible that such a small and pretty thing could be the source of so much woe.

The curse pressed close, so close the thunder of the river was suddenly loud in our ears. The room grew dim apart from that one gleaming, almost glowing, thing.

Tian was nearly as strong as the blind Bezal down below. The stone of his will shook under the onslaught of magic, but like the outcropping at the base of the falls he shuddered but did not shift.

"Will you, speaking for Mae Irión, return this mirror to me?"

The third time of asking was the ritual one.

Tian looked me in the eyes: his dark as the river-stone, adamant; mine no doubt gold with magic, banked no longer.

His voice shook but did not falter as he replied. "I do, and I will, and I am."

With swift steps he crossed the room, picked up the cursed mirror, and deposited it into my hastily outstretched hands. There could have been no better action.

I spared a brief thought of gleeful anticipation for all that I might learn from them, when we had the leisure, and then the curse required the entirety of my attention.

~

With the mirror in my hands I was quite suddenly and quite literally the centre point of the curse's spiderweb net.

I substituted myself in smoothly, if I may say so myself. That was the last metacognitive thought I was aware of for a while.

Fire is my element, fire and air. Opposites to water and earth, it was easy enough to misdirect the curse into taking my purifying fire as a further development of the blight upon the stone-and-water of Mae Irión. The curse thus welcomed my magic, sending the fire along each and every strand. Most of them I had already noted in my earlier assessment, but not all.

I could not have done it were I a hair less powerful or a whit less certain of my blood kinship to the original setters of the curse. As it was, I was very glad I had removed myself from any active workings as Lord of Zunidh before I had left the Palace, for my personal power was—just—sufficient to replace the thunderous engine of the river, if only for a moment. But a moment was all I needed.

My fire ran to the end of each strand and crouched there in readiness, poised for my will to twist the good to the evil once again. The curse waited for the next iteration of its terrible beauty. The land trembled in fearful anticipation, and the stone boulders holding it off the last few clusters of remaining living men were groaning under the fire.

A curse is the inverse of a blessing. What sort of deity could I even pretend to be if I could not return good for evil on behalf of my own people?

Here is the final fulfilment of your work, I told the curse, utterly honestly, and showed it the walls of the world finally crashing together because there was nothing left between them.

The curse did not *think*. It twisted what was good into its evil. Pride into isolation, wisdom into despair, a life-giving sacred river into the flood of malignancy. It demanded a new shape of me.

I am a great mage, one of the greatest. But I am a better poet, for it is by words that I have transformed the world for the better.

I sang a verse in the mode of the *Saga of the Sons of Morning*, recalling childhood exercises in composition. It was not as smooth as versification in my own Modern Shaian, but it had a certain sinewy strength, and the curse settled into the curves of my meaning as if they were Yr's. I made them lapidary as gemstones, the answer to that ancient elegy for the lost last free city.

Ai! Mae Irión, Queen of Cities!
  For ninety generations and nine
  Were you lost to history and to time
  The walls of the world enclosed you
  The words of Yr and Damar bound you
  The death of Lazunar was heavy on your hearts
  The Sun was pitiless
  The Moon merciless
  Your works and your walls forgotten.

Ai! Mae Irión, Queen of Cities!
  Never did you yield
  Never did you fall
  Unconquered, unbowed, unbroken
  Remorseful for the death of Lazunar
  Grieving your lost loved ones
  You learned patience
  Fortitude you showed and strength

Though the world lay forgotten, out of your reach.

Ai! Mae Irión, Queen of Cities!
  Return to the world, proud citadel!
  The walls of the world are held
  Against you no longer
  The words of Damar and of Yr
  Harden hearts no longer
  The guilt of the death of Lazunar
  Stains your hands no longer
  For ninety generations and nine
  May the Sun shine in his glory
  And the Moon in her beauty
  And the stars in their passages
  On Mae Irión the golden
  Free at last once more, Queen of Cities

My words echoed along each strand of the spiderweb, the fire burning out corruption and curse until the river ran free and the air clear of its taint. The curse twisted itself to my will, twisted to fulfil my words, twisted again, and with a feeling absurdly like a *pop* it twisted inside out and floated away, no longer a tightly-woven curse but free-floating blessing.

I opened my eyes. Tian, that solid stone, looked a good thirty years younger, and he had tears running down his face.

"There," I said, patting the magic into place, and sat down hard on the floor.

I suppose one might, if one were so inclined, go so far as to call it a *swoon*. Personally I prefer *an hysterical fit*; as I do not physically possess a uterus it underlines the silliness of the phrase admirably.

"I think punch-drunk might be the phrase you're going for," Masseo said in an amused tone.

I pushed myself up on my elbow, mindful of my sore wrist only because of the sling, and blinked around. I was reclining on a mat laid on one of the raised platforms the Mae Irioni (Irionese? Irionians?) seemed fond of. My head had been supported by something solid; I twisted to look at it. It was one of the wooden spools Masseo and I had not been sure the use of.

"A head rest, of course," I murmured, staring at it.

"They were much taken with your splendid cushions, if their expressions when they came to fetch me were anything to go by," Masseo said. He was seated next to me, legs stretched out on the floor below the platform.

I smiled up at him. "There will be a lot of new things for them to discover."

He smiled back. I thought absently that I could get used to this smiling, happy Masseo. Of course, I would have to, but it was nice that it was such a pleasant, positive change in him.

"You look the very image of a dissolute emperor of old," he told me, then laughed when I sat up immediately. "Oh, we can't have that?"

I gripped the edge of the platform as my head swam. "Is there any water?"

"Here," he said, more soberly, and passed me a wooden cup. "Do you want something to eat?"

"In a moment." I sipped the water gratefully. It had been flavoured with a leaf of something that was almost but not quite familiar mint. "What time is it?"

"Mid-afternoon, I should say. You've been in your hysteric fit for about two hours. I'd call it a faint, myself."

"It's good to be precise," I agreed, and let my gaze wander around the room.

It was probably the one I'd collapsed in, formerly the centre of the curse. Yes, there was the wooden stool the mirror had rested on, under a window. The mirror itself was on the floor next to me. I could hardly blame Tian for not wanting to touch it.

I leaned over to pick the mirror up. As soon as my hand touched the handle the whole thing dissolved into a pile of dust.

"I hope you didn't have a strong *need* to unlock any hearts with that," Masseo said after a moment.

"It was only mine," I reolied lightly, brushing bronze dust off my fingers. The motes glittered in the air, and the skin of my hand glimmered more subtly. There were occasions when I wore cosmetics made of gold dust and even powdered diamonds (which look impressive and feel horrible, in case you were wondering), so I was familiar with the grit and knew it would take days to feel clean.

The room seemed to be some sort of treasury. A few chests were clustered awkwardly together, no doubt moved from the platform to make room for me. Other stools and benches stood here and there, with various intriguing and beautiful items on them. I looked at Masseo, who was regarding me with a strange fondness in his eye.

"What?" he asked.

I could have asked him what he was thinking, but I wasn't sure I was quite ready to know the answer. I gestured at the room instead. "What do you make of their treasures?"

"I think they reckon you've given them their greatest," he replied, entirely seriously. "You didn't have to do that in one fell swoop, did you? Not that it wasn't impressive. I was going through some items in my pack when the curse unravelled. You could almost *see* it: like the sun coming out from behind a cloud."

"I had all the information I needed, and Tian, the elder, set up the situation perfectly. I could have done it more slowly and less extravagantly, but not any better."

"I do love how the showiest option is always the *best* one when it comes to you," Masseo said, chuckling. "There are some lovely pieces here. No iron, of course, but there's a splendid gold mazer, and a really remarkable shell necklace."

"Really?" I levered myself up, feeling all of my bruises, and tottered nearly as badly as Bezal before my muscles loosened. Alas, removing the curse had not removed thirty years from *me*. Masseo jumped up more fluidly.

We paced around the room, admiring the objects. A few symbols and shapes were familiar from the very oldest items in the Palace Treasury. I had a bronze sculpture of a horse in my study that was said to have come from these parts and, I supposed, these days. Its pair stood on a table here, sleek and proud if hardly larger than the palm of my hand.

Footsteps proclaimed an arrival: Tian, along with one of the bearded young men, apathetic no more but bright-eyed with relief and wonder. It seemed I had not had been dreaming of Tian as rejuvenated, for the tall man striding up behind the youth was in his prime, not his dotage. Still a strong and steady rock, but no longer battered by the storm.

He had tied his hair back into a simple plait, and combed his long beard. They were still silvery-grey, but even they seemed brighter, healthier, more alive. His dark eyes flashed, and his smile was broad.

"O *Khainos*!" he cried, crossing the room with his arms outstretched. He halted a few feet away when I instinctively retreated, arms still out but no longer liable to enclose me in an embrace. I grimaced inwardly and kept my face court-serene.

"What a deed you have done for us, *Khainos*! When we hoped for the easement of our pain we never dared hope for such a day as this! What can we do? What can we say? You have saved us."

They still needed *so much*. Women willing to marry into their culture, for one thing, and salt at the very least (I was sure it had something important to do with health, and if they were missing salt what other vital nutrients might they also be lacking?); not to mention five thousand years of technological and magical innovations. They might not want all of them, but if they wished to join the world—

And that was still a question. I smiled at Tian. "My heart is gladdened to see you so much recovered already," I said. "I will do all I can to see you again great."

Tian met my gaze for a long moment, then heaved a great sigh. "*Khainos*, you need do nothing more—"

"Did you not hear me when I said I was *Saavelor* Zunidh? You are my people, Tian of Mae Irión."

He paused, then offered: "We have called the council together to speak of what must be. It will be soon, over what feast we can offer in this day."

My stomach, well-schooled as it was, rumbled only quietly. Masseo heard it, and laughed softly. "And once you were the first of us to speak of food! No, don't worry about translating—I don't understand more than one word in ten but I don't need to."

That was surely boring, but I trusted Masseo to know what he liked, so I nodded and returned my attention to Tian. I gestured at the horse. "I have seen another horse such as this, but the story of its origin is long lost. Can you tell me more?"

"You have the pair? Ah, so Aurdar fell in the end." Tian sighed again. "They were gifts of alliance. The Aurdaréz were great bronze-casters, sculptors, and loved horses. They raised them on the plains to the west, over the mountains. There was a pass in the south once ..."

The ruins of Aurdar had been in Kavanor, long since now fallen into the sea. But I did know something about the city, from the research I had undertaken before my quest. "The bronze hammers of Aurdar remain, taken into the Palace of Stars—the capital of the empire—and made into bells. They ring in each dawn and sunset."

"So pass all good things. I saw Aurdar once, in my youth. I was a great traveller then."

"Will you tell me of the other things here?"

He looked at me and saw, I hoped, my genuine curiosity, and agreed quietly. We spent the next half hour going around the room, looking at the treasures of the deep past of Zunidh. Some were similar to items I had seen in museums or the Palace Treasury, but in those cases they were old and often worn; most of these had been made or given within Tian's memory, and were bright and new.

On the far side of the room was a basket with a shell necklace in it. Tian lifted it up carefully, his eyes soft with memories. The shells glimmered softly in the indirect light: nacre, tortoiseshell cowries, red and purple shells I could not name, and pearls white and gold and the gold marked with white that was called flame.

I did not recognize it, but I was familiar with shell necklaces of the sort. "This is an *efela* from the Wide Seas," I said, surprised. "Did you trade there?"

"Across the Great Ocean? No!" Tian laughed. "We were not seafarers, us. We had enough with our great rivers. But once the seafarers came across the Great Ocean to visit us. I remember them well! They said they had followed the *jijie*—it is a kind of bird, I do not know if your language has a name for them—they fly out to sea, we know not where, and return to our jungles to nest and breed. The seafarers, the Keluléz they called themselves, followed them one day. They thought nothing of sailing across an ocean because they were curious where the birds went."

"They are a remarkable people," I agreed.

Tian's face fell. "They were conquered, then?"

It was too much to go into all the long and complicated history of Astandalan imperialism here, but I could answer that question, at least—Kip had ensured that! "They came as allies of the Emperor Aurelius Magnus, when a terrible war was being fought and he needed great sailors."

"They were a proud and merry people," Tian said. "I am glad to hear they have not failed."

"My vizier," there being no word for viceroy; but actually *vizier* might be a better term, and I wished we'd thought of it earlier, "is of that people. He is a great man."

Tian put the shell necklace back into its basket with gentle hands. "I am glad," he said simply.

"You will meet him one day," I promised, knowing how much Kip would appreciate a *free* people, and we went down to the feast.

17

IN WHICH WE CONSIDER MAPS

They had slaughtered what was probably one of the last large animals for the feast, though I was sorry to say that I had no idea what a *ahuacu* was. It tasted good roasted, anyway, even without salt.

Their music was very strange.

~

After the feast had finished, it was not yet sunset. Masseo and I returned to the guest-house accompanied by Tian, Bezal, and Bezal's attendant, along with Ezan and another man of about thirty who also spoke Antique Shaian. It had become evident over the course of the feast that fewer of the populace were fluent than I had thought at first.

In the downstairs room we settled at the table. Masseo made tea, his smokey caravan tea in the silver teapot, and I produced enough porcelain cups for everyone. I also pulled the maps of Zunidh out of my bag.

"These are beautiful," Masseo said, helping me to anchor the corners after I had unrolled the one showing what was called the Eastern Hemisphere. Solaara, a quarter of the world away, was the central point from which official directions were calculated. Kip always grumbled about Amboloyo being *east* when, as everyone knew, it was actually in the Far West. This is not an argument he has so far tried to make to anyone else yet, for good or for ill. Kip is very persistent when he gets an idea in his head.

"What are these?" Tian asked. Bezal was blind, of course, and the third, angriest elder, the one with the scarred face, had been so overcome by the breaking of the curse that he had gone home to recover, even to the point of missing the feast. I was not entirely convinced by this explanation, but let it go.

I explained what a map was, and the most basic concept of writing. Ezan came forward, eyes alight with curiosity, and pored over the fine parchment. (Maps, like important proclamations, were usually done on magically-imbued parchment rather than paper, preventing unlawful alteration or destruction.)

"So the designs represent words? Sounds?" he asked. "How ingenious! Like the marks the magicians use, but more useful."

"Exactly."

He was so visibly enthused by the whole concept that I eventually got out a notebook and a pen and wrote out the modern alphabet for him to study. It was just as well, I reflected as I explained the letters and their sounds, that he could skip over the entire long and complicated development from the ancient ideographs through the somewhat simplified hieratic scripts of the early Empire to the great spelling reforms of Dangora/Zangora V's time (I sometimes wondered if she had just preferred *Z* over *D* and the whole thing got out of hand; it wouldn't have been the first, nor the last, such occurrence), to the eventual relatively coherent semi-phonetic alphabet currently in use.

I didn't explain any of that. I just told him that A was for *ah*, and left out the fact that I had been informed it was currently taught with *A is for Artorin* by a smarmy educator who thought I would appreciate it. It would have been funnier if they had also used *F is for Fitzroy*.

Masseo eventually took Ezan over to a corner to teach him how to write phonetically, which was the sort of cross-cultural communication Kip would adore. Tian was examining the map with wonder. "These are the mountains?" he said, pointing at the jagged lines. "And this a river?"

It was a beautiful map, in strong black ink and delicately tinted colours. The rivers were shaded with blue, their names written in impossibly fine calligraphy along their curling lengths.

"Yes." I found Mosgul and pointed it out. "This is Mosgul, once Mae Osgilian." I walked my fingers across the plateaus between Mosgul and the Qavaliun Basin. It was remarkable that I had never before noticed how blank and empty this portion of the map was. And I hadn't. I had spent many hours with maps of Zunidh and other regions of the empire, as part of the Red Company and before and after, learning of far-off places I might or might not ever get to see, and yet ruled. Yet I had never noticed even in passing how there was a great blank spot between Central Damara and the New Sea where Kavanor had once been.

Even the name—Central Damara—had never suggested itself as strange. No one ever spoke of Southern Damara, for there was nothing there. Just the gorges, and the impenetrable and to all accounts uninhabited jungle, and then the westernmost coast of the Wide Seas that covered half of Zunidh.

Tian touched the spot where I had said Mosgul lay with hesitant fingers. Even to an untutored eye the blankness labelled only "the Qavaliun Basin" must be striking.

I looked seriously up at him and at Bezal, who lifted his blind eyes to meet mine, stone touching fire until both curled up purring like sibling cats.

"What do you want?" I asked them. "Do you wish to remove yourselves from the world, and be no more a part of Zunidh? I can shift the Borders to enclose you."

I did not *want* to—the world wished to stay entire, not lose any of its lands or native magics—but I *could*.

"Or?" Bezal said, unworried.

"Or I can draw you fully into the magic of the world, and rejoin you into the wider society. It is up to you."

"You have said you will help us without requiring us to become a part of your empire."

"My empire is gone. Yet the world has a government, built upon the foundations of the broken empire but not of it. I am even now on a quest to find my heir, as the Lady of the Peacock Throne quested, or Ialo before her, or …"

Bezal still looked very old, but a hale old, no longer as if he were about to collapse into dust and bones. He wheezed out a laugh. "Ah, so you are following the old tradition? It was old in our days; it must be truly ancient now. Odd that you would need to."

"I wanted to," I said, entirely honestly.

Tian laughed then too. Masseo looked up at us, at me, with a bright smile, then turned back to Ezan and the sounds that went with *o*.

They were stone-aligned, truth-telling and truth-hearing. I wasn't quite sure what to make of them laughing to hear me speak so honestly.

"Tell me more about this Keluléz seafarer to whom you entrusted your people," Tian requested, and so I told him about the brilliant, humble Kip, whose pride lay in submitting himself to his art. I spoke about the annual stipend and the tension between the central authority of the Palace and the regional princes, about education and opportunity and the length of time it had been since our last wars.

Tian and Bezal listened intently. And at the end Tian said, "You recognized the shell necklace of the Keluléz immediately. If your vizier can keep his culture so much his own, then we can trust you, and him, to let us be ourselves again."

"We will stand as your people, and your heir's," added Bezal.

"Ninety generations and nine you promised us; ninety generations and nine may your own name be known and beloved!"

I was glad he hadn't said anything about my line, which was nearly spent. "I thank you," I said gravely instead, and took up the pen loaded with the ink I used for formal proclamations. "Mae Irión is here," I said, pointing at a spot between the edge of the gorges and the confluence with the river Dimiter Mdang had called the Artorin.

Though after my earlier exertions my own power was at a low ebb, the magic of the world was eager and excited. It had waited at the old boundaries, piling up like water behind a dam, and rushed eagerly to me when I reached out to it. I pinched a thread of magic —like calls to like—and focused it on the map, visible representation of the world. This was the hybrid magic I had worked for so long, and even though I could feel something like an inward sigh from my magic, it came obediently to the summons.

I drew a tiny icon of a citadel and wrote *Mae Irión* as close to the accurate position as I could do without a team of surveyors and a dozen minor wizards. The magic surged through the room and then suddenly was *familiar*.

Bezal drew a sharp breath. He looked again younger, albeit still blind and his hands still shook. Tian asked him something in their own language, to which the elder shook his head. "All is well," he said firmly. "All is better than well."

"If you say so," said Tian, his eyes fierce as he regarded me,

I smiled at him and readied my pen. "Let me right my map. What is the name you give the rivers?"

"The Ghuerayo is our mother," Tian said, "and this great one coming from the north is the Huahualopo ..."

I spent the evening writing letters on behalf of the Mae Irionéz: several short explanatory ones to whomever they first encountered, briefly explaining the situation and requesting the recipient to accompany the ambassadors to the nearest university with a scholar of Antique Shaian; and a rather longer one to Kip.

As I didn't know when he might receive it, I confined my topic to the situation here and what I thought the broad outlines of a resolution should be. I had long since found that Kip worked best with an overarching directive and the freedom to achieve it according to his own ideas and intuition. He had satisfactorily created a stable and peaceful world government out of disparate and occasionally violent components, so I was sure he could handle this complex affair.

Even if it did involve creating a new self-governing province that was emphatically not to be subsumed under Amboloyo or Old Damara.

Oh, there was no doubt about it. He would be utterly *delighted* to do so. Kip is no friend of hereditary oligarchs, Prince Rufus of Amboloyo least of all.

Masseo watched me write for a while until he pulled out a small knife and a block of wood and began to whittle. His expression reminded me a great deal of Ludvic Omo, the commander of my guards, who was a stolid man of few words and great hidden poetry. He, too, whittled.

"What are you carving?" I asked as I folded the letters and dug in my bag for the special sealing wax that would, imprinted with the signet ring, ensure that the recipient knew this was a genuine letter from me.

He tipped the block of golden-brown wood towards me, showing the beginnings of a fish of some form. "Just playing," he said. "It's been a while since I last did anything like this, but I get antsy if I don't do something with my hands every day or two. You're probably the same with poetry?"

Antsy was one way of putting it.

"Yes," I agreed, thinking of how my near-complete inability to write, to create, had been the worst part of being Emperor of Astandalas. The enchantments on the position had forced me to suppress my own magic entirely, and with my magic so too, it seemed, had fled my muse. I had, with great effort, written a handful of sonnets through that period, in my precious daily half-hour of privacy in my tiny, nearly windowless study.

"Blacksmithing isn't a particularly good indoor activity," Masseo went on, "and I've enough fishing lures even for Gadarved and Faleron when we meet up with them."

"You're very confident," I observed, warming the sealing wax with a spark of magic.

"I am with you," he replied complacently. "I'm sure you have a plan."

I grinned at this very old joke. "I, a plan? Don't be absurd! I have a method."

He laughed. "My mistake."

We set off the next morning along one of the ancient roads. Tian told me that it had once led *somewhere*. They did not know the name of the world or even the nation who had lived there, only that it had closed down in the year of their curse. I suspected that even if *The Jifuréz* had meant anything to us that it wouldn't matter much, as apart from the four thousand certain years of intervening history there was also the Fall, which had rearranged many of the Borders, and however long since.

The road was similar to the one leading down from the falls, snugly fitted blocks of stone, once wide and smooth, now narrow with the encroaching greenery. Masseo and I were accompanied across the fields by a cheerful throng of Mae Irionéz until we reached an archway marking the end of the raised stone vegetable beds.

"This road led to the meeting-place," Tian told us. "We marked it with pillars. The passage used to be open at dawn of each day, for the length of time it took for the sun to clear the horizon. You should be able to reach the pillars before sunset tonight, and all going well, pass through tomorrow."

"Thank you," I said, sure that things would not be anywhere near so straightforward as that.

But what did that matter? The route I had found and marked was somewhere in the gorge system high above the Qavaliun (or rather Ghuerayo) basin, and neither Masseo nor I were keen to try the "old stair" that theoretically led up the cliff.

Anyway, now that the curse was lifted and I was becoming accustomed to the magic hereabouts I could feel a certain dissonance indicative of a Border passage ahead of us. My heart lifted at the thought. Soon the *real* adventure would begin.

"Farewell," Tian said gravely. "I hope to meet you again in your own place."

"I look forward to it," I replied, and after a few more formalities Tian bowed, I inclined my head regally in return, and Masseo and I left the crowd and entered the jungle.

It would be nice, I reflected, to have my *own* place, not a palace but a home.

I confess I cheated.

I had not recovered magically from the breaking of the curse, and as a result was deeply disinclined to holding my power in check. I was therefore radiating a certain low level of magic, which in other places and circumstances would have been a terrible idea —there are many things that find such displays greatly attractive— but here I walked on land newly reclaimed for Zunidh as Zunidh's lord magus.

Each step echoed magically, not binding the land but greeting it, welcoming it, reassuring it. The magic woke to my touch, eager and beneficent. Masseo was humming to himself, and I felt secure in letting my mind drift as I strode along, my stout stick thumping down pleasingly on the hard stone beneath the soft leaf-litter covering it, letting the magic get to know me.

Whatever dangers there might be in the unexplored jungle that had swallowed up half the river-basin, and I was certain there were many, man-eating tigers amongst them, nothing was likely to challenge a great mage in the course of his work.

As I said, cheating. That is not the way to have an adventure.

We stopped in a clearing for lunch. The path following the old road was clear if close-grown. Masseo had pulled out a machete from his bag (saying, a little shame-faced, that he had not thought to introduce the Mae Irionéz to iron and steel with such a useful object as a three-foot jungle knife) and struck at overhanging branches and vines. We saw many birds, heard the rustles of various small animals, and surprised a large green python sunning itself in a sunny gap, but otherwise the most noticeable evidence of fauna came from the sounds of a great multitude of insects.

It was hot and sticky walking, even at a relatively easy pace, and even with Masseo to clear the way and my magic to keep away the mosquitos. I was glad for the rest, and glad for the fresh fruit with which we had been supplied.

I peeled a pineapple carefully with a small knife. Masseo, halfway through his portion of the meal-cakes we'd also been given, regarded me with an expression that suggested he very much wanted to take it out of my hands and do the job more efficiently. I appreciated his restraint.

"You should have some of the cakes as well," he urged when I finally got to the point of cutting off chunks of pineapple to eat. "Not just fruit. They're not sweet."

It was easier to eat one or two of the bland, boring cakes than to argue or explain why the pineapple was so precious. It was not just the fact that it was fresh, and thus the greatest of luxuries to me who had had food taboos seemingly without end; it was that *I* had peeled it, I who had been ritually forbidden holding an edged blade for so long I had almost forgotten how to handle one.

I was not quite so circumscribed as Lord of Zunidh, but as Emperor nearly everything I touched had to be purified and ritually and magically acceptable within the network of enchantments. A knife, intended to cut and to harm, had very specific and terrible meanings within that context.

And despite many efforts on my part, even after the Fall most of those taboos had only been relaxed, not removed. No one was blinded for meeting my eyes, or killed by my touch; but only Kip ever dared meet them, and I had still permanently scarred the one person I had touched before the great purification in preparation for my quest.

"Shall we?" Masseo asked. "I think I hear water ahead, so we can wash our hands."

In other circumstances we might have had an adventure in that stream, where strange toothy fish swirled in ominous schools, but they were busy with the corpse of a pig-like animal that had fallen in downstream, and did not bother us.

We reached the circle of pillars after the sun had gone behind the mountains, but before night had fallen. The jungle had not encroached on the stone pavement between them. There was something eerie about the very emptiness, as if someone carefully tended the space and removed every weed or questing vine.

These pillars showed their age. They had been finely carved once, but the carvings were blurred and softened with the effects of time. A greenish scurf in the deeper grooves was all that delineated shapes.

We walked around the perimeter slowly. Every other pillar seemed to represent the Mae Irionéz and their kin: dolphins and tigers predominated, and long-tailed monkeys and something like an egret or ibis. Those were made of the dark stone of the roads and the outcroppings in the river.

The alternate pillars were a pale pink sandstone of a sort I had not seen anywhere local. They depicted elephants and horses and some sort of bear-like creature. I touched one of the pillars and felt a deep, quiescent link to a different world. "Ysthar," I murmured, for a moment tasting roses. I looked at the carvings, and this time saw the difference in the length and shape of the tusks, the height of the head, the suggestion of long fur. "Not elephants. Mammoths."

"Is that where it goes?" Masseo asked.

"Where it went, once upon a time. Now ..." We continued circling around. My magic was touching the magic here, waking up a slumbering enchantment. Sparks jumped from pillar to pillar.

Masseo said, "Fitzroy ..."

I smiled at him, the magic fizzing happily. "It still leads somewhere. It's waking up."

We completed the circuit and the stuttering, sparking magic steadied. It was still waiting for something: the best I could imagine it was a dancer reaching out for a partner who had not yet reached back. But there *was* a partner out there, a hand reaching back.

"It will open for us with the dawn," I said, feeling the circle's eagerness to fulfil its ancient function.

"And lead us where?"

"Our company was from each of the Nine Worlds," I reminded him. "It doesn't really matter, does it?"

"Sometimes I find your method discomfiting. Did you bring a tent in that remarkable bag of yours?'

I blinked at this non sequitur and had to think for a moment. Tents were not something on Conju's usual register; and I hadn't thought to ask him for one. (For a brief moment the picture of his face if I had done so warmed me greatly.) "I don't believe so. Did you?"

"You watched me do all my packing!"

237

"I don't think you should sound so superior. You had a spare anvil ready to go, but not a tent?"

Masseo set down his bag in the middle of the circle and gave me a familiar frown before still-unexpectedly erupting with laughter.

"And you had all those pillows! What we need is Jullanar. I bet *she* has a tent all packed and ready to go."

"She always was the most practical of us," I agreed. "Even you had your moments of divine carelessness."

He gave me a mocking bow. "Thank you!"

I sat down on a cushion I pulled out from my bag (and I did get him one as well, I assure you) and then pulled out a reasonable cache of firewood, as I hadn't come *entirely* unprepared for camping. Just … mostly.

18

IN WHICH WE THROW CAUTION TO THE WINDS

*I*t started to rain around midnight.

As we'd gone to bed shortly after full dark and I'd slept my usual amount, I was half-awake, dreamily watching the magic moving in and around and through the pillars.

We'd set up our blankets and pillows in the middle of the space, somewhat to Masseo's concern. I had assured him that magically it was the most neutral spot, better than being either on the outside or near the edge. He'd muttered something about *ancient places of magic* before brightening and noting that I was, myself, an *ancient being of magic*, and thus he probably didn't need to worry.

For all that I regularly spend a third of each day working magic, great magic, I had not experienced such wild and impetuous forces as this week in so many years. The circle of pillars was as intoxicating as the sky forest had been.

The rain began with a fine sifting mist, then before I had even sat up suddenly transitioned to full tropical downpour. It was entirely unexpected. The orderly magic of Solaara, like Astandalas before it, ensured rain fell at night, and never when it might inconvenience *me*. It was night now, obviously, but I had barely *seen* rain since my time with the Red Company, only on that one holiday to the Vangavaye-ve, and the thought of it never crossed my mind.

It took me a few moments to raise a canopy sufficient to protect us. By that point Masseo had woken up, and looked at me with sleepy displeasure.

"You're really not quick off the mark, are you?" he said.

I frowned at him, wanting to protest, but it was true. "I'm out of practice," I said, perhaps a little grudgingly. And I was still magically exhausted: that small effort, which should have been hardly more taxing than shooing away the mosquitos, left me feeling quivery.

He rubbed his face, grimacing at the water that ran down his arm, and reached over to stir up the coals and mend the fire. It sputtered from the rain, but had not entirely gone out.

"Not with magic, surely? You were splendid with that curse."

I wondered about siphoning off the water, but that's the sort of magic that tends to end disastrously where I'm concerned, even without the over-exertion. It was much more likely that I would set our belongings on fire than dry them off.

"No small magics, quick responses. It's all been carefully regulated great workings for me."

The fire stirred sluggishly. I could help with that, at least, a magic entirely instinctual, and even remembered to wait until he had withdrawn his hands before I helped the new wood catch.

"Thank you," he said, and helped me shake out our bedding. Most of the water seemed to have beaded up and run off, and I truly did have a more than ample sufficiency of pillows and blankets, so was able to provide us with a new set, arranging the others in proximity to the fire to dry off.

Masseo watched me settle down on a new down pillow enclosed in what seemed to be a sumptuous dark purple velvet. "How many pillows do you normally sleep with?"

"I can't say I've counted them recently. Three or four, I suppose." I visualized my bed. "Perhaps six."

"Six!"

"Why, how many do you have?"

He was laughing now. "One."

"How restrained of you."

The fire was burning brightly and cast off a goodly warmth. The air was not cold, but the dowsing had chilled me and the fire felt lovely. The magic was moving more quickly as the world turned towards morning.

"You've changed a lot," Masseo said.

I wanted to say, *So have you*, but I just looked at him, his face softly illuminated by the firelight. He smiled crookedly.

"Like that: exactly like that. When would you have *ever* let an opening like that go without a return comment?"

He stretched out on his blankets and cushions, still watching me, the light dancing in his eyes. I stayed where I was, thinking that even if I didn't particularly like the old eating couch style, it was good to know how to recline on one elbow in situations like these.

"It's not bad," he said, a note of concern creeping into his voice. "Merely … different. That you're so calm and collected now."

Serene, my inner, sarcastic voice commented. I could have said it aloud: there were no guards or servants or courtiers or flunkies or attendants or ministers here, just a dear friend. But my tongue would not move. His hilarity and disbelief at discovering me an emperor of Astandalas was too fresh.

Masseo shifted and looked into the fire. I could see he was smiling. In so many ways it was a lovely change. He had been so dour.

"You're much happier."

He rolled over onto his back, looking up at where my invisible canopy blocked the rain, the firelight catching the water in sheets of gold. "You're not going to go back to sleep, are you?'

"I've slept my usual amount."

He sighed, a put-on sigh that made me smile. My wrist had started to throb so I lay down, stretching out on my back, mirroring his position. I felt oddly vulnerable, the magic moving below us, reaching out beyond the bounds of the world, the dark jungle shadowy and invisible beyond the circle of pillars, the sky opaque. The air moved softly around us, bearing fine droplets of water at times, and the green, musky scent of the jungle.

Masseo's voice came quietly, meditatively, out of the dark.

"That last night in the Silver Forest ... The magic leapt up suddenly, at least as far as I was concerned. We were waiting for you to come back from the river. It was such a strange place ... all silver and brown. I'd expected it to be like the Moon's country, but it wasn't. It was magical, but a different sort of magic."

Ancient Shaian magic not dissimilar from that on this land, woven in and through with later developments of Schooled magic. That forest was one of the great protections around Astandalas, silently guarding the once-vulnerable northern approach to the city and (as I found out later) housing in its innermost groves a summer palace for the Imperial family.

"There was something like an earthquake, though I don't remember if the ground actually moved or if it just felt as if it had. Like a ripple through the world, as if the trees and land were nothing more than reflections or those illusions you used to do. We all looked at each other, and I remember that Pharia took a step towards Damian and then—she wasn't *there*. Just gone. He stepped towards her, crying her name, and he hadn't even finished speaking when *he* disappeared.

"I was sitting on my pack while I undid my bootlaces, so I grabbed it. By then it was clear something had happened. I looked across the camp at Sardeet even as Gadarved and Pali and Ayasha all disappeared. She smiled at me, and I remember thinking it wasn't a sad expression, even though I knew it was the end—I don't know why but I did—and she said, 'He will come back as unexpectedly as he has left. Until we meet again—fare well!' And even as I was thinking, of course, this was something to do with you, she was gone."

The canopy above me was blurring. I squinted my eyes shut against the bright reflections. How many times had I wondered what they had thought, in those final moments when the Silver Forest was roused against them?

"Masseo," I said, but my voice cracked.

"Hush," he said, gently. "I'm speaking now."

That had been a joke, older than Masseo's friendship even. Jullanar used to say it in exasperation and then as a joking-but-serious indication that I was interrupting too often, too excited to listen, too ... *much*.

"Jullanar and I were the last ones. It seemed it was taking a step that caused everyone to disappear, so we gathered everything we could reach without moving, and then Jullanar said to me, bravely, 'See you on the other side!'—and—and she was gone. And then it was just me, and I took a breath and stepped and ... and then I was in far western Voonra."

The Silver Forest protections, once roused, dispersed any enemies randomly across the breadth of the Empire.

"I suppose I could have looked for the others, but Sardeet was a bit of a Seer, you remember, and there was something in the way she said *Farewell*, and the way the magic felt, and the way ... we'd been arguing quite a bit, that last month or two, hadn't we? We'd been a little *too* successful. We were entering our thirties, well, except for Ayasha and Gadarved who were already older, and I know Pharia and Damian were wanting to settle down, at least. But you were so adamantly adventurous ..."

I had somehow forgotten those arguments. I dug my fingers into the velvet and silk of the cushions under me. The textures, even the scents rising from the fabric, were familiar. I could have been lying on my bed in the Palace, staring up at the canopy, drapes shutting out sight of my attendants though they could hear me and I them.

A breeze swirled over my hot face and brought with it the definitely outdoor odour of the jungle, green and growing and muck and something creamy and warm, like vanilla or chocolate, some night-blooming flower. And it was Masseo I could hear breathing, not Pikabe or Ato or Zeraphin or any of the others, and beneath the velvet and the silk were not the smooth antique linens of my sheets but a thin mat and below that stone.

The magic pressed close.

"I suppose," Masseo went on thoughtfully, "that I had always felt that being part of the Red Company was a gift—a reprieve—it never seemed quite *real*, though it was also the most real part of my life. Everything about it was so absurdly extravagant. ... Once I was by myself again it felt like a dream, and I was awake in the real world again.

"I didn't go looking. I wandered around the hinterlands of western Voonra for a while. It was a place I'd never been to before, strange and wonderful in many ways, though very insular and suspicious of strangers. I acquired some tools and a pony-cart and became a travelling farrier and blacksmith, going from village to village plying my trade. It wasn't exciting work, by any means, but it took a long time to adjust to being just *Tika Smith*, as they called me there, no one special at all, not *Masseo Umrit of the Red Company*, hero of a dozen songs and participant in many, many more.

"It was a happy time, those years before the Fall. Artorin Damara was a good emperor, as far as those things go."

"Thank you," I said dryly.

He chuckled.

I wished I understood what he thought I *did* mean by these comments.

"I was in Voonra during the Fall. Where I was, it mostly took the form of a series of earthquakes, and the collapse of anything that had been built by magic. One building would dissolve into bricks and mortar dust, the next one to it would be perfectly fine except for the plumbing having melted and run out of the building ... some roads and bridges were fine, other times the rivers themselves had been diverted with magic and they ran backwards or upside down or turned all the fish in them into air-breathers. There are places there where fish come swimming through the air towards you. It was all very odd.

"I worked where I was, a city called Vaelorjel, to help with the reconstruction, rebuilding a town, a country, a world. It was hard but satisfying work … lots for a smith to do." He fell silent for a few moments, and when he continued his voice was softer, regretful. "I had a neighbour, a widow. She was very lovely and took a fancy to me. It should have been—"

He stopped, took an audible breath, and started again. "It should have been simple. I loved her dearly, and she returned my affections, but … when it came to the point of courting, I … couldn't. How was I to tell her that I had been lying the whole time? Or that … Fitzroy, do you know where I'm from?"

"You never said," I replied.

"That wasn't what I asked you."

I lay there for a while. "I was under an enchantment that prevented me from telling you, from telling anyone, who I truly was. You were all so kind about letting me keep my secrets. I knew from the magic that you were born on Zunidh, but that's it. I never quite figured out your accent."

"I always wondered why you never pressed about that, when you were willing to ask impudent questions about literally everything else. I took it as you being raised with rather different social mores than normal people."

"That was true enough."

The fire crackled. Something beyond the circle of firelight, beyond the pillars, made a deep *hurr hurr* noise. I touched the magic and felt a wash of reassurance. Whatever it was meant us no harm.

Masseo seemed to be focused on his own thoughts, for he made no indication he'd heard anything. I felt obscurely pleased I'd noticed something he hadn't. Then I remembered he was not one of my guards, that we were *equals*, and that I too had my responsibilities for his safety.

"I am from Zunidh," he said into the quiet. "The Azilint. It doesn't matter where exactly."

His voice made it clear it did matter, and also that he wasn't going to tell me.

The Azilint is an archipelago off the eastern coast of Southern Dair, mountainous and well-forested. The islands tend to be large, but they are so craggy that communication across ridges has always been difficult and it is specific valleys that hold identity. The Azilinti were not at all related to the Wide Sea Islanders, but they shared something of the fierce local pride.

People from the Azilint said: *I am so-and-so from such-and-such village. The head of my carving is such-and-such.* If pressed, they would name their valley, then their mountain, and finally, reluctantly, their island. And when they had done so it was always clear that the island was so fundamental a part of their identity that they could barely conceive of being unattached to it. Most Azilinti carried long wooden staffs, carved with the emblems of their place and their own doings. Each island had its own particular wood that no one else would use.

"When I was a very young man," Masseo said, "I was infatuated with a girl in my village. We fancied ourselves in love— perhaps we were. We thought our passions strong enough, pure enough, to protect us from all the social censure. We were caught, of course."

The cultures of Zunidh are, and always have been, many and various. Some had no issues with any form of sex, so long as all parties consented; others held much stricter views, down to those for whom it was only within the specific bonds of marriage that it was acceptable.

Clearly Masseo's village was one of the stricter ones. I knew some horrifically strong laws from the Azilint. Sexual crimes were almost always punished as harshly as possible, often with execution. Not that I condoned rape or assault in any form, but some of the Azilinti islanders held very narrow ideas of what forms of attraction were permissible, and it had required a great deal of effort to persuade them not to execute out of hand two men or two women who loved each other. They were still usually exiled, but at least they could fashion a life for themselves.

"I was sixteen, and legally a man," Masseo said. "She was fifteen, and legally a child. According to our laws, it was rape."

I curled my fingers until my nails pressed through the cloth onto the hard stone, and willed my heart to stop stuttering. Somehow, in all the years we had travelled with each other, this had never come up.

His voice was flat. I felt the magic pause, listening. I would have been worried if I had not known Masseo for ten years, and seen him in his village more recently, for wakeful magic *judges*, and answers like to like. What door opened for us at dawn would be a response to this midnight confession.

"The village convened a council. The law stated that rapists were executed, thrown over the cliff to be eaten by sharks. They knew it was mutual, consensual; that we had thought it love. But they knew that I knew it was wrong, that we should have waited a year, that we should have been married. … They decided that I was no longer and nevermore would be a part of their village. They stripped my family name from me, broke my staff, and cast me out in exile. *Umrit* means no-name."

In those dozens of songs I had written about him, about the Red Company, I named him thus. Masseo Umrit: a name known even to the halls of heaven.

"They tried to be merciful, in their own way. They did not kill me; and they did not refuse me my first name. The last thing my father said to me was that I would never again be a son of his, but that perhaps I could one day be a man."

I would have expected his voice to be savage, but although it was flat the pain seemed muted. I listened carefully. I am considered a good judge of character; and I remembered that dour, unhappy journeyman blacksmith outside his master's forge, who shoed our horses and looked so wistfully at us when I spontaneously invited him along to adventure.

He had come, all the way to the divine lands on the other side of the Sea of Stars, where we dallied in the Moon's garden and drank honey-wine from the meads of the Sun.

"I had nothing, knew nothing, was nothing. I was so angry and lost. I fled, stowed away on the first ship I found, stole food and money ... found myself falling further and further into crimes I would never have imagined myself able to commit, a month before. I hated myself more and more, but what else was I to do?"

If that happened nowadays—and I was not so certain it did not, could not, happen, in the Azilint or elsewhere—there was the annual stipend. A net to catch one falling, whoever and wherever they were.

Back then there had been nothing except the kindness of strangers, and a strong young man fallen into crime would not be considered a worthy recipient of kindness.

"Along the way I stole from a man who caught me. He was a blacksmith, a hard man, and he said that he would exact every ounce of bread and every penny of coin from me in hard work."

He was silent for long enough that I ventured a question. "You stayed?"

"I didn't have any choice. He chained me to the anvil for the first six months."

That startled me into laughing. "Really? Surely that was illegal even in Eritanyr's day."

"No one cared. My master paid his taxes and no one liked him much, but he was a talented smith and reckoned a most upright man. Six months incarcerated for petty thievery *was* legal punishment, and the local authorities didn't mind him feeding me in return for heavy labour. And it was heavy, fourteen, fifteen hours a day. For the first two months I was so tired all the time I couldn't think. And then, as I started to get used to the work, and my muscles developed, I discovered I ... liked it. It was something I could *do*. At the end of the six months, when my master unchained me, I asked him to take me on as a formal apprentice."

His voice quirked. "He was an even harder master when I was free than when I'd been chained to his anvil. But I learned a great deal from him. He was exceedingly moral in a narrow way, very much *this is right* and *that is wrong*, nothing in the middle. Either the work was done right, or it was done again until it was. Nothing less than that. Either the iron held, or it shattered and was reforged until it was strong again. He reforged me."

"Until one day Damian and Jullanar and Pali and I came gallivanting along—"

"And showed me how bright the soul could be. How bright *I* could shine. You wrote all those wonderful songs about me, about us, and gave me—oh, Fitzroy, you gave us all the means and the opportunity to be *great*. Most of us don't start where you did, you know, or Damian or Pali. Jullanar and I used to talk about it. We needed to be pushed."

I had my own thoughts about Jullanar, who was my very first friend and did more to support my following of my vocation than Masseo or possibly even she herself knew, but the creature out beyond the circle of pillars made its *hurr hurr* noise again and I remained silent, listening.

Masseo sighed. "I tried to become a man my father might have been proud to have for his son, but I could never forgive them for casting me out, killing me in every way except the final one. I can *understand* it, but I could never accept it."

He breathed hard for a few moments before he collected himself enough to continue.

"When Larima, the Voonran widow, talked to me about courting, I realized that I had misconstrued the friendship I had valued so much, and I—I had never told her that I was Masseo Umrit of the Red Company, and I don't think she ever guessed. I am not so flamboyant as you.

"No one is as flamboyant as you, not even Sardeet, and she tried. Oh, Fitzroy, I have missed you so!" His voice wavered, then he continued. "I couldn't tell Larima the truth—I wasn't brave enough—and I couldn't stay, not when I had hurt her so despite my good intentions. I left, travelling again, but this time not happily. I was pursued by the ghosts I thought I had long since laid to rest.

"Eventually I stumbled through a passage between the worlds. I was lost in the Borderwood for a while—I will have to tell you about that another time—and eventually I found myself on Zunidh. I wanted badly to go home, but it was a permanent exile. They would have turned their backs on me, pretended I was invisible, ignored me. I was no son of theirs. *No-name of no-where.* When I came out of the gorges—"

"What!" I exclaimed. "You knew where to go?"

"You were having so much fun I didn't feel like I should say anything."

I spluttered a bit, glad to have lightened the moment however briefly. Masseo's voice was less flat when he continued. "I came out in Stolkitz, a village on the lower plateau, and heard about the Mother of the Mountains. I was heartsick and so tired of not being true to myself. I went up as a petitioner and told her everything."

"Everything?"

"Everything. About all the things I'd done as a young man, about being part of the Red Company, everything. I told her at the beginning that I would accept whatever penance she gave me. If she turned me in to the authorities, so be it. I would go up before the Lord Emperor with my head high, if that was what she decided."

He had never come up before me; I had never had that test.

"Obviously she had a different penance in mind."

"Yes. She listened to it all, and at the end she told me that I had served my time with my master smith for the petty crimes I had committed beforehand, and I had been punished enough by my village for their laws and those of the Empire.

"As for being a member of the Red Company, she said that as I had spent seven years—at least according to official records—as the infamous, even notorious, wanted criminal Masseo Umrit, then I should serve twice seven years anonymously in penance. And so *Master Smith* I became, and gave no other name. Kenna came along at the end of the first seven years and I accepted her as my apprentice, hoping that when her and my seven-year terms were up that something would change."

"When were they up?" I asked.

There was humour in his voice as he replied. "That's why I wasn't packed yet. You were two days early."

He fell asleep again. I felt thoroughly rested, and spent the rest of the night watching the fire burn down. The sky began to lighten incrementally. The rain had stopped, and a silvery mist was rising.

The magic stirred eagerly in its dance. I was about to waken Masseo when I heard the creature utter its *hurr hurr* a third time.

Out of the mist came the soft padding of a very large cat. It circled around the pillars, a shape of soft ashes-over-embers orange and black. When it came close enough I saw that it was a tiger.

It was truly enormous.

The magic pressed hard against me. I stood up slowly, as gracefully as I could, maintaining eye contact. This was a being as ancient and powerful as the Tigara.

"Good morning," I said quietly.

The tiger stopped just before it crossed between two pillars. Its eyes were almost exactly the same colour as the coals I had been staring into.

"Good morning," it replied at last. Its voice was a deep, velvety rumble, as attractive and as perilous as its fur. I wanted to sink my hands into that fur, feel the great cat's heart beating against my skin. Nothing I had ever encountered before—not even the great bronze bells made out of the hammers of Aurdar—had ever felt so deeply and incontestably *Zunidh*.

It said nothing else: just watched me for a long, long moment. The magic crowded close and exuberant, sparkling just below visible sight. At last the tiger made its *hurr hurr* sound again and with silent steps disappeared back into the jungle. My last sight of it was the tip of a flame-and-black tail twitching aside a curl of mist.

I let out a deep sigh as the magic ran after it and then subsided, like a wave cresting and falling away.

Masseo said, "What was that all about?"

I looked down at him. Somewhere beyond the mist the Sun had nearly reached our horizon.

"A visitor," I said. "Come: it's nearly sunrise."

He shook his head and quickly helped me gather up our assorted cushions and other belongings. The mist swirled, catching lights from other worlds, partners reaching out. Masseo stood next to me over the ashes of our nearly-extinguished fire, looking from pillar to pillar.

"Which do we take?"

I took a deep, slow breath in, tasting the air, the magic, the faintest hint of musk lingering from the great tiger. The magic sang in my senses, reaching out hands to the hands reaching back. I felt the magic of all the worlds swirling towards us, even far-distant Eahh and Kaphyrn.

"It's up to you," I said, knowing it was true. He had made his confession in the dark of the night: now it was time to see where that led.

He looked uncertainly at me, then around the circle of pillars. In the unseen distance the sun was rising. The magic swirled more strongly, the wind picking up and the mist whirling around us. Each gap between two pillars was a gateway to another world.

"That one," Masseo said at last, gesturing to the one the tiger had visited. "If—"

He stopped. Light was streaking the sky, magic woken fully, bright sunlight leaping from pillar to pillar in a net of power. The gateway he had chosen glowed a fine bright silver-gold, like the line of the sun on the sea.

"Excellent choice," I said, taking him gingerly by the arm and stepping forward just as the sun crested the horizon and the magic pulsed into dazzling brilliance.

And then we were gone.

III

AN EVENTFUL MIDSUMMER DAY

19

IN WHICH THERE IS A CHANCE ENCOUNTER

We stepped from steaming jungle to cool temperate woodland, and before we could catch our bearings were immediately run into by a young man.

We all fell over, Masseo, the young man, and I. Masseo had still been holding one of the cushions, and he sprawled over it, a study in old-gold and brown and bronze against green, green grass.

"Stop smiling at the picture we make, Fitzroy," he said crossly.

The young man stopped spluttering apologies and gasped.

There might be other people named Fitzroy in the Nine Worlds —in fact, I would be considerably surprised if there weren't—but it was highly unlikely this young man would think of that when confronted by two men stepping out of nowhere in front of him.

I sighed extravagantly and pushed myself up, not immediately remembering to avoid using my still-sore wrist. I was not graceful rising; it's not something I do often; but I managed without too much trouble. Masseo and the young man scrambled up rather more quickly, and we regarded each other for a brief, anticipatory moment.

The young man was perhaps twenty or a bit older, rather short, lean, with disheveled dark brown hair and intelligent brown eyes. He was pale-skinned, lightly tanned, and I could see the wild remnants of a quite extraordinary array of magic still lingering about him. He was dressed in dusty, useful clothing, blue and brown hose and tunic, and carried nothing. His glance was skittering back and forth from Masseo to me, obviously going through the members of the Red Company in his mind to figure out which one Masseo must be.

"We're on Alinor," I informed Masseo, and smiled brilliantly at the young man. "Where precisely do we find ourselves?"

His face lit with a shy, delighted smile. "Where *precisely*? We are beside the Dragon Stone on the Greenway running from Dartington to the old Imperial Highway, in the southernmost barony of the duchy of Fiellan in the kingdom of Rondé."

"Thank you," I said gravely, and looked around curiously. It was, I took it, summer: the trees were in full green leaf and the birds were singing. The air, while cool compared to the jungle we had just left, was warm and bore the hint of coming heat. It was just past dawn here as well, a sparkling morning.

We were standing on a level green bridleway that ran straight off in one direction between two high hedges, full trees behind them. The other direction contained a constructed reflecting pool, circular in shape and edged with dark grey stone coping, in the middle of which were two rough-hewn stones, one vertical and the other lying flat just above water level. It appeared we had walked through the gap between the hedges where they widened to encircle the pool.

I turned back to the young man. "Do you know why it is called the Dragon Stone?"

"Not exactly," he answered readily, if disappointingly. "Though I can tell you that the Green Dragon is the name of the public house yonder, at the end of the Greenway, and that when a dragon came out of the Woods Noirell last year, I encountered it here, perching on those stones as if they were made for it. More usually we understand that they are sacred to the Lady of the Green and White—particularly in her aspect as Lady of Summer."

This was more intriguing, and also set some distant memories waking. Someone had mentioned something about a dragon in Northwestern Oriole to me, not very long ago ...

Masseo said, "What did you do, encountering it?"

The young man flushed, which he did magnificently. There is something about the ability of pale-skinned people to blush all shades of pink and scarlet that delights me inordinately. In the past I often did my best to provoke Damian, who was blond as a sunbeam, and Jullanar, who blushed at almost everything.

The young man said, a little quickly, "At that time it gave me a riddle, which I set about answering. Then—"

The memory unfurled. "Aha!" I cried, interrupting his continued explanation. "Are you Jemis Greenwing?"

The young man startled severely. His voice came out in a squeak. "Er—what—how did—that is—Yes?"

Well, it is not every day that Fitzroy Angursell unexpectedly knows who you are.

Although in truth this was something I knew as Artorin Damara, Last Emperor of Astandalas and Lord of Zunidh. That would probably discombobulate him even more, if such a thing were possible.

I beamed at him; behind him, Masseo had rolled his eyes and was now grinning in amusement.

"Yes: you attended Morrowlea, if I understand correctly?"

If anything, Jemis Greenwing looked even more astonished. "I did, yes. How—" He cleared his throat as his voice squeaked again. "Er, excuse me, sir. How do you know?"

Very rarely, there is a guest of sufficient rank to sit beside me at a table who is also a great conversationalist. The Chancellor of Morrowlea was one such, and she had chosen to tell me a tale about her students that was not as tall as it seemed.

I replied with blithe airiness. "I had a lovely conversation not long ago with Lady Rusticiana, the Chancellor of Morrowlea, and she told me all about you and your doings." I looked at Masseo, who gamely tried to straighten his face. "Young Mr. Greenwing here slew the dragon—with a bread knife, I understood?"

"A cake knife," the young man muttered.

"The details are critical," I agreed solemnly. "Are you related to that Jack Greenwing who received the Heart of Glory?"

"My father," he said, with commendable pride.

"An extraordinary man. What are your mother's people?"

Jemis Greenwing said, "My mother was the only child of the Marchioness of the Woods Noirell. My mother died some years ago, but my grandmother lives."

One thing I was very well educated in was the manifold titles of my extensive demesne. Why I needed to know all of them when I was intended for a life in isolated exile I never understood as a boy; but learn them I did.

Admittedly, most of the time it was in punishment for some misdeed or other.

By the time I was sixteen I had memorized the entirety of the nine-volume *Manual of Imperial Titles and Honorifics*.

I well remembered his grandmother from her days at court, where the rumours were that she was much subdued from her debut in the Empress Anyoë's day. I gave him a commiserating nod. "That sort of witch never dies."

He appeared scandalized but also in agreement, and ventured, "Er, you've met?"

"I would very much doubt that she has any idea it was *I*," I said, most truthfully. "You, I believe, would therefore be the Viscount St-Noire."

"I prefer Mr. Greenwing."

"Morrowlea continues radical, then? I entirely approve."

"Yes," said Mr. Greenwing, looking as if he found himself greatly daring, "I do suppose *you* would."

"Indeed! Now: you have situated us admirably with respect to the two ends of this ancient turf road, and that within the wider context of the barony, but it has been many years since I last passed this way—unless you are familiar with it, Masseo?"

Masseo shook his head, mirth brimming in his eyes as Mr. Greenwing mouthed *Masseo Umrit* to himself with obvious wonder.

"I don't know your intended destination," Mr. Greenwing began.

"Oh, that is far ahead of us yet," I assured him.

"I ... see."

"Most perspicacious of you. We are headed more immediately towards Stoneybridge."

His eyes glimmered with understanding. "You can get there by taking the road to Chare that leads southeast from the Coombe, south of town. Er, sir, if I may say so—if you go past the stones to the highway and turn south, that is, left, you will shortly come to a road leading west, which will take you to Ragnor Bella, the local town. It's market-day and the first day of the Midsomer Assizes today: I will be there later."

"We could do with replenishing a few supplies," I acknowledged.

"You will not find it far out of your way—you can take the road leading out of town through Ragglebridge and it will lead you to the crossroads that takes you to the Coombe."

"Even better."

He bit his lip. "There's a bookstore in town that I think you would very much like to see, sir. It's called Elderflower Books—"

My attention sharpened instantly. I knew someone from Fiellan whose great ambition had been to open a bookstore by that name. "*Is* it now? And is its owner a woman, by any chance? A little shorter than you, I think, somewhat comfortable of figure, with flyway gingery-mouse hair, freckles, and a tendency to be much more incisive than she looks?"

Jemis Greenwing burst out laughing. "You do know her!"

"My oldest friend," I proclaimed. "Does she still make those most excellent gingersnaps?"

"Yes—"

I clapped Masseo on the shoulder. "Come! We must away! Adventures await. I thank you for your directions and your advice, Mr. Greenwing. In return—" I wove the most egregious tatters of magic into a more coherent pattern, flicked off the lingering remnants of three distinct curses and two separate enchantments (I was going to have to ask Jullanar about *that*), and finally said, "Shall I write a song about your dragon-slaying?"

His eyes were nearly glowing with excitement; his voice squeaked again. "Yes! Er, I mean—yes, please, sir, thank you!"

"I assume I can get the details from my friend," I said, and inclined my head in dismissal. "I am sure we shall meet again: till then, speed well!"

Masseo said nothing until we were on the other side of the round pool. Looking back, we could see that Jemis Greenwing was still staring after us, though when he saw us looking he lifted his hand in acknowledgement and then set off running back the other direction. Then Masseo said, "How *do* you do it?"

"Do what?" I pulled my walking stick out of my bag and then said, "Actually, I think I'd like to take advantage of this pool and wash my face."

"In the sacred pool: why not?"

"I'm sure the Lady of Summer won't begrudge me a splash of water. Anyhow, what do you mean?"

"How can you get *me* to pick our route, and manage to bring us out so we land more or less on top of Jullanar's protégé?"

I set my bag down on the stone coping and thought about what outfit I should put on for the momentous events about to occur. I grinned at Masseo.

"Oh, it's a gift. What do you think? The blue or the red?"

"You don't even have anything in your hands—oh, very well! The red!"

"Excellent choice," I said, and pulled out a set of knee-length robes in embroidered crimson silk. Then I cursed mildly, for I had forgotten to dry out my splendid new boots properly after all.

~

It took us about an hour to walk to the town. Mostly this was due to a minor blister I had contracted the day before from my sandals. The boots chafed in a different place, which was moderately preferential, but I did explain to Masseo that I would need to buy socks once we arrived at the market.

"You didn't bring enough with you?"

"I haven't worn socks since before the Fall. My costumier did her best, but a dozen pairs isn't enough, is it?"

"Not when it comes to you, no. Tell me about your costumier."

I eyed him, but his expression was gently encouraging, neither mocking nor credulous.

Perhaps he was not wrong to think that all confidence men and fraudsters had costumiers, too. I knew from our past activities that it is not simply emperors and folk heroes who can have a certain iconography about them.

And so I told him about Lady Ylette, who was exceedingly talented and concealed a tyrannical disposition behind her perfectly-coiffed petite frame. The description of how she'd chased Kip around half the Palace to design a new court costume had Masseo wheezing with laughter, which I confess was deeply satisfying. Even with his new, brighter demeanour, it was still a challenge to make him laugh outright.

It was a beautiful morning. The Greenway was very pleasant to walk on, springy turf underfoot, with the birds singing and flowers blooming in the verges. It was too early for the Green Dragon Public House to be open, so (a little ruefully) we decided to forgo breakfast until we reached the town. The Imperial Highway was in excellent repair, if a little dustier than it would have been in times gone by.

"It's surprisingly quiet for a market day," I observed. The highway was also nearly empty, but for a distant carter well ahead of us.

"All the vendors will have been setting up since before dawn, I expect," Masseo pointed out. "Is that the road?"

There was a sign pointing to *Ragnor Bella, 2* ("Miles, do you think?" "It's unlikely to be Collian leagues"). This road was beaten earth, dusty but with mud lingering in the deeper ruts from earlier rain. It led down at a long slant across the face of a slope towards a river-valley where we could see a cluster of houses gathered in the spit of land between the confluence of two rivers. A flock of pigeons wheeled over the slate and thatched roofs.

The brow of the hill afforded a fine prospect of the whole area. I looked around, orienting myself according to maps I vaguely remembered from years past. I couldn't remember the name of the undulating, thickly forested hills in the west, but the mountains to the south and east were the Crosslains. The Imperial Highway we had just left went straight south: once it had passed through a permanent gateway between worlds and led to Astandalas the Golden.

The sky was blue, with a multitude of small white clouds scudding across on a stiff upper wind. Down here it was just on the cusp between breezy and windy, making the temperature just about perfect. The trees tossed their leaves gaily, multitudes of pennons in every shade of green. Down below us the rivers sparkled silver.

"Well?" Masseo said.

"Well, indeed," I replied, smiling, and we set off down the hill.

~

I liked Ragnor Bella immediately, though I probably would have gone mad in short order had I been obliged to live there.

We crossed into the town proper over a humpbacked bridge, after which the road became cobbled. From our approach it had been clear that, like many towns in this part of Alinor, Ragnor Bella was arranged along a central spine of a main road, with a series of wider squares in front of the principal buildings.

As we climbed up the cobbled street we began to see people, in twos and threes, most of them also heading towards the centre. They looked askance at us, taking in our foreign clothing and whispering to their companions, but no one asked any questions.

The market square itself was busy. We came out surprisingly near the bookstore, which we only realized because of how overwhelmingly busy its doorway was. I glanced at Masseo, who said, "Breakfast first?"

"Let's," I agreed, and we circled around the slightly less thronged perimeter of the square. The stalls in the centre seemed to be organized in rough lines radiating out from a fountain set next to a tall carved stone pillar on a plinth. The pillar had a shield on its top, which presumably bore the town's coat of arms, or perhaps the barony's if the town didn't warrant one.

We found the bakery nearly opposite the bookstore, in a permanent building with pleasant mullioned windows and a propped-open door. Though there was a queue, any initial morning rush of customers seemed to have died down.

We joined the end of the line, occasioning another surge of murmurs, and regarded the variety of breads and other pastries on offer. The baker seemed to be talented: a full dozen different shapes and sizes of bread were piled up on shelves along the back wall, and the front, glassed-in counter, had another dozen of pastries. All of them were unfamiliar and all appeared delicious; but then we were both rather famished by this point.

"It occurs to me," Masseo said as we shuffled up a few steps in the wake of a woman who had bought a large sackful of plump round loaves, "that I don't have any Alinorel money."

"Oh! I do," I said, remembering, and reached into my bag for the little purse Aelian had given me so long ago. (All of three days, was it?) I tipped a few coins into my hand and gave them to Masseo.

He accepted them with bemusement. "Do I want to know where you got this from?"

"The post office in your village, as it happens," I returned blithely.

"Did you really—the stipend?" He began to snicker. "You *didn't*! Did you put down your actual name?"

"My legal one, anyway," I replied off-handedly. "It wouldn't take nicknames."

Masseo sighed gustily, his face creased with good humour. (I really *did* like this light-hearted Masseo; to think he had been holding all that remorse in his heart before!) "Do you even know where these coins are from?"

I examined the ones I held. My own face stared back at me, serene, rather handsomer than in reality, and apparently humour-less. "Somewhere in the old Empire, at any rate."

Two young boys scampered off with an iced roll each, the scent of cinnamon wafting back in their wake. We moved forward another two steps, and I smelled the delicious aroma of coffee.

I inhaled deeply. I prefer tea, as any right-thinking aristocrat should, but the scent of good coffee is glorious. And it was prob-ably unlikely I should find the former here; I was fairly certain the last round of trade negotiations between Alinor and Zunidh had involved the question of the Ystharian tea trade and access thereto.

I missed what the three giggling schoolgirls two ahead of us purchased, but the saturnine man in good tweed immediately ahead asked for, and received, a large mug of coffee together with another cinnamon spiral roll. He stepped aside but did not leave the shop, though it was not immediately clear whether this was out of curiosity as to our presence or because of the ceramic mug. He certainly made no pretence about not observing us closely.

The baker, a short, balding man with a cheerful round face and a white apron, looked at us with his mouth briefly agape. Professionalism took over shortly: "What can I do for you, gentlemen?"

"We're strangers here," I began with a bright smile, and deposited the coins on the counter. "We have some Alinorel money, though we're not entirely certain from which country, and we were hoping to acquire some breakfast and perhaps bread, if we have enough." I regarded the coins doubtfully. There were several different copper and silver coins, and one larger gold-alloy one. "Bread used to be two pennies a loaf, didn't it?"

The baker and several other people in the shop burst out laughing. "When on earth did you last buy bread?" the baker said. "It hasn't cost under a wheatear for, oh, decades."

"I think the last time he bought anything was in the Emperor Eritanyr's day," Masseo interjected.

"I am aware of the concept of inflation," I said, a little indignantly—between Kip and the Lord Treasurer I was well instructed in such key financial concepts—then I grinned. "But I have to admit that no, I haven't bought anything since then. I've been living on the fat of the land, as I believe is the phrase. I did acquire some books a year or two ago, but thinking about it I traded magic for those. I'm quite accomplished at illusions."

"Illusions?" the baker said curiously.

"One vendor wished to see a tiger, another a dragon. But I understand you've already seen one of *those* in real life."

Several people chuckled. The man with the coffee raised his eyebrows and appeared most thoughtful.

"You strongly resemble the Last Emperor," he said in well-educated accents, gesturing at a small copy of one of my early state portraits that the baker had placed to one side, in a clear position of honour. I cast an appraising glance at it: given that it had been done when I was all of thirty-five, and the fact that this was Alinor, it was not very likely anyone would actually connect me directly to it.

"It's true," I said agreeably. "Indeed, in the past week alone I have been taken for Yr the Conqueror, his father Harbut Zalarin, Aurelius Magnus, and Artorin Damara. And while I cannot claim to the muscles of the conqueror," and here I grinned with one of those sly sideways winks, "I *am* rather good at magic, if I do say so myself."

"And he does," Masseo interjected, though his attention was still directed mostly to the pastries.

"I cannot help it if I am also one of the great poets of the last age of the Nine Worlds," I said. "Or rather, I suppose I could, but it would be a sore disappointment to everyone except my late parents. And I heard from the Chancellor of Morrowlea that there are some stories here worth singing far and wide …"

"Not on an empty stomach, I hope?" the baker said when I paused.

"I certainly hope not, but you have not yet said what, if anything, our coin can buy. I should very much like one of those spiral cinnamon rolls and the coffee smells divine—and I can tell you I know whereof I speak on such matters, for not only have I been worshipped as a god, I have had access to the best coffee beans on Zunidh, where they originated, as you may know."

"You talk as much as Jemis Greenwing," the baker said, in apparent awe.

I favoured him with another grin. "I knew I liked the young man when he apologized so handsomely for running into us, and that after we had emerged from a passage between the worlds with no warning whatsoever."

"I am beginning to think all the stories are true," said the man who'd commented on the portrait. "I'll stand them their breakfast, Mr. Inglesides, if their coin is too foreign."

"I shan't reject a good Taran florin," Mr. Inglesides replied, taking one of the larger silver coins and pushing the rest back to me. "For a florin and—if you don't mind—perhaps a song?"

Masseo was laughing silently now.

I reached into my bag with due solemnity and drew out my harp. "We have not yet gotten to your side of the bargain, master baker, but I shall tell you that we also require directions to anyone in this village who might be able to furnish us with socks, a tent, and what was the other thing you wanted, Masseo, besides breakfast?"

"It is Alinor—"

"A book, of course. Though we were visiting the bookstore in any case."

"I'm sure you were," Mr. Inglesides said, his eyes gleaming with delight. "I'm not sure about a tent—"

"We could do with two," Masseo put in.

I cocked my head at him. "Two?"

"Two," he reiterated firmly.

I was sure he had some good reason in his mind, even if he were disinclined to share it. "Very well: two. I think we can assume *some* of our friends are organized."

"Why? Your concept of practicality has not improved in thirty years, except that instead of inexplicable quantities of felt slippers you brought cushions."

"I note that we used the felt slippers *and* have already made use of the cushions." I turned back to the baker, who was gamely trying not to laugh out loud, at the risk of his eyes watering. I regarded him doubtfully and then tilted my head at the saturnine man as I strummed an arpeggio to check the tuning. "Any particular request?"

The air was suddenly crystalline with expectancy, but as on the sky ship, no one quite wanted to be the one to name names.

"I think," the saturnine man said, with a sly glance at the baker, "that we should really have one about Jullanar of the Sea."

"A capital idea," I said, fiddling with a few of the necessary tuning knobs. The baker set on the counter a neat parcel of cinnamon rolls, some other sort of raisin-and-custard pastry that Masseo seemed interested in, several more savoury cheese-and-onion things, and three stout loaves of bread. The coffee came next, and I took a mouthful.

Divine. The Mae Irionéz had not possessed the drink, which might have been discovered after their disappearance under the curse, come to think of it, as coffee trees were originally native to Southern Dair and it had been a century or two after Yr had conquered Kavanduru that the young empire had turned its attention south.

"Now," I began, playing a few scales to warm up my fingers as I thought which of all those songs about my dear Jullanar I should begin with—

And then there was a great ruckus from outside the shop as a hugely loud gong suddenly reverberated through the air.

Someone at the end of the queue hastily shoved the door as wide as it could go, and we all stared to see that the very person most present in our minds had climbed up on the plinth of the stone pillar in the middle of the square, hammered on the metal shield that was placed at its height, and was staring down at a man in uniform who was pleading with her to stop making a scene.

I could have told him his pleas were useless, as once Jullanar got it into her head to do something she was almost as persistent as Kip about seeing it through; but I didn't need to.

"Be quiet? Be *quiet*?" she cried, fury crackling through her voice. "That is the last straw—no! That is *beyond* that last straw! Benneret Etaris, in the sight of these witnesses on this the first day of the Midsummer Assizes: I divorce you, I divorce you, *I divorce you!*"

"You can't divorce me!" the erstwhile Mr. Jullanar cried in utter shock.

Jullanar was hanging on the stone pillar with one hand, the other still gripping the hammer she'd used to whack the shield with, and now leaned down over him in a menacing fashion. Her voice came out in an angry hiss.

"Watch me."

Jullanar, to be honest, appeared almost exactly as she had when she was eighteen, if slightly plumper and with a few strands of grey twisting through her hair. She looked in her late forties or early fifties, which made me a touch envious; but then I wasn't married to someone I felt the need to divorce in the middle of a marketplace.

"Can she, do you know?" Masseo asked me in a low voice.

"It's the first day of the Midsummer Assizes?" I asked, looking around for confirmation, which I received from the saturnine man. "Then, assuming she meets the criteria, absolutely."

"The criteria?"

The question, interestingly, came from Mr. Inglesides the baker.

"A few specific sorts of witnesses," I said. "Will you excuse us? I shall try to perform a song for you later—"

"I reckon the coming performance will be most entertaining," the baker replied, with a slow wink.

"Oh, I expect that can be assured," I said, and hastily collected our comestibles and the coins the baker had not chosen, to stuff them in my bag for later. (I may be lacking in certain practicalities, but not *all* of them.)

The baker came out from behind his counter and shooed out the remaining customers who had been hovering between the rival attractions of us and the angry divorce proceedings in the middle of the square.

Masseo forced his way through the crowd, which parted reluctantly for him. I followed in his wake, and the saturnine man followed me, still holding his mug of coffee. I saw out of the corner of my eye that he'd also collected mine, which I found a pleasing encouragement.

Jullanar was castigating the morals of her husband in riper language than he seemed to have heard from her before, judging by his pole-axed expression. He kept trying to interject, but Jullanar on a tear was a force to be reckoned with.

"—I stood by for your infidelities, your infelicities, your ineptitude, your inebriation. I solved your cases for you when you were too sozzled to notice I rewrote your notes until they made actual sense. I was polite to your mother and your sisters and your misogynistic moron of a brother. But I will stand by no longer!"

"But, Jules," he said, with an unfortunate whine.

"My name," she said in frigid tones, "is *Jullanar*."

"You know that's not—seemly," he said.

Jullanar tossed her head back, her hair flying out of its previously neat bun and spiralling up around her head. Her eyes narrowed and her nostrils flared.

Unwisely, he seemed to take her brief pause as an opening. "Jules," he said, "be sensible now. It was just a little peccadillo—"

"A little peccadillo?" Her voice went up into a high shriek. Masseo and I exchanged a grimace, remembering a few unfortunate occasions when we'd been the recipients of such ire. "A peccadillo, you say? Listen," she said, gesturing wildly with the hammer at the crowd, some of whose members flinched. "Listen to your chief constable! A peccadillo, he thinks: like gambling on a race at the Harvest Fair, or having a barrel of illegal whiskey, or *conniving at framing a good woman for adultery*."

There was an unimpressed murmur from the gathered townspeople. I studied their body language and expressions carefully, if discreetly, collecting impressions. About a quarter sided with the husband; almost the remainder were on Jullanar's side, with a handful finding the scene entirely distasteful and another, larger, handful simply gleeful at seeing two respectable citizens going at it hammer-and-tongs.

Well enough, I thought phlegmatically, and mentally ran down the list of requirements for an open-air divorce in the duchy of Fiellan.

Of course, I could have done it by fiat. Apart from being the

272

still-more-or-less recognized emperor, I was also the definitely-still-technically High King of Rondé, as that wasn't dependent on my imperial titles but actually descended from my father's side. As eldest son of the house of Damara I was granted that title irrevocably.

But of course people would know that, and I had already made it clear I was Fitzroy Angursell.

"You've never said anything before," the husband said, with amazing obtuseness. I eyed him. He was handsome enough, in a dirty-blond and hearty kind of way, but Jullanar had been courted by fairy princes, so I doubted that was enough reason for her to marry him.

"Your mother was alive before."

"My mother? What does she have to do with anything?"

His bewilderment appeared genuine. Jullanar gave him an utterly disdainful look. "She blackmailed me into marrying you, for one thing. The only good thing that came out of it was our children."

Beside me, Masseo coughed. I had to admit that blackmail made more sense.

Not, apparently, to the husband. "Blackmail? But—what on earth could *you* have done—" His brow furrowed suddenly. "You never did graduate university, did you?"

Jullanar erupted into incredulous cackles. "Graduate university? You think I would be blackmailed by *that*? No, husband of mine: your mother is dead and so is mine, and so with an apology to my sister—"

She cast a not-at-all apologetic glance at someone whose face I couldn't quite see from my angle, but who was one of those I had allocated as being on the husband's side and who by her bearing looked to be entirely and genuinely appalled—

"I," she declared proudly, "am Jullanar of the Sea."

20

IN WHICH I ADVISE ON A DIVORCE

The response to this was varied.

I watched carefully with the corners of my eyes, as if I were observing courtiers without seeming to notice them. Two thirds of the crowd were utterly flabbergasted by this claim, and many of them doubted. Another third had knowing, smug looks, as if they'd suspected long ago. A full half, on either side, were visibly delighted.

Only the husband, who presumably knew her the best, verbalized his disbelief aloud.

"Don't be absurd, Jules," he said. "I know you—"

"I am increasingly beginning to doubt it."

"Look," he said, visibly starting to get angry. "It's all very well for you to have an hysterical moment, but—"

"An hysterical moment? An *hysterical moment*?" Jullanar's tone of voice went up another octave in indignation so absolute she choked on her own words and simply stared at him aghast.

He began what looked like it might turn into a smirk, and in the interests of avoiding homicide I decided it was time to intervene.

"I should weigh your thought carefully, and then be silent," I told the husband in my court voice, which I had practiced until it could cut through a crowd's noise with all the ease of the proverbial hot knife through butter.

He spun around to look at me and gape. "Who the *hell* are you?"

I smiled at him with lazy menace, but was forestalled by Jullanar. Her voice rang out: "Fitzroy Angursell!"

I bowed (not something I was well practiced in) as the crowd murmured. "In the flesh."

"Where," she demanded, "have you been?"

It was as if I'd gone off with a fishing rod and come back three days late with a story about the Salmon of Wisdom; or gone to collect firewood and returned two hours late with a lovesick elemental salamander in tow; or gone to fetch water and shown up thirty-odd years late with a story that—well.

The crowd was silent with breathless enjoyment of the scene.

Come to that, I felt a certain breathless enjoyment of the scene.

I grinned up at her. "I was caught by a dire curse laid upon my family, enchanted, entrammelled, enslaved, and finally was only able to escape because one of my guards took pity on me and the Moon woke my slumbering heart."

Masseo raised his eyebrows. Jullanar stared at me. Everyone else just looked at each other in confusion.

"Do you know," said Jullanar with vast sarcasm, "that makes perfect sense."

"As does your desire to divorce this fool," I said, gesturing rudely at the erstwhile husband, who said, "Hey," when he realized that I meant him.

I raised my eyebrow at him. "Did you have something to say besides a fulsome apology?"

"A what? Why should I apologize—she's the one making the scene, not me!"

Jullanar's face flushed a dangerous pink. I nodded at her and focused the considerable weight of my attention on the husband.

He was remarkably insensitive to it, so I gradually increased my magical presence while addressing him.

"You, sir, are a fool. You will be fortunate indeed to be only a footnote in history. No—no. Do not speak. Every word you say is fuel to my fire; if Jullanar only speaks the word, I can ensure that you are a laughingstock on three worlds."

Probably four, and possibly five, but I wasn't sure about either Ysthar's or Colhélhé's linguistic status. Alinor, Zunidh, and Voonra all still used Shaian as their primary common tongue.

The husband spluttered out something to the effect that the pack of us were criminals, and to be arrested.

"Criminals?" I said, flinging out my magic so the air sang with it. At the edge of the crowd I felt the recently-familiar mess of magic around Jullanar's protégé Jemis Greenwing as he came up, but the rest of the populace was unfamiliar except for Masseo's forge-fire and Jullanar's gloriously homely garden-earth.

"Criminals?" I laughed, a high ringing laugh I had almost forgotten I knew how to utter. The air was nearly luminescent with my magic. Even the husband was sweating under it now.

"Criminals? Us? I am Fitzroy Angursell of the Red Company: poet, revolutionary, magus, fool. My poetry was banned on five worlds for being too excellent, and moving people's souls too greatly.

"This is Masseo Umrit, whose hands wrought legends, weapons fit for the gods and those who would assail the gods, as we did in the Holy Desert of Kaph, when we championed the Wind Lords against their enemies. And this woman, your former wife, my oldest friend and my first editor: Jullanar of the Sea, who sparked the revolution of Galderon, who taught Astandalas what it meant to be true to one's soul, who was courted by three fairy princes and the sea-king of the North, who held up her very ordinariness up as a banner to fly before our glory.

"Our deeds stand larger than mere criminality. Our names sound forth in the halls of heaven: the very gods of the dreamtime know us. We stole boats from the house of the Sun and sailed them down the River of Stars; we poached game from the Dark Forest on the far side of the Moon's country; we gate-crashed a party in the very heart of the Palace of Stars and mocked the Emperor to his face.

"Criminals? If you insist. Rather more people would call us folk heroes."

The husband's face was going an interesting shade of puce, just the colour of a flea one is about to squish.

He spluttered and finally said: "I am the chief constable of this town! You—you—you are not welcome here! I don't know if you're crazy or serious or—or—or what, but it's indecent and wrong and you can't come here and say these things—"

"You, sir, are incoherent," I said, cutting him off and turning back to Jullanar, who was looking particularly gratified. "Regarding your plea for divorce: you are obviously aware of the first steps, namely that it must be the first day of the Midsummer Assizes, and you must make your declaration threefold at the market-cross."

Jullanar cocked her head at me. "I am capable of doing research."

"Don't I know it! While odd laws, particularly odd marriage laws, are something of a hobby of mine."

I turned slowly around, observing the crowd. The disgusted few were clustering but hadn't left this splendid mess of a display; the undecided were generally swinging towards Jullanar's side out of enjoyment in seeing local authority brought low. Which was fair enough.

And there was Jemis Greenwing, who was hovering near the bookstore trying hard not to look entirely gleeful. I met his eyes and gestured towards him. He pushed through the crowd with puzzlement on his features. He had changed clothes, into a long swinging blue coat, neatly tailored, with a foamy cravat at his throat. "Yes, sir?"

"The next requirement is a witness holding imperial title, Viscount St-Noire."

"I am hardly impartial," he said. Jullanar was regarding him with a sharp fondness.

"Oh, I must say that I am not always fully convinced of the merits of impartiality," I said, "though I have certainly heard many advocate for it. Now—a witness holding a Rondelan title?"

The man from the bakery sauntered up and handed me my coffee. "I was granted a knighthood for my portraiture; will that do?"

I resolutely did not worry about the far higher likelihood of a portraitist correctly identifying me. As with Aelian the post officer in Masseo's village: who would believe him?

And really, I didn't mind that rumour running rampant around Alinor. It would take time to reach Zunidh, and by then be much garbled.

"Very good," I said, and turned to Jullanar. "As a woman, I believe under Rondelan law you would have taken your husband's name?"

"Etaris," she replied, nodding, then scowled at her husband. "It's his best feature."

"He's not entirely ill-favoured to look upon," I pointed out fairly.

Someone in the crowd tittered. Jullanar herself just gave me a reluctant smile and murmured *Damian* almost too quietly to catch.

"It is a good name," I said, fixing him with a sharp stare. By this point even he felt my magic and authority, and was shivering under its force. Then I looked around at the crowd and particularly at my two witnesses. "Is the Chief Magistrate around?"

"Here," said a pleasant baritone voice, and a stocky roan-haired man emerged from the crowd. He nodded at Jemis Greenwing, the portraitist in tweed, Jullanar, Mr. Etaris, and Masseo before giving me an impressively meaningful glance. "I know what law you are following, and I am impressed by your knowledge, sir—"

"Thank you!" I said brightly. "I expect you're about to move on to the various reasons why I ought to be arrested immediately by someone I hope is not the chief constable whose morals both professional and personal have just been soundly denigrated by his soon-to-be former wife?'

The Chief Magistrate gave me an appreciative smile. "Although I have nothing but your fine words to condemn you, the law does still stand ..."

I sighed extravagantly. "We worked hard on our reputations, and so I must confess to being *slightly* chagrinned at this, but in the interests of not entirely damaging my dear Jullanar's reputation in this town ..." I pulled out a sealed parchment scroll from my bag and presented it to the Chief Magistrate.

He examined the seal with rising eyebrows, then broke it carefully to read the enclosure with an increasingly astonished expression.

It was a writ of pardon for the crimes committed in the days and demesne of the Empire of Astandalas by the *Notorious Outlaw Fitzroy Angursell and those of his companions so-called of the Red Company, namely the following* from the hand and seal of His Serene and Radiant Holiness, Artorin Damara, Last Emperor of Astandalas and Present Lord of Zunidh.

The Chief Magistrate looked at me, his professional calm slipping. "How—"

I smiled lazily at him. "How did I come by this? Artorin Damara, Last Emperor of Astandalas and present Lord of Zunidh, requested my advice on the pursuance of a quest. You may be aware from the stories that I am one of the great experts on the subject of adventuring."

Beside me, Jemis Greenwing jerked.

The Chief Magistrate said, "This is a pardon for the Red Company under the Imperial Seal."

The silence grew electric.

"Forgery!" the chief constable spluttered.

I raised my eyebrows at him "Forge the Imperial Seal? You underestimate the efforts put into making that as unforgeable as anything in the Nine Worlds. And even if it were not so, neither forgery nor flight are skills of mine, sirrah, and I may tell you that I have spent a great deal more time and effort on the latter."

Masseo snickered nearly silently beside me, which made Jullanar's face change in astonishment. I felt a surge of affection for her.

"This does seem to be in order," the Chief Magistrate said, reading it over again. "May I ask what the advice was?"

I laughed. "What! That advice was worth a writ of pardon for the most illustrious criminals of the late Empire of Astandalas! You can hardly expect me to provide it to you gratis."

"Oh, don't be absurd, Fitzroy," Jullanar said. "Your advice on questing is always the same: decide on your object and then go look for something else entirely."

"There are refinements," I said with dignity, even as Jemis Greenwing and the knighted portraitist both laughed. "Anyhow: the Last Emperor was satisfied with my advice."

The Chief Magistrate rolled up the scroll and returned it to me. I took it with care to ensure that my signet ring did not touch the parchment or wax, as it would reset the broken seal on so doing and undoubtedly give the game away. "Then, by all means, let us finish this divorce proceeding," he said. "If you would, sir?"

"Indeed!" I turned to Jullanar. "There are three possible outcomes. Do you wish for the simple divorce, where you keep his name and half your shared belongings? For the second, you return to your father's name and house, and only those items which are demonstrably yours may come with you."

"Etaris is a better name than Thistlethwaite," Jullanar allowed.

"The third option is to reject the patriarchy entirely and walk away a free woman with neither surname nor anything appertaining to one."

The crowd went suddenly dead silent. Jullanar looked down at me, and I saw a painful pride in her eyes.

"Of course," I went on, "you have by your own merits already earned an epithet and entrance into the halls of heroes."

There was a long, silent hesitation. Then Jullanar smiled slowly, tremulously, a little wanly, like dawn on a cloudy day. I watched her, silently offering my support; her expression turned resolute. She reached into the pocket of her sensible gown and pulled out an iron key. She looked at her protégé. "Mr. Greenwing, are you interested in business ownership?"

Mr. Greenwing caught himself from gaping and smiled back. "The Duke of Fillering Pool has mentioned that I should think about diversifying my portfolio. Is there anything you'd like me to set aside?"

Mr. Etaris was spluttering and had passed from puce to something approaching vermilion. I leaned forward and whispered to him, "Take a deep breath. You don't want to suffer an apoplexy." I also relaxed the magic from weighing on him, which probably helped more than my words.

Jullanar said, "There is a bag you found when you took over the upstairs flat, and another under the counter. The cost of the store and its contents is—ah—" she grinned suddenly at me. "A gold emperor seems fair, does it not?"

"Proverbially so," Mr. Greenwing agreed, and reached into the pocket of his long coat (which looked like something I had seen from Alinorel courtiers in my early days as emperor; I wondered when and why it had come back into fashion, and wanted one for myself) for a large coin that shone true-gold in the sunlight. He held it up to her, and she exchanged the key for it with slightly trembling fingers.

She looked at the crowd, finishing with the Chief Magistrate. "Let this transaction be witnessed by all here, that I have sold Elderflower Books to Jemis Greenwing, Viscount St-Noire."

"So witnessed," the Chief Magistrate said. "I will see that the proper documents are noted in the court records."

"Thank you," she said with dignity. She looked at the coin and then tossed it to him. "Please use this for the good of the village poor."

They were both ignoring her nearly-ex-husband with splendid insouciance. "I shall," agreed the Chief Magistrate.

Jullanar now looked at me. "I'm ready," she said, "to be Jullanar of the Sea again."

～

We didn't find a tent, and no one apparently sold good wool socks in midsummer. I couldn't determine why, as it was agreed that people who wore shoes and boots (as did all the people of Ragnor Bella I had observed) continued to need socks or stockings in the summer; but they did not buy them at the market. At least we were able to stock up our small library of reading material.

Jemis Greenwing, it transpired, had been Jullanar's assistant for most of the past year, the viscountcy being something of a surprise. He was almost painfully delighted to assist us in finding interesting things to read while Jullanar went and reassured her children that she was not permanently abandoning them.

This was not a concern either Masseo or I had had, so we left it to her discretion and occupied ourselves with the contents of her bookstore.

Masseo found several three-volume novels that appealed, and I found two volumes of poetry and a collection of essays on the art of pottery-making that intrigued me. Both Masseo and Jemis Greenwing regarded this choice with surprise when I set my selections on the counter.

"That's very modest," Masseo said, indicating his rather larger stack.

I patted my bag. "You doubt my carrying capacity even after stashing your spare anvil and all those ingots in it?"

"My mistake! You probably have a substantial library in there."

"A reasonable travelling one," I agreed, and turned to Jullanar, who had just come in. "All set?"

Her expression was sad. "Mostly." She glanced at her protégé. "Will you keep an eye on my children, Mr. Greenwing? My son is of an age and disposition to follow his father in all things, alas, but my daughter is in a rebellious phase, and much put out by the fact that mine is outshining hers."

"It is difficult to be the child of greatness," said Jack Greenwing's son. He reached below the counter and pulled out two bags. One of them was exceedingly familiar.

"Jullanar! Can that possibly be *my* Bag of Unusual Capacity?"

She shoved it towards me with a fond exasperation. "You did ask me to take care of it in your absence, as you may or may not recall."

The enchantments I had wrought on the bag, in what had been nearly my first deliberate working, had possessed (I could see now) one of the two great weaknesses of inexperienced magi. One is simple lack of skill and power; the other is overcompensation.

I have always been far more prone to overcompensating.

I reached my hand in, thinking of Jullanar. My fingers closed around something hard, rounded, and cold.

I drew it out to find I was holding a wickedly sharp and preternaturally brilliant silver sword. It was perhaps three feet long, narrow-bladed as a fencing foil, runes etched down the middle speaking of light, courage, beauty. It spangled the bookstore walls with radiance, making the vase of high-summer flowers set on top of the unlit iron stove in the middle of the room glow.

"Dear Lady," breathed Jemis Greenwing, dragon-slayer and hero's son.

I turned the sword around so the hilt was pointing towards Jullanar and the blade lay flat on my forearm. "I believe this is yours, my lady."

She reached out a trembling hand. Her fingers curled around the hilt, fitting in between the quillons, taking their once familiar positions. Her eyes met mine. I'd forgotten how soft a blue hers were, especially when they were luminous with unshed tears.

She lifted the sword gently from my grip and then stood there, feet moving automatically to those positions Damian had spent so long drilling us in, turning the sword this way and that.

She might have looked ridiculous, this small-town bourgeois woman, but there had always been a certain quality to her spirit that precluded any such superficial judgment. Jullanar had never let her essential ordinariness stop her from having follies as great as any of the rest of us. Greater, perhaps, for she had to break a narrower circle of presumptions.

"With this sword," she said softly, "I cut the webs of those giant spiders in the forest on the Dark Side of the Moon."

"With that sword," Masseo said, "you taught many fools the error of their ways."

I gazed at her with love so overwhelming I thought my heart would break from it. "With that sword, you rescued all of us when we were caught by the stratagems of the Wizard of the Labyrinth."

The more magic each of personally possessed, the worse off we had been. Masseo was not a wizard or a magus, but he had already begun his long study of runes, and had forged this sword out of starlight and the water blessed by the unicorns who live in the valleys of the Moon's country. Ayasha and Gadarved both came of cultures where all were practitioners, however small; Faleron had been cursed with levity and gifted with tongues; Pharia and Damian, Tanteyr both, had their people's strange magic of the soul; Sardeet had married and borne a divinity, and had the gift of Sight; Pali had already by then long since earned her reputation as one who would walk unflinching into the realms of the gods, with a holy vocation to vengeance; and I, of course, was an incipient great mage.

And that left Jullanar, who try as she might had never been able to light a candle or recognize a subtle enchantment, but who never let that stop her.

I reached my hand into my bag again and pulled out a leather strap that turned out to be attached the corner of a grimoire I was sure I'd lost in the volcanic eruption of Figur.

"Now this is more like it," I exclaimed, stuffing the books into my much more prosaic New Bag and enthusiastically reaching into the other. "Any bets I can find the scabbard before we find the next member of our company?"

Masseo said, "A tent would be more useful. I'm sure you had at least one in there."

"It's summer here," I said, dismissing this concern, and pulling out a leather sack of coins that were not legal tender anywhere in the old Empire and weren't even made of a useful metal that could be melted down.

Jemis Greenwing watched me with fascination. Jullanar shook her head and handed me the sword to stow away again so she could shrug into the sturdy rucksack she'd already had packed.

"Fortunately I was prepared for things to go sideways," Jullanar said. "Though admittedly I can't say I was expecting *you* to show up out of nowhere."

"That was for your protégé," I murmured, finding a singular shoe that certainly hadn't ever fit me. I put it back and retrieved a saddle instead.

"Stop playing," Jullanar ordered. "I've got clothes, money, a little food, some medicines, a notebook, pen and ink, and a book to read. What am I missing? Don't say a tent, Masseo, we're old enough that we can stay at inns."

"How much money did you squirrel away before you decided to divorce your husband?"

She smiled mysteriously, then snickered. "I was thinking Fitzroy here could pay for things."

I looked up from a small pile of miscellaneous leather goods, including a belt that looked as if it might just fit me if I got Masseo to fix the buckle. "You have an interesting notion of what being enslaved and entrammelled by magic involves. I have not held

285

coins in my hand since the parting of the Red Company till just over a week ago."

I had nearly forgotten the necessity, in fact, until Kip sat me down to go over certain preparations he'd made, and solemnly discussed appropriate daily budgets for people who were not travelling with an entourage of five hundred.

Both of us barely managed to keep a straight face through the conversation, though I suspected for quite different reasons.

Jullanar looked pensive. "A week ago I came out of formal mourning for my mother-in-law and began serious preparations. Though I wasn't planning on leaving until I discovered that law in a book of particularly obscure regional legalities that came in the store and had to be catalogued." She gestured at a book on a high shelf that managed to look immediately tedious despite being slim and well-bound. I considered the effect and decided it was the particular shade of dusty brown cloth.

Masseo leaned up against the counter. "A week ago I was thinking that it was ten days before my apprentice finished her term, and that I should probably start thinking about planning for an adventure."

They both looked at me. I counted back the days and then grinned at them. "A week ago I broke into Yr the Conqueror's tomb and then set the Solamen Fens on fire. Speaking of which: Jullanar, do you remember the bronze mirror you bought in the Great Bazaar in Yedoen?"

Jullanar was well used to my apparent non sequiturs, and did not let this confound her. "Wasn't it the Grand Bazaar? And yes: I gave it to Pali."

"Not Sardeet?"

Jullanar gave me a speaking glance. "Sardeet abhorred mirrors, magical ones especially. Pali thought the engravings were interesting. Why?"

As the one mirror was still in its tomb, and the second one had disintegrated when I'd undone the curse, I wasn't sure why I was bothering, and hesitated.

"He's taking his own advice on questing," Masseo said, snickering.

"Ah! Are these the first or the second object?" Jullanar asked.

I laughed. "Oh, third at the very least. Shall we?"

IN WHICH THERE ARE FAR TOO MANY EMOTIONS

*J*ullanar led us through town with her head held high and her eyes resolutely focused forward. Very few of the townspeople said anything directly, though they were all watching, and many murmured to each other as we passed.

We walked down the long winding main street away from the market square, past a second square where an important hotel faced the post office (its livery, I thought, nowhere near so fine as the one Kip and I had chosen for Zunidh's), and on until a cross street took us through houses and small stores towards the edge of town.

The architecture of Ragnor Bella was fairly evenly divided between a dark red brick and white-plastered walls, both usually framed with heavy timbers. The roofs were thatched or shingled, the windows mullioned, and boxes of bright flowers were at nearly every window and every door, though the gardens seemed to be hidden behind the houses.

Outside the open door of one of the houses a thin woman in a blue dress stood with her arms folded and her face pinched in disapproval. Jullanar's step faltered as we approached.

The woman waited until we were very close before speaking. "Well, you've made a right spectacle of yourself today, sister."

Jullanar put her shoulders back and her chin up. "Yes."

There was a little silence, before the woman in the blue dress relaxed very slightly. Her lips upturned in what wasn't quite a smile, more of a grimace. "You know I can't approve."

"I know," Jullanar replied, rather sadly.

The woman paused, then took a deep, resolute breath. "But that doesn't matter. Will you introduce your friends?"

Jullanar's face flickered with an array of emotions that passed too quickly for me to read them. "This is Fitzroy Angursell," she said, "and this Masseo Umrit. My sister Lavinia Landry."

I inclined my head; Masseo bowed. Lavinia curtsied stiffly, her posture and her expression both unyielding. But I saw in her eyes something just slightly wistful as she looked at her sister.

"Here," she said awkwardly, unfolding her arms and thrusting a bundle at Jullanar. "For your travels."

Jullanar took it, visibly moved. "Lavinia—"

"Go," Lavinia replied, as stiff and sour as before. "You've made enough of a fuss already."

And we went.

Jullanar's sister was the last person who spoke at length to us, though we—particularly Jullanar, of course—were hailed by various passers-by of a wide range of social classes and ages. Jullanar returned the greetings with a bright, fixed smile.

She maintained this through Ragnor Bella, across a bridge over the river Raggle, and into a community unimaginatively called Ragglebridge. I did appreciate the evident dedication to the point, as along with the bridge and the hamlet there was also a public house of the same name. The road, conversely, was called *Coombe.*

We headed out at Jullanar's brisk pace, which was just slightly faster than my own natural stride. I thumped the walking stick down, humming very quietly to myself, and wondered what might be necessary to turn the stick into a proper wizard's staff

Not—as you will have gathered—that I am in any way a proper wizard, but sometimes one wishes to convey a certain image.

A bit of shaping at the tip, perhaps a mystic stone in cunningly wrought wooden grips. I had already begun to wear one section smooth, so that could be made more deliberate, and there was a spiral scar running down that could be emphasized.

We crested a rise that seemed to mark a boundary, for an old laid hedge wandered off to our right—southwest, possibly—down into the valley of the Raggle. On the town side there had been pastures, green grass and white-and-brown cattle with short horns; on this side was a sort of uncultivated heath.

Ahead of us the land undulated towards a forested ridge. The mountains rose up behind it, lower than those to the south but still tall and bare-shouldered. There were a handful of houses visible, but the land nevertheless held a certain desolation about it that reminded me a little of the land about Mae Irión.

I glanced up at a fine wooden church on a hillock near us; on closer examination it was clearly derelict, with a large tree pushing branches up against its windows and slumping outbuildings.

Overall there was a certain shrunkenness about the landscape. Not quite as if it had once been *bigger*, but as if it had been … more. More inhabited, perhaps.

The magic here was foreign to me, being Alinorel, though still mostly of the fabric wrought by Astandalan wizards. It was excited and more aware than usual, as if great and unusual things had been stirring it up. I thought of the strange magics enveloping Jemis Greenwing and wondered what else besides errant dragons had been happening here.

I turned to ask Jullanar, only to discover she and Masseo had drawn ahead. I hastened to catch up to them, noting now that I was looking that there were all sorts of overgrown or half-ruined structures around. A half-tumbled stone wall, a tilting wooden shed, a stone trough just barely visible beneath an overcoat of brambles.

Jullanar and Masseo were conversing; from her quick look over her shoulder as I approached, followed by a bright peal of laughter, I deduced it was about me.

I decided to ignore this, which somehow made the both of them laugh even harder.

"Fitzroy!"

"Jullanar!"

She looked at me, eyes bright, stumbled a step, and put her hand on my arm to steady herself. I flinched but caught myself before moving. Even as I was silently congratulating myself for this development her face clouded over.

"What's wrong? Is your arm bruised? Did I hurt you?"

"No, no," I assured her, smiling. I had forgotten to put the sling on that morning, but my wrist, while still a bit sore, was not at fault.

Her hand slid down to grasp mine tightly. "Fitzroy—good heavens! Your pulse is *racing*. What's wrong?"

I looked down at our entwined hands and carefully loosened mine. "I am not accustomed to being touched," I said simply.

Something flashed in her eyes. Not pity, but—I blinked and looked away, cursing (not for the first time!) my magic and its effect when I was unwary. "I apologize," I said, gripping the walking stick. "I'm still getting used to casual …"

I trailed off, for once at a loss for words.

"Casual touch?"

I smiled wryly. "That too."

"I see," she said, exchanging a glance with Masseo. Then turning back to me: "I suppose a hug is out of the question? I always thought yours were the best," she added, a little wistfully.

I had to brace myself, but I handed my walking stick to Masseo and carefully enfolded her in my arms. "Never," I said, as she turned her face to my breast.

Her head fit just below my chin, so my nose was full of the scent of her hair, perfumed like hyacinths. I could feel my heart racing, traitorous organ that it was, but I refused to let it govern me. Jullanar's arms came around my waist, pressing against my ribs.

I closed my eyes against tears that surely would never fall. But I had not held anyone since we had last met; and Jullanar had been the first one ever to embrace me, many years ago now as it was.

If my eyes were damp so too was the front of my scarlet robes, but none of us said anything when Jullanar at last released me. She looked at me for a long, searching moment, which I could not sustain.

I jumped when Masseo clapped his hands lightly. "There seems to be a nice grassy lawn in the churchyard yonder. Do you think we can sit there for a bite? I don't know about you, Jullanar, but I'm hungry."

"What about me?" I protested. "I might be hungry, too. And I'm the one with our breakfast."

"You haven't had breakfast?" Jullanar cried in mock horror. "It's nearly eleven! You haven't said a word of your famishment."

Masseo shook his head. "Fitzroy has not been very good at taking care of himself. I presumed he would join us, of course, if we made obvious the opportunity."

I didn't really know what he meant—I had thought to bring the food, *and* money, and bedding, had I not?—but quietly followed them up a footpath that led to the church.

It was a lovely picnic, as the market square baker was talented and Masseo had secretly bought a punnet of cherries, which do not grow near Solaara and which I hadn't had eaten since before the Empire fell.

He'd bought them for Jullanar, whose favourite fruit they were and who had had a difficult morning. I was greatly touched that she was willing to share them with me.

After our breakfast we set off at a more moderate pace, and this time we talked.

"I don't want to talk about me," Jullanar declared, a touch angrily. "You saw my life!"

"It was a delightful bookstore, and Mr. Greenwing seems a most estimable young man," I agreed.

"Oh—*you*! You know what I mean. Tell me about you, Fitzroy. Though I'm surprised you need the invitation."

"It's because he's actually Aurelius Magnus," Masseo said, with no hint of a joke.

Jullanar considered this. "Like Aurelius Magnus and the Seafarer King?"

"The Islanders never had kings," I said, because Kip had made this *very clear* over the years.

Masseo ignored me. "Exactly."

"Do you know, that explains *so much*."

"Doesn't it!" Masseo replied. "Don't let him apologize for leaving us in the Silver Forest, he'll make a great hash of it."

I was hardly likely to improve without practice, my inner sarcastic voice pointed out, but Jullanar had already started to retell a story she half-remembered about Aurelius Magnus, and I confess I didn't really want to interrupt.

"There's that story about the cabbages, weren't they," she said. "You know, when he was trying to be incognito but since he had no idea what part anyone even used it was terribly obvious he couldn't have actually been a farmer as he'd claimed."

"You don't say," Masseo replied, deadpan.

There were any number of incidents I would have preferred to gloss over. Jullanar began with my initial reaction to discovering peas in their pods (which really, if one isn't brought up with gardening or preparing food, is fairly marvellous), and continued on from there through any number of foodstuffs both delectable and decidedly not.

"One could have farmed places were cabbages *aren't* grown," I said, feeling sympathy for my distant ancestor.

"Have you since learned what a cabbage is?" Jullanar asked after a deliberate pause.

"It's a vegetable," I replied readily, though that was about all I could claim to know about it. "Jullanar, I'm actually—"

"Don't disillusion me just yet! I've had enough of that today. Not to mention it's outrageously out of character. Will you sing us a song instead? Please?"

Well, if she put it that way ... "With pleasure. Any requests?"

With Jullanar, it was always going to be something from *Aurora and the Peacock*.

We walked for a couple of hours at a pleasant pace. I developed a hot spot on my left foot to match the blister on my right, and was reminded by Jullanar of the names of various north-temperate climate trees, flowers, and birds. For most of the time we talked about our shared past.

I contributed to the stories and occasional songs, but for the most part was inclined to listen. Jullanar obviously found this at odds with her memory of me, and kept trying to prompt me to talk. Masseo, hitherto always one of the quieter members of our company, usually responded in my place.

"Do you remember when—"

"Of course, Sardeet said—"

And off they would go.

I wondered why it was not harder for them to tell these stories. Surely they had spent as long as I had keeping their mouths shut?

Only a few people in Jullanar's community had *known*, and none in Masseo's. Yet now, reunited, the stories flowed for them, and not for me, the once-great storyteller.

Some time not long after noon we climbed up and over the wooded ridge and, after descending to the subsequent valley, took a break at a tiny roadside public house. Jullanar recommended a pint of bright coppery ale (not something I had drunk in the Palace; it felt a strange luxury to have alcoholic drink in the middle of the day) and a 'ploughman's lunch', which consisted of strong brown bread, fresh butter, pickled vegetables, hard yellow cheese, and cold meats along with grainy mustard and a spiced fruit-and-onion chutney. It was all entirely foreign and quite delicious.

The 'Garden Hut' public house was located not far from a small, fast-moving river. We were now far enough from Ragnor Bella that the publican merely expressed astonishment that 'Mrs. Etaris' wasn't in town for market-day. The strangers she was keeping company with were regarded with fascination but not mentioned explicitly.

Jullanar replied boldly that she had sold her store to Mr. Green-wing, divorced her husband, and was off travelling with old friends to have an adventure.

Someone in the corner said something about *Galderon*, and that was that.

Perhaps it had always been a performance, and I was just remembering wrong that once this had been … easy.

My heart felt queer.

"I thought you only attended Galderon for that one year?" I enquired as we set off again.

Jullanar blushed lightly. "After—after the Silver Forest, I found myself in East Oriole, and after dithering around for a bit decided to go back to the university to see if I could resume my studies. They were just coming out from the siege by the time I got there, and had decided to hold oral exams before granting degrees. I had been expelled but there were those who remembered me …"

"You were the reason for the revolution, you mean," Masseo said.

The University of Galderon had seceded from their province of the Empire after the governor of East Oriole had interfered excessively with their organization and teaching. They had fired our Ayasha (then the more respectable Professor Ash) without even veiling the bigotry, and expelled Jullanar when she bravely stood up for the professor. She had brought Ayasha to meet Damian, Pali, and me, and we became the Red Company, and went off on our adventures.

Galderon, as we found out when swinging back by it a year or two later so Jullanar and Ayasha could see what had happened to their friends, had taken the two unjust expulsions as grounds for a revolution. The governor had responded with violence, and settled into a protracted siege of the university.

They had not managed to resolve their differences until over a decade later, when the university had sent an embassy to the Emperor, by that time myself, who had, naturally (if inexplicably to many), been on their side.

"Well—I suppose I was, yes. Poor Marianne! All she wanted was to marry a good man, and she ended up starting a revolution and becoming a general and a scholar. She told me how heartened they had all been by the songs and stories they managed to hear of our doings. At any rate, I *had* been a student, and though expelled it was under the Old Regime, and so they agreed to reinstate my status and let me sit whatever exams I pleased."

"And?" I asked, when she did not immediately tell us the result.

Her flush darkened to a fine deep rose. "It's possible I have a Doctorate in Geography for my surpassingly excellent knowledge of the physical and political geographies of the Nine Worlds."

We all laughed, and Masseo said, "We did travel widely!"

"Yes, they asked me to write up an account of Eahh and Kaphyrn as my dissertation." She looked off at the distant mountains. The morning's puffy clouds had given way to a clear cerulean blue, against which the peaks stood in sharp brown-grey relief. "My family were not certain what to make of it, but they were willing to believe I'd spent those ten years stuck inside the walls of Galderon. It was hardly *respectable* to be a revolutionary, but it was better than their suspicions that I was Jullanar of the Sea. They couldn't understand how I'd ended up in Geography, but I told them I'd been responsible for the maps."

She had always been responsible for *our* maps, being fascinated with the art of cartography.

"Fitzroy has some beautiful ones of Zunidh," Masseo told her. "I've never seen finer."

"One would expect the great travelling emperor to have good charts," she agreed, giving me a merry grin.

"Would one?" I replied with great haughtiness, but they just laughed and she slid her hand into the crook of my arm. I took a breath but did not skitter away, nor ask her to move, and instead willed my heart to stop over-reacting so.

We walked upstream along the river until the road forked, one continuing on and the other turning a sharp left across the water. Jullanar smiled at me as we drew near the bridge. "Where exactly are we going?"

"We've been following you for ages," I exclaimed.

She and Masseo exchanged humour-filled glances. "I'm sure I was following *you*," Jullanar replied primly.

"And I certainly was not leading the way," Masseo added.

I huffed silently. "I was informed by your Mr. Greenwing that the road to Chare led out of the Coombe."

"I cannot believe you have an actual destination—unless we want only the *road* to Chare, and not to reach Chare itself?"

I was minded of Masseo wanting the highfaluting explanation.

"Fitzroy said something about Stoneybridge," Masseo said before I could come up with an appropriate one.

She blinked innocently. "Stoneybridge?"

"Jullanar," I said sternly, "that was a *terrible* pretence at igno-

rance. I know you already know why we're going there; Mr. Greenwing gave you away."

Masseo looked surprised. "He did?"

"It was in his eyes when I asked him directions."

"It's possible that Pali and I may have encountered each other
this spring," Jullanar allowed. "We go this way, in that case."

Which was the road across the river, naturally.

It was another hump-backed stone-built affair; looking down at
the water as we crossed I could see the narrow shadows of fish in
the clear water in the shadow of the bridge.

Off upstream was a hamlet, presumably reached by the road we
had just left. Ours went parallel to the river for a few hundred
yards before veering uphill along a smaller stream.

"We should be able to reach the pass today, at least," Jullanar
said as the road dwindled to a path.

"As Fitzroy neglected to bring a tent—"

"So did you!"

Masseo chuckled. Jullanar laughed aloud. "I believe there's a
refuge up there—a little building, rustic, but better than no shelter.
Even at midsummer it'll be chilly up there at night."

"And we do have provisions, bedding, and water," Masseo
acknowledged.

Practical matters thus attended to, up we began to climb.

As we went I pondered what Pali might have told Jullanar
about her disastrous visit to me in Solaara. But Jullanar said
nothing about it at all.

The side road was not designed for any form of wheeled vehicle,
though some travellers came by horseback, judging by the tracks
and droppings left behind. It was wide enough for the three of us to
walk abreast, which we did with Jullanar in the middle. I was on

the left so I didn't whack anyone with the walking stick by accident.

We wound up and down, more up than down, through a pleasant woodland full of small birds. There were more flies than midges or mosquitos, easy enough to shoo away from the three of us with a faint impulse of magic. The tiny magic still felt an untoward strain, as despite the gentle activity of the day I had clearly not recovered.

It was hard to know whether this was actually untoward or not. Usually I would spend weeks not doing anything after such a great work as undoing the curse, as I hardly had to perform any small magics as part of my daily activity as Lord of Zunidh and it would take that long at the least to plan the next great one.

After an hour or so we climbed out of the woods and onto sloping green pastures full of sheep. Jullanar informed us that the Coombe sheep were noted for their wool, which was particularly fleecy. I regarded the animals as we passed. They looked like sheep.

At other times I might have asked questions about the sheep and what particularly fleecy wool was used for, but Masseo told a joke about shepherds, and I didn't want to force the conversation.

I listened a little wistfully to their easy banter, how first Jullanar and then Masseo (or first Masseo and then Jullanar) would say something, a comment or an observation or a pun, and the other would return with a question or a story or an encouragement, and so the conversation would flow smoothly.

It made me acutely aware of just how few *conversations* I'd had.

I spoke: and was obeyed.

I had long since learned to be careful of what I said. It was perilously easy for over-enthusiastic courtiers to take comments or observations (to say nothing of questions or encouragements) as instructions.

Comment on the beauty of cherry blossoms, quoting a well-known poet on the poignancy of their ephemerality, and the audience came back to present a new *season* for my pleasure. The weather-workers of Astandalas had been stupendously skilled at their craft; but I still cringed inwardly at the memory of just what that folly had cost.

Not that I thought either Masseo or Jullanar were the sort of person to do such a thing—we were, after all, half folk heroes, half iconoclasts, and the two of them in particular quite sensible—but—

That *but* niggled at me, and kept me silent.

I had talked about clothing with Ylette and Conju, about guard rotations and Palace gossip with Ludvic and Rhodin, about art and books and politics with Kip.

I *wanted* to be friends with them; *wanted* them to look on me as their equal, and they mine. I knew at least Ludvic and Kip wanted the same, and Kip especially tried, but the whole structure of the Palace, the government, society at large, was designed to ensure everybody knew and treated the person at the centre as an ostensible and inviolate god.

All this to say that I was afraid of ruining the conversation. Surely I was unconsciously, unconscionably arrogant, accustomed as I was to instant obedience, instant service, instant deference. I walked beside them, listening carefully, and said little even when their comments jogged a memory for me.

My inner sarcastic voice said I was being foolish, but I had long since learned to disregard that voice. A week's adventures had helped me get over myself, at least in the moment, but now that Masseo had Jullanar to talk with, and there was no other audience to perform for, I found myself falling back into those old habits of observing without participating.

There were stone walls snaking improbably up the face of the mountains. These were more common farther north, Jullanar said, where stone and sheep were the only the things the land produced in any abundance. Down here the walls related to a territorial dispute between the people of the Coombe, who did not consider themselves part of Ragnor barony, and Baron Ragnor, who did.

We came to an ingenious swinging gate set into one of these

stone walls, wide enough for a horse to be taken through but impenetrable, apparently, to sheep. On the other side of it was a stone bench next to a spring whose flow had been channelled into a stone basin.

"Let's rest here for a bit," Jullanar said, swinging off her rucksack before either of us responded. She washed her face in the spring water and then pulled out a wooden cup for a drink. I watched, feeling a painful nostalgia at the way her hair was escaping its braid, at her flushed but happy face, at ... being there, and yet not being *first*.

"Have a drink, Fitzroy," Masseo urged me. "Do you need a cup?"

I shook my head slowly, reaching into the New Bag for one of the ones Conju had packed for me. It was an absurdly delicate piece of bone china rimmed with gold, a coffee cup fit for an Emperor. I had to be careful not to knock it against the stone as I filled it.

"That's beautiful," Jullanar said, as I leaned against the wall while I sipped the water and listened to my heart beat in my ears. She slid over on the bench and patted the stone beside her. "Sit down."

Masseo had found another stone for his seat. "Thank you," I replied carefully, and sat down.

Jullanar and Masseo looked at each other again. I looked out at the surroundings, breathing slowly and deeply. The air was nowhere near so thin as it had been in Masseo's village, but we had climbed higher than I'd realized: the valley of the Coombe was already distant, and we could see over the wooden ridge we'd crossed earlier to the broader valley in which Ragnor Bella lay.

From here the geography of the region was clear. We were climbing up the eastern ridge of the foothills of the Crosslains; the valley the road followed led up between two great outthrust flanks towards a low saddle that was presumably the pass. The land undulated down to the Coombe, over the ridge, down to the wide valley. To the south the land was forested to the feet of the mountains, while to the north fields gave way to yet another wood before the blue haze of distance dissolved distinction.

There was a hawk cruising across the sloping green pastures, pale grey with a long tail and narrow wings and a flashing white rump. It swung in wide shallow arcs low above the grass, as if it were quartering the fields in a search pattern.

The stone was cold and hard through my silk and cotton clothes. I rather wanted to take off my boots and bathe my feet, but knew that would be asking for trouble when it came to putting them back on.

Masseo took my cup and refilled it for me, then offered a handful of dried cherries he pulled out of his bag. Jullanar exclaimed softly and dug in her rucksack for a linen handkerchief which she unfolded with a ceremonious air to reveal pale-brown biscuits from which the sharp scent of ginger rose up.

I had to turn my head to keep the tears from springing to my eyes. How often had I tried to describe those ginger biscuits to my attendants! Chefs the glory of their civilizations had presented me with ginger confections of every sort, but none of them were Jullanar's.

I took one of the biscuits with a hand I would swear resolutely was not trembling, and hardly dared to bite into it for fear it would fall short of my memory. Sugar crystals sparkled in the sunlight like diamond dust.

"They were fresh this morning," Jullanar said, misinterpreting my reluctance. "I needed to make something to distract myself."

"They're delicious," Masseo said with his mouth still full.

"It won't bite you," Jullanar said to me, her eyes gleaming impishly.

Masseo swallowed his mouthful. "I suppose that emperors do not get this sort of cookie."

"Not the ones that were stolen away by the Sun and travel through the sky fighting monsters," Jullanar agreed.

"You should have been there for his arrival, Jullanar! He came in clothes the colour of the midnight sky, just as if he'd stepped out of the shrine painting, ready to answer prayers and scatter largesse."

"He fell out of the sky on top of me the first time I met him," replied Jullanar, who had never grown tired of that story in all the years I had known her. "Come to think of it, your outfit that time could have been made out of the sky—it was a fine enough blue velvet cloak to be a piece of the heavens."

I forced a smile, but my heart stuttered.

To cover the moment of weakness I took a bite of the biscuit.

It was even better than I had remembered.

"Fitzroy!" Jullanar exclaimed, leaving off a description of some outfit I'd once worn. "You're crying?"

I brushed my hand against my eyes and stared to find it came away wet. When was the last time I had wept?

I could answer that: that day Pali had come, and I had not been able to go with her.

I turned away from them, staring fiercely out at the landscape, but Jullanar made a huffing noise and pulled me over until I was tight against her side. Masseo grumbled almost inaudibly before squeezing between the end of the bench and the stone wall, his strong arm along the back of my shoulders.

His clothes still smelled of the forge, as Jullanar's of the garden. I listened to my heart beating too wildly, trying to calm down. My chest felt too tight.

It had been more than a year since the heart attack that had made everyone so sharply aware that I was not, as custom would have it, actually immortal.

What had the physicians said to do when I was in danger of excessive sentiment? (Not that they had put it that way, not to me.)

Five things I could see, four things I could hear, three things I could smell, one emotion I felt.

Five things I could see: green grass and white sheep and grey mountains and blue sky and the sunlight reflecting on the spring-water at our feet.

Four things I could hear: the wind whistling around the rocks, Jullanar humming a lullaby, some bird cheeping, Masseo's deep, even breathing.

Three things I could smell: ginger, and roses, and hot metal.

One emotion I felt:

By all the gods who were not *me*! Once I had been able to describe for other people the emotions they had never known they felt before!

22

IN WHICH WE TAKE REFUGE

I used to adore secrets.

I collected them, as some men collect birds or butterflies: carefully, and with great attention to detail. An attention to detail was, I fancied, one of my great skills as a poet, that ability to make another *be* just as I wished. With the strokes of my pen I could carry them to the Divine Lands, or to the bottom of the sea, or into the furthest reaches of my imagination, following characters who were not, quite, anybody I had ever met.

Blackmail was never an interest of mine, nor a thief's possessiveness or a gossip's desire to *tell*. I learned the secrets given to me freely, esoteric magic or humble mysteries or whispered confessions, and I transmuted them in my art into something truer than any scholar's fact.

When at last my heart stopped palpitating and the tears receded and I could pretend myself composed, we started walking again, more slowly, to the ever-nearing ridge. Jullanar pointed out several notable geographic features—the hills across the valley were the Gorbelow Hills, and the valley was carved by the two rivers of the

East and West Rag, which came to a confluence just to the north of Ragnor Bella, south of the Arguty Forest.

We were climbing up the Crosslains, which were called the Linder Mountains on the Linder side of the border and the Craslins on the Charese side. The saddle we were ascending towards led to a high ridge that wound between three mountains, two visible and the third hidden to the east. Up there the road forked, one branch leading down to Lind, the other to Chare.

I absorbed all this knowledge as best I could, connecting it to what I already knew of the countries named. (Lind was a kingdom; it produced excellent sausages and good cheese; the Church of the Lady of the Green and White had one of its main centres in Mark-fen, the capital. Chare, a parliamentary republic, had no fewer than seventeen universities within its borders, including the famous Stoneybridge; it produced wine, almonds, saffron, and mules; it had a much stronger mercantile class than Lind and a solid, some might say entrenched, guild system.)

"I always wanted to go to university," I said apropos of nothing, which surprised all of us.

Jullanar recovered first. "What would you like to study?"

"It's a bit late now, surely."

"They probably wouldn't deny *you* a place," Masseo said.

At some point this morning I had twisted my signet ring so the flat bezel was once more visible. I clenched my hand around the walking staff, looking at the way the skin tautened over the knuckles. "I suppose not," I said, trying not to sound too dispirited at the thought of what attending a university as the heir to the Empire would have been like, and how much worse it would be to attend as the Last Emperor.

"Literature?" Jullanar asked.

I had to recollect my thoughts. "I can study that well enough on my own."

She laughed. "So no languages, geography, politics, magic, runes—"

Masseo joined in gleefully. "Enchantment, disenchantment, fashion, theatre, rhetoric—"

"*Or* poetics. What does that leave? Maths?"

Mathematics is not one of my strong points. I shook my head, looking down at some plants with round pleated green leaves, each with a dewdrop like a bead of quicksilver nestled into the folds, and chartreuse-green froths of flowers. "I've always wanted to know more about plants," I murmured.

"Those are lady's mantle," Jullanar told me. "I have—had—some in my garden. I love how the dew beads like that."

I stooped down to pluck a leaf. The dew ran off, leaving the leaf dry. I rubbed it between my fingers; the texture was soft, almost velvety, and there was a faint silvery sheen as I tilted the leaf at various angles, both the result of a multitude of fine hairs covering the surface.

"What new songs have you written?" Jullanar asked after we climbed up a steep portion and stopped with one accord at the top to catch our breath.

I turned around slowly. We'd climbed another few hundred feet above the stone bench now, and were only one very steep climb away from the saddle. I regarded it doubtfully. The evidence lower down the path suggested people managed to get their horses up and down that hill, but even if had been many years since I'd last been on horseback, I couldn't imagine this passage was very pleasant for either the horse or the rider.

They were still waiting for an answer. I spoke far more nonchalantly than I felt. "Nothing yet."

Jullanar's expression was a study in shock. "Fitzroy—"

"I have a distinct style," I said sharply, as if that were an answer for half of a lifetime of listening for a muse that never came.

Albeit it was true. I had not signed my songs, when I released them into the world, teaching fellow musicians or ardent listeners, publishing a few in various cities, but yet people had been able to say *this one* was by the same artist as *that one*, and on and on until I had published *Aurora and the Peacock* under my own name.

"I wonder," I said, because Jullanar and Masseo were still frowning in distress, "what ever happened to the royalties from *Aurora.*"

"They probably have been accumulating vast riches over the years," Jullanar said. "It's still in print, as you may or may not know."

"Isn't it banned here?" Masseo asked.

"Of course, but that doesn't stop anyone except the unimaginative. Most of the new editions I've seen since the Fall have been published by Jacinth, which otherwise specializes in the most resolutely dull and respectable works of comparative philology. Clever of them."

My publisher had been based out of Colhélhé, out of Yedoen of the Great Bazaar, one of the great centres of learning in that world. They had had several partnerships with other printing houses elsewhere in the Empire, but I couldn't name them off the top of my head. Not to mention they used false imprints for my works to keep them out of the censors' hands.

"Perhaps we will pass through Yedoen in our travels," I said, and on that reminder (and because Jullanar no longer looked dangerously flushed), suggested we start off again.

They agreed, though we all looked at the steep incline ahead of us with displeasure. "Where *are* we going?" Jullanar asked, then laughed at her own words.

I liked her laugh, richer and less shrill than her younger self's occasional giggle. This was a woman in her prime, solid and secure in her sense of self.

"That is," she went on, "what is the ostensible object of our quest? Oh yes—those mirrors. What then? Dare I ask what they're for?"

I concentrated on my footing as I crossed a little rivulet with muddy patches, the end of the staff squelching as it sank an inch down. Once safely on the other side I offered my hand back to Jullanar, who accepted it with a happy smile and a little hop.

"The mirrors are supposed to show the past, the present, and the future, and united can show the truth of any enchantment or ensorcellment. Not that it matters, what with Lazunar's destroyed."

"Do you need the assistance?" Masseo asked in evidently genuine surprise. "You seemed to know exactly how to undo that curse on Mae Irión."

I considered how to answer that as we started up the steep section. It was easier now that I wasn't looking at them. "That wasn't on *myself*, Masseo."

There was a silence as we laboured up a few yards. The path went up nearly vertically, only passable by virtue of rough stairs formed out of large stones that zigzagged up a kind of chimney between two outcroppings of a rough dark grey stone. Little tufts of grass and pretty four-petalled pink and white flowers adorned every tiny crevice containing soil.

I paused at a marginally wider ledge to catch my breath. Looking back down on Jullanar and Masseo I realized how high we were, and how steep a drop it was. Masseo was close on my heels, but Jullanar was coming more slowly, with her eyes fixed on the ground and using her hands to support herself. When she reached our level she leaned into the rock, eyes closed.

"Perhaps Masseo should go up first, and then you, and me last," I said.

"I'm sorry to be so slow."

"Nonsense! You've never liked heights. And this way you *know* I'll see you, and I can catch you if you slip."

"Er," said Masseo.

"With *magic*," I went on, glaring at him. "I do not need the muscles of Yr the Conqueror for that!"

Jullanar giggled with surprise, but she did open her eyes to smile at me in relief. "Fitzroy, you've never had the muscles for that! Thank you."

"My great pleasure," I replied, with a regal nod.

Masseo appeared more dubious, but continued up first without saying anything further. "Would you like my staff?" I asked Jullanar.

"No, I feel better touching the stone. I'll—it'll be better once I'm up, won't it?"

"Assuredly."

"Will you—will you keep talking, please?"

"If you'd like." I pondered a moment. "It amazes me that people take horses up and down this path. Not something I'd enjoy! Not that I've been on horseback since … the old days. Which is an uncomfortable number of years for me. Fewer for you, it would seem."

She nodded, took a deep breath, and started up, leaning well forward. "Thirteen years since the Interim after the Fall, and before that Artorin Damara's reign was fourteen years, wasn't it?"

"Fourteen years, four months, and four days, in fact," I informed her. "Not that I was counting or anything."

She chuckled tiredly. "I don't suppose you really *are* Aurelius Magnus? Or were?"

"I'm not sure that I believe in reincarnation."

"I suppose I was thinking more of an immortal deity coming to the mortal worlds every once in a while."

I thought of the Tigara whispering of Crow to me. "Why *do* people insist I'm divine? You know me better than that!"

"You fell out of the sky on top of Damian and me."

Masseo was high above us by this point, at the stone pillar that appeared to mark the top of the path. He shouted down to us something with great excitement that got stolen away by the wind. I waved; he waved back with wide gestures and moved out of sight.

"I tripped and fell out of one world into another. It wasn't actually on purpose."

She sighed. "I know. It's just … I suppose it's easier to think of you being *other* in some way."

There were many things I wanted to say to that, but I had already thoroughly embarrassed myself over the ginger biscuits, and so I only said, "Jullanar, I hate to break it to you, but we *are* ancient heroes out of legend."

She wheezed out a laugh, and accepted Masseo's strong arm to get up over the brink of the cliff. I followed her expeditiously, for even if I didn't mind heights, climbing up that steep of a slope was no picnic—we'd had one earlier, so I had an easy comparison—and was grateful to find someone had placed another bench up there, and sat on it.

After a few minutes of recovering I looked around to see the view back over the valley of Fiellan. From up here the haze was more pronounced but the panorama splendid. After satisfying my curiosity about the courses of the rivers Rag I turned my attention to the mountains and the saddle we had just reached.

The sheep were up here too, leaving shiny brown pellets scattered in the grass. A small bird—a lark, perhaps? I could hear a high thin song pouring down—hovered high above us. The saddle was a broad grassy meadow that led at a much gentler slope upwards to a ridge where another stone pillar stood sentinel. The path was clear, if not much more than a footpath.

"I thought you said this was the main route to Chare?" I asked Jullanar, puzzled. I was sure at some point that had come up.

"It is *now*," she explained. "In Astandalan days there was a route that led by a southern pass, a proper road, but it was badly damaged during the Fall. People speculate that it actually led through part of the Borderwood and that's why it became so strangely impassable."

"How curious."

The Border between Alinor and Ysthar had once lain in the woods south of Ragnor Bella. Even now I could feel the tendrils of other worlds' magics curling through the air, tenuous as a distant smell but just barely perceptible. One was of Zunidh, but I could not trace its origin without going into the deep trance. It wasn't the same as the passage that had led Masseo and me here, for that had quite clearly been a one-way opening, at least at that time and for us.

"And I didn't say it earlier, but people go round with their horses—there's a longer path further up the Coombe, that reconnects with this one further along, by the refuge. It's much farther, though, miles, that way. The refuge is another hour and a half or two hours' walk—will that be all right, Fitzroy?"

I felt mildly offended that she thought I wasn't fit enough for this. And while it might be true that my exercise was usually quite constrained, it's not as if I didn't do *anything*—quite apart from the pacing, I swam regularly.

I looked, I reminded myself (and felt, and … was), considerably older than she. And she had always been one to cosset. I'd found it such a baffling, if pleasant, habit, back when we'd first met.

"I'm fine, thank you," I replied. "It's all this fresh air and fun— I'm not accustomed to it in these quantities."

Any quantities, really, but that was another matter.

"Tell us if you want to take a break," she instructed.

"Of course, my lady," I replied, bowing grandly, which made her laugh.

But when we reached the refuge two hours later she told me I should set up beds and then lie down to rest while she and Masseo saw to supper.

I was more than a little confused. The last portion of the walk had been delightful, what with the cool air and the bright sunlight and the springy close-cropped grass underfoot. I had once again been tempted to take off my boots, and only the frequent presence of the sheep pellets discouraged the idea. We had walked at a gentle pace, an amble really, and Masseo had talked about his apprentice Kenna and his little cottage with its waterwheel and forge.

"You're alarmingly pale, which is quite the trick for you," she said bluntly.

"And no matter what you say, you can't possibly pretend you've been hiking up mountains on a regular basis," Masseo added. "Go on, bestrew your multitudes of cushions and we'll light a fire and make supper and so on."

The refuge was a small stone building with wood-framed windows and a slate roof. It was all one room inside, with a wooden platform across one end where the ceiling slanted down into a kind of alcove that I supposed was meant to be for sleeping. The other end of the room had a fireplace with a basket of wood next to it as well as a rough table and four chairs.

"I can help," I said quietly. "I'm not … unwilling. Or incapable."

Jullanar patted me on the arm empathetically. "Don't worry! We'll conscript you to work other days. Just—tonight, Fitzroy, let us take care of you?"

Everyone took care of me, I thought a little dismally, but they seemed adamant in their insistence that I didn't need to do anything, and so I left them to chopping wood and fetching water.

I did have to remove the dust off the platform, which I did by magic since I couldn't see a broom. Jullanar came back inside holding one and laughed to see me directing a spiral of dust motes out the window with my not-yet-a-wizard's staff. I smiled back, ignoring how I really ought to stop doing these little, unaccustomed magics until I'd recovered properly. This was not Zunidh, and I might need the strength. Even on Zunidh I'd needed it for that unexpected plunge over the waterfall.

As she got to the work of sweeping the area around the hearth, I pulled out the bedding Conju had packed for me. There were three down-filled cloth pallets (out of at least a dozen, for Conju had not been sanguine about the likely comfort of beds I might encounter along the way, nor anyone's ability to clean the mattresses), and sheets in antique ivory linen, and woollen blankets in bright colours woven by skilled artists, and more of the cushions Masseo had decried but also enjoyed.

I arranged these into three beds—blue for Jullanar, orange for

Masseo, green for me—and was pleased at how they transformed the space into something strange and wonderful, like a grotto. I spread out a length of cloth that had come out of my private study and wished I hadn't had the thought, for now the place reminded me of that small room, burrowed deep in the heart of the Palace where I could be considered safe.

The poets who called power its own worst imprisonment were not far wrong.

I sat down on my bed, legs hanging over the edge of the platform, and wearily struggled with my boots. Masseo came in with a load of wood for the fire, saw me, and hurried over to help without being solicited.

"Thank you," I said awkwardly.

"No worries." He set the boots neatly to one side. I stripped off my socks and rubbed the hot spot. At least the upward climb had changed the angle of chafing and not compounded the problem into a blister. "Do you want some water? It's from a marked spring, so it should be clean."

I nodded, and he regarded me for a long moment without saying anything. I set my New Bag on the platform beside me and wondered about pulling out my Old Bag to see what I could find.

"Lie down," he said gently. "I'll bring you the water."

"It's still early," I said, looking out the window—Jullanar had opened the shutters—at the bright sunlight.

"We're north," he reminded me, "and it's midsummer. The longest day. Jullanar said it won't get dark till half past nine."

"I'd forgotten," I said, a natural enough thing to say, I thought, but he quirked his lips before Jullanar called him from outside and he apologized and went off.

It seemed much easier just to lie down and contemplate how much nicer it felt to have my feet up.

～

I must have fallen asleep, for when I opened my eyes next the light outside the window was a rich gold and the fire was burning brightly in the hearth. I sat up slowly, feeling unwarrantedly dizzy. One of them had left a cup of water beside my bags. I sipped it, looking at the two of them sitting at the table, chatting quietly. Jullanar had undone her braids so her hair waved down her back, while Masseo had his whittling knife and block of wood out. Jullanar's back was to me so I couldn't see what she was doing.

When I set the cup down it made a click. Jullanar twisted around to look at me, then came over when she saw I was sitting up. "Are you awake? You look much better!" She reached out towards my forehead, then paused when I recoiled. "Sorry, Fitzroy. I … Do you mind if I check for fever? You really did look unwell earlier. It occurred to us it might have been sunstroke."

I braced myself and nodded permission. Her hand was gentle and cool, and she didn't linger.

"Well?"

She smiled gently. "It seems a normal temperature. A little warm, perhaps. Do you feel better?"

I nodded.

"That's good. Do you want to join us for a cup of tea? Masseo has some lovely smoked stuff."

He had produced the silver teapot as well. I considered his pack, which was larger than Jullanar's—he was a smith, broad-shouldered and strong—and marvelled at the choice of bringing a silver teapot instead of anything else. Not that I disagreed with bringing the lovely instead of the merely useful; sometimes such delights made all the difference.

The tea made me feel better, as coffee never did. We had three mismatched cups, a wooden one for Masseo, an enamelled tin one for Jullanar, a gold-rimmed porcelain one for me. Jullanar laughed when she saw what I'd brought to be filled, though she poured easily enough.

"My dear Fitzroy! What a cup that is! Fit for an emperor!"

"Especially a legendary one," Masseo put in, pushing over a plate with more of the ginger biscuits on it. I took one and tried not to appear miffed at their mockery.

I didn't succeed, for Jullanar stopped laughing and said, "Are we—I'm sorry, did I hurt your feelings?"

"It's nothing. I'm ... unaccustomed to ... teasing."

"Oh, *no*." Her face went aghast. Masseo, when I looked at him, appeared almost as distraught.

I went over her words, and mine, in my mind, but couldn't see what there was to be so upset over. "It's nothing, truly," I assured them, knowing I was awkward in every way. "It's the same as being touched. ... I've forgotten ..." I trailed off. It was hard to articulate what I'd forgotten; or rather what I *knew* I had forgotten. "It has all been very formal," I concluded. "I will remember how to behave among friends soon."

Jullanar regarded me as if this was the most distressing thing I'd ever said to her, which was surely not warranted, and Masseo turned away with a gruff clearing of his throat to put another piece of wood on the fire.

My inner sarcastic voice pointed out that I was demonstrating just why the very definition of *pathetic* is *the emperor with no empire*.

Time to change the subject, which I did without pretending otherwise. "What are you making?" I asked Jullanar, gesturing at the small skeins of wool in soft purplish-red and fine ivory that lay before her. "Are you knitting something?"

Jullanar lifted the short implement, a straight handle with a small hooked point, with which she was doing some sort of clever knotting trick. "It's called crochet. Similar to knitting in the end result, but it only uses the one hook. I'm making a scarf." She bit her lip. "Do you have any new hobbies?"

I smiled wryly at her. "Does running a government count?"

23

IN WHICH I LOSE MY TEMPER

*A*fter I finished my cup of tea I went outside to where Masseo had indicated a privy was located. It was marginally more civilized than the outhouse the Mae Irionéz had given us to use; there were wood-pulp rags to use to wipe oneself, rather than a shared sponge on a stick. I shuddered again at the thought (personal sponges were bad enough) and did my business hastily before finding the spring so I could wash my hands thoroughly. There was no telling when the *door* had last been cleaned, given the state of the interior.

That done I surveyed the surroundings more carefully than earlier. The track we'd come by was met just below the hut by another, wider path that came up from the south. Both turned—I walked around the building to see the route—and headed nearly due east to where a tall standing stone marked a crossroads perhaps a mile away. That, I guessed, was the fork proper, with one road leading north and east to Lind and the other south and east to Chare. I could only see three roads, as nothing led due south from the crossroads.

Coming up the Charese road was a rider on a black horse. I stood at the corner of the hut, watching the horse canter with a steady, beautiful pace. The lingering sunlight slanted through gaps between the mountains, bathing the rider in gold.

There was no one else visible for miles. Just the wide green heath and the rider and their horse, splendid and solitary. I stood with tears once again in my eyes, for this too had once been familiar, and now was entirely strange.

The rider came up to the cross-roads standing stone and performed a marvellously graceful feat in which she directed her horse to circle tightly around the standing stone while she leaned down to one side, one foot in the stirrup and one hand on the saddle, and collected something from the ground without stopping, falling, or even slowing from the canter.

I had only seen a handful of people able to do that, and one of them lived down that road.

The wind had freshened, and I shivered a little; which was as good a reason as any to hastily return inside and change my clothes to the apricot wool robes with the green hose and a pair of half-boots in a fine dark brown leather.

Jullanar and Masseo regarded my action with amusement. "Is there an occasion?" Jullanar asked with a dimpled smile.

"We are about to have a visitor," I replied.

"Oh? Shall I put the kettle on?"

"I think that would be appreciated."

They looked at each other, before Masseo shook his head and refilled the kettle from the bucket of water Jullanar had brought in earlier. There was a pot of something else on the fire, but he hooked it off the tripod with practiced ease and set it to the side of the hearth so he could put the kettle to boil instead.

I went over to my luggage and hesitated before putting my hand into the Old Bag. I pulled out a cup I had thought lost in the Sea of Stars. When I studied the ceramic glaze cautiously I saw it had a faint smudge of silver on it, the suggestion of a glimmer. I focused my magical attention on it and felt only waves of good fortune and good friendship.

I set it down in front of the fourth chair at the table even as Masseo fussed with his teapot and fresh tea leaves, and Jullanar arranged the biscuits to make it less evident we'd already eaten half of them.

The thunder of horse hooves grew loud, the steady *da-da-dump* of a canter or a waltz, before coming to an abrupt halt with a clatter as horseshoes hit the stones around the base of the refuge. The horse neighed, and a woman's voice murmured something gently to it before there was a creak from the steps and a slim, petite woman, black-haired and copper-skinned, still one of the most beautiful I have ever seen, peeked in the door with a perfunctory knock on its frame.

"Excuse me, I was hoping—"

But she stopped then, dark eyes wide, strong black brows winging up, one hand coming up to her mouth in shock, for she had seen just who waited for her there.

She looked at Jullanar, and at Masseo, and then she looked at me, and I could not help but be reminded of how angry she had been the last time we spoke.

"You," she said flatly.

I tried so hard to smile at her as myself, not as emperor or lord magus or legendary folk hero or trickster god or anything of the sort. "Pali. Would you like a cup of tea?"

"Only if it's served in a cup from heaven," she said, embracing first Jullanar and then Masseo fiercely, and giving me a wry smile and a deep curtsey.

I realized I had not stood up to greet her, and did so hastily enough that the chair fell over. She gave me an even wryer smile, which faded into surprise when I came all the way around the table, though my courage faltered at that point and instead of giving her an embrace I handed her the cup, which she took with a dumbfounded expression.

"It's not really—?"

"He keeps telling us he's not *actually* a semi-apotheosized god," Masseo complained.

What did that even mean?

I indicated the cup. "I'm pretty certain I stole this from the Moon and dropped it into the Sea of Stars, so … close enough?"

The kettle chose this moment to start to boil. Jullanar and Masseo both turned to fuss with it. Pali and I stared at each other.

She said, with a strange tentativeness, "You're not helping your case any."

A thousand retorts were on my tongue, but I could only think of the expression on her face when she had asked me those last three devastating questions.

Is there anything left of you but the Last Emperor?

How can I believe that you ever told us the truth about anything?

And, worst of all:

Will you prove it, then, and come with me?

To which I had been unable to say anything but the most tremendous and final and unwanted *no* of my life.

"By the all gods," Jullanar said crossly, "and that includes *you*, Fitzroy, sit down and let's talk this out like the adults we are."

I looked in polite bewilderment at Jullanar, but did return to my seat, which Masseo had set upright for me. I murmured my thanks to him—it was getting easier to remember to do so—and sat down across from Pali, who had barely taken her eyes off me.

There was an awkward silence. I thought about what to say, but curiosity overrode any other thought, and I said to Jullanar, "*Do* people talk out their emotions, in your experience?"

She raised her eyebrows at me. "Don't they in yours?"

I thought about Kip, who had (as far as I could tell) never actually told his beloved family that he was the unofficial head of the world's government until I had made him the official one, for fear of what they might say.

No one else even came close.

I shook my head. "No."

She blinked. Masseo moved his teapot so the fragrant steam eddied around the table, smokey and rich and reminiscent of so many past conversations.

"Fitzroy," he said slowly and seriously, "have *you* ever told someone what you were truly thinking?"

I could have said something flippant, one of those truths that no one ever believed—I could have told them *about* those truths that no one ever believed—but I was tired, and spoke a hard truth instead. "Masseo, people have committed suicide because I told them what I actually thought."

I could name four people who had done so, in the early days of my reign as Emperor, before I knew what that sort of criticism meant at the Imperial court. Half a dozen more had been executed for crossing some boundary-line of etiquette. *Wars* had started because I had spoken too openly.

I didn't have any personal compunction against telling the truth, but it was not as if I didn't have plenty of evidence for why I *should* not. It was better to smile benignly and serenely and say nothing.

I was, I had been told once, an institution, and institutions did not have feelings.

They looked at me as if I were joking; Pali particularly appeared to think it in very poor taste. I folded my hands on the table before me and resolutely held my magic in control. I was still tired after the curse-breaking in Mae Irión, but, *as everyone knew*, high emotions and wild magic mix far too well.

"Desur of Erldan," I said. "Goroghen the Tailor. Nina Firunzky. Lord Saiverdell. That was in the first six months, before I learned what not to say."

Jullanar shrank back slightly. Pali's face was stern, but her eyes were troubled. Masseo reached out as if to pat my hand, but I folded my hands in my lap, and he poured us all tea instead.

The great difference between sitting here in this refuge high on a mountain and any other uncomfortable tea party I had ever been to —and I have been to many—was that here it was not *my* burden to ensure the conversation flowed. None of my friends knew, or cared if they did, that as the highest-ranking party it was up to me to set the tone and content of the discussion. If I had given *any* such indications that this was a subject I didn't want to talk about, not even Kip would have pushed.

(It was true that I had become *friends* with Kip after he and I had had several conversations in which we told each other true things about our emotions, even if both of us retreated quickly thereafter to easier topics, like world governance and the eradication of poverty.)

Masseo said, "You told me you'd made at least one apology. At the time I thought … well, I thought perhaps you were joking, but you weren't, were you?"

"I dislike lying, it's true."

Pali stirred and spoke for nearly the first time. "A nice evasion, but what does Masseo mean?"

I considered how to answer that. How could I tell them about that afternoon, evening, day, when Ludvic suggested I retire and I seized at the idea like a drowning man, and hurt Conju's feelings so terribly? Conju had not laughed at my attempt at an apology, but he had found it nearly impossible to accept nevertheless.

Masseo spoke before I had fully gathered my thoughts together.

"When he first arrived—well, the first bit of privacy we had—he tried to apologize to me for abandoning us in the Silver Forest. I told him not to be absurd, that it was hardly his desire that the protections rose up, but mostly I made fun for how awkward an apology it was." He looked at me with a strange expression in his eyes and a soft, rueful smile. "I'm sorry for laughing at you, Fitzroy. I wasn't thinking how hard that must have been for you."

Being condescended *to* was not a common experience of mine, and I didn't like it much. "It's fine," I said shortly.

"It's not fine," Jullanar said, setting her cup down loudly, and when I looked at her I could see her ire was roused again, her face flushed and her eyes bright and flashing. "Fitzroy, I've only spent half a *day* with you, and already I can see—"

She stopped there. I waited, but nothing more seemed to be forthcoming. I glanced at Pali, whose expression was uncomfortably close to grim. "We've all changed," I said quietly. "It's been … a long time."

Longer, it was clear, for me than for them, but long enough regardless.

Jullanar tossed her head in exasperation. "Of course we've all changed, but we're also all the same *people* we were before. Pali is still Pali for all that she's a great scholar now. Masseo isn't a different person for all that he's learned how to laugh, and *you're* not a different person for all that you've forgotten how to."

If she had been any member of my household, my posture and expression would have told her in no uncertain terms to *back off immediately*.

Because they were (had been?) my friends, they paid no attention whatsoever to my demeanour, and persisted.

For my part, I tried but could not prevent the wash of furious indignation that I was being so disregarded. Jullanar kept speaking but I heard only the voice in my mind saying, in my coldest and harshest imperial tone, *Does she not know that we are the Emperor of Astandalas?*

It was more with horror at myself than anger at them that I pushed back from the table and stormed outside.

Storm was, alas, the correct word.

It was only the second time in my life that my temper had translated itself into tempest. I walked away from the refuge, into he teeth of a storm that would not bite me.

The wind was a solid force, sweeping down the valley, driving magic before it. I bent my head and pushed against the wind, the magic, the long-learned indignation, letting the brute force of the wind tear the moisture from my eyes before it had any other reason to form.

At length I grew tired of walking against the pressure and turned, leaning against it, letting it support me, letting it blow all the fury out of my heart and mind.

When I was younger I had been a skilled and powerful mage— or rather, I had *become* one over the course of our adventures. Masseo was not, after all, the only one to study strange books in obscure libraries.

My affinity had always been first to fire and secondarily to air. I set things on fire when my emotions were roused beyond control; I did not make storms.

Yet when I had tried, and nearly failed, to make my household *see* that I was a man, and not merely a god, it was a tempest I had called up, a wall of rain and a storm of winds.

These winds were not those tropical airs, that heavy humid somnolence ready to rouse to lightning. These were high montane winds, thin and cold and crackling with their own power. They spoke of throwing stones to one another, playing with the snow on the highest peaks, the solitude of the high places that was not loneliness.

Why did this *hurt* so? I had spent so long wishing to be treated as a person, a friend, a human being.

I leaned back into the wind. The sun was going down behind the mountains whose western face we had climbed that afternoon. The land was dimming, not yet dark, but greyer, softer, less distinct. For all the rocks around me, the wind seemed the hardest thing in the world.

It was a bare country up here, all grass bent flat and some low shrubby plant with pink-purple blossoms. Farther up the valley I had taken was some sort of small tree, twisted and gnarled from the wind, gleaming white in the gloaming.

I would walk to the tree, I decided, and then return to the hut and apologize for losing my temper.

They might be grateful, I thought wryly, that I had spent much more of the past thousand years on weather magic than anything to do with fire.

It took me longer to reach the tree than I'd expected. There was a stream in the way, shallow and chattering noisily even over the wind, which I forded awkwardly, soaking one foot.

The tree had white blossoms, with a heavy, musky scent, and many ribbons tied along its branches. They fluttered madly in the wind, strips of cloth of all lengths and colours and ages, some faded, others bright.

I circled the tree, questioning it with my magic. It was planted on a node of sorts, anchoring several streams of magic that joined here. Sometimes, the magic whispered, the road to Fairyland left from here.

It was Midsummer's night. The passage would have been easy to open.

I hastily withdrew my magic and tucked it away. It was rather harder to avoid opening, in fact, given the circumstances. Only sunrise on Midsummer morning would have been more propitious for the passage.

It was getting dark, and I had left my friends to wait and perhaps to worry, and …

And I did not want to go to Fairyland without them.

I put my hand on the gnarled trunk of the tree, gifting it with a drop of my own magic in gratitude, for even if the wind was still awesome in its strength I no longer felt so roiled inside myself.

After a moment I felt ready, and started to walk back to the refuge.

I had told my household that time, Conju and Ludvic and Kip, that we always wanted others to know our hearts, but how could they if we did not tell them?

Those three men had spent half a lifetime in intimate proximity to me, yet what did I know of their hearts or they of mine?

Enough, and never a sufficiency, I supposed. And yet, I presumed, assumed even, that Jullanar would *know* to interpret the subtleties of behaviour that were all I had been allowed, or allowed myself, at court.

How arrogant of me to assume she would look on me the way my guards and attendants did, or be able to read me the way Kip did, after our decades (centuries) of working so closely together, our more recent deep friendship.

It occurred to me that it had not taken me this long to reach the tree from the stream going the other direction.

I stopped to look around. The mountains were dim masses against a luminous royal-blue sky, and the heath or upper valley of the path was already in quite deep shadow.

I sent out my magic, but the wind was so strong it overwhelmed any more subtle or delicate indications. I had not, I could be sure, strayed into Fairyland, as someone not a great mage attuned to the borders between worlds almost certainly would have. Otherwise …

The stars were still faint and also unfamiliar. I had known the skies of each world well enough once, enough to pick out a handful of constellations, but that had been a long time ago, and I doubted that waiting until full dark and visible stars would be of much use.

Eventually it occurred to me that I had been walking *into* the wind on my way out, and therefore if I turned my back to it I should be going in the correct direction to return.

I did so, and nearly immediately fell into the stream. After picking myself up I reoriented myself to the wind at my back, and squelched onwards, up and over a slight rise. There before me in the distance was a faint light.

I felt quite proud of myself. I'd been known to get much more thoroughly lost on slighter grounds. (Though in my defence: the universe is full of invitations, some of which are irresistible.)

It was nearly full dark when I reached the refuge, and despite the mild season I was shivering from the chill of wet clothing and mountain winds and, I admit, exhaustion. It had been a very full day even by my standards.

It wasn't till I stood at the steps that I realized the light was not shining from the window of the refuge but was actually a lantern set above the door of a small wooden caravan.

24

IN WHICH I RECEIVE SOME ADVICE

I knocked on the door.

After a moment it opened, revealing a white-haired old woman, all wrinkles and weathered ruddy skin and the powerful scent of sheep and tobacco and some other herb that made me want to sneeze.

She surveyed me thoughtfully and without visible surprise. She was smoking a pipe, a short stout thing, and puffed on it several times before speaking.

"Lost, ar' tha?" she said at last, her accent broad.

It was probably obvious, but I nodded anyway.

"Come in. Leave thy shoes and any ill-wishes outside the door."

I complied—not that I had any ill wishes at the moment—and found myself in a brightly lit, cheerful sort of place. The fug of sheep wool, tobacco, and the strange herb was briefly intense, before it overpowered my nose and became the background.

The old shepherdess, or so I presumed she was, pointed me to a blanket thrown over a built-in bench or chest of some form. There was a small pot-bellied iron stove at the end opposite the door, with a single bed tucked on one side and cabinets on the other. A folding table filled the middle of the space, an oil lantern swung from the curved ceiling, and a slumbering black-and-white dog took up most of the floor. After opening one eye to look at me, the dog thumped its tail twice and returned to sleep. Everything was brightly painted, and although it should have been entirely claustrophobic, instead I felt immediately heartened.

The stove was lit; in other circumstances I should probably have found it unbearably hot. As it was, I was grateful for the blanket to absorb some of the stream water. The shepherdess put a kettle on to boil and set a loaf of bread and a round of white cheese on the table. A knife and two plates followed.

"There," she said. "Be welcome, stranger."

She eyed me, and an odd expression flitted across her face. "Belike no stranger. Thy face is familiar."

It had been on every coin for twenty or thirty years, of course.

I opened my mouth to brazen it out, but felt suddenly, inexplicably, unutterably weary. I wanted to be only Fitzroy Angursell—oh, how badly!—but if the last three days in Masseo's and now Jullanar's company had shown me anything, it was that I could not quite help but wish to be Artorin Damara as well.

I might in truth have been a good emperor only in comparison to my uncle Eritanyr but I had *tried*, dammit, and I was tired of pretending otherwise.

And even if it was largely due to recognizing and assisting Kip's genius, I had not done so ill as Lord of Zunidh, all in all. Even Pali had granted me that much.

"You'll have seen pictures of me," I told the shepherdess. "I'm Artorin Damara, Last Emperor of Astandalas and Lord of Zunidh."

She puffed at her pipe. "Strange place to find thee all alone, then."

I laughed, a choked sort of thing unlike my usual laughter. "You have no idea."

She cut me a slice of bread and a wedge of cheese, and made me a tisane with the boiling water over sage leaves. ("For clarity," she

329

said, not clarifying anything.) And then she said, "Well, I won't ask it of thee, but it seems to me tha wants to tell the story, and I'll listen if tha does."

It had been a long day: I did.

~

It had started, I told her, a few years back, when my then-secretary and unofficial head of government, Kip—

"Busy man," she said, puffing away.

I had overworked him terribly for years before realizing it. "Yes," I agreed.

—Kip had invited me to take a holiday in the remote Outer Ring of the Vangavaye-ve with him, and there, far from the Palace, I had finally been able to break loose of the confines and constraints of my position, and reach towards genuine friendship.

And Ludvic, my chief guard, had respond by suggesting I retire.

"Don't hear much about emperors retiring," observed the shepherdess. "More often dying on the job."

"Exactly. But being the Lord of Zunidh ... there was precedent there. And as we found out later, there is a ceremony, a ritual, and a spell to do before setting out on a quest to find an heir."

"And that's why th'art here?"

I hesitated. "Officially, yes."

The shepherdess's eyes twinkled. "And *unofficially*, belike?"

I hesitated again, but ... "Well, you see," strengthening my resolution, "I wasn't supposed to become emperor. I was the back-up heir. I had a magical role but not a political one. I was exiled, to a tower on the edge of the Colhélhé, far away from everywhere, where I was supposed to spend out my days."

"But?" said the shepherdess after an interval.

"But I didn't stay there," I told her. "I went off searching for adventures, and friends, and—and I found them, for I am—I was— I am also Fitzroy Angursell of the Red Company."

A slightly faster and more prolonged series of puffs was all the reaction the shepherdess made to this revelation. I was greatly relieved that she didn't laugh with disbelieving appreciation for the joke.

I drank the sage tea (which tasted more vaguely minty than anything) and waited.

Eventually she spoke. "So, th'art looking for thy old friends, then."

"Yes. And ... I've found three of them."

I told her about Masseo and Jullanar and how neither of them seemed to believe me when I told them the truth; and then how no one ever seemed to believe me when I told them the deeply true things; and then about Pali, who was sharp as a desert wind; and then about the argument that had led to me storming off and getting lost.

At the end the shepherdess poured me more of the tea and then reflected, puffing gently at her pipe. I considered what I had just said and disliked how confused I was.

"Do you have any advice?" I asked, not thinking until after I had said the words how ridiculous the question was. But really—who else ought I to ask?

Her eyes were twinkling, probably at the absurdity. "It seems to me that thy friends hurt thy feelings and tha doesn't know how to tell them so."

"It's not that simple," I protested.

She smiled at me, all her wrinkles crinkling. "No? Art tha not allowed to have feelings of thy own, then?"

I felt even more confused, and didn't know what to say. And that was not a situation in which I often found myself.

"Look, lad," the old shepherdess said, taking her pipe out of her mouth and gesturing at me with it. "I don't know much about emperors, and I don't know much about poets, and I don't know much about learned men like thy own self, but I reckon I know a bit about people, belike."

"I would welcome hearing your advice," I replied politely.

"Be the first time!" She cackled. "Now, listen here, laddie. Th'art making an ocean out of a drop of rain. Aye, it's wet, but two raindrops don't make a puddle. Thy friends were teasing thee, I reckon, and I reckon emperors don't get much of that, do they?"

I smiled reluctantly. "Very little."

"So then. Tha'rt used to being the centre, I guess, and so tha'rt been trying to keep the side, so's not to be too much the emperor, belike?"

I sat back while I absorbed this. Aelian the post officer had read me this clearly, this *easily*, too.

Was it just that my courtiers were too preoccupied with their own games to pay attention to my moods?

No, that surely wasn't it. At court I instinctively retreated, all my defences up, my face nothing more than the image of the idol they expected. And once alone and free—

"I was trying," I said, and added, ruefully, "I'm sure I'm doing a poor job of it. Being … ordinary."

The shepherdess puffed at her pipe. "Can't say as any of the songs or stories ever made Fitzroy Angursell out to be *that*."

"I must seem so so arrogant."

The sleeping dog muttered a soft bark, feet twitching, as it dreamed. Its tailed thumped against my foot.

I'd wanted a dog, once. Somehow it had never seemed the right time.

"I reckon I never thought the Last Emperor of Astandalas would come knocking on *my* door for advice," the shepherdess said. "Though tha'rt hardly the first! And I'll tell thee what I've told many a young man on the outs with his friends: that honesty is best, and no one likes either the braggart or the falsely humble. As for thee, lad, thou hast no business pretending to be anything but what thou art."

It was only the only time she'd said *thou* clearly, and it struck me.

The Tigara had said, *Fly with joy, Old Crow*, and even if I wasn't
—for surely I would know, if I were?—the Crow of his imaginings,
the Tigara's advice was almost exactly the same as what Aelian had
given me, and now this shepherdess.

I thought how Masseo had probably expected me to join him in
the great flight of fancies and hypotheticals with which he'd
regaled Jullanar, and how sad Jullanar had seemed when I did not
join in on their reminiscing. I'd been trying not to take over; and
they'd responded with anxious queries about whether I had
sunstroke.

And it must be said that I *wanted* to talk! Just that as with touching, it was hard to know how to start after so long.

I drank my tea and watched the dog breathing and felt myself
unravel a tight stitch or two. Eventually some inner doubt
shifted.

"Is it far to the refuge from here? The one on the road?" I asked.
"I think ... they'll be worried if I don't come back soon."

And that *wasn't* due to my being the centre of things, but
because I was their friend, and so they cared.

It was an appallingly simple point, really. I can only claim that
courts are so complex it becomes easy to miss seeing the simple.

"Tha came up the wrong side," she replied. "I'll show thee—
come on, then."

She got up, nudging the dog with her foot. It sighed but leaped
nimbly to its feet to follow us out. I sat on the steps to put on my
shoes, but they were so disagreeably wet in the end I decided just
to walk in my stockinged feet instead.

The stars had come out and were magnificent. The western sky
was still faintly green with the long lingering twilight of these
northern latitudes. The wind had gentled considerably, and was
hardly more than brisk. A stream was quite audible.

"Tha'rt a wizard, right?" the shepherdess asked.

"A mage, yes."

"Good for a light?"

I produced a golden mage-light to hover in the air between us. The dog lifted its nose to investigate and sneezed.

"Good boy," the shepherdess said absently before turning to me. "Go down the hill here to the stream, and take it left, down the water, to the stone bridge. It's just a stone, not anything fancy, all right? Cross over and there'll be a path that leads to the refuge. Can't miss it."

I had my doubts about that—last night the edges of Fairyland would have been very permeable indeed—but it did seem straightforward enough even for me.

"Thank you," I said, and then, more tentatively: "Is there anything you would ask of me in return?"

She puffed away at her pipe. "I reckon tha'st already done quite enough for me, one way or another, and I ain't one to want more than I have."

"May I write you into a song?"

She cackled, the sound of it echoing into the night. "Always ask, does tha?"

I flushed, not that she could see it. "Not always."

"Me dog's name is Pip," she said; the dog's ears perked alertly. "That's enough fame for the likes o'me."

"Thank you," I said again, with a half-bow whose awkwardness would have spelled social death to any newcomer to my courts.

"Get thee home to thy friends before tha finds any more trouble," the shepherdess ordered, and, obediently, I went.

With my light illuminating my path, I did not stray. Down the hill to the stream; downstream to the stone slab of a bridge; across the bridge and up the path that led from it. In short order I duly arrived at the refuge, where my three friends were sitting on the steps, waiting.

They watched me arrive with expressions mildly troubled, torn,

I rather thought, between relief and anger. A clear thread of amusement (even on Pali's face) was less immediately comprehensible.

I stood at the foot of the steps and looked up at them.

The last time this had happened, that time in the Vangavaye-ve, my friends—Kip and Conju—had folded themselves down into the full formal prostration, as if my anger and frustration were their fault. Conju had even resigned, if reluctantly, in apology.

Jullanar started to smirk, and elbowed Masseo. "You owe me a wheatear. He's back before dawn."

Masseo grunted. "And you owe me a penny. He didn't bring anyone back with him."

"True," Jullanar said, and grinned at me. "You didn't run across a mermaid in distress or a long-thought-dead soldier or a mysterious heir?"

I shook my head. "Just the road to Fairyland and a shepherdess with a dog by the name of Pip, I'm afraid."

"And you didn't bring them back with you?"

"No. She gave me some advice about talking to you."

Pali said, "Come in, then." It was brusque, but her tone was warmer than before, and I took a breath and followed them into the refuge, where the fire was still burning merrily and the air was aromatic with peppermint.

We settled once more around the fire. I was by this point mostly dry, but collected a richly woven blanket (silk and cashmere wool in stripes from coral to crimson) before taking my seat. Jullanar poured us the mint tea.

"I'm sorry for storming off in a temper," I began, then hastened on before they could say anything in response. "I am not accustomed to teasing or being teased, and ..."

And this was *legitimate*, and *normal*, not merely injured pride, the old shepherdess had assured me.

"And it hurt my feelings that you didn't take me seriously," I said resolutely.

Jullanar regarded me with a frown creasing her forehead.

"Fitzroy, you spent all the time I knew you joking about being under an enchantment and how you're secretly the heir of gods and myths and legendary wizards."

I pulled the blanket more tightly around my shoulders, as if I sat alone in my private study, closed away from the world, not an institution or a god but a man, lonely as only someone surrounded by people could be. "Jullanar, I spent all the time you knew me under an enchantment and trying every way I could to get you to guess the truth yourself."

Masseo still seemed inclined to laugh, but I turned on him fiercely. "Masseo, please! I listened to you when you spoke the truth of your past—will you not extend me the same courtesy? Why is *my* heart a laughing-matter?"

He subsided, pressing his hand to his eyes. Pali's face was very still.

"My name," I bit out, "is Artorin Damara. I am the eldest son of the Imperial Princess Lamissa of the house of Yr and Grand Duke Mantorin Damara. I am the direct descendant of ninety-eight Emperors of Astandalas and was the hundredth and last. I am a descendant in a right line of the Sun, of Harbut Zalarin and of Aurelius Magnus. I am the Lord of Five Thousand Lands and Ten Thousand Titles. I am the present Lord Magus of Zunidh, High King of Rondé and yes, Prince of the White Forest. And *yes*, I am Fitzroy Angursell of the Red Company, whom no one *ever* believes when he speaks the truth."

That came out snidely, but I stopped there.

Jullanar said, "You always said—" And then she stopped, and looked at me sharply. "You always *did* say, didn't you?"

"I tried," I said, looking away from her sympathy. "I was exiled, enchanted ... I found out my *name* when I was crowned emperor. Sometimes what I think is worse is that I didn't even realize I didn't have one until I was eighteen."

"I am beginning to understand why you have difficulties being touched," Masseo said thoughtfully. Then he gave me a warm

expression, not quite a smile. "I'm sorry I didn't listen before. You told me but I was so excited to see you again I paid hardly any attention. And," he went on with an impish grin I'd never seen from him before, "I have to say you did a spectacular job of implying you were actually Aurelius Magnus come down from heaven to answer prayers!"

Pali mouthed *Aurelius Magnus* to herself, but said nothing out loud. I could feel myself retreating behind my serene public face, and tried hard not to. My heart felt jittery and wrong. I breathed deeply, firmly grounding myself, refusing to let the fire flare up or the storm rouse again.

"What was your apology for?" Masseo asked. "The one you gave before."

"That's rather personal, isn't it?" Jullanar replied doubtfully. "Fitzroy, we're not trying to pry—"

I couldn't help the snort of disbelief, and she laughed, though it came out a bit choked.

"All right, yes, we are! You didn't seem at all surprised to see Pali arrive. Why not?"

That was a question I knew how to answer. "Didn't you arrange to meet her here?"

"No!" Jullanar turned to Pali in surprise. "Unless you wrote to me? I must have missed that letter if you did!"

Pali shook her head. "I received your letter of last week two days ago, saying that you had found a means to divorce your husband on the first day of midsummer, and I left yesterday. I hoped to reach Ragnor Bella before you left, but I wasn't anticipating you would have found Masseo and Fitzroy already."

"I hardly found them; they came to me." Jullanar looked at Masseo and me. "I should have been more surprised, but it's been a day of impossible things. How *did* you find me?"

"Jemis Greenwing told us to go to the bookstore," I supplied, but that was the sort of misleading truth Masseo disliked.

"Fitzroy found *me* first and we headed off to a passage between

Zunidh and the Borderwood he knew about, but we, er, overshot our mark and ended up going over a waterfall into a cursed pre-Astandalan jungle kingdom and … how was this just the day before yesterday? Anyway, we, or rather Fitzroy, undid their curse and were told of a stone circle where they'd marked the passageway out. And then," and Masseo gave me a suspicious glance, "there was some sort of magic tiger, and he told me to pick which of the pillars we walked through—"

"The tiger did?" Jullanar interjected.

"No, Fitzroy. But I picked the one the tiger had come to, as I figured it was probably good luck, and we walked through and then we ran into your protégé."

"Were run into," I corrected. "Details are important."

"Yes, like the kind of knife he used to kill a dragon … How did you even *know* that? I thought you might have known Jullanar was here already, but did you?"

I was on firmer ground with this sort of discussion. "Of course not; I merely recognized the name of the bookstore she'd always wanted to have, and of course I knew she was from Fiellan, so it was hardly inconceivable. As for hearing about the dragon-slaying, as I told Mr. Greenwing, the Chancellor of Morrowlea told me. She'd come to do some research in the Imperial Archives and visit her sister, and we had supper together one day."

"Really?" said Masseo.

"Really," I said dryly. "Even the last Emperor of Astandalas and present Lord of Zunidh can desire interesting dinner companions, you know."

"Wait, wait, wait," said Jullanar, fixing me with a stern glare. "What do you mean, you're the Lord of Zunidh?"

I confess I stared at her.

"Oh," she said, going rather pink. "So when Masseo and I were joking earlier about … oh."

She subsided, apparently to reconcile her thoughts of me with this new knowledge. I disliked intensely how bewildered I felt, and turned sternly to Pali. "Didn't you tell her?"

"I didn't think it was something to write in a letter," she replied evenly.

She and Jullanar had met up in the spring, and it was midsummer already, and—

And that had not been news worth sharing.

"Oh," I said, in a small voice, feeling more utterly humiliated than at any other point of my life.

Had I been fair as Jullanar I would no doubt have been scarlet. As it was I felt very hot and my heart seemed very loud.

It took me a moment to collect myself and address Jullanar's question, but when I did look up it was to find they were all regarding me with various expressions of alarm. I automatically assessed my posture and expression, which were that well-practiced benign serenity, and raised my eyebrow in silent query.

It was Pali who spoke next. "What—what is that for?" she demanded. "Surely you didn't want me to convey that sort of news to Jullanar in a letter that anyone could have opened? There were troubles with the post this spring."

"Troubles with everything," Jullanar muttered.

Pali glared at me with her eyes bright and her head held high. "So please forgive me for preferring to wait until I saw her next! We were planning on meeting up this summer and going to look for everyone, and I thought it would be better to tell her that news in person. I should have told *you* I'd found her, yes, but you can't pretend that we had much opportunity for any sort of *real* conversation."

It was hard-learned habit not to respond immediately. I took a breath, thinking over what she had said, what I should say in response, and the discrepancy stood out clear.

"I thought," I said evenly, "that you and Jullanar met this spring."

"Yes, right before I went to Zunidh and saw you. I only got back a fortnight ago—gods, Fitzroy, you think I'd sit on that news for long? I could hardly—I hardly knew what to think, and I would have ridden to Ragnor Bella immediately if I hadn't had to arrange for an indefinite leave of absence and sort out my house and things first."

She continued to glare fiercely at me, meeting my eyes fearlessly. I could still feel my heart beating too loudly, but with a different emotion.

"In fact," she said, her eyes softening, "I am utterly *amazed* to find you so close behind me. I'm sorry for doubting you. I ..." She bit her lip, and glanced at Jullanar, who nodded encouragingly. Pali squared her shoulders and regarded me with solemn courage. "I have been going over what I said to you, and I must apologize. I was sore shocked to encounter you, and I said things that must have hurt you deeply. Hear my sorrow, I beg you."

The final words were ritual, and in her own language.

I might not be very good at making apologies, but I know how to accept them. I met her eyes with equal solemnity. "I hear your sorrow, and I say it is a shadow cast by a swift-moving bird, here and gone."

I hesitated there, but what could I say? Those words had been harsh and hard to hear, but I could not say it had not been beneficial to be asked those questions, to be accused of that pusillanimity of spirit.

And it had been a year for me since she had come.

Jullanar said, "That's a good beginning, but perhaps ... Fitzroy, may I advise you to *tell* Pali how that made you feel?"

I twisted in my seat to regard her. "Why?"

She regarded me with almost as much bewilderment as I felt at her question. "What do you mean, why? So you can resolve whatever it was. Which I admit I'm curious about, but you don't have to go into details if it's, er, private."

"But we have resolved it," I said, looking at Pali for confirma-

THE RETURN OF FITZROY ANGURSELL

tion. "She apologized, and I accepted the apology. There's not ... that's what you *do*."

Jullanar looked at me, and then at Pali, who was smiling crookedly, and then at Masseo, who shrugged his magnificent smith's shoulders.

"Oh, I give up!" Jullanar said, and went to the fireplace to deal with whatever the pot Masseo had set to the side contained.

Masseo said, "I found it very helpful to talk out my emotions with the Mother of the Mountains, regarding what I told you. There were things I thought I had long since resolved, but were still lingering and still painful."

"There is a difference," I acknowledged warily, "between how you are now and then."

He nodded in encouragement. "Yes, exactly. It was a combination of what I did as penance and having the Mother Superior listen to me as I talked it all out, the big and the small, that helped. You know me, Fitzroy. I was never one for *talking*!"

"There does seem something unnatural about you pleading with me to talk more."

That made them all laugh, not unkindly or sycophantically, but with great good humour.

And did I then, thus invited, need be afraid?

It was true that Masseo was a much happier person than he'd been before.

"It's been over a year for me," I blurted to Pali. "Did you—did you *know* before you came that you would find me?"

She shook her head. "No, not at all. I was genuinely there to do research. I wondered if you knew it was me, and that was why you'd granted me the audience ...?"

I smiled wryly at her. "No, not at all. I'd read your books, and Cliopher brought up your request. I was having a difficult day ... the cleansing rituals were very involved and tiresome."

"And I came in and I was so shocked to realize it was *you* that I said—those things." Her voice was rueful. "I truly am sorry. I shouldn't have said ..." She glanced at Jullanar, and smiled even more wryly than I had. "I shouldn't have been so antagonistic. Your Lord Chancellor put me right when he came down after. I deserved the chastening. I have been worrying about how you might have taken it ... It wasn't clear at the time to me. You seemed so distant."

I nodded, not sure what to say. Masseo was right, and I did feel better for having clarified this, but also somehow emptied and uncertain.

Jullanar said tentatively, "You told me you were going to research in the Imperial Archives, Pali?"

"Yes, looking up a few things ..." She turned to Masseo. "I'm a professor of Late Astandalan History at Stoneybridge, if no one mentioned. It's strange to think of the subject of one's books reading them!"

"Meaning you didn't go and read all the books about the Red Company in the Stoneybridge library?" I asked, smiling genuinely for what felt like the first time in hours. "I read all the ones in the Archives!"

Pali laughed, and then gave me a contemplative but far less challenging glance. "May I ask about the touching?"

I tried not to flinch. "Is it that obvious?"

"To be honest," Jullanar said, "yes."

I took a sip of my now-cold tea. "There was a taboo on the person of the Emperor," I said. "You were blinded for looking into the Emperor's eyes, burned to death for touching. There were some long and painful cleansing ceremonies for consorts and, and so on, but I never ..."

I stopped for a moment. Politically significant as my marital status might long have been, it was one of the few areas of my life where it was understood I might have some desire for human emotion.

"You never married," Jullanar said, for whom this was a matter of state gossip.

"No." I couldn't look at Pali, who had been the only one I ever wanted to marry, and who had rejected all of my grand proposals with the statement that one day she might say yes.

According to Masseo, in an off-hand comment that might not have been referring to this at all, she had been about to say yes when the Empire fell upon me.

I looked down at the table, which had nicks and odd burns on its unpolished surface. The chairs were hardly less comfortable than the ones I habitually sat upon, which said something about the sacrifices of comfort for impressiveness of imperial furniture.

"After the Fall, some of those taboos were relaxed. There were others ... No going out-of-doors under the open light of the Sun or the Moon, for instance. No eating uncooked food. No touching impure items. No holding of knives or anything edged. No ... There were many. After the Fall I tried to reduce them, but the only ones I was at all successful regarding were the strictures against being outside and meeting eyes. Not though many people chose to go against that custom."

For so long it had been Kip and Kip alone, who had done more than he could possibly realize to keep me sane.

I looked at Masseo, who gave me a look full of deep sympathy and encouragement. I took heart from the knowledge that he had spoken a worse secret to a harsher judge, and come out far the better for it.

"I have touched or been touched by five people since I was anointed Emperor," I said, clenching my hands together as I had long since stopped doing.

(What was I, thirty-two and abruptly thrust from being a great revolutionary folk hero and renegade to being the Emperor of Astandalas?)

The Moon, Ludvic, Kip, Masseo, and Jullanar.

I looked at Pali, knowing I was pleading such as I had pleaded with no one; there had been no one to plead to, save the One Above, and though I believed in the god above all gods I had never had more than poetic inspiration from him.

Pali had furrowed her perfect crow's-wing brows, her dark eyes steady and sad. She had a few strands of silver in her shining black hair, matching the white freckles along one side of her face from when she had walked unafraid through the dark regions between the mortal and divine worlds to save her sister Sardeet from the god who had stolen her away.

"I am trying," I said, and reached out across the table with a hand we all politely pretended wasn't trembling.

Pali took my hand with both of hers, and drew it up to her lips. She brushed the back of my knuckles so lightly I could barely feel the touch.

"You," she said, her eyes bright and brilliant, "are utterly impossible."

We looked at each other for a long moment. For the first time that day I felt my heart beat steadily, joyously.

I turned then to Jullanar, who was openly crying and obviously trying to hold herself back from embracing me fiercely.

"We can't have that," I said sternly, brushing a few strands of hair back from her cheek with my left hand.

"I've always cried too easily, you know that," she said, smiling tremulously. Then she caught my hand with hers and turned it over so she could look at my signet ring. "Is this—are you actually *wearing* the Imperial Seal?"

I raised my eyebrows at her, grateful beyond measure to move on from all that emoting. "No one else should be."

She started to giggle, with the kind of release from heavy emotions that was hard to resist for laugher or listener. "I can't *believe* you actually said you'd traded your advice on questing for a writ of pardon for the Red Company."

I withdrew my hands from both my friends and sipped my stone-cold tea with enormous dignity. "Don't be absurd, Jullanar. It was perfectly true."

IN WHICH I REMOVE ANOTHER CURSE

$\mathcal{M}$asseo did something with the pot and pronounced the food ready, which relieved all of us.

During the bustle of setting the table—my contribution being a loaf of the bread we'd bought in Ragnor Bella—Pali came up to me and said quietly, "Fitzroy."

I smiled down at her. "Pali."

She didn't say anything, just twirled the end of her waist-long braid with her hand, something she always used to do when she was nervous.

"I don't suppose—"

If I had not had Jullanar's comments and example earlier that day, I probably would not have known what she was about, but I had, and did, and so I opened my arms wide and enfolded her.

A week ago I had spent half an hour nervously asking Kip how to greet people. He had sensibly suggested that hugs were not usual between strangers, and thus not to worry if I felt awkward about them.

Despite my heart's excitement, I found I liked them just as much as I remembered.

And then we sat down to supper, which was an excellent hearty soup containing ingredients I did not recognize either in or out of their original form. With mischief in her eyes Jullanar made a traditional grace to the gods and the Lord Emperor.

I replied with the appropriate short benediction, because I might be a very indifferent god but I do know my duty, though all of us were smiling as I did so, as if this might become a recurring joke.

For a while we ate quietly without speaking much but for requests to pass the bread and so on. After serving us all seconds (Jullanar paused over her own bowl as if debating with herself, then muttered something defiantly about being a free woman and no slave to the patriarchy, which I decided probably had to do with her figure, and therefore was entirely her own business), we settled into that time of the evening when we could enjoy the fire and the conversation.

Jullanar and Pali whispered to each other as I contemplated going over to fetch my bag and the bottles of wine I knew was in it. There's an upside to being waited on hand on foot, I mused, eyeing the ten feet separating me from it with displeasure.

Masseo put another piece of wood on the fire, the dishes in a pile, and sat down next to me. "All right there?"

"Oh, I expect I shall recover forthwith, thank you."

He huffed instead of laughing, so I reckoned it a half point. "What do you think the girls are gossiping about?"

"We could ask them to be forthright and so on," I said lazily, stretching out my legs. I really did like these robes. I glanced at Masseo. "Do you think anyone will mind if I take off my socks?"

That did make him laugh, heartily and long, which wasn't entirely intentional. His laughter drew Pali and Jullanar to rejoin us, even as I used one foot and then the other to pry off my socks so I could wriggle my toes before the fire.

"This is not something I get to do very often," I said with great satisfaction.

"Too indecorous?" Jullanar asked.

"More a lack of fireplaces. Most of them were blocked off when the Palace ended up in Solaara after the Fall."

"I truly want to ask you all about being the Emperor and Lord of Zunidh, and how exactly they managed to lose track of you to the point you could come gallivanting around with us, but I—that is, Pali and I—" Pali sighed, but acknowledged the comment, as Jullanar went on, a little nervously. "That is, Pali and I wanted to say ..."

"Oh, let me," Pali said crossly. "Fitzroy, do you remember the diamond you stole from That Party?"

"The Diamond of Gaesion, the Star of the North, yes." I regarded my Old Bag pensively. "I'm afraid I lost it ..." And then, since we had just spent that excruciating period *talking about feelings like adults* (even if like no other adults I had ever spent any time with or observed), I added, "That's why I particularly wanted those three mirrors."

"What mirrors?" Pali asked alertly.

Jullanar leaned forward. "Do you remember the one I gave you, the one I found in the Grand Bazaar of Yedoen?"

"Wasn't it the Great Bazaar?" Pali replied, frowning. (I felt pleasingly validated.) "Yes, of course. I didn't bring it with me, I'm afraid. It's packed away. Not to say we couldn't go to Stoneybridge and fetch it out if necessary." She looked at Jullanar and then me with evident curiosity. "Did you find out something out about it?"

"Did he ever," said Masseo. "It's apparently one of the Three Mirrors of Harbut Zalarin, and together they show the past, the present, and the future."

I nodded. "Also how to undo curses and open hearts."

"A princely gift, Jullanar," Pali said, laughing at the thought. "I do apologize for not bringing it with me! I had no bag such as Fitzroy enchanted, and mostly chose practical items over sentimental."

"Did you bring a tent?" I asked, diverted.

"Of course."

"We should have taken bets," I said to Masseo, who said he knew better.

"Is that what we're searching after? The other two mirrors?"

"No, I already have them," I said. "Or rather, I left one where it was and managed to destroy the second. It's been a busy week, but I have to admit I was rather more efficient in finding them than I anticipated."

"It's probably all that running of governments," Jullanar suggested solemnly.

"That," said Pali, "does not generally lead to efficiency."

This sort of banter made my heart sing, but Jullanar seemed to have been reminded of whatever she was thinking about with respect to the diamond, and didn't smile.

"Jullanar, if you want the Diamond of Gaesion, we can look for that next. We need something to look for, anyway, and that's something I wanted to find."

She and Pali exchanged one of their glances again.

I needed Damian or Sardeet to be with us so I would have someone to exchange glances with Jullanar and Pali about.

Pali appeared to lose this time, for she was the one to utter the delicately suggestive, "Oh? Was there a curse on the diamond?"

"Not exactly. You see …" I settled myself in my chair, then shook my head and stood up to fetch the New Bag instead. While I was over there I collected the Old Bag and set them both beside my chair, where I could pull out random objects of loose association as might strike my fancy. Masseo and Jullanar had both taken my momentary absence to bring out their handicrafts from wherever they'd stashed them earlier, though Pali simply fiddled with the end of her braid.

"I think I need wine for this, even if the rest of you don't."

"I'll have some," Pali said, raising her hand.

"Me too," Jullanar added. "Today I divorced my husband, sold my store, discovered I have an official pardon for half a lifetime of crimes, and reunited with many old friends, one of whom has unexpectedly turned out to be not the trickster god we all half-thought he was but actually the Last Emperor of Astandalas. I think a glass of wine is perfectly in order."

"Masseo?" I invited politely, assuming (correctly) that he wouldn't want any.

"I'll put the kettle on again for myself. Do you have any tea fit for an emperor in there that you'd be willing to share?"

"Most certainly," I replied, and from the New Bag drew out a bottle of fine Amboloyan red wine, three crystal goblets, and a small metal tin, enamelled with gold phoenixes flying on a blue background, containing a gift of tea from the Lord of Ysthar. When Masseo opened it the fragrance poured out, rich and full of magic.

"Oh, perhaps I'll have some of that instead," Pali murmured.

"You can have both." I poured the wine for the three of us as Masseo refilled the kettle, and Jullanar brought out her few remaining ginger biscuits, and finally I was ready to explain something that probably didn't need anything like the folderol surrounding it.

But the small ceremony of opening the wine and pouring it for my friends helped, even if Jullanar unhelpfully commented that she was surprised I didn't have any difficulties with the cork, given my servants.

"Attendants," I corrected, a distinction I always tried to keep in my own mind and one which many in my household cared about deeply. I also have servants: but Conju is not one. "I can tell you more about that, but you sounded as if you particularly wanted to know about the diamond."

"Yes. Why you stole it, primarily."

I sipped my wine. "I've never been quite certain whether to consider that as truly *theft* or not. Admittedly it was never given to me, but that diamond was an heirloom of the house of Damara, and attached to the eldest son, like the title of High King of Rondé—" I

349

tipped my glass to Jullanar, who lived within that kingdom, "or Prince of the White Forest."

"You always said—" Jullanar exclaimed, and then flushed. "You always *did* say, didn't you?"

I tried not to look smug. "Indeed."

"And so, this diamond? You thought it should be yours, so you took it?"

I glared lightly at Pali. "You cannot think me so crude? No. The short answer is that when I was a boy, my tutor used to punish my misbehaviour by making me memorize dead languages and etiquette manuals."

Jullanar appeared arrested at this thought. "When I first met you, you knew nine languages."

"What can I say? I was a troublesome child. Which is relevant, for when I was around thirteen and in a rebellious mood, I went exploring in the forbidden east wing of the house, which was usually closed off. No one lived in the house but for my tutor and the servants, but it was a large building intended as the main seat of the Grand Dukes of Damara. The east wing was where they'd put all sorts of important but unfashionable items, including a collection of unset stones. One of these was what I thought a large crystal. It appealed to me, and I decided to take it so I could examine it at my leisure."

"I begin to see where this is going," Masseo said, amused.

"My daughter is thirteen," Jullanar said thoughtfully. "I'm not sure what I would do if I caught her pilfering family heirlooms in the attic."

"You'd be pleased she was following after her mother's example, no doubt," Pali said, with a fond smile.

I hoped Jullanar wouldn't become upset by the thought of her children, so I hurried on. "You probably would not force them to memorize, recite, and then paraphrase the first five books of *The Saga of the Sons of Morning* in Antique Shaian to prove they've learned the language."

"No wonder you didn't have any problems with the Mae Irionéz," Masseo muttered, using a green and yellow striped scarf he pulled from the Old Bag to wrap around the handle of the kettle, since Jullanar was wringing the cloth they'd been using before between her hands.

I have to admit I was becoming most curious as to what significance the Diamond of Gaesion had taken on for her.

"The *Saga of the Sons of Morning* describes the semi-legendary history of Zunidh until the early conquests of Yr and Damar. One of the stories in the third book mentions the sorcerer Ajuwar, who was called the Master of the Birds."

"Oh, I've heard of him!" Jullanar cried, brightening. "Wasn't he the one who put 'all the heaviness in his heart' into a stone so he would be light enough to fly? And then it turned out this made him immortal, and that was all very well at first until everyone he loved died and eventually he begged the gods to put him out of his suffering, so they turned him into the Morning Star to warn people about overreaching themselves."

They all looked at me and tried to keep their faces straight, which effort, however ineffectual, I applauded.

"Sadly," I said, "when I was thirteen I didn't heed the latter part of the story, and I very much wanted to fly."

It took them a few moments to work through what I meant. "You tried to put the heaviness of your heart into a stone?" Jullanar said tentatively.

"I put *something* into the Diamond of Gaesion, the Star of the North," I corrected. "You can see why I wasn't too keen on it disappearing into the Imperial Treasury as part of my sister's dowry ... Admittedly it probably would have been safer to leave it there, where I knew where it was. What was anyone going to do with it besides put it on display, or perhaps make it the centrepiece of a crown or the like? Instead I took it with me, and when I was thrown out of the high tower of the Moon into the Sea of Stars, if you remember that occasion, it was one of the things that I think fell out of my bag."

I looked at Pali's silver-glimmering cup, which sat beside her wine glass and caught the light innocently. "Mind you, I thought I lost that cup then, too, and here it is. So I'm game to make that the next ostensible object of our quest, if you'd really like to find it. I was hoping to undo the curse I inflicted on myself through the three mirrors, but of course it would be easier with the thing itself, especially since I have managed not to acquire them after all." I smiled brightly at Jullanar and Pali.

They both looked stricken with horror.

"Dear Lady," Jullanar said in a hollow voice. "We broke your heart."

In Jullanar's capacious although not enchanted pack there was a small velvet bag, in which was a silk handkerchief, in which were a dozen shards of one of the largest diamonds ever discovered. She spread the handkerchief out on the table, smoothing out the corners with anxious fingers, and we all stared at it.

The magic was achingly familiar and incredibly strange. It was not like the spirit houses anchoring the bindings on the Solamen Fens, which were made foreign by the many generations of local witches adding their own magic to the mix. It was not even like the great magics I had performed as Lord of Zunidh, the hybrid Schooled and wild magic that I could now hardly bear to touch.

No, this was me, and yet not me. If I were a thousand and thirty years old, as the Ouranatha claimed, it had been a thousand and seventeen years since this had been a part of me. Yet I had not missed it when I was a young man, or perhaps I had not known to miss it. I was lacking in so much that other people took for granted, from a name on up, that it was quite possible I had been missing something all along, and never realized.

I might have been unwilling to reclaim whatever it was, except that if the timelines of Alinor and Zunidh were as unrelated as Pali's account indicated, it was possible, probable even, that it was their smashing of the diamond that had caused my heart attack a year ago—

Or not.

"You're scowling?" Jullanar asked tentatively.

"I had a heart attack," I said, most of my attention on the diamond shards and the magic swirling around them. "I thought perhaps it was from you breaking this, but it was before Pali came, not after."

I held my hand, palm down and fingers spread, a few inches above the shards. The light they reflected seemed to be pulsing. I regarded the light and the feel of the magic, and the feel of my own body pushed to the forefront of my attention in a way it normally did not. My heart certainly was beating in time with the light.

"I think I understand why my heart has been so erratic today," I murmured.

"Fitzroy," Pali said.

I blinked at her, teetering on the edge of the deep trance.

Jullanar still appeared horrified. Pali said, "Remember: I met Jullanar before I met you. She was caught up in some odd events after I left—I had to reach the gate to Zunidh by a certain date."

"I have so much to tell you," Jullanar said. "I thought ... This part of Fiellan has always been considered the least affected by the Fall of Astandalas, as you may know, and I thought it might have something to do with this, the diamond I mean, when we had troubles in the winter and spring. I looked in your bag, and pulled out the diamond without any trouble at all, as if it wished to be found ..."

Whatever it was, my heart or my soul or something else, I could say that yes, indeed, I had wanted to be found.

I thought of the roused magic of Ragnor Bella, the strange

remnants around Jemis Greenwing, and knew it had to be a long story indeed.

"I think this is why I survived the Fall myself," I told them.

"Oh," Jullanar said in a small voice. "Fitzroy, I smashed it with a *hammer*."

This seemed improbable as well as impressive. "Why? and also, how?"

"Why ... is a long story, but in short it was to keep it out of enemy hands."

Masseo looked about as surprised as I felt. "What enemies did you have in Ragnor Bella that you thought might want the diamond?"

"Who *didn't* want the Heart of the Moon!" Jullanar said in exasperation. "Between the Dark Kings and the vanguard of Faerie and the excessive number of criminal groups operating out of the Arguty Forest, not to mention the Indrillines from Tara and the Knockermen from Ghilousette ... Oh, in the end the only thing that seemed to be likely to stop an outright war was to get rid of it."

Masseo reached out to poke at one of the shards with his finger. I felt a strange twist in my heart and nearly lost track of the conversation.

"Please don't do that," I murmured.

He removed his hand with a startled oath. "How did you smash it, then?"

I nearly smirked. "And with what kind of hammer?"

"One of Masseo's old ones from out of your bag," she replied. "It wasn't nearly as hard as I expected. One tap and it just ... fell apart."

"Of course," I nearly whispered.

Institutions may not have feelings, but people do.

Some years, before I had Kip, it was only the memory of their friendship that sustained me at all. That my heart could be so fragile as that, to shatter with the lightest tap, did not surprise me at all.

It was cowardly of me, but I retreated from their appalled, curious faces by sinking down into the deep trance.

And there they were, in my soul's mindscape as in the room beside me: Masseo's forge-fire and Jullanar's garden-earth and Pali's wind-horse. Under their care the fire of my soul was blazing high and strong, as I had not seen it for years.

Point to Jullanar's *talking through our emotions*, I thought in distant amusement, turning my inner gaze in and out until I was focused on the pile of diamond shards.

In this vision it was painfully obvious the diamond shards were a missing part of me. They reached out to the bonfire, the same colour and fire, but deeper, richer, *more*.

I had been a foolish youth, if a powerful one, little though I had understood my power. I had thought it a game of make-believe until I saw the diamond again as part of the betrothal gifts laid out in the Throne Room of the Palace of Stars when we crashed That Party, and I had been so aghast at what I had done that I snatched the diamond without thinking, wanting only to keep it safe and secure and close to me.

I had been thirteen, and thought I was exchanging a power I didn't believe I had for an ability to fly I didn't think I would get.

What, I wondered, had I *actually* done?

There was only one way to find out.

I scooped up the diamond shards with my both my hands, in that vision where what I was picking up was diamond-edged fire, and the fire burned and the diamonds cut but I knew what I had to do, for I am a wild mage and my heart sings when the deed is right and the time is now.

I held the burning diamonds in my cupped hands until my hands caught fire, and then I endured the pain as whatever it was I had given up burned itself back into me.

And then it was done, and I opened my eyes to see that my friends were still sitting around me, though now they were staring open-mouthed at my hands in the centre of the table.

I looked down, where the diamonds had disappeared entirely, and at my hands which looked just the same as usual, and I took a deep breath, and another, and then I said, "Well, that was a bit unexpected, wasn't it?"

Jullanar said, somewhat incredulously, "You mean you didn't intend the diamonds to catch fire in your hands?"

"Is that what it looked like?" I picked up my wineglass and lifted it to my lips, or tried to, but my hands were trembling so much with the aftereffects of the magic that I set the glass down again hastily.

"I think," I said, "that I might need to lie down again."

"I think," Masseo said in a very good imitation of my tone and timbre, "that that is a good idea."

And he and Jullanar between them carried me over to my bed, where Pali tucked me in. I tried to say there were more cushions for her in my New Bag, but fell asleep in the middle of the thought that Pali had been organized enough to bring a tent, and so assuredly would also have a bedroll.

IN WHICH THERE IS A CROW

That night I dreamed I was flying.

I flew hard and fast, in a direction I knew at some deep instinctual level. The land below me was familiar, though in the way of dreams it was not always the same place.

I flew over the blackened grasses of the Solamen Fens. The Tigara reared up its head from the secretive pool at the centre of the marshes and winked at me but said nothing before plunging its head down and down in water that never rippled. I called something back to it, a fierce exultant cry without words, and flew harder.

The land changed. It was the circle of the Vangavaye-ve, atolls and high islands, lagoons and deep sink-holes, coral reefs and palm trees. It was patchwork fields and cattle beside a river, the land soft and well-watered, which could have been anywhere with a temperate climate. It was a desert with horses running down the dunes, their manes and tails waving like flags. It was a series of rocky islets like stepping stones leading to the sunrise. It was the Pale of Astandalas, and the miles-high wall of ice on the northern marches.

It was the Empire, I realized eventually, recognizing a Voonran city, an Alinorel vineyard, Yedoen of Colhélhé with its vast bazaar. I flew, through the night and day, world to world. Gradually I realized that I was following the arc of the River of Stars through the night, and ever eastward in the day.

East across Zunidh, east across Alinor, east across Voonra, east across Ysthar, and east across Colhélhé, over its endless encircling Ocean, which they said had no shores but the Divine Lands.

I flew on tireless wings, black shadow invisible, until finally I came to a tall and mossy tower I knew, where once I had found a riddle and a key and a way to learn who I might be.

It was the Tower of Harbut Zalarin, to which I had been exiled at sixteen, and returned once with the Red Company, and once on my own when the Empire fell upon me like a tsunami and plunged me so deep under its waters that it took me a thousand years to resurface.

I landed on the uppermost windowsill of the tower with a flutter of wings and as much ease as if I had done it a thousand times before.

The room within took up the entire floor. It had windows in each of the eight directions; from it I had once seen the Sun rise to my west.

There was a woman in the room, standing in the middle of the eight-pointed star inscribed in silver on the wooden floor. She had lit candles at every point, and another seven within and another nine without. I knew without seeing any more that she was performing the original version of Harbut Zalarin's Spell for Seeking.

The woman was perhaps in her early thirties. She had skin nearly as black as mine, and wild corkscrew curls, and her eyes were a lucid golden amber when she opened them to look directly at me. Her face was indescribably familiar, like my sister's or my mother's or my grandmother's or any of our other relations, but I had never seen her before in my life.

She tilted her head in a way that reminded me of someone else entirely, and a small smile touched her lips. "Somehow," she said, "I wasn't expecting to be related to a crow."

~

I woke before any of the others, just as dawn was spreading her rosy fingers above the mountains to the east. I tiptoed outside to wash my face in the spring and make use of the rustic facilities. Pali's horse was dozing with one hoof cocked close to the building, and came over to be greeted. I stroked the soft, warm velvet of its nose, letting it snort hot, hay-scented air on my hand, and tentatively examined my own magic.

It was easier this third time to slip into the inner deep trance. My inner campfire really was more of a bonfire now, and was looking increasingly well tended. A pile of chopped wood was stacked neatly to one side, and there were richly woven carpets with bright cushions to sit on, and instead of a vaguely delineated clearing in a woods, there was the beginnings of a riotously blooming flowering mead.

Jullanar, I thought fondly, and put another log onto the bonfire.

I looked at it again. The strange dead, empty space was glimmering softly, like embers about to catch. I crouched before it, and might have reached my hand in but was interrupted by something that was not any known part of my soul.

A crow cawed on the other side of the fire. I walked around it, wondering in the back of my mind what this metaphor meant with respect to my magic, and found that the other side of the clearing held a dead tree stump on which was perched a black crow.

I regarded its intelligent eye, and wondered if I should amend that thought to Crow.

But something in me, new and yet so very old, strange and yet entirely *mine*, knew that that was wrong. I touched the thought and backed away, not yet ready to address it.

359

The crow cawed again, a little derisively, and offered me a small golden item, about the length of my forefinger. I took the object from the bird, which flew off, and examined it carefully.

To all appearances it was the golden key I had found in a seagull's nest on a gargoyle sticking out from the Tower of Harbut Zalarin over the boundary between Ocean and Sky, and which I had lost somewhere in the depths of my Bag of Unusual Capacities and Intermittent Returns.

And what, I wondered, as I had always wondered, was this the lost key *to*?

I opened my eyes out of the trance and blinked to see the world a different place. The horse loomed enormous beside me, its ears pricked forward in confusion. I stepped back, stumbled as my legs did not work as I thought they should, flung out my arms to catch my balance, and a gust of wind caught me and I was aloft.

It was even better than my dream, for this was real.

I circled up and around in a wide lazy loop, keeping an eye on the hut. When smoke started to rise from its chimney I knew the others were awake, and slid instinctively down the wind-roads back to them. There was something so impossibly natural about this transformation that I was, to be frank, a little frightened.

The three of them came out and appeared to be looking for me, for they walked around the building and to separate little hillocks before reconvening at the door to discuss the matter. I slanted down and fluttered to a too-easy transformation back into my human form a few feet from them.

They were gratifyingly amazed.

I grinned at them. "My thirteen year-old-self was an utter *idiot*."

Jullanar tried hard not to laugh, really she did. "You gave up your ability to turn into a crow?"

"Apparently."

"I didn't know crows were any emblem of the imperial lineage," Pali said, mildly suspicious.

I gave her a very serious look. "Pali, I'm not sure if you've ever noticed this before, but I am not a very typical member of my family."

Jullanar lifted her hand to her mouth, her eyes sparkling, even as Pali heaved a great put-upon sigh that made her horse come trotting up with reassurances. I regarded the horse, but it gave no evidence of any uncanniness beyond the superb training Pali had always given her steeds. Pali petted the mare absently, watching me.

Finally she said, "Did you happen to see that there's a new road that wasn't there yesterday?"

I turned to look where she pointed, at the crossroads where there was, indeed, a new path leading due east, towards the mountain that rose between the roads to Lind and to Chare.

I thought of my dream, and how I had travelled instinctively *east* for the past week, and thus found three of my friends all unexpectedly, and how in the dream I had therefore found the woman who looked like me in the tower at the uttermost east of Colhélhé, and that I was, technically and officially, on a quest for an heir, and I nodded. "Obviously we go that way next."

"But after breakfast?" Masseo asked tentatively.

"After breakfast," I agreed.

Jullanar and Masseo went in, leaving Pali and me to stand there looking at each other. My heart was beating hard, but not in the unpleasant fashion of the day before. I felt full of energy and life from my toes to my surely-soon-to-grow-out hair.

Pali tilted her head to regard me with narrowed eyes. I grinned at her. She hadn't yet braided her hair back, and it swirled below her waist in the light breeze. She was wearing the indigo robes with a sky-blue sash of her own people, albeit of a rank and station she had long since surpassed, and her scimitar was at her side. I thought it was marvellous that she was even more beautiful than she had been when I first met her.

I smiled at her as I had smiled at her so often, and said what I had said to her on that first encounter.

"You are *magnificent*," I said, and then, looking her straight in the eyes, "We should get married."

Her lips parted and for a moment her eyes widened hugely.

Then her eyes lit with a sly amusement, and she repeated the words she had said on that memorable occasion. "But how do I know you're magnificent enough for me?"

My smile broadened and I could feel my newly settled magic swirl around us, bedecking the air with sparkles like tiny fireflies. "I am the poet Fitzroy Angursell," I said, as I had said then.

That time she had said, *Ask me again when you're famous.*

Every other occasion she'd said, *Hmm, perhaps next time.*

This time she said, "Oh, you're impossible!" and took my arm to pull me inside.

I followed, laughing. It's not like I could with any honesty deny it.

AUTHOR'S NOTE

The Return of Fitzroy Angursell follows on from *The Hands of the Emperor* and is only the beginning of Fitzroy's various quests. The next book in the Zunidh saga will return to Cliopher (Kip) Mdang's story with *At the Feet of the Sun*.

Earlier stories about the Red Company include *The Bride of the Blue Wind* and *The Warrior of the Third Veil* (The Sisters Avramapul 1 and 2), and *The Tower at the Edge of the World*, in which Fitzroy gives himself a name.

If you haven't yet read the Greenwing & Dart series, some of the mysteries surrounding Jemis Greenwing of dragon-slaying fame begin with *Stargazy Pie*.

For information about coming sequels and other books, please visit my website www.victoriagoddard.ca, where you can also join my newsletter.